Firestorm 2034

The fourth volume in
a collection of writings by

C.J.S. Hayward

C.J.S. Hayward Publications, Wheaton

1. Profound giftedness--literature. 2. Profound giftedness--education. 3. Profound giftedness--social interaction. 4. Profound giftedness--interests and experience. 5. Mnemotechnics. 6. Science fiction.

ISBN 978-0-6152-0216-7

The reader is invited to visit CJSHayward.com.

Contents

Contents

Procedures for the Adjustment and Repair of Televisions

A Glimpse Through a Crystal

I lay on my bed, half-awake, half-asleep, the spectres of dreams beginning to flit through my mind. I saw a castle, a bog, a car with computer screens for its wheels, and many other fleeting images before my mind, when the forms and images began to coalesce.

I saw myself a little boy, blonde-haired, blue-eyed, filthy, and clothed in tattered rags. I was at the end of a pathway, at a pair of massive iron doors, set in a wall of granite that reached as far and as high as the eye could see. On these doors were bronze knockers. I reached, and struck the door; it resounded, as of thunder. I struck the door a second time; it resounded again, and I could sense something -- a presence? I know not how to name it. Then my hand reached and knocked the door a third time, and the sound echoed, grew louder, stronger. I stood in place only because I was too terrified to run, and then a blast of light seared the air and shattered the doors. A god came out -- he looked majestic enough to be a god, although I could not see his face, for it was covered with a veil -- and reached his hand down to me, and said, "Welcome, traveler. I am come to show you the world that is to come. I am to show you Heaven."

I stared in awe and fear, a thousand questions on my mind. And he stood, with a repose that drove away fear. This time, something of the little boy was not only as I saw myself appear on the outside, but inside me; I somehow lost my guile and dignity, and said, "You know what every theologian dreamed of. Can you give me theology from Heaven?"

He laughed, a laugh that burned me and yet was somehow good. He said, "I am sorry, Jonathan. I cannot give you that, because there is no theology in Heaven. It isn't needed. It is one of the brightest lamps that is no more because the Lamb of God himself is our light. When the perfect comes, the imperfect will pass away. Did you want an answer to some area that Christians debate?"

I thought, and answered truthfully, "No. I -- I don't know how to explain it. I want something bigger than that."

The god looked at me, and said, "You have answered well. Calvin, Beza, and Arminius are all up here, all in accordance with each other, and none of them has changed his mind. At least not over the points that Calvinists and Arminians debate. There were plenty of other points where they were wrong. Theology is work well worth doing; it contributes to God's glory, but the best of theologians make quite a few errors. Keep seeking the heart of God, the something bigger, and you will find it. What else do you want to know?"

"Do you have laughter still, I hope?"

"Yes, certainly."

"Could you tell me a few jokes from Heaven?"

"No. I will not mock you with things that are too heavy for you. Your funniest jokes have the barest seed the full-grown plant that lives in Heaven and nourishes everyone; you would be destroyed by our humor."

I looked around, and saw a faint emanation of light from beyond the doorway, a vanishing light; mist and darkness were beginning to appear, and the image looked vague and hazy. I asked, "Why can't I see?"

The being before me said, "You don't see. Or, rather, I am seeing with you and for you. Your eyes cannot bear the load of even my veiled face. I appear to you as you are asleep, beginning to dream, but no such thing exists with us. Sleep is an image of death, and has no place in Heaven. Yet only when you are sleeping is your guard down low enough to let Heaven in."

I asked, "Why should I be granted the special privilege of seeing Heaven?"

He said to me, "It is not nearly so rare a privilege as you think. Heaven is breathed by much of art, literature, music, by friendships, deeds, prayer; in many of these things, the people have insights of Heaven, only not consciously. A great many works you ignore breathe Heaven in a way you will never come close to. The Father is dealing with you as he chooses to deal with you, just as he is dealing with others as he chooses to deal with them. Are you ready to come in?"

I hesitated and said, "One more question. Theology won't exist in Heaven; laughter will exist aplenty, too real for me to bear its form. I have some guesses about mathematics, which I will not venture to guess. Will I see anything that I know in Heaven?"

He said, "Yes, indeed, a great many things. You will come to see things in Heaven that will make you wonder how you ever saw them on earth without seeing Heaven in them. The custom among believers of holding hands when praying -- community and touch (yes, I know you've written a treatise on touch) naturally accompanying communion with God -- exists here, filled with the resurrection life as never before. The blessed here who join hands in prayer are totally present to God and totally present to each other -- save that it is not only soul-body touching soul-body, but resurrected spirit-body touching resurrected spirit-body. It is a form of communion with God and man. At least that is as much of it as I can tell you in the words of your language. You who wield your language with skill and power have struggled with its limitations, while still a mortal who has never touched the lifegiving energy of the Great River -- nor shall you see it tonight. You may see Heaven when you are with me, as you may see Brazil by riding about Rio de Janeiro for an hour on a bus -- that is to say, you cannot see one part in a thousand of what is there, nor can you comprehend one part in a thousand of what you see. You will still learn much. Jonathan, you are really not that far off from joining us; your life on earth is passing, fleeting, however many times it may appear to drag; when you will die, you will look around you and say, 'Am I in God's presence already? That was short.' Then you will drink in full from the wellspring of truth --

"Jonathan, I know why you thought but did not ask about mathematics. Mathematics exists here, as an art form -- you were right when you thought of all mortal mathematics having to pass through the gates of finiteness. It has to be decidable in a finite time. That is no longer part of man; we can look and immediately know the answer to any of your great unsolved questions. As to how there can still be mathematics when every person can immediately see the answer to the hardest question -- I can't explain it to you, but I assure you that God provides an answer to that more stunning than anything a mathematician on earth will ever know. Eye has not seen, ear has not heard, nor has any mind imagined what God has done with the things his children treasure.

"Come, take my hand. We will pass through the doorway together."

I gasped as he took my hand. It was as if I was holding a burning coal. I looked at my hand, and saw to my surprise that I was looking at the hands of a man again, one whom the fire did not wound. Then the god gave me a pull, and I passed through the blazing portal.

It was with a disappointment that I looked around and saw that I was only in a candy store.

I looked at the wall of glass bowls skeptically, not being in a particular mood for candy. My host said, "Come on! Take as much as you want! It's on me." I took a colorful assortment of candies, and then went out into a sunny field. We stood, looked at the clouds for a while, and then dove into a pool of water. After swimming, he asked me, "Do you want to come to an amusement park? There are roller coasters there unlike any you've seen on earth."

I hesitated, and said, "This isn't much like what I expected in Heaven. This is like what one of my professors called a Utopia of spoiled children. I expect to see pleasure in Heaven, but if Heaven only offers early pleasure -- is this all there is to Heaven?"

My host looked at me and said, "You are quite the philosopher. Pleasure is not all there is to Heaven, but God told me to bring you in by this gateway. You need to become as a little child to enter the Kingdom of Heaven, and there is something a little boy sees when he is told, 'In Heaven you can eat all the candy you want,' that you do not. Become as a little child. Would you like some cotton candy?"

I tried to submit to God's will; I'm not sure I got my attitude right, but I tried at least to do the right thing. So I took the candy, and -- have I been blind all these years? I know it sounds presumptuous, but I think I really did taste that candy as a little boy would. It left me thirsty, and I am sure it is only because I was in Heaven that it did not leave a big sticky mess all over my face and clothes, but I *tasted* it -- sheer, simple bliss. I've heard the old quotation about how a child can't believe that making love is better than ice cream; at that point, perhaps only partly because I am not married, I began to suspect that that statement stems from a forgetfulness of what a child experiences when he eats ice cream -- something that is the highlight of a day, the highlight of a week, something that can make a bad day into a good day.

Some people came along, and we began talking, and it wasn't until a good bit into the conversation when I realized that the conversation was switching fluidly between languages -- Italian one moment, Arabic the next, then Sanskrit, then the unbroken language from before the Curse of Babel, the language of the Dawn of Creation -- and I began to cry. One of the things I know I can never have in this life is a mastery of all languages -- and something in Heaven, perhaps even that cheap candy, had affected me so that I was able to move among languages and cultures among the gods and the goddesses that surrounded me. There was something else I don't know how to describe -- a change that was beginning to be wrought in me. It wasn't so much that I was enjoying what was around me, as that I had an enjoyment coming through who I was. And it was not a cause of pride.

Then, as it were, a veil was torn, and I saw one -- what can I call it? a rock, or a flame, or a pulsing mound of energy, unmoved and yet dancing, and around it a constellation of little rocks, each one both like the first rock and totally unlike any other. They were all part of a dance, a dance which combined total order with total freedom -- and I was part of the dance! I was aware of a kind of communion with the other dancers; space did not separate us. I would not have been more honored if they had all been spinning about me; there is something about it that I cannot describe, even badly.

The dance continued, and as it continued I saw myself walking through a vast hallway, with floors of marble and shimmering golden trees. There was a stand, and on it lay open a massive book. My host opened it, and I only glanced at the pages -- enough to see that it recorded the entire story of creation, from Eden to the Second Coming. My life was written on it, every pure thought and action, every sin; I sat stunned that such a thing could be.

"Every place in Heaven is special, unique," my guest said, "and this is a place of remembrance, of story. The special, sweet, fleeting time on earth that each of us had, is remembered for the goods it had that will not exist here. Choosing the right when one's nature is warped and sinful, making disciples of unbelievers, penitence, forgiveness, and ten thousand other things, from marriage to even theology -- they do not exist for us, except as a far off memory. We stand clothed in the good deeds of our life on earth -- what we could do in the limited time we had. You have a very special place, part of the tiny minority of runners who approach the finish line, while the rest stood outside, cheering. This is the Story of how we came to be, and it is your Story too. Cherish your time as mortal man; it will not last long. You have not long before the perfect comes and the imperfect disappears. You know how children always wish to grow up, how they rush on, and how adults see childhood as a special time. You want to be through with the race, to have received your crown. Rightly so. At the same time, wish to make the best use of the fleeting moments, of the scarce time before you enter into glory. Before you will know it, many of the goods you know now will be only a memory.

"I would like to show you one more thing. Walk this way." He took me, and opened a door, to a place that seemed to open out onto a countryside, or a palace. The palace had a courtyard, a pool in which to swim, a view onto forest. Inside were books, and meeting places, and a tinkering room, and a gallery of artwork. "You know that our Lord said, 'In my Father's house there are many rooms.' This is one of those rooms. It is a room that the Father has prepared for a believer, knowing all of his life and his virtues and his good works. Each one holds things in common with others, and is different. And they're connected, though you can't see the connections now. Would you like to know whose room you are looking at?"

"Yes, very much. I would like to meet him," I said.

"It's your room, Jonathan. And you haven't seen the tenth part of it. You will forever be king over a corner of Heaven, having this place in which to commune with God and invite other people over -- and visit their rooms. It is impossible on earth to be friends with a great many people -- but not here."

As I was listening to my guide, I heard footsteps behind me. I looked, and saw a Lamb next to me, soft and gentle. I took it into my arms, and it nestled against my heart. I held the Lamb for a while, and then said, "This guardian fills me with the terror of his majesty; how is it that you do not?" The Lamb looked into my eyes and said, "All this in time you shall understand -- when you do not need to. I will hold you in my heart then, as I hold you in my heart now. Would you like to come here? For real?"

I thought and said, "It would not be the best thing. I have longed many times for Heaven, but then where would my creations be? I hope that the time will pass quickly, but I have work to do on earth. Lord, please help me bear the time until then, and let it be fruitful! But I want to enter into Heaven after living to the full the lifetime of work you have for me -- whether it is a long lifetime or being killed in a car accident on the road to work tomorrow. I want to come to Heaven through earth."

He said, "You have chosen well, mystic. It will not be that long. And I will always be with you."

I awoke with a jerk, and looked around. 9:58 PM. Time to get a good night's sleep and be rested for tomorrow. And pray for God's providence in my work.

Game Review: Meatspace

Game: *Meatspace*

Score: ¤ ¤ ¤ ¤ ¤ ¤ ¤ (7 out of 5 possible!)

Category: First Person Immersive/Puzzle/Real Life Adventure

---

meatspace: /meet'spays/, n.

> The physical world, where the meat lives — as opposed to *cyberspace*. Hackers are actually more willing to use this term than 'cyberspace', because it's not speculative — we already have a running meatspace implementation (the universe). Compare *RL*.

The New Hacker's Dictionary, "*meatspace*"

I am faced with the daunting task of reviewing Meatspace. The temptation is to say, "This is stunning! It makes [*insert name of classic*] look like a bad Pong clone! I want to play it again and again!" It's a *temptation*, not because the game doesn't live up to that praise, but because discerning readers read reviews like that and their defenses go up against a reviewer who is, to put it delicately, getting slightly carried away.

So I'll let go of the obvious temptation, and talk about how Meatspace handles physics. There's another game we all know where player slang for a smoke grenade is "lag bomb", because the physics of the smoke is so taxing that it slows the other player's computer to a crawl: a smoke grenade, aka lag bomb, is a cheap way to half-paralyze other players. Maybe that's an extreme example, but haven't we all dealt with games where things get choppy (maybe just a little) when there's a lot going on?

That doesn't happen in Meatspace. End of discussion. Period. For one example, one of a million little effects done *perfectly* is a squirrel running across your path. It's a throwaway effect, really: the game would appear quite convincing without it, but every single detail, from how the furry little body changes shape as it moves to the artificial intelligence controlling its motion to every single perfectly rendered hair, is flawless. Trying to find something that works as a lag bomb simply doesn't work. Move over, physics engines that have a reasonably convincing rag doll effect. Move over, for that matter, the supercomputers I used at the National Center for Supercomputing Applications. The physics is absolutely stunning.

But to say that and stop there is to paint a deceptive picture. Very deceptive. The physics and the graphics are the best I've seen, but there is more to the game than the physics. Many players don't give the physics a second thought. However well done the physics may be, and however stunningly advanced, the physics is one piece among a million. A beautiful piece, admittedly, but not even one of the biggest. At least to most players; there are some players who play only for the sight and sound aspect, but you can play the game well without those things even being much of a consideration. As impressive as the physics are, and as impressive as every sensory effect is, it would be deceptive at best to say that the game is driven by sight and sound.

In *The Hitchhiker's Guide to the Galaxy* (the book, but unfortunately not the movie), Zaphod Beeblebrox is drawn towards the Total Perspective Vortex, which we learn is a horrifying death, before learning *why* it is a horrifying death. The Total Perspective Vortex shows a person's absolute (in)significance within the universe as an insignificant and forgettable item in a universe that is vast beyond measure. And that is such a horrifying experience that people die from the trauma. Except that Zaphod walks into the Total Perspective Vortex and walks out not only not dead, but contented, happy, proud, and even more full of himself than usual.

What has been happening is that Zaphod has been in an alternate universe, and more specifically an alternate universe that completely revolves around him. *He* is the most important feature of the universe, and the universe knows it. Had he been thrown into the *real* universe's Total Perspective Vortex, he would have been destroyed by it.

And in fact with the other computer games I've played and written, the player is the center of the universe. And that's not the end of it. The universe revolves around the player, and in fact nothing is put into the game but things that are for the player. In a room in a first person shooter, there are millions and in fact billions of ways to see the room. But, if there is a player in the room, only one of those perspectives or angles is calculated: the player's. Everything else is simply ignored. If there isn't a player in the room, the room might as well not be visible. And the rooms themselves exist for the player. The player is a good deal more than the center of the universe: if it's not there for the player, it's not there.

Maybe I've been the center of the universe in other games I've played. In Meatspace, I am *not* the center of the universe. Meatspace has such an immense, fathomless universe that you or I could never be its center.

In Meatspace, if I am in a room and I can see, the light goes just as well where I can't see it as where I can see it. If I leave the light on and walk out of the room, the room is visible--the physics calculations go on--just as well as I am in the room. There are places I could get to, and places I could never get to, and both are developed in full detail--even though there are many more places

I couldn't get to than places I could (conceivably) travel to. When I play the game--or, to be more exact, when I *join* the game--there are billions of others in the game, the vast, vast majority of whom have no idea that I am there. If I'm the center of a game's universe, the universe is miserably small. In Meatspace, there is a universe with so many stars that no one inside the game knows exactly how many, and one planet on one of those stars is a rich enough world that no matter how long you played you could never see more than a tiny slice of its treasures.

And AI in the game... To talk about artificial intelligence, I need to draw an analogy with anime. When people watch anime, they are not so imperceptive that they think that the pictures look exactly like people, or cars, or whatever. What they do is cooperate with pictures that most people would never confuse with the real thing, and make believe with some not-very-realistic cartoons, and in their minds give something that isn't really there. The pictures certainly *suggest* people, or whatever else they are supposed to represent. But people watching it cooperate and overlook some rather vast differences between the pictures and what people pretend the pictures are.

In games, the artificial intelligence is like this. You can pretend that you're really having a conversation, or even that the non-player characters move around in a natural way. You can cooperate with the artificial intelligence the way anime enthusiasts cooperate with the cartoon. But you're being generous.

I didn't have to pretend the Meatspace people were intelligent. They *were* intelligent, without my pretending. The game was much more interesting than if the universe, and everybody's life, revolved around me. People had an infinite wealth of experiences, stories, goals, projects, desires, habits, and I may have been part of the picture, but the picture was far bigger than me. When I talked with people, I was not pretending they were intelligent. There was no need. I was stepping into a larger world. In a fantasy world, characters talk about selling magic items, rumors, joining a party, and other things that revolve around a cramped player. I can't list all the things people talk about in Meatspace (my hard drive only has 30 gigabytes of free space), but talking with another person is an encounter with a larger world that includes more than your priorities. The way other people appear in Meatspace is something I've never seen in another game: an opportunity to step into something deeper and vaster than "Me! Me! Me!"

And this is deceptive, because it generally describes something in a game where nothing is generic--everything is always specific. I'd like to give a slice of specifically what I encountered.

I went through a meandering course that took me through shops with sundry wares, ended up purchasing a few square feet of something very much like leather, and settled down at a place where I could get a food ration. Except "food ration" is a generic and therefore inappropriate term; they did not sell me a "food ration", but (in this case) a delightfully spiced beef curry with vegetables and rice.

As I was waiting for them to make my food, there were pictures around. There was one picture of a beautiful Asian woman sitting on a low stone wall in front of a French formal garden and chateau, one picture of a beautiful Asian woman sitting on a camel in front of an Egyptian pyramid, and one picture of a beautiful Asian woman sitting against a powerful red sports car. There were other pictures obscured by stacked boxes of soda. The women, as well as being beautiful and wearing flattering Western clothes, had the general build and almost the complexion of a Western ideal of beauty.

I had seen this kind of artwork in previous levels of Meatspace--in one large area, there was simply no other kind of picture you could buy on a calendar--but I'd always been puzzled by it. This time, there was something else I could see. They were almost like religious icons. This is not to say that people specifically believed religious doctrines about them, or that there was some failure of perceivedly due reverence in stacking boxes of soda in front of them, or some other things like that, but it *is* to say that they aren't just pictures of what they show. What they show is not only exotic but the emblem of something transcendent that's shining through. And I can be saddened by some things about them--those pictures can easily slide into the pornographic--but there is something I was saddened by that I am no longer bothered by.

The image of beauty and transcendence is Western much for some of the same reasons that (for a tongue in cheek example) we have a Great White Ninja played by Chris Farley in *Beverly Hills Ninja*. The West is exotic to the East, and the East is exotic to the West. The pictures are misunderstood if they are not seen as a sort of stained glass window that people look at because they see something shining through it.

There's probably a lot more to be said. If I spent several more years of play just to investigate the question, I might also be able to tell you why the shops allowed me to purchase about a square yard of an artificial surrogate for leather, and a few yards of cord, for less money than I would earn in an hour. For now, my game play has included little research into how communities can produce or fail to produce wealth. I just know enough to know that a detail like that, like the kind of system where there are poor people who eat meat with every meal, is a balancing act that has never before been managed in two and a half million years of human community, and quite probably a balancing act that will not survive longer than its civilization, any more than a tree can keep growing once its river runs dry.

There is something about the Meatspace levels we find ourselves in that makes it harder to see the gems around us. The medieval and the Arthurian looks a certain way to us after they no longer exist. What do things look like if we look at our placement in Meatspace as it might appear when our technological society is but a memory?

My avatar (but one could take a long time explaining how it is more than an avatar) was just in a place with Gothic lettering on a sign on the ground, saying, "Spaccarelli Meditation Garden." A pale, almost luminous statue of the Virgin overlooks a waterfall, rocks, plants, and a bench. The garden is small, but in its enclosed space one can be drawn into the quiet of the waterfall's song, forget about the outside world, even the nearby Gothic buildings--Gothic buildings that did not exist in the Middle Ages but do exist on a level that didn't exist in the Middle Ages. I have since moved to a building that combines the Gothic with the modern: I can see stonework that evokes the Gothic, and I see it through a glass wall which would have been extremely unlikely at a time when glass cost as much as a precious metal.

Some players entered the game wishing they were set in the future instead of the past--anything but where they are now. What would my life have been like if I were born in the Middle Ages? That's simple enough. I would have died in infancy, and my mother with me. Usually when I imagine myself in the Middle Ages, I take any number of things for granted.

The Middle Ages--the knights in armor of Arthurian legend, a picture which becomes even more interesting when it is deepened with scholarly resources to include a different way of perceiving time and space, the shadow of Plato, minstrels singing love songs, precursors to scientific method which become all the more interesting if one looks not at what they became but what they came from--all of this makes for a lost world that is all the more haunting because it can only be entered as a memory.

The character I play is studying theology at a university. "University" means a tradition that began in the Middle Ages, and it means living in community with other students and scholars, free to use technology but always connecting face-to-face and meeting as flesh and blood. As well as the older kind of university, the technology in Meatspace has allowed another kind of education which is a new enough possibility that many players remember when it would have been impossible. In the new model, a student may never meet any of his teachers; there is no sense of living together in community and no real sense that a path or way which has defined teaching since before the ancients is necessary. Not everyone in the ancient model understood or even would accepted the idea that a university should be an embodied community. But the only alternative, the older kind of correspondence school, never enjoyed the same prestige. Now there is another model, not so much another kind of community as a way to substitute for community and embodied presence, and it is gaining a massive ground in a short time. It is a real threat to the older university.

Given the rapid ascent of the "bodiless university", it seems to me quite possible that by the end of my game, I will have seen the old order of a university as an embodied community as it has been since its medieval birth, will have vanished as the horse-drawn carriage vanished after Henry Ford introduced what seemed to simply be another option (besides riding a horse). Perhaps this will never happen, but if you consider how much could vanish, and how much is easy to take for granted, the scholarly community has something as hauntingly beautiful as the knight in shining armor, or perhaps more beautiful, and this is not only because the university is a medieval institution and some universities have Gothic architecture. The roots run much deeper than that. And that is only one slice of the game--a rather small slice, all things considered.

Technology in this area of the game is interesting, and more importantly than just the technology, the cultural forces surrounding technology are interesting. They hold a tragic beauty, in its own way as tragic and as beautiful as the tale of Arthur's death: two armies stood across from each other, and each had been ordered not to attack unless the other side drew a sword. Then one soldier saw a snake in the grass, drew his sword to protect himself. Then the battle began, and King Arthur was mortally wounded. On the side of technology, the community had achieved technology that opened up possibilities that never existed before partly because it had oriented itself toward technology as no such community had done before. That made for a sorceror's bargain that made it difficult to perceive other kinds of beauty in other cultures--or for that matter, their own. The full cultural story--were it possible to fully understand--is even deeper in its tragic beauty than the bittersweet hypothesis of a disembodied university opening up something new while hurting the older tradition. One cannot seriously examine technology without seeing its power--and even its *beauty*--yet in this society, it is a minority at best who know what it means, and what the beauty would consist of, for a society ordered around other principles like contemplation.

Yet to say that is silly. It's like reviewing a chess program by describing the art history behind the pictures representing the pawns. Interesting, perhaps, and perhaps impressive, but it falls short of the mark, as does any serious attempt to review Meatspace. I haven't discussed 99% of an expanse of pavement stretching as far as the eye can see and then further, nor a room that lets me look out over trees and buildings as if I were suspended in the sky, nor a melting pot which combines the wealth of Africa, indigenous Americans, Europe, and Asia and which is believed to be the birthplace of hip hop, nor indeed what it means to be in an outer borough in the "capital of the world," nor why some dismiss the Bronx as being not a very nice place to live. I believe I have deeply failed to capture the global spirit of Meatspace because I gave too little attention to the unique local character of my level--and you cannot play Meatspace without encountering such a unique local character. To play Meatspace is to enter a world rich with apples and appearances, books and buttercups, children and cats, drivel and daydreams, electronics and excellence, fables and fairy tales, grandeur and giggles, horses (yes, they still exist!) and houses, igloos and imagination, jumping and justice, kites and katana, languages and laughter, microscopes and megaphones, noses and noise, operas and obverses, porpoises and porcupines, quiet and quickness, roaches and Russia, Swiss Army Knives and spirit, transportation and tummies, understanding and understatements, vowels and vices, water and wisdom, xanthan gum and xylophones, yule logs and youth, zebras and zits. It is far beyond my power to describe them.

The Monastery

It was late in the day, and my feet were hurting.

I had spent the past three hours on the winding path up the foothills, and you will excuse me if I was not paying attention to the beauty around me.

I saw it, and then wondered how I had not seen it--an alabaster palace rising out of the dark rock around it, hidden in a niche as foothill became mountain. After I saw it, I realized--I could not tell if the plants around me were wild or garden, but there was a grassy spot around it. Some of my fatigue eased as I looked into a pond and saw koi and goldfish swimming.

I looked around and saw the Gothic buildings, the trees, the stone path and walkways. I was beginning to relax, when I heard a voice say, "Good evening," and looked, and realized there was a man on the bench in front of me.

He was wearing a grey-green monk's robe, and cleaning a gun. He looked at me for a moment, tucked the gun into a shack, and welcomed me in.

Outside, the sun was setting. At the time, I thought of the last rays of the dying sun--but it was not that, so much as day giving birth to night. We passed inside to a hallway, with wooden chairs and a round wooden table. It seemed brightly enough lit, if by torchlight.

My guide disappeared into a hallway, and returned with two

silver chalices, and set one before me. He raised his chalice, and took a sip.

The wine was a dry white wine--refreshing and cold as ice. It must have gone to my head faster than I expected; I gave a long list of complaints, about how inaccessible this place was, and how hard the road. He listened silently, and I burst out, "Can you get the master of this place to come to me? I need to see him personally."

The servant softly replied, "He knows you are coming, and he will see you before you leave. In the mean time, may I show you around his corner of the world?"

I felt anger flaring within me; I am a busy man, and do not like to waste my time with subordinates. If it was only one of his underlings who would be available, I would have sent a subordinate myself. As I thought this, I was surprised to hear myself say, "Please."

We set down the chalices, and started walking through a maze of passageways. He took a small oil lamp, one that seemed to burn brightly, and we passed through a few doors before stepping into a massive room.

The room blazed with intense brilliance; I covered my eyes, and wondered how they made a flame to burn so bright. Then I realized that the chandaliers were lit with incandescent light. The shelves had illuminated manuscripts next to books with plastic covers--computer science next to bestiaries. My guide went over by one place, tapped with his finger--and I realized that he was at a computer.

Perhaps reading the look on my face, my guide told me, "The master uses computers as much as you do. Do you need to check your e-mail?"

I asked, "Why are there torches in the room you left me in, and electric light here?"

He said, "Is a person not permitted to use both? The master, as you call him, believes that technology is like alcohol--good within proper limits--and not something you have to use as much as you can. There are electric lights here because their brilliance makes reading easier on the eyes. Other rooms have torches, or nothing at all, because a flame has a different meaning, one that we prefer. Never mind; I can get you a flashlight if you like. Oh, and you can take off your watch now. It won't work here."

"It won't work? Look, it keeps track of time to the second, and it is working as we speak!"

The man studied my watch, though I think he was humoring me, and said, "It will give a number as well here as anywhere else. But that number means very little here, and you would do just as well to put it in your pocket."

I looked at my watch, and kept it on. He asked, "What time is it?"

I looked, and said, "19:58."

"Is that all?"

I told him the seconds, and then the date and year, and added, "But it doesn't feel like the 21st century here." I was beginning to feel a little nervous.

He said, "What century do you think it is here?"

I said, "Like a medieval time that someone's taken a scissors to. You have a garden with perfect gothic architecture, and you in a monk's robe, holding an expensive-looking rifle. And a computer in a library that doesn't even try to organize books by subject or time."

I looked around on the wall, and noticed a hunting trophy. Or at least that's what I took it for at first. There was a large sheild-shaped piece of wood, such as would come with a beautiful stag--but no animal's head. Instead, there were hundreds upon hundreds of bullet holes in the wood--enough that the wood should have shattered. I walked over, and read the glass plate: "This magnificent deer shot 1-4-98 in Wisconsin with an AK-47. God bless the NRA."

I laughed a minute, and said, "What is this doing in here?"

The servant said, "What is anything doing here? Does it surprise you?"

I said, "From what I have heard, the master of this place is very serious about life."

My guide said, "Of course he is. And he cherishes laughter."

I looked around a bit, but could not understand why the other things were there--only be puzzled at how anyone could arrange a computer and other oddments to make a room that felt unmistably medieval. Or was it? "What time is it here? To you?"

My guide said, "Every time and no time. We do not measure time by numbers here; to the extent that time is 'measured', we 'measure' by what fills it--something qualitative and not quantiative. Your culture measures a place's niche in history by how many physical years have passed before it; we understand that well enough, but we reckon time, not by its place in the march of seconds, but by the content of its character. You may think of this place as medieval if you want; others view it as ancient, and not a small part is postmodern--more than the computer is contemporary."

I looked at my watch. Only five minutes had passed. I felt frustration and puzzlement, and wondered how long this could go on.

"When can we move on from here?"

"When you are ready. You aren't ready yet."

I looked at my watch. Not even ten seconds had passed. The second hand seemed to be moving very slowly.

I felt something moving in the back of my mind, but I tried to push it back. The second hand continued on its lazy journey, and then--I took off my watch and put it in my pocket.

My guide stood up and said, "Walk this way, please."

He led me to a doorway, opening a door, and warning me not to step over the threshold. I looked, and saw why--there was a drop of about a foot, into a pool of water. The walls were blue, and there was sand at the far end. Two children--a little boy and a little girl--were making sand castles.

He led me through the mazelike passages to rooms I cannot describe. One room had mechanical devices in all stages of assembly and disassembly. Another was bare and clean. The kitchen had pepperoni and peppers hanging, and was filled with an orange glow that was more than torchlight. There was a deserted classroom filled with flickering blue light, and then we walked into a theatre.

The chamber was small, and this theatre had more than the usual slanted floor. The best way I could describe it is to say that it was a wall, at times vertical, with handholds and outcroppings. There were three women and two men on the stage, but not standing--or sitting, for that matter. They were climbing, shifting about as they talked.

I could not understand their language, but there was something about it that fascinated me. I was surprised to find myself listening to it. I was even more surprised to realize that, if I could not understand the words, I could no less grasp the story. It was a story of friendship, and there is something important in that words melted into song, and climbing into dance.

I watched to the end. The actors and actresses did not disappear backstage, but simply climbed down into the audience, and began talking with people. I could not tell if the conversation was part of the act, or if they were just seeing friends. I wondered if it really made any difference--and then realized, with a flash, that I had caught a glimpse into how this place worked.

When I wanted to go, the servant led me to a room filled with pipes. He cranked a wheel, and I heard gears turning, and began to see the jet black keys of an organ. He played a musical fragment; it sounded incomplete.

He said, "Play."

I closed my eyes and said, "I don't know how to play any instrument."

He repeated the fragment and said, "That doesn't matter. Play."

There followed a game of question and answer--he would improvise a snatch of music, and I would follow. I would say that it was beautiful, but I couldn't really put it that way. It would be better to say that his music was mediocre, and mine didn't quite reach that standard.

We walked out into a cloister. I gasped. There was a sheltered pathway around a grassy court and a pool stirred by fish.

It was illumined by moon and star, and the brilliance was dazzling.

We walked around, and I looked. In my mind's eye I could see white marble statues of saints praying--I wasn't sure, but I made up my mind to suggest that to the master. After a time we stopped walking on the grass, and entered another door.

Not too far into the hallway, he turned, set the oil lamp into a small alcove, and began to rise up the wall. Shortly before disappearing into the blackness above, he said, "Climb."

I learn a little, I think. I did not protest; I put my hands and feet on the wall, and felt nothing. I leaned against it, and felt something give way--something yielding to give a handhold. Then I started climbing. I fell a couple of times, but reached the shadows where he disappeared. He took me by the hand and began to lead me along a path.

I could feel a wall on either side, and then nothing, save his hand and my feet. Where was I? I said, "I can't see!"

A woman's voice said, "No one can see here. Eyes aren't needed." I felt an arm around my waist, and a gentle squeeze.

I felt that warmth, and said, "I came to this place because I wanted to see the master of this house, and I wanted to see him personally. Now--I am ready to leave without seeing him. I have seen enough, and I no longer want to trouble him."

I felt my guide's hand on my shoulder, and heard his voice as he said, "You have seen me personally, and you are not troubling me. You are here at my invitation. You will always be welcome here."

When I first entered the house, I would have been stunned. Now, it seemed the last puzzle piece in something I had been gathering since I started hiking.

The conversation was deep, and I cannot tell you what was said. I don't mean that I forgot it--I remember it clearly enough. I don't really mean that it would be a breach of confidence--it might be that as well. What I mean is that there was something special in that room, and it would not make much sense to you even if I could explain it. If I were to say that we talked in a room without light, where you had to feel around to move about--it would be literally true, but beside the point. When I remember the room, I do not think about what wasn't there, but what was there. I was glad I took off my watch--but I cannot say why. The best thing I can say is that if you can figure out how a person could be aware of a succession of moments, and at the same time have time sense that is not entirely linear--or at very least not *just* linear--you have a glimpse of what I found in that room.

We talked long, and it was late into the next day when I got up from a perfectly ordinary guestroom, packed, and left. I put on my watch, returned to my business, and started working on the backlog of invoices and meetings that accumulated in my absence. I'm still pretty busy, but I have never left that room.

Seven-Sided Gem

This lecture was given Oct. 26, 2001 during the Midwestern Mensa regional gathering, at the Arlington Heights Sheraton.

Introductory remarks by Dr. Mike Doyle, CEO and Founder of Eolas Technologies: I first met Jonathan Hayward on the MegaList about a year and a half ago. I was impressed enough by his abilities to hire him at the first opportunity, and he now works as a software developer for Eolas Technologies. Jonathan, in one year, did an independent study of calculus, programmed a four-dimensional maze, and ranked 7th nationally in the 1989 MathCounts competition. Then he turned 14 and turned his attention to deeper challenges. He has studied at Wheaton College, the Sorbonne, and the University of Illinois. Like many profoundly gifted, Jonathan moves among a wide range of interests. He is now focused on writing. He has been published in Ubiquity, *Noesis*, *Inner Sanctum*, *Perfection*, and now *Vidya*, with Religion Within the Bounds of Amusement. Please welcome him as he speaks about his experiences as a profoundly gifted individual.

Jonathan: Thank you. It is a privilege to be here; I have been looking forward to this night, a time when we can connect and share--not only through our costumes. More on my costume later. Before I begin my speech proper, I'd like to deal with a couple of preliminaries. I have a slight speech impediment; I'll try to speak clearly, but you may have to work a little harder to understand me. Second, I'd like to review the seven points of my speech, the seven facets of the seven-sided gem:

- Metaculture: a term which I coined and which I'll explain.
- Ages and cultures: by 'ages' I mean different temporal ages, not how old a person is.
- Beyond the Binet-Simon: alternative approaches to intelligence estimation.
- Inside the glass wall: a private symbol I'll explain.
- A musing life: Do I mean a life that is amusing or a life that has musing? I'll explain that.
- Thinking inside the box: lessons learned from living among IQ normals.
- Mystic, Artist, Christian.

Don't talk about the things you're interested in with someone you've just met. Never mind that, to you, abstract conversation is a staple of acquaintanceship and friendship. To the other person, it may be boring, unpleasant, or a sign of unwanted romantic interest.

Never mind that you have five points of great subtlety and complexity. Pick one, and when you have simplified past the point of distortion, be ready for the other person to say, "Excuse me. Could you say that in English?"

Don't assume that the person in authority believes, "The rules exist for the betterment of the community and are therefore negotiable when they do not contribute to that end." Even if the rules do not consider your case, even if they end up hurting you, expect, "The rules are the rules and I am not here to make exceptions."

Never mind that you can shift your culture at will, or that it is something you must do to connect with others. Don't try explaining it to others, and whatever you do don't ask them to do so. If you do, they will experience culture shock and react accordingly. Never mind that to you, foreign cultures are familiar and familiar cultures foreign. Don't try to explain this either. It asks them to do something completely unfair.

Be very careful in sharing accomplishments, or even things you don't think of as accomplishments, just cherished moments. To the other person, they may well be intimidating to the point of alienation.

Grieve a thousand wounds, but don't fall prey to the worst wound of all. Don't come to believe, "I will never connect with them, and they will never understand me." If you do, you will find yourself in a sort of Hell--not in the world to come, but here on earth. You will be in a Hell of isolation, an alien in an alien land.

They can joke. That's why you're frustrated they don't understand your humor. They can think. That's why you're hurt and upset when they never fathom your deepest thoughts. To those separated by the greatest chasm, is given the greatest ability to bridge chasms.

Perhaps it is harder than doing calculus in middle school or creating a language. It is still something you can do. That intellect that leaves people dazed is the intellect you can use to communicate--connect--in ways that aren't open to them. That burning intensity that's gotten you into so much trouble can put fire in your friendships such as many of your friends would never have otherwise known. That unique inner world, that you've closed the doors to, after being burned time and time again, is a place you may learn to draw people into. I cannot tell you how, but with a lot of hard work, a lot of patience, a lot of humility, a lot of forgiveness given *and received*, you may come to a point of synergy past the point where you wished you were not quite so gifted.

An anthropologist at this point might make the case that there is an unbridgeable chasm between the already very bright minds associated with Mensa, and the severely gifted. *I'd rather say something different.* I'd rather say the severely gifted experience is a crystallization of many things that make the Mensa experience distinctive, and there is a common bond of giftedness as well as the bond of being human. I'd rather say that what gap does exist is one that can be bridged. That is the premise this whole talk is based on.

A much better speaker than I am might be able to explain, in the abstract and in entirety, what the inner world and experience of the severely gifted is like. I can't do that, but I have my sights set on a much more modest goal: to share something of my own inner world and experience, and light a candle of illumination.

When I was a student at Wheaton College, there was a chapel where students lined up and shared some of the, ahem, *interesting* questions they'd been asked: "You grew up in Japan? Say something in Chinese!" "Say something in African!" "What did it *feel* like growing up in Finland?" (Uh, I don't know. Slight tingling sensation around the toes?) The chapel was given by *missionary's kids/third culture kids*, sometimes abbreviated MK/TCK. A third culture kid is a kid who grows up surrounded by one host culture--let us say, blue--to parents who belong to another culture--let us say, yellow. They are neither properly blue nor properly yellow, but create a *third culture* that draws on both. This is not a simple average of the two cultures; there are common similarities, whether it's a U.S. kid growing up in Kenya, or a Japanese growing up in the U.S. It is a different mode of experience, a different way of being human. Third culture kids tend to have a tremendous ability to adapt to new cultures, but at times a cost: the price of never being completely at home in a culture, as a fish in water. When I heard that chapel, I said, "That's me!"

It is the characteristic of very creative minds to hit a very large nail not quite on the head. I am not literally a third culture kid; by the time I heard that chapel, I had not lived abroad. There was something deep that resonated, however. The best way I can describe it is that a third culture kid creates a third culture after being shaped by the outer forces of the host culture on one hand and his parents on the other, and a severely gifted individual is shaped by the outer forces of an IQ-normal world and an inner world from a different kind of mind: the higher you go on the IQ spectrum, there is less and less more of the same intelligence, and more and more of a different kind of intelligence altogether. I coined the term 'metaculture' to refer to the commonality of experience, a way of not ever being in a culture as a fish is in water. It brings pain, a sense of never fitting in, and at the same time a freedom from some of the blindnesses others can't escape.

In talking about cultures, I'm hesitant to say that they've left an imprint on me, because the metaphor is deficient. It evokes an image of an active, solid, definite culture that leaves a mark on hot wax which is simply there to receive an imprint. The truth is much more interesting: the cultures are themselves, yes, but I am actively drawing, discerning, seeing what in them is of interest to me and can be drawn into myself. Anyone who knows cultures knows that conveying even one culture in five hours is impossible; I hope not to convey the cultures I visited, so much as give a sense of what sort of thing is interesting.

The summer after that chapel, I lived in Malaysia. My father spent the year teaching, and the rest of the family lived there. I got to spend the summer. I understand why my Mom said it was the best year of her life.

In American culture, there is always a clock tick-tick-ticking. It's not just there when you look down at your watch; it may be more present when you're not looking: when you're visiting your friend and distracted with twenty other things to do that day, or on the road where you move faster than any human athlete can run, and one second's needless delay is one second's torment. In Malaysia, the clock's constant ticking stops. This is not unique to Malaysia; those of you familiar with African cultures, or Latin American, will know something similar, but it is at any rate different from the U.S. It's not exactly true that the Malaysians perceive time slowly where we perceive it quickly, as that the U.S. is conscious of time where Malaysians are conscious of other things. I have continued to shape my sense of time after leaving Malaysia, and come to focus not on time but on people, creation, and some work. If I try to spend a half an hour on my third novel, what will dominate is the half hour, not the novel; I try to give focused presence to what I am doing now and not have a clock cut up my emotions. It is a tremendous boon in writing, or being with people. I try to keep enough of an American time sense to not be needlessly rude by being late to appointments, but on the inside I seek a different time, and I believe my friendships and my creations are the better for it. *Dost thou love life? Then do not quantize time, for numbers are not the stuff life's made of.*

Some time after that, I studied in Paris at the Sorbonne. It was a wonderful time; part of my heart is still there. During my time as a student, I acquired a taste for alcohol. One thing I realized rather quickly is that five ounces of wine is not much. If I had a glass of wine with dinner and tossed it back after my first bites, I could have another... and another... and another... and become rather quickly inebriated. Or I could simply not have any more wine. *Or*--there is an alternative--I could sip my wine, savor it.

In doing that, I tasted wine as I had not tasted any beverage before. Because there was so little, I learned to be present and enjoy much more than absently having a hazy awareness that something I liked was passing through my mouth. My absent awareness of sodas was not a bad thing; one thing I learned upon returning is that American soft drinks are not intended to be consumed that way. If you sip a small glass of Mountain Don't, you will soon learn that Mountain Don't isn't meant to be so sipped. I learned to be present, not just to wine and non-alcoholic beverages like fruit drinks and Mocha, but also to food, and to a much broader circle. If I am in a public place, and music I like comes across the air, it is transient; it is fleeting. I cannot make it last any longer, but I can be present to it in the short time it does last. When a friend comes from out of town, in all likelihood her visit will be over before it has begun--but I can be present in that time as well. This presence has added something to my life complimentary to the time sense I acquired from Malaysia.

What's the last culture? One that will take a bit more explaining, as I have to swim upstream against more than one thread of American culture. What is it that I have to swim up against? "This is an idea whose time has come." "It's the wave of the future." "We're entering the third millenium."

If I were to speak of "an idea whose time has come, and gone," or "the wave of the past," it would be less clear that I was speaking a compliment. If I were to say, in the most reverent of tones, "We're standing at the forty-second latitude and eighty-seventh longitude.", you'd have every right to accuse me of a non sequitur. I believe that "We're entering the third millenium." is also a non sequitur, even though it is spoken as a statement of great significance.

There are two ideas closely intertwined: the doctrine of progress, which says we are better, nobler, wiser people than those who came before--a temporal version of ethnocentrism, which says that ideas like machines grow rust and need to be replaced--and period awareness, which goes beyond the historicist observation that all of us, past and present, exist in a historical-cultural context and are affected by it; period awareness fixes an unbridgeable chasm between the people who walked before and us; they are in a hermetically sealed box. The net respect is to believe that the peoples of the past cannot talk with us: we can point out how they were less enlightened times, but they certainly cannot criticize us.

My second novel, Firestorm 2034, is the story of a medieval in 21st century America. In the course of researching medieval culture, thinking about it, and trying to convey it, it left a mark on me in many ways similar to Malaysia and France. Mark Twain's A Connecticut Yankee in King Arthur's Court is a masterpiece of humor that is often mistaken for a reasonable treatment of medieval culture; my novel reverses it in more ways than one. Not only is it a medieval in America, but more deeply I reject the belief that the most significant difference between the medievals and us is that we have better technology. There is a wealth of culture and wisdom that has been largely lost.

What is one such area? The present issue of My Generation, the magazine of the American Association of Retired Persons, has a cover story about "Jeff Bridges: Beautiful Dreamer." On the cover, he has black hair tinged with silver, although I would forgive you if you glanced and said it was brown. It's a few inches longer than mine. He's curled up, slouching, with his arms over his knees, wearing faded jeans, white socks, and tennis shoes. *The man looks like a teenager.* This is not an accident. I have never seen a My Generation cover with a woman who looks old enough to be admitted to the AARP, and when I first saw that periodical, I mistook it for a GenX magazine.

Why? The core idea is that there is a short period of glory--I'll say from fifteen to twenty-five years, although some of you might place the beginning and end a little differently--and before that point, you're only a child, meaning curiously enough that you don't have access to adult pleasures; you can't drink, you can't drive--and after that point, you're a has-been. This message is ubiquitous, present not only in children's TV shows but equally in a magazine for retired people. And, in a certain manner, it makes perfect sense.

It makes perfect sense if there is nothing more to have in life than physical pleasure. Before fifteen, you can't acquire as much pleasure as someone with adult resources; after twenty-five, your capacity for youthful pleasure diminishes. And so, if one starts by assuming that the whole point of life is to have pleasure, that the point of science is to create a Utopia of spoiled children, then it follows quite simply that a child is nothing much and someone past the age of thirty is a has-been. It follows quite simply for us, but the medievals saw it differently.

The medievals believed that the entire purpose of this life is as a preparation, an apprenticeship, a beginning, to an eternity gazing on God's glory. It means that, even in this life, there is infinitely more to seek than physical pleasure. There is more to desire. There is virtue, both earthly, natural virtues, and the merry, heavenly, deiform virtues. One can begin to be a heavenly person, enjoy Heaven's joys, and know God.

The words, "Eat, drink, and be merry, for tomorrow we may die," voice a pessimistic philosophy: enjoy pleasure because there's nothing more and we have a grim life. The medieval view sought much more than pleasure, and in following it, I want to grow more. I don't believe I'm leaving the time when I can enjoy the only good in life, pleasure. I believe I have different fruits in season coming. Some people dread their thirtieth birthday. I'm looking forward to it. I'm looking forward to turning thirty, forty, fifty, to when my hair turns tweed and then white. I'm looking forward to growing in wisdom: the interesting part of *my* life isn't ending, but just beginning.

What about intelligence testing? I like Madeleine l'Engle's A Wind in the Door; it's a children's book with a little boy, Charles Wallace, whose IQ is "so high it's untestable by normal means." I like the story and Charles Wallace; I identify with him, and in reference to that passage began to wish the same were true of me, that my IQ were so high it was untestable by normal means. I even tried to convince myself, in moments of pride, that this was true.

It came as a great disappointment to learn not only was this literally true, that my IQ was literally so high as to be untestable by normal means, but that the threshold was so low. If the authors of the Binet-Simon test, paradigm example of the good IQ test, were to be told, "This test you've made, doesn't really distinguish average from below average, but shows a remarkably fine discrimination at the upper strata of human intelligence," they would have regarded the test as a failure, pure and simple. The Binet-Simon test is a test for inferiority. Sources I've seen differ as to why; one gently states that it was meant to identify special needs people and give them that extra boost of special education they need to function in life. Another says, less charitably, that it's to identify certain people as inferior: exclude them; stop 'wasting' resources on them. In either case, it is less than clear to me that this is the model of test for organizations like Mensa.

Some other high-IQ societies use an adjusted model of test, where they take off the time limit, because they recognize that rushing people doesn't get best behavior, and put all the problems on anabolic steroids. This can probably boost the ceiling a little, but it has its own problems. It's a bit like taking an office where work isn't getting done, and making everybody work twenty more hours a week: if work isn't getting done, five more hours might help a little, but twenty won't fix the problem. Howard Gardner, multiple intelligence theorist, spends most of Extraordinary Minds arguing for a multiplicity of genius; in the beginning, he asks if there's anything common to all kinds of genius, and says, yes, he'd identify three things:

- There is some domain of performance.
- There is a community that appreciates the genius's performance in this domain.
- Failures.

According to Gardner, a genius fails more, and more spectacularly, than an average person.

This notwithstanding, if you're trying to get into Mega Society East, what counts on the test is not what you get right; it's what you get wrong. It's not the absolutely brilliant answers you had to questions two, five, and seven; it's the fact that you missed something on questions one, four, and nine. Given the cognitive diversity at the upper end of the spectrum, there are limitations to even high-ceiling tests.

Is there any alternative? I would say yes, and I believe a hint of it comes from a story about a high school physics student. After the unit covering air pressure, the teacher wrote on an exam, "Explain how to use a barometer to determine the height of a tall building." The student wrote, "Tie a rope around the barometer, lower it from the top of the building until it hits the ground, make a mark on the rope, pull it up, and measure the length of the rope. (There are other ways of doing this.)"

This put the teacher in a bit of a bind. He called in one of his colleagues, and explained what had happened. The colleague said, "*In a way that demonstrates your knowledge of physics*, explain how to use a barometer to determine the height of a tall building." The student said, "Go to the top of the building with a barometer and a stopwatch. Drop the barometer, and measure the time before the barometer splatters on the ground beneath. Then use the formula $y = {}^1/_2\, at^2$ to calculate the height of the building." The teachers conferred and gave him almost full credit.

The teacher asked what some of the other ways were: "Go outside on a sunny day, and measure the height of the barometer, the length of the barometer's shadow, and the length of the building's shadows, and use ratios to determine the height of the building." "This probably isn't the best way, but go into the basement, knock on the superintendent's door, and say, 'Mr. Superintendent! I have a fine barometer for you if you will only tell me the height of the building!'"

What this story screams out to me is not just that the student is bright enough that he could see the desired answer about calculating from the difference in air pressure. I'm positive of that. It's not just that he *could* give several alternate approaches. It's that he *would*. It's that he behaved like a gifted mind does when it's been completely insulted.

That gives a hint of an indirect approach: don't try IQ-normal-style cognitive strain questions, but look for a very different *kind* of thinking, and the effects of living in a world where most other people are two, three, four, five sigma below you. I wrote up the basic ideas, and e-mailed Paul Cooijmans, head of *Giga* and Glia. He suggested I start my own high-IQ society. I thought that was a little more ambitious than I wanted to take on now, but I did create a test. I wrote it up, gave it to heads of some high-IQ societies to distribute, received very kind responses from Gina LoSasso of the Mega Foundation and Nik Lygeros of the *Pi Society*... and have gotten two tests filled out, which I haven't looked at because I want to read them together. The test may turn out to be nothing more than an interesting fizzle. Even then, I thought it might be interesting enough to share.

What about the glass wall? The symbol relates to me to three layers, or levels, of maturity in dealing with others. The first layer is not recognizing there is a difference. In childhood, even when I scored high in the MathCounts competition, I might have realized there was something called intelligence and I had more of it, but not that I thought all that differently: I treated others as if they were the same as me underneath. *That is a recipe for giving and receiving hurt.*

When I finally let myself see that there were differences, I tried to fit in through blending in. In the short run, that's much better; there are far fewer incidents. Over time, it costs--the cost of a false self. There were some things in myself I wasn't showing anyone, not even myself.

After that, I began to erect a glass wall about myself, something that would keep things out of view before I was confident people were ready, but not permanently--and would let me draw others in. I don't think this is a final resting place--in fact, I'm almost positive it *isn't*--but it seems a definite step ahead of the other two steps.

What's inside the glass wall? Much of this speech hints at things inside the glass wall, but I'd like to give one concrete example.

In the book Fearfully and Wonderfully Made, Phillip Yancey helps draw out stories and insights from Paul Brand, the doctor who discovered that leprosy ravages the body by destroying the sense of touch, and with it the ability to feel pain. In one of these stories, Dr. Brand tells how he left a speaking engagement sick, sat hunched in the corner of a train car, wishing the interminable train ride would be over, and finally staggered to his hotel room. He began to undress, and realized to his horror that there was no feeling in his left heel.

He pricked himself with a pin and felt nothing. He jabbed himself harder, watched a drop of blood form, and moaned for the pain that would not come. That night, he lay dressed on his bed. He knew that sulfone drugs would probably stop the spread of the disease quite quickly, but he still could not help imagine it spreading to his hands, his feet. As a doctor who worked with patients who'd lost their sense of touch, he cherished the feel of earth in his fingers, the feel of a puppy's fur, the affection of a friend. His career as a surgeon would soon end. What's more, what would become of his movement? He, their leader, had assured others that leprosy was the least contagious of all communicable diseases, and careful hygeine could almost ensure that they would not get it. What would it mean if he, their leader, was a *leper*? That ugly word he'd banished from his vocabulary rose like a monster with new strength.

After a long and sleepless night, Dr. Brand got up, and took a pin to face the gristly task of mapping out the affected area. He took a breath, jabbed himself--and roared in pain. Nothing had ever felt so delicious to him as that one electric jolt of pain.

He realized what had happened. He was sick, with something mundane, and as a sick traveller had forgone his usual motion. *His foot had fallen asleep.* Dr. Brand was for a time too ashamed to recount that dismal experience, but I'm glad he did. The experience changed his life, and the story has impacted me.

As far as perception goes, I'm not sure if my sense of touch is more perceptive than most people's. Probably a little bit. I can say that it is integrated with other senses. There was one time I was at the supermarket, and the woman in front of me in the checkout line dropped a soda bottle a short distance. Being bored, I gently pinched the bottle, and then made a comment that seemed to me almost too obvious to be worth saying: if you pinch a soda bottle, you can tell if it's safe to open. A bottle that can be safely opened will give slightly to moderate pressure; a bottle that's shaken up is firm as a rock. Her reply, "Oh, is that the trick that you use?" caught me off guard. Feeling a shaken soda bottle like that is no more a *trick* to me than looking at the stove for dancing orange spots is a trick to see if I've started a grease fire.

As an American who's lived in France, I like to give my friends hugs and kisses. I'm careful how and when I ask, particularly about a kiss on the cheek, and I listen to people with my intuition before asking those questions... but that invitation (accepted or not) is usually tied to when I pull someone inside the glass wall.

What about a musing life? Neil Postman, in Amusing Ourselves to Death: Public Discourse in an Age of Show Business talks about the dark side of television's effects on culture. Without going into a full analysis of Plato's Allegory of the Television, I will say that television blinds the inner eye by stimulating the surface and starving the depths. *A home without a television is like a slice of chocolate cake without tartar sauce.*

Without television, what happens? At times, you get bored, and then more bored, and then you come to a place *on the other side of boredom* with renewed creativity, sensitivity, and insight. I try to live there; like my time sense and the presence learned through wine, it gives focus to musings, such as this talk was woven from. It is a sort of fast for the mind, and makes room for a considerable degree of depth.

What is my interest in thinking inside the box? There's been a lot of homage paid to the many virtues of thinking outside the box. Perhaps many of you have stories to tell of a time when someone was extolling the many virtues of thinking outside the box, but that's not where I'm going. The praises of thinking outside the box are sung because thinking inside and outside the box complement each other, and most people are so often inside the box that it's hard for them to step out. With severely gifted individuals, the real challenge is not thinking outside the box, but thinking inside the box.

There are many times that it's better to think inside the box. Driving to work, for instance. More deeply, communicating and negotiating requires one to understand and think like the other person, and for many people, this means thinking inside the box. I'd also like to give one very concrete example of where it's important to think inside the box: manners.

Manners are an arbitrary collection of rules, and there is no unifying principle that everything else flows from. Respecting and valuing the person will not tell you why you should hold a fork like a pen instead of how a little boy wants to hold a knife. Something that meaningless may be very difficult for you and me to learn, but it is important. Why? To many people, manners are the very foundation of civilized interaction, and it presents them with a needless and pointless obstacle if you say, "I respect you and I do not feel the need to observe manners in your presence."

It's been said, "Never offend people with style when you can offend them with substance;" if people are going to walk away from you offended, let them be offended by something of substance, not by crude manners.

And lastly: mystic, artist, Christian. Why do I group these together? Does being a mystic make one an artist and a Christian? No; nothing like that holds directly, but there is a common thread. It's illuminated by a conversation I had with one friend, where I said that pragmatism was a philosophical disease. I learned shortly thereafter that pragmatism was quite important to her.

Why would I say something like that? In one conversation a few years earlier, at Calvin College, one of my friends asked me why I wanted something, and didn't like my response. A little probing, and I knew why: while the words he used were, "Why do you want it?", what he meant by it, the only thing he could mean at that time, was, "What do you find it useful for?" The item, whatever it was (I don't remember), was not something I wanted for its usefulness in letting me get something else; it was something I valued in itself. He couldn't see that.

So I asked him, "Do you value having that arm on your body?" "Uh, yes..." "Why?" "Because if I have an arm, I can grab an apple." "Why do you want that?" "Because if I grab an apple, I can eat an apple." "Why do you want that?" "Because if I eat an apple, I can live and not die!" "Why do you want that?" At *that* point, he gave the response I'd been waiting for: an impassioned explanation that living and not dying was not simply valued as a means to something else, but something he wanted for itself.

Pragmatism and utilitarianism have a very small circle of things that are valued outside of their usefulness to something else: the *Oxford Companion to Philosophy* lists only pleasure, which seems a dismally small selection to me. Franky Schaeffer's Addicted to Mediocrity: 20th Century Christians and the Arts talks about the insipid banality in the Christian art tradition: the tradition that once produced Dante and Bach has now produced John's Christian Stores, and a large part of that is because Christians sold their birthright to embrace pragmatism. Where pragmatism draws a small circle of things that are embraced, Christianity, mysticism, and art draw a much larger circle: there's something there that isn't in Dewey and Mill's practical world.

Madeleine l'Engle, in Walking on Water: Reflections on Faith and Art, tells of a time in college when her professor asked on a test how Chaucer chose a particular literary device in a passage, and she wrote in a white heat of fury that Chaucer did not "choose a literary device;" that's not how an artist works at all! I had a loosely similar experience, if not involving anger; I was sharing something I was writing with a new acquaintance, and she complimented my use of personification at a specific point. I had to reread the passage more than once to see what she meant; she made a straightforward statement, but I had not thought in those terms. A good artist may have excellent technique, but the technique is there because the art is good; the art is not good just because of the technique. Good art comes through something much more, and much more interesting, than technique: listening to the work, serving it, cooperating with it, helping an unformed idea have a shape that others can see.

What about mysticism? There is a problem here; you might say that insofar as mysticism can be explained, it is not mysticism. I will say that the characters I identify with most in literature have been characters who've had a foot in another world. Charles Wallace from Madeleine l'Engle's A Wind in the Door is not the boy genius, Dexter from *Dexter's Laboratory*, an abstract personification of intelligence; he is a very real and believable person. He is open to another world, not surprised to think he's seen dragons in the twins' vegetable garden, and he *kythes*; that is, he has a real and present communication, something beyond communication, with others. You can read about kything in the 100 ways of kything on my webpage.

In Robert Heinlein's Stranger in a Strange Land, Michael Valentine Smith is born as a baby boy on Mars, orphaned by all human travellers, raised on Mars by Martians in Martian culture, and brought to earth as a young man. Let's talk about culture shock for a moment. Smith causes and receives quite a lot of it, as the story narrates his progression from a Martian with the genes and ancestry of a man to a character who is both human and Martian. There are quite a few stumbling points along the way to this. At one point, early in the story, someone asks Michael what is intended to be a very routine question, but Michael doesn't get it. He has heard the words before, but he's a bit like a top-notch English professor trying to decipher a math paper: even with a glossary to all the symbol, there's a whole way of thinking that goes with the strange words, and Michael doesn't understand it. Heinlein says that half a million years' wildly alien abstractions raced through his mind. I don't have half a million years' worth of much of anything, but I do have wildly alien abstractions. I first became a philosopher as a boy, too young to touch any of my thoughts in language; one of the questions I thought of was, "Am I human?", or, "Am I a being of the same class as those I observe around me?" I observed that my parents were linguistic creatures who moved naturally in language, that I was not linguistic in any comparable way, and concluded that I was not human. Another question I pondered was a short, simple question that could be rendered, "Can there be a perpetual motion machine, and if so, how can it be started?" The second part of the question was tied to the first; the best way I can explain it is that, given time-symmetric laws of physics, if there's a machine that will keep on going forever, then the other side of the coin is that it has been going on forever, and there's no way to start it. In middle school, I started French at about the age of ten, and in a few years was able to think more fluently in French than in English. My accent sounded more typical of a native Parisian French speaker than a Midwestern American English speaker. Why? There are a couple of reasons, differences in how the two languages were taught, but one of the basic ones is that English was here, French was there, and my way of thinking was way out there, and happened to be closer to French than English.

Blajeny, also from A Wind in the Door, is a Teacher from another galaxy, and the lessons he brings are sometimes difficult: not as, "Face your worst fear ever," but as different from what they'd expect. He tells the children they will be in his class, and Meg is elated that her brother Charles will never have to go to the red schoolhouse again; then he says something that leaves her wondering where his classroom is. Blajeny retreats inside himself, and when she's decided he won't answer, he says, "Here, there, everywhere. In the schoolyard in first-grade recess. With the cherubim and seraphim. Among the farandolae." I am wearing the costume you see me in because of how I identify with Blajeny, because there's something of me that shines through him.

Last, what about being a Christian? There's one music professor who said that, rather than thinking that we sing a song one and then it's over, and we sing it later, and so on, we should rather thing that as long as there have been created beings, there is an eternal song rising before God, a song rising as incense that will never go out, and that when we sing we step into that song. Christianity is the foundation this whole edifice of thought is built upon, and its crowning jewel. It is the soil in which other things grow, and the thoughts I have given are an example of how Christians may think.

So now in this brief time I have shared a little bit about myself; I have answered a few questions and raised many more. Come visit my website, at Jonathan's Corner (Search & Sitemap); it's in your program. Of course I'd like to hear from an editor who'd like me to write something, or would like an existing manuscript, or someone who'd like to hear me speak, or someone who'd like a website built, but more than any of that I have given this talk for the same reason I've built my website: to connect. What have I left you wondering about?

An Abstract Art of Memory

Abstract. Author briefly describes classic mnemotechnics, indicates a possible weakness in their ability to deal with abstractions, and suggests a parallel development of related principles designed to work well with abstractions.

Frances Yates opens *The Art of Memory* with a tale from ancient Greece[1]:

> At a banquet given by a nobleman of Thessaly named Scopas, the poet Simonides of Ceos chanted a lyric poem in honor of his post but including a passage in praise of Castor and Pollux. Scopas meanly told the poet that he would only pay him half the sum agreed upon for the panegyric and that he must obtain the balance from the twin gods to whom he had devoted half the poem. A little later, a message was brought in to Simonides that two young men were waiting outside who wished to see him. He rose from the banquet and went out but could find no one. During his absence the roof of the banqueting hall fell in, crushing Scopas and all the guests beneath the ruins; the corpses were so mangled that the relatives who came to take them away for burial were unable to identify them. But Simonides remembered the places at which they had been sitting at the table and

was therefore able to indicate to the relatives which were their dead.

After his spatial memory in this event, Simonides is credited with having created an art of memory: start with a building full of distinct places. If you want to remember something, imagine a striking image with a token of what you wish to remember at the place. To recall something naval, you might imagine a giant nail driven into your front door, with an anchor hanging from it; if you visualize this intensely, then when in your mind's eye you go through your house and imagine your front door, then the anchor will come to mind and you will remember the boats. Imagining a striking image on a remembered place is called *pegging*: when you do this, you fasten a piece of information on a given peg, and can pick it up later. Yates uses the terms *art of memory* and *artificial memory* as essentially interchangeable with *mnemotechnics*, and I will follow a similar usage.

There is a little more than this to the technique, and it allows people to do things that seem staggering to someone not familiar with the phenomenon[2]. Being able to look at a list of twenty items and recite it forwards and backwards is more than a party trick. The technique is phenomenally well-adapted to language acquisition. It is possible for a person skilled in the technique to learn to read a language in weeks. It is the foundation to some people learning an amount of folklore so that today they would be considered walking encyclopedias. This art of memory was an important part of the ancient Greek rhetorical tradition[3], drawn by medieval Europe into the cardinal virtue of wisdom[4], and then transformed into an occult art by the Renaissance[5]. Medieval and renaissance variations put the technique to vastly different use, and understood it to signify greatly different things, but outside of Lullism[6] and Ramism[7], the essential technique was the same.

In my own efforts to learn the classical form of the art of memory, I have noticed something curious. I'm better at remembering people's names, and I no longer need to write call numbers down when I go to the library. I was able, without difficulty, to deliver an hour-long speech from memory. Learning vocabulary for foreign languages has come much more quickly; it only took me about a month to learn to read the Latin Vulgate. My weaknesses in memory are not nearly so great as they were, and I know other people have been much better at the art than I am. At the same time, I've found one surprise, something different from the all-around better memory I suspected the art would give me. What is it? If there is a problem, it is most likely subtle: the system has obvious benefits. To tease it out, I'd like to recall a famous passage from Plato's *Phaedrus*[8]:

> *Socrates:* At the Egyptian city of Naucratis, there was a famous old god, whose name was Theuth; the bird which is called the Ibis was sacred to him, and he was the inventor of many arts, such as arithmetic and calculation and geometry and astronomy and draughts and dice, but his great discovery was the use of letters. Now in those days Thamus was the king of the whole of Upper Egypt, which is in the district surrounding that great city which is called by the Hellenes Egyptian Thebes, and they call the god himself Ammon. To him came Theuth and showed his inventions, desiring that the other Egyptians might be allowed to have the benefit of them; he went through them, and Thamus inquired about their several uses, and praised some of them and censured others, as he approved or disapproved of them. There would be no use in repeating all that Thamus said to Theuth in praise or blame of the various arts. But when they came to letters, This, said Theuth, will make the Egyptians wiser and give them better memories; for this is the cure of forgetfulness and folly. Thamus replied: O most ingenious Theuth, he who has the gift of invention is not always the best judge of the utility or inutility of his own inventions to the users of them. And in this instance a paternal love of your own child has led you to say what is

> not the fact: for this invention of yours will create forgetfulness in the learners' souls, because they will not use their memories; they will trust to the external written characters. You have found a specific, not for memory but for reminiscence, and you give your disciples only the pretence of wisdom; they will be hearers of many things and will have learned nothing; they will appear to be omniscient and will generally know nothing; they will be tiresome, having the reputation of knowledge without the reality.

There is clear concern that writing is not what it appears, and it will endanger or destroy the knowledge people keep in memory; a case can be made that the phenomenon of Renaissance artificial memory as an occult practice occurred because only someone involved in the occult would have occasion to keep such memory after books were so easily available.

What kind of things might one wish to have in memory? Let me quote one classic example: the argument by which Cantor proved that there are more real numbers between 0 and 1 than there are counting numbers (1, 2, 3...). I paraphrase the basic argument here:

1. Two sets are said to have the same number of elements if you can always pair them up, with nothing left over on either side. If one set always has something left over after the matching up, it has more elements.
2. Suppose, for the sake of argument, that there are at least as many counting numbers as real numbers between 0 and 1. Then you can make a list of the numbers between 0 and 1:

```
1:  .012343289889...
2:  .328932198323...
3:  .438724328743...
4:  .988733287923...
5:  .324432003442...
6:  .213443765001...
7:  .321010320030...
```

```
8:   .323983213298...
9:   .982133982198...
10:  .321932198904...
11:  .000321321278...
12:  .032103217832...
```

3. Now, take the first decimal place of the first number, the second of the second number, and so on and so forth, and make them into a number:

```
1:   .012343289889...
2:   .328932198323...
3:   .438724328743...
4:   .988733287923...
5:   .324432003442...
6:   .213443765001...
7:   .321010320030...
8:   .323983213298...
9:   .982133982198...
10:  .321932198904...
11:  .000321321278...
12:  .032103217832...
```

   Result:

```
.028733312972...
```

4. Now make another number between 0 and 1 that is different at every decimal place from the number just computed:

```
.139844423083...
```

5. Now, remember that we assumed that the list has all the numbers between 0 and 1: every single one, without exception. Therefore, if this assumption is true, then the latter number we constructed must be on the list. But where?

   The number can't be the first number on the list, because it was constructed to be different at the first decimal place from the first number on the list. It can't be the second number on the list, because it was constructed to be different at the second decimal place from the second number on the list. Nor can it be the third, fourth, fifth... in fact, it can't be *anywhere* on the list because it was constructed to be different. So we have one number left over. (Can we put that number on the list? Certainly, but the argument shows that the new list will leave out another number.)

6. The list of numbers between 0 and 1 doesn't have all the numbers between 0 and 1.
7. We have a contradiction.
8. We started by assuming that you can make a list that contains all the numbers between 0 and 1, but there's a contradiction: any list leaves numbers left over. Therefore, our assumption must be wrong. Therefore, there must be too many real numbers between 0 and 1 to assign a separate counting number to each of them.

Let's say we want to commit this argument to memory. A mathematician with artificial memory might say, "That's easy! You just imagine a chessboard with distorted mirrors along its diagonal." That is indeed a good image if you are a mathematician who already understands the concept. If you find the argument hard to follow, it is at best a difficult thing to store via the artificial memory. Even if it can be done, storing this argument in artificial memory is probably much more trouble than learning it as a mathematician would.

Let me repeat the quotation from the Phaedrus, while changing a few words:

> *Jefferson:* At the Greek region of Thessaly, there was a famous old poet, whose name was Simonides; totems seen with the inner eye were devoted to him, and he was the inventor of a great art, greater than arithmetic and calculation and geometry and astronomy and draughts. Now

in those days Rousseau was a sage revered throughout the West, and they called the god himself *Rationis*. To him came Simonides and showed his invention, desiring that the rest of the world might be allowed to have the benefit of it; he went through it, and Rousseau inquired about its several uses, and praised some of them and censured others, as he approved or disapproved of them. There would be no use in repeating all that Rousseau said to Simonides in praise or blame of various facets. But when they came to inner writing, This, said Simonides, will make the West wiser and give it better memory; for this is the cure of forgetfulness and of folly. Rousseau replied: O most ingenious Simonides, he who has the gift of invention is not always the best judge of utility or inutility of his own inventions to the users of them. And in this instance a paternal love of your own child has led you to say what is not the fact; for this invention will create forgetfulness in the learner's souls, because they will not remember abstract things; they will trust to mere mnemonic symbols and not remember things of depth. You have found a specific, not for memory but for reminiscence, and you give your disciples only the pretence of wisdom; they will be hearers of many things and will have learned nothing; they will appear to be omniscient and will generally know nothing; they will be tiresome, having the reputation and outer shell of knowledge without the reality of deep thought.

It is clear that if we follow Thomas Aquinas's instructions on memory to visualize a woman for wisdom, we may recall wisdom. *What is less clear is that this inner writing particularly helps an abstract recollection of wisdom.* It may be able to recall an understanding of wisdom acquired without the help of artificial memory, but this art which allows at times stunning performance in the memorization of concrete data is of more debatable merit in learning abstraction. It has been my own experience that abstractions can be forced through the gate of concreteness in artificial memory, but it is like forcing a sponge through a funnel. While I admittedly don't have a medieval practitioner's inner vocabulary to deal with abstractions, using the artificial memory to deal with abstractions seems awkward in much the same way that storing individual letters through artificial memory[9] is awkward. The standard artificial memory is a tool for being reminded of abstractions, but not for remembering them. It offers the abstract thinker a seductive way to recall a great many concrete facts instead of learning deep thought.

The overall impression I receive of the artificial memory is not so much a failed attempt at a tool to store abstractions as a successful attempt at a concrete tool which was not intended to store abstractions. It is my belief that some of its principles, in modified form, suggest the beginnings of an art of memory well-fitted to dealing with abstractions. The mature form of such an endeavor will not simply be an abstract mirror image of a concrete artificial memory, but it is appropriate enough for the first steps I might hazard.

Consider the following four paragraphs:

1. Physics is like music. Both owe something of substance to the Pythagoreans. Both are aesthetic endeavors that in some way represent nature in highly abstracted form. Both are interested in mechanical waves. Many good physicists are closet musicians, and all musical instruments operate on physical principle.

2. Physics is like literature. Both are written in books that vary from moderately easy to very hard. Both deal with a distinction between action and what is acted on, be it plot and character or force and particle, and both allow complex entities to be built of simpler ones. Practitioners of both want to be thought of as insightful people who understand reality.

3. Physics is like an adventure. Both involve a venture into the unknown, where the protagonist tries to discover what

is happening. Both have a mystique that exists despite most people's fear to experience such things themselves. To succeed in either, one is expected to have impressive strengths.

4. Physics is like magic. Both flourished in the West, at the same time, out of the same desire: a desire to understand nature so as to control it. Both attract abstract thinkers, are practiced in part through the manipulation of arcane symbols, and may be found in the same person, from Newton to Feynman[10]. Magical theory claims matter to be composed of earth, air, fire, and water, while physics finds matter to be composed of solid, liquid, gas, and plasma.

What is the merit of these comparisons? They recall a story in which a literature professor asked Feynman if he thought physics was like literature. Feynman led him on with an elaborate analogy of how physics was like literature, and then said, "But it seems to me you can make such an analogy between any two subjects, so I don't find such analogies helpful." He observed that one can make a reasonably compelling analogy even if there's no philosophically substantial connection.

The laws of logic and philosophy are not the laws of memory. What is a liability to Feynman's implicit philosophical method is a strength to memory. The philosophical merit of the above comparisons is debatable. The benefit to memory is different: it appears to me that this is an abstract analogue to pegging. A connection, real or spurious, aids the memory even if it doesn't aid a rigorous philosophical understanding. In pegging, it is considered an advantage to visualize a ludicrously illogical scene: it is much more memorable than something routine and sensible. Early psychological experiments in memory involved memorization of nonsense syllables. The experimenters intentionally chose meaningless material to memorize. Why? Well, if the subject perceived meaning, that would provide a spurious way for the subject to remember the data, and so proper

Ebbinghausian memory study meant investigating how people investigate memory material which was as meaningless as possible. Without pausing to develop an obvious critique, I'd suggest that this spurious route to memory is of great interest to us. Meaningful data is more memorable than meaningless, and this is true whether the meaning perceived is philosophically sound or obviously contrived. I might suggest that interesting meaning provides a direct abstract parallel to the striking, special-effect appearance of effective images in pegging.

I intentionally chose not to compare physics to astronomy, chemistry, computer science, engineering, mathematics, metaphysics, or statistics, because I wanted to show how a different concept can be used to establish connections to a new one. Or, more properly, different concept*s*. *Having a new concept connected to three very different ones will capture different facets than one anchor point, and possibly cancel out some of each other's biases.* A multiplicity of perspectives lends balance and depth. This isn't to say similar concepts can't be used, only that searching for a partial or full isomorphism to a known concept is easier than encoding from scratch. If memorable connections can be made between physics and adventure, music, English, and magic, what might be obtained from comparison with mathematics, chemistry, and engineering? A comparison between physics and these last three disciplines is left as an exercise to the reader, and one that may be quite fruitful.

Is this a desirable way to remember things? I would make two different comments on this score. First, when learning Latin words, I would first peg it to an English word with a vivid image, then later recall the image and reconstruct the English equivalent, then recall the image and remember the English, then the image would drop out so I would directly remember the English, and finally the English word would drop out too, leaving me with a Latin usage often different from the English equivalent used. Artificial memory does not circumvent natural memory; instead it streamlines the process and short-circuits many of the disruptive trips to the dictionary. Pegs vanish with use; they are not an alternate final product but a more efficient route for concepts more frequently used, and a cache of reference material. Therefore, even if remembered comparisons between physics and adventure/music/English/magic fall short of how one would desire to understand the concept, a similar flattening of the learning curve is possible. Second, I would say that *even if you fail to peg something, you may succeed*. How? In trying to peg a person's name, I hold that name and face in an intense focus--quite the opposite how I once reacted: "I'll never remember that," a belief which chased other people's names out of my mind in seconds. That focus is relevant to memory, and it has happened more than once that I completely failed to create a peg, but my failure used enough mental energy that I still remembered. If you search through your memory and fail to make even forced connections between a new concept and existing concepts, the mental focus given to the concept will leave you much better off than if you had thrown up your hands and thought the self-fulfilling prophecy: "I will never remember that!"

Certain kinds of emotional intelligence are part of the discipline. Learning to cultivate *presence* has to do with an emotional side, and I have written elsewhere about activities that can help to cultivate such presence[11]. We learn material better if we are interested in it; therefore consciously cultivating an interest in the material and seeing how it can be fascinating is another edge. Cultivating and guarding your inner emotional state can have substantial impact on memory and learning abstractions. Much of it has to do with keeping a state of presence. Shutting out abstractions is one obvious way to do this; another, perhaps less obvious, is to avoid cramming and simply ploughing through material unless it's something you don't really need to learn. Why?

If there is a sprinkler that disperses a fine mist, it will slowly moisten the ground. What if there's a high-volume sprinkler that shoots big, heavy drops of water high up in the air? With all that water pounding on the ground, it looks like the ground is quickly saturated. The appearance is deceptive. What has happened is that the heavy drops have pounded the surface of the ground into a beaten shield, so there really is water rolling off of a very wet surface, but go an inch down and the soil is as parched as ever. This sort of thing happens in studying, when people think that the more force they use, the better the results. Up to a point, definitely, and perseverance counts--but I have found myself to learn much more when I paid attention to my mental and emotional state and backed off if I sensed that I was leaving that optimal zone. I learn something if I say "This is important, so I'll plough through as much as I can as quickly as I can," but it's not as much, and keeping on task needs to be balanced with getting off task when that is helpful.

Consider the following problem:[12]

> In the inns of certain Himalayan villages is practiced a most civilized and refined tea ceremony. The ceremony involves a host and exactly two guests, neither more nor less. When his guests have arrived and have seated themselves at his table, the host performs five services for them. These services are listed in order of the nobility which the Himalayan attribute to them: (1) Stoking the Fire, (2) Fanning the Flames, (3) Passing the Rice Cakes, (4) Pouring the Tea, and (5) Reciting Poetry. During the ceremony, any of those present may ask another, "Honored Sir, may I perform this onerous task for you?" However, a person may request of another only the least noble of the tasks which the other is performing. Further, if a person is performing any tasks, then he may not request a task which is nobler than the least noble task he is already performing. Custom requires that by the time the tea ceremony is over, all the tasks will have been transferred from the host to the most senior of the guests. How may this be accomplished?

Incomprehensible appearances notwithstanding, this is a very simple problem, the Towers of Hanoi. Someone who has learned the Towers of Hanoi may still solve the tea ceremony formulation as slowly as someone who's never seen any form of the problem[13]. A failure to recognize isomorphisms provides one of the more interesting passages in Feynman's memoirs[14]:

> I often liked to play tricks on people when I was at MIT. One time, in a mechanical drawing class, some joker picked up a French curve (a piece of plastic for drawing smooth curves--a curly, funny-looking thing) and said, "I wonder if the curves on this thing have some special formula?"
>
> I thought for a moment and said, "Sure they do. The curves are very special curves. Lemme show ya," and I picked up my French curve and began to turn it slowly. "The French curve is made so that at the lowest point on each curve, no matter how you turn it, the tangent is horizontal."
>
> All the guys in the class were holding their French curve up at different angles, holding their pencil up to it at the lowest point and laying it along, and discovering that, sure enough, the tangent is horizontal. They were all excited by this "discovery"--even though they had already gone through a certain amount of calculus and had already "learned" that the derivative (tangent) of the minimum (lowest point) of *any* curve is zero (horizontal). They didn't put two and two together. They didn't even know what they "knew."

What is going on here is that Feynman perceives an isomorphism where the others do not. There may be a natural bent to or away from perceiving isomorphisms, and cognitive science suggests most people have a bent away. The finding, as best I can tell, is not so much that people *can't* look for isomorphisms, as that they *don't*. The practice of looking for and finding isomorphisms has something to give, because something can be treated as already known instead of learned from scratch. I might wonder in passing if the ultra-high-IQ rapid learning and interdisciplinary proclivities stem in part from the perception and application of isomorphisms, which may *reduce* the amount of material actually learned in picking up a new skill.

The classical art of memory derives strength from a mind that works visually; a background in abstract thought will help one learn abstractions. It has been thought[15] that people can more effectively encode and remember material in a given domain if it's one they have worked with; I would suggest that this abstract pegging also creates a way to encode material with background from other domains. An elaborate, intense, and distinct encoding is believed to help recall[16]. Heightening of memorable features, in what is striking or humorous[17], should help, and mimetics seems likely to contain jewels in its accounts of how a meme makes itself striking.

Someone familiar with artificial memory may ask, "What about places (*loci*)?" Part of the art of memory, be it ancient, medieval, or renaissance, involved having an inner building of sorts that one could imagine going through in order and recalling items. I have two basic comments here. First, a connection could use traditional artificial memory techniques as an index: imagine a muscular man with a tremendous physique running onto the scene, grabbing an adventurer's sword, shield, and pack, sitting down at a pipe organ which has a large illuminated manuscript on top, and clumsily playing music until a giant gold ring engraved with fiery letters falls on the scene and turns it to dust. You have pegged physics to adventure, music, literature, and magic; if you wanted to reconstruct an understanding of physics, you could see what it was pegged to, and then try to recall the given similarities. Second and more deeply, *I believe that a person's entire edifice of previously acquired concepts may serve as an immense memory palace*. It is not spatial in the traditional sense, and I am not here concerned with the senses in which it might be considered a topological space, but it is a deeply qualitative place, and accessible if one uses traditional artificial memory for an index: these adaptations are intended to expand the repertoire of what disciplined artificial memory can do, not abolish the traditional discipline.

Symbols are the last unexplored facet. Earlier I suggested that a chessboard with mirrors along its diagonal may be a good token to represent Cantor's diagonal argument, but does not bring memory of the whole proof. Now I would like to give the other side: an abstraction may not be fully captured by a symbol, but a good symbol helps. A sign/symbol distinction has been made, where a sign represents while a symbol represents and embodies. In this sense I suggest that tokens be as symbolic as possible.

Why use a token? Aren't the deepest thoughts beyond words? Yes, but recall depends on being able to encode. I have found my deepest thoughts to not be worded and often difficult to translate to words, but I have also found that I lose them if I cannot put them in words. As such, thinking and choosing a good, mentally manipulable symbol for an abstraction is both difficult and desirable. My own discipline of formation, mathematics, chooses names for variables like 'x', 'y', and 'z' which software engineers are taught not to use because they impede comprehension: a computer program with variable names like 'x' and 'y' is harder to understand or even write to completion than one which with names like 'trucks_remaining' or 'customers_last_name'. The authors of *Design Patterns*[18] comment that naming a pattern is one of the hardest parts of writing it down. The art of creating a manipulable symbol for an abstraction is hard, but worth the trouble. This, too, may also help you to probe an abstraction in a way that will aid recall.

To test these principles, I decided to spend a week[19] seeing what I could learn of a physics text[20] and Kant's *Critique of Pure Reason*[21]. I considered myself to have understood a portion of the physics text after being able to solve the last of the list of questions. I had originally decided to see how quickly I could absorb material. After working through 10% of the physics text in one day, I decided to shift emphasis and pursue depth more than speed. In reading Kant, the tendency to barely grasp a difficult concept forgotten in grasping the next difficult concept gave way, with artificial memory, to understanding the concepts better and grasping them in a way that had a more permanent effect. I read through page 108 of 607 in the physics text and 144 of 669 in Kant's *Critique of Pure Reason*.

The first day's physics ventures saw two interesting ways of storing concepts, and one comment worth mentioning. There is a classic skit, in which two rescuers are performing two-person CPR on a patient. Then one of the rescuers says, "I'm getting tired. Let's switch," and the patient gets up, the tired rescuer lies down, and the other two perform CPR on him. This was used to store the interchangeability of point of effort, point of resistance, and fulcrum on a lever, based on an isomorphism to the skit's humor element.

The rule given later, that along any axis the sum of forces for a body in equilibrium is always zero, was symbolized by an image of a knife cutting a circle through the center: no matter what angle of cutting there was, the cut leaves two equal halves.

These both involved images, but the images differed from pegging images as a schematic diagram differs from a computer animated advertisement. They seemed a combination of an isomorphism and a symbol, and in both cases the power stemmed not only from the resultant image but the process of creation. The images functioned in a sense related to pegging, but most of the images so far developed have been abstract images unlike anything I've read about in historical or how-to discussion of the art of memory.

The following was logged that night. The problem referred to is a somewhat complex lever problem given in three parts:

> In reviewing the day's thoughts at night, I recognized that the problems seem to admit a shortcut solution that does not rigorously apply the principles but obtains the correct answer: problem 12 on page 31 gives two weights and other information, and all three subproblems can be answered by assuming that there are two parts in the same ratio [as] the weights, and applying a little horse sense as to which goes where. It's a bit like general relativity, which

condenses to "Everything changes by a factor of the square root of (1 - (v^2/c^2))." I am not sure whether this is a property of physics itself or a socially emergent property of problems used in physics texts.

I believe this suggests that I was interacting with the material deeply and quite probably in a fashion not anticipated by the authors.

In reading Kant, I can't as easily say "I solved the last exercises in each section" and don't simply want to just say, "I read these pages." I would like to demonstrate interaction with the material with excerpts from my log:

> ...I am now in the introduction to the second edition, and there are two images in reference to Kant's treatment of subjective and objective. One is of a disc which has been cut in half, sliced again along a perpendicular axis and brought together along the first axis so that the direction of the cut has been changed. The other is of a sphere being turned out by [topologically] compactifying R3 [Euclidean three-space] by the addition of a single point, and then shifting so the vast outside has become the cramped inside and the cramped inside has become the vast outside. Both images are inadequate to the text, indicating at best what sort of thing may be thought about in what sort of shift Kant tries to introduce, and I want to reread the last couple of pages. Closer to the mark is a story about three umpires who say, in turn, "I calls them as they are," "I calls them as I see them," and "They may be strikes, they may be balls, but they ain't nothing until I calls them!"

> Having reread, I believe that the topological example is truer than I realized. I made it on almost superficial grounds, after reading a footnote which gave as example scientific progress after Copernicus proposed, rather than that the observer be fixed and the heavens rotate, the heavens are fixed and the observer rotate. The deeper

significance is this: prior accounts had apparently not given sufficient account to subjective factors, treating subjective differences as practically unimportant--what mattered for investigation was the things in themselves. Thus the subjective was the unexamined inside of the sphere. Then, after the transformation, the objective was the unexaminable inside of the new sphere: we may investigate what is now outside, our subjective states and the appearances conformed to them, but things in themselves are more sealed than our filters before: before, we didn't look; after, we can't look. What is stated [in Kant] so far is a gross overextension of a profound observation.

The below passages refer to pp. 68-70:

Kant's arguments that space is an *a priori* concept can be framed as showing that there exists a chicken-and-egg or bootstrapping gap between them and sense data.

What is a chicken-and-egg/bootstrapping gap? In assisting with English as a Second Language instruction, I was faced with a difficulty in explanation. Assuming certain background, it is possible for a person not to know something while there is a straightforward way of explaining--perhaps a very long way of explaining, but it's obvious enough how to explain it in terms of communicable concepts. Then there is the case where there is no direct way to explain something: one example is how to explain to a small child what air is. One can point to water, wood, metal, stone, food, and a great many other things, but the same procedure may not yield understanding of air. It may be possible with a Zen-like cleverness to circumvent it--in saying, for example, that air is what presses on your skin on a windy day--but it is not as straightforward as even an involved and difficult explanation where you know how to use the other person's concepts to build the one you want.

In English as a Second Language instruction, this

kind of gap is a significant phenomenon in dealing with students who have no beginning English knowledge, and in dealing with concepts that cannot obviously be demonstrated: 'sister' and 'woman', when both terms refer to an adult, differ in a way that is almost certainly understood in the student's native tongue but is nonetheless extremely difficult to explain. When I first made the musing, I envisioned a Zen-like solution. Koans immortalize incidents in which Zen masters bypassed chicken-and-egg gaps in trying to convey enlightenment that cannot be straightforwardly explained, and therefore show a powerful kind of communication. That is what I envisioned, but it is not how English is taught to speakers of other languages. What happens in ESL classes, and with younger children, is a gradual emergence that is difficult to account for in the terms of analytic philosophy--a straightforward explanation sounds like hand-waving and sloppy thinking--but with enough repetition, material is picked up. It may have something to do with a mechanism of learning outlined in Polanyi's *Personal Knowledge*, which talks about how i.e. swimmers learn from coaches to inhale more air and exhale less completely so that their lungs act more as a flotation device than a non-swimmers, *even though neither swimmer nor coach is likely aware of what is going on on any conscious level*. People pick things up through at least one route besides grasping a concept consciously synthesized from sense data.

Kant's proof that a given concept is *a priori* essentially consists of argument that the concept that cannot be synthesized from sense data through the obvious means of central route processing. He is probably right in that the concepts he classifies as *a priori*, and presumably others as well, cannot just be synthesized from sense data through central route processing. It does not follow that a concept must be *a priori*: there are other possibilities besides the route Kant investigates that one can acquire a belief. I do believe, though, that we come with some kind of innate or *a priori* knowledge: the difficulties experienced in visualizing four dimensional objects suggest that our dealing with three-dimensional space is not simply the result of a completely amorphous central nervous system which we happen to condition to deal with three dimensions; there is something of substance, comparable in character to a psychologist's broader understanding of memory, that we are born to. An investigation of that would take me too far afield.

P. 87. "Now a thing in itself cannot be known throu[g]h mere relations; and we may therefore conclude that since outer science gives us nothing but mere relations, this sense can contain in its representation only the relation of an object to the subject, and not the inner properties of the object in itself."

There is a near-compatibility between this and realist philosophy of science. How?

Recall my observation about chicken-and-egg gaps and how they may be surmounted (here I think of Zenlike short-circuiting of the gap rather than the vaguely indicated gradual emergence of concepts which haven't been subject to a detailed and understood explanation). What goes on in a physics experiment? The truly famous ones since 1900--I think of the Millikin oil-drop experiment--include a very clever hack that tricks nature into revealing herself. People, not even experimental physicists, can grab a handful of household items and prove that electric charge is quantized. [22] Perhaps that was possible in Galileo's day, but a groundbreaking experiment involves a brilliant, clever, unexpected trickery of nature that is isomorphic to a Zen short-circuiting in a chicken-and-egg gap, or a clever hack, and so on and so forth. Even a routine classroom experiment uses technology that is the fruit of this kind of resourcefulness. People do something they "shouldn't" be able to do. This is possibly how we might learn intuitions

Kant classifies as *a priori*, and how experimental scientists cleverly circumvent the roadblock Kant describes here. It might be said that understanding this basic problem is prerequisite to a good realist philosophy of science.

'Hack', in this context, refers to the programming cleverness described in *Programming Pearls*[23]. I analyzed that fundamental mode of problem solving and compared it with its counterpart in "Of Technology, Magic, and Channels"[24]. There are other observations and interactions with the text, but I believe these should adequately make the point.

I chose Kant because of his reputation as an impenetrable analytic philosopher. With the aid of a good translation and these principles, I was at times surprised at how easy it was to read. By the end of the week, I had another surprise when I decided to reread George MacDonald's *Phantastes*[25], a work which I have greatly enjoyed. This time, my experience was different. I felt my mind working differently despite a high degree of mental fatigue. The evocative metaphor fell dead, and I found myself reading the text as I would read Kant, thinking in a manner deeply influenced by reading Kant, and in the end setting it down because my mind had shifted deeply into a mode quite different from what allows me to enjoy *Phantastes*. I was surprised at how deeply using abstract memory to read Kant had affected not only conscious recall of ideas but also ways of thought itself.

I do not consider my recorded observations to be in any sense a rigorous experiment, but I believe the experience suggests it's interesting enough to be worth a good experiment.

Here are twelve proposed principles, or rules of thumb, of abstract memory:

1. Be wholly present. Want to know the material. Make it emotionally relevant and connected to something that concerns you. Don't take notes[26].
2. Encode material in multiple ways. Some different ways to encode are: analogies to different abstractions, list

distinctions from similar abstractions, paraphrase, search for isomorphisms, use the concepts, and create visual symbols.[27]

3. At least in the beginning, mix a little bit of reading material with a lot of processing. Don't plough through anything you want to remember. Work on drawing a lot of mist in, not pounding with heavy drops that will create a beaten shield.
4. Don't read out of a desire to finish reading a text. Read to draw the materials through processed thought.
5. Process in a way that is striking, stunning, novel, and counter-intuitive: in a word, memorable.
6. Process material on as deep a level as you can.[28]
7. Search for subtle distinctions between a concept under study and its near neighbors.
8. Converse, interact with, and respond to the abstractions. What would you say if an acquaintance said that in a discussion? What questions would you ask? Write it down.
9. Know how much mental energy you have, and choose battles wisely. Given a limited amount of energy, it is better to fully remember a smaller number of critical abstractions than to have diffuse knowledge of many random ideas.
10. Guard your emotions. Be aware of what emotional states you learn well in, and put being in those states before passing your eyes over such-and-such many pages of reading material.
11. Review material after study, seeking to find a different way of putting it.
12. Metacogitate. Be your own coach.

Committing these principles to memory is left as an

exercise to the reader.

What can I say to conclude this monograph? I can think of one or two brief addenda, such as the programmer's virtue of laziness[29], but in a very real sense I can't conclude now. I can sketch out a couple of critiques that may be of interest. Jerry Mander[30] critiques the artificial unusuality of television and especially advertising, in a way that has direct bearing on traditional mnemotechnics. He suggests that giving otherwise uninteresting sensation a strained and artificial unusuality has undesirable impact on how people perceive life as seen outside of TV, and the angle of his critique is the main reason why I was hesitant to learn artificial memory. There may be room for similar critiques about why making ridiculous comparisons to remember ideas creates a bad habit for someone who wishes to think rigorously. There is also the cognitive critique that the search for isomorphisms will introduce unnoted distortion. One thinks of the person who says, "All the religions in the world say the same thing." There is a common and problematic tendency to be astute in perceiving substantial similarities among world religions and all but blind in perceiving even more substantial differences. That is why I suggest comparing with multiple and different familiar concepts, rather than one. I could give other thoughts about critiques, but I'm trying to explain an art of memory, not especially to defend it.My intention here is not to settle all questions, but open the biggest one and suggest a direction of inquiry by which an emerging investigation may find a more powerful way to learn abstractions.[31]

Notes

1. Yates, Frances A., *The Art of Memory*, hereafter *AM*, Chicago: University of Chicago Press, 1966, pp. 1-2. The text is a treasure trove on the development of mnemotechnics, also referred to here as artificial memory or the art of memory.
2. Trudeau, Kevin, *Kevin Trudeau's Mega Memory*, hereafter

KTMM, New York: William Morrow & Co., 1995 is one of several practical manuals for someone who thinks the classical art of memory interesting and would like to be able to use it.

3. *AM*, pp. 27ff.

4. *Ibid.*, pp. 50ff.

5. *Ibid.*, pp. 129ff.

6. *Ibid.*, pp. 173ff.

7. *Ibid.*, pp. 231ff.

8. Jowett, B., *The Dialogues of Plato*, Vol. III, hereafter *DP*, New York: National Library Company, pp. 442-443.

9. *AM*, pp. 112ff describes one popularizer whose somewhat debased form advocated memorizing individual letters. This practice is awkward, much as it would be awkward to record the appearance of a room by taking a notepad and writing one letter on each sheet of paper.

10. Feynman, Richard, *Surely You're Joking, Mr. Feynman*, hereafter *SYJMF*, New York: W. W. Norton & Company, 1985, pp. 338ff and other places in the text. He began his famous "Cargo Cult Science" address by talking about his occult diversions from scientific endeavors, and it is arguable that Newton's groundbreaking work in physics and optics was a scientific diversion from his main occult endeavors. I find it revealing that, even with Feynman's occult forays left in the book, the index shows curious lacunae for "ESP", "Hallicunation", "New Age", "Reflexology", "Sensory deprivation", etc.

11. *100 Ways of Kything*, hereafter *1WK*, by Jonathan Hayward, at http://JonathansCorner.com/writing/kything describes a number of activities which can embody presence and focus.

12. Hayes, J.R., and Simon, H.A., "Understanding Written

Problem Instructions", 1974, in Gregg, L.W. ed., *Knowledge and Cognition*, hereafter *KC*, Hillsdale: Erlbaum. Quoted in Posner, Michael I. ed., *Foundations of Cognitive Science*, hereafter *FCS*, Cambridge: The MIT Press, 1989, pp. 534-535.

13. *FCS*, pp. 559-560.

14. *SYJMF*, pp. 36-37. A more scholarly, if more pedestrian, mention of the phenomenon is provided in *FCS*, pp. 559-560.

15. *FCS*, p. 690. The authors do not necessarily subscribe to this view, but acknowledge influence among many in the field.

16. *Ibid.*, p. 691.

17. "A Picture of Evil", hereafter *APE*, by Jonathan Hayward, at http://JonathansCorner.com/writing/evil/ provides an example of communication which is striking in this manner.

18. Gamma, Erich; Helm, Richard; Johnson, Ralph; Vlissides, John, *Design Patterns: Elements of Reusable Object-Oriented Software*, hereafter *DP*, Reading: Addison-Wesley, p. 3. The book describes recurring good practices that are known to many expert practitioners, but often only on a tacit level--and tries to explain how this tacit knowledge can be made explicit. The book is commonly called 'GoF' ("Gang of Four") by software developers. Thanks to Ron Miles for locating the page number.

19. February 9-15 2002. Testing abstract artificial and honing this article were juggled with other responsibilities.

20. Black, Newton Henry; Davis, Harvey Nathaniel, *New Practical Physics: Fundamental Principles and Applications to Daily Life*, hereafter *NPP*, New York: Macmillan, 1929. Given to me as a whimsical Christmas gift in 2001. At the time of beginning, I was significantly

out of practice in both physics and mathematics.

21. Smith, Norman Kemp tr., *Immanuel Kant's Critique of Pure Reason*, hereafter *IKCPR*, London: Macmillan, 1929. I had not previously read Kant.

22. I knew that science doesn't deal in proof; experiments may corroborate a theory, but not establish it as something to never again doubt. I was thinking at that point along another dimension, to convey a quality of physics experiments today.

23. Bentley, Jon Louis, *Programming Pearls*, hereafter *PP*, Reading: Addison-Wesley, 1986.

24. Hayward, Jonathan, "Of Technology, Magic, and Channels", in *Gift of Fire*, June 2001, number 126.

25. MacDonald, George, *Phantastes*, hereafter *P*, reprinted Grand Rapids: Wm. B. Eerdmans, 1999.

26. Despite widespread endorsement of this practice, taking notes taxes limited mental energy that can better be used to understand the material, and acts to the mind as a signal of, "This can safely be forgotten." *KTMM*, very early on, makes a point of telling readers not to take notes (p. 5). The purpose of attending a lecture or reading a book is to make internal comprehension rather than external reference materials.

27. Tulving, Endel; Craik, Fergus I.M., *The Oxford Handbook of Memory*, hereafter *OHM*, Oxford: Oxford University Press, 2000, refers on p. 98 to the *picture superiority effect*, which states that pictures are better remembered because of a dual coding where they are encoded as image and words and therefore have two chances at being stored rather than the one chance when material is presented only as words.

28. *OHM* mentions on p. 94 the "levels of processing" view, a significant perspective which states that material is

retained better the more deeply it is processed.

29. Wall, Larry; Christiansen, Tom; Schwartz, Randal L., *Programming Perl*, Second Edition, hereafter *PP2*, Sebastopol: O'Reilly, pp. 217ff and other places throughout the book. Known by the affectionate nickname of "the camel book" among software developers. (This book is distinct from *PP*).
30. Mander, Jerry, *Four Arguments for the Elimination of Television*, hereafter *FAET*, New York: Morrow Quill, 1978, pp. 299ff.
31. I would like to thank Robin Munn for giving me my first serious introduction to the art of memory, Linda Washington and Martin Harris for looking at my manuscript, William Struthers for valuable comments about source material, and Chris Tessone, Angela Zielinski, Kent and Theo Nebergall, and people from Wheaton College and International Christian Mensa for prayer. I would also like to thank those who read this article, apply it, perhaps extend it, and perhaps tell others about them.

The Mindstorm

The Alumnus: Hello. I was in town, and I wanted to stop in for a visit.

The Visionary: How good to see you! What have you been up to? We're all interested in hearing what our alumni are doing.

The Alumnus: Well, that would take a bit of explaining. I had a good experience with college.

The Visionary: That's lovely to hear.

The Alumnus: Yes, and I know that some alumni from our Illinois Mathematics and Science Academy, also known as IMSA, didn't. I got through college the same way I got through gradeschool, playing by the law of the jungle. I stopped and thought about how to approach college. I realized soon that higher numbered courses were easier than lower numbered courses, and how to find professors I could work with. And I understand why one alumna said, "IMSA didn't prepare me for college. It prepared me for graduate school." College will not automatically be a good experience for IMSA students, but there are choices the college won't advertise but could be made.

The Visionary: I wish you could speak to some of our students.

The Alumnus: I'd like the opportunity. There are a lot of things to say--that there's a normal scale of elementary-junior high-high school-undergraduate-graduate school, and IMSA doesn't fit on it. It has high school aged students, but it's not a modified high school; it's close in ways to graduate school, but there's something about it that is missed if you put it at any one point on the scale. And this has the result that IMSA students need to realize that when they enter college, they are not going from high school to the next step after high school; they're going from IMSA to something that was not meant to follow IMSA. But something that has opportunities if they knock on back doors and take advantage of some things the university doesn't know they need.

The Visionary: If you're serious about talking to our students, I mean talking with our students, I can introduce you to the appropriate people.

The Alumnus: Thank you. I was mentioning this to lead up to a gem of a class I took, one on what you need to know to make user-friendly computer programs, i.e. usability. There was something that set me thinking, nettled me, when I was reading through some of the jargon file's Hell desk slang, um, I mean help desk slang. The term "pilot error" meant much the same thing as "ID ten T error".

The Visionary: I know what "pilot error" means in some contexts, but what does "ID ten T error" mean?

The Alumnus: It's easiest to see if you write it out.

The Visionary [goes to a markerboard and writes, "*I D 1 0 T*"]: Um... I assume there's a reason you started to say, "Hell desk." Aren't they just blowing off steam?

The Alumnus: Yes. Unfortunately, one of the ways many help desk employees have blown off steam is to say, "Ok. If you'll hold for a minute, I'm going to transfer you to my supervisor. Would you tell her that you appear to have an 'eye dee ten tee' error?" And they all gloat over what they've gotten the customer to say. No, seriously, you don't need to keep a straight face.

But what really struck me was the entry for PEBKAC, acronym for "Problem Exists Between Keyboard and Chair." There was an example given of,

> Did you figure out why that guy couldn't print?
>
> Yeah, he kept canceling the print operation before it could finish. PEBKAC.

This was philosophically interesting.

The Visionary: How?

The Alumnus: In a computer, you get these time wasting messages where a little window pops up and you can't do any useful work until you click on the button. It becomes noise for the sake of noise; like the boy who cried, "Wolf!", we have the computer that cries, "Worth your attention." After a while, the normal thing most people do is click on the button automatically so they can get back to their work. It's a waste of time to try to decipher the cryptic messages.

So when people go to print, another one of these waste-of-time windows pops up, except that this time, when you do the right thing and click on the button and make it go away, your print job fails. And this specific example is chosen as a paradigm example of PEBKAC.

For a lot of these errors, there is a problem between a

keyboard and chair. But the problem isn't between the user's keyboard and chair. The problem is between the programmer's keyboard and chair.

The Visionary: Ouch.

The Alumnus: That course was what led to what I did for my Ph.D.

The Visionary: And that was?

The Alumnus: My discipline of record is philosophy of mind/cognitive science.

The Visionary: "Discipline of record?" I'm curious to hear you drop the other shoe.

The Alumnus: Usability is connected to cognitive science--an amalgam of computer science, psychology, philosophy, neuroscience, linguistics, and other areas, all trying to understand human thought so we can re-implement it on a computer. It's a fascinating area for interdisciplinary study, and usability draws on it, just from a different angle: instead of making computers intelligent, it tries to make computers friendly to people who don't understand how they are built. And a lot of things which are clear as day if you built the system aren't automatically clear to customers. A system which is usable lets the user have an illusory cognitive model of how the system works that is far, far simpler than how a programmer would understand it. And programmers don't consciously believe that customers understand the innards of their system, but there's an assumption that creeps in, an assumption of, "My way of thinking about it is how a person thinks about it."

The Visionary: That way of putting it makes the programmers sound ego-centric.

The Alumnus: I wouldn't put it in such crude terms as that; they are thinking in a way that is human.

With languages, there is a lot of diversity. Aside from the variety of languages, there's a difference between the U.S., where the majority only speak one language, and Sénégal, where it is common for people to speak five or six languages. There's a difference between Italy, where people speak one national language in a fairly pure form, and India, where English and Hindi are spliced together seamlessly. For that matter, there's the deaf outlet of speaking with your hands instead of your mouth. But with all these differences, language itself is not something which is added to being human. Language is not a custom that cultures may happen to include. There are exceptional cases where people do not learn a language, and these are tragic cases where people are deprived of a human birthright. The specifics of language may vary, but language itself is not adding something to being human. It is something that is basically human. The details and even diversity of languages are details of how language works out.

And a lot of things are like that. Understanding something that you're working on is not something added to being human; it's an interpretation of something basic. How one thinks, about technology and other things, is not something added to being human. It's something basically human.

One very natural tendency is to think that "I" or "we" or "people like us" are just being human; we just have what is natural to being human. The "them" group has all sorts of things that are added to being human, but "we" are just being human. So we expect other people to think like us. We assume it so deeply and unconsciously that we are shocked by their perversity when they violate this expectation.

The Visionary: Wow. I hadn't thought of it in those terms before. Do you think IMSA provided a safe haven from this kind of lockstep thinking for its students?

The Alumnus: I think it provides a safe haven for quite a lot of its students. But getting back to my Ph.D. program--

The Visionary: Yes?

The Alumnus: So I began, encouraged by some initial successes, to try and make the first artificial mind. For a while I thought I would succeed, after overcoming some obstacles that couldn't have been that bad.

The Visionary: What were these obstacles?

The Alumnus: Just a special case here and there, an unrepresentative anomaly. But when I worked, I had a sneaking suspicion dawn on me.

Freshman year, I had a college roommate who was brilliant and eccentric. He turned out stunning proofs in math classes. He was also trying to build a perpetual motion machine. He was adjusting this and that; I listened, entranced, when he traced the history of great experiments in physics, and talked about how across the centuries they went from observing obvious behavior to find subtle ways to trick nature into showing you something you weren't supposed to see. Think of the ingenuity of the Millikan oil drop experiment. And so he went on, trying to adjust this and that, seeking to get things just right for a perpetual motion machine. There were times when he seemed to almost have it. It seemed there were ten things you needed for a perpetual motion machine, and he had an almost working machine for any nine of them. But that tenth one seemed never to fall into place.

And I had a sneaking suspicion, one that I was going to try awfully hard to ignore, that for a long time I convinced myself I didn't know what I was expecting. But deja vu kept creeping in. I had just succeeded with a project that met every clearly defined goal I set for it... but I had just found another way not to make artificial intelligence.

The crusher was when I read von Neumann's 1958 The Computer and the Brain. Then I stopped running from deja vu. Here was crass confidence that in 1958 we discoved the basis for all human thought, and all human thought is add, subtract, multiply, and divide. Here was an assumption in lieu of argument. And here was the air I breathed as a cognitive science.

The Visionary: But I've looked at some reports, and artificial intelligence seems to be just around the corner.

The Alumnus: Full artificial intelligence is just around the corner, and it's been just around the corner since at least the fifties--arguably much longer, because for a hundred years before the brain was a computer, it was a telephone exchange. (I think that's why we talk about a person being "wired" a particular way.) The brain is always understood as the state of the art technology we're most proud of.

I hit rock bottom after thinking about how I had convinced myself I was creating a working artificial intelligence by obtaining results and reinterpreting results as success. It's very seductive, and I was thinking about what some skeptics had said about magic.

What emerged was... The effort to make computers think has found ways that the human mind is much more interesting than we thought. And I began to push in a new direction. Instead of trying to understand human intelligence to make computers more intelligent, I began to try to understand human intelligence to make humans more intelligent.

The Visionary: What exactly do you mean?

The Alumnus: There are a lot of disciplines that teach you how to think. I think scholars in many disciplines see their discipline as the discipline that teaches you how to think, where truly different disciplines are a sort of no-man's land that doesn't qualify as "how to think." But these are a coupled subject matter and how to think about the subject matter. This was, in abstracted, crystalline, and universal form, "How to think." The analogy I used at the time was that it was the elementary school number line (1, 2, 3, ...), abstracted from sets of one physical object, two physical objects, three physical objects...

The Visionary [pausing]**:** It sounds like you're pioneering a new academic discipline. Would you like IMSA to highlight this?

The Alumnus: I am working that out. Not exactly whether what I am doing would qualify as an academic discipline--I'm pretty sure of that--but whether going down that route would be the wisest choice. For now, I'd rather wait.

The Visionary: Are you sure you wouldn't want the prestige? Hmm... on second thought, I can see that.

What are the scientific underpinnings of your discipline?

The Alumnus [pause]**:** That question is one of the first ones people ask me. It's automatic.

In tandem with what you might call my loss of faith in cognitive science, I began to question the cultural place of science. Including that in a question like this, the nearly immediate question people ask is one that assumes the answers are fed by science. Three of the most difficult mental accomplishments I've made are learning to think like a scientist, crafting this discipline of how to think, and learning to genuinely ask "How else could it be?" when people automatically go charging in with science.

The Visionary: But don't you think it's important to understand what's going on in the body?

The Alumnus: Both your questions, "What are the scientific underpinnings of your discipline?" and "But don't you think it's important to understand what's going on in the body?" are examples of the tendency I'm talking about. Your latter question assumes that "understanding the body" and "study the science of the body" are interchangeable terms; they often are treated that way in Western culture, but they need not be.

The Visionary: But how else could it be?

The Alumnus: In journalism and some writing classes, students are taught a technique of cubing, which asks six questions, one for each side of the cube. The six questions are all "w" words: who, what, when, where, and how.

In most aboriginal cultures, for instance, people ask more than one question, but the big question is, "Why?" The stories provide explanations for why the world is as it is.

In science, the big question is, "How?" Laws and theories provide mechanisms for how things happen. "Why?" isn't just de-emphasized; it's something people learn not to ask, something that is subtly stamped out like much of a child's creativity. Asking "Why?" is a basic error, like asking how much an idea weighs. One philosopher of science I read gave an example of a father asking a teenaged son, "Why is the living room light on?" and getting the answer, "Because the switch is in the 'on' position, closing the circuit and causing electricity to flow through the bulb." That isn't why, that's how. And if students are taught science without being taught how to be independent from science, or for that matter if they are in a culture influenced by science as ours has been, they'll come to share the assumption that this is the one and only serious answer to, "Why is the living room light on?"

That puts things too simply, but my point is that science does not represent the full range of inquiry. Science has cast a powerful shadow, not just in that science is scientific (which is as it should be) but in that non-scientific inquiry is not as independent as it should be.

But I'm getting off topic. What I was meaning to say was that I use science, but my discipline is dependent on an independence from science as well.

The Visionary: Could I backtrack a fair distance?

The Alumnus: Sure, to what?

The Visionary: There was something in the back of my mind when you answered my question about IMSA shielding its students from a lockstep environment. May I ask a more specific question?

The Alumnus: Certainly.

The Visionary: Did IMSA shield you from a lockstep environment?

The Alumnus: IMSA was unquestionably a better environment for me than a mainstream school.

The Visionary: You're being diplomatic.

The Alumnus: Ok. IMSA tries to be a magnet school serving the gifted population. Instead of memorization, it tries to produce critical observers, right?

The Visionary: Yes, and this isn't just for IMSA. We want to be a beacon of hope, for educational progress to the state and to the world.

The Alumnus: IMSA still doesn't have a football program, right?

The Visionary: IMSA students still don't really want one. If there was enough demand, we'd have one.

The Alumnus: What would you say to a football coach who wanted to liberate the tough, aggressive quarterback struggling to get out of every IMSA bookworm?

The Visionary: I think I see where you're going. Let me play devil's advocate for the moment. Our society has recognized football as an endeavor for some. But don't we recognize that education is a goal for all?

The Alumnus: All analogies break down, and I can't force you to see my point if you don't want to. My reason for drawing that analogy is that the average mind learns by memorization of given material, and that mind is ill-served by trying to liberate that critical observer just as many bookworms would be ill-served by trying to liberate that hidden quarterback. The kind of student that does well at IMSA doesn't do so well with the memorization that serves the average student. But it's a two-way street.

The Visionary: And I think I see a connection to what you said about programmers assume that how they think about a product is how everybody will think about it. And...

The Alumnus: Yes. But there's something else.

The Visionary: So how do you think IMSA's outreach should be changed? Should we stop outreach?

The Alumnus: I'd want to give that some thought. That isn't why I brought this up. I brought up this two-edged sword to make it easier to see another two-edged sword.

The two-edged sword I've suggested is that, just as IMSA students tend to be uncomfortable with the instructional methods at most schools, average students would be uncomfortable with instruction that seeks to liberate a hidden critical observer. It's a bad match both ways. The other two-edged sword has to do with the nature of giftedness. How would you define giftedness?

The Visionary: I try not to, at least in not as strong terms as you do. IMSA is trying to liberate the genius of every child.

The Alumnus: I think your actions are wiser than your rhetoric. How much thought goes into your admissions decisions?

The Visionary: Our admissions staff give a great deal of thought! Do you think we're careless?

The Alumnus: I would have been disturbed if IMSA made a random choice from among the students whose genius would be nurtured. Are you sure you don't want to define giftedness?

The Visionary: Every child has some talent.

The Alumnus: I agree, although your words sound suspiciously like words that many IMSA parents have learned to wince at. There are a lot of parents who have bright children who have learned that "All of our children are gifted." means, in practical terms, "Your daughter will be educated according to our idealization of an average student, no matter how much it hurts her, and we won't make accomodation."

But you are, unlike me, an administrator whom everybody blames for problems, and you know that there are many occasions where coming out and expressing your candid opinions is an invitation to disaster. I groused about the administration to no end as a student; it is only as an adult that I've come to appreciate the difficult and delicate task of being an administrator, and what kind of performance on an administration's part lets me focus on my work.

I'm going to put on my suspicious and mistrustful observer cap and read into your actions that it would be politically dangerous for you to say "This is the kind of gifted student we look for at IMSA." But I am not an administrator. I am more of a private person than you can afford to be, and there are more degrees of freedom offered to me. Would you mind my giving my opinion on a matter where you in particular need to be very careful in what you say?

The Visionary: I'm always open to listen, and I'm not just saying this as an administrator.

The Alumnus: I should also say that because something is politic, I don't automatically translate "politic" to "insincere." I believe you've been as successful as you have partly because you sincerely want to hear what people have to say. When someone says, "political sensitivity," I've learned to stop being a cynic and automatically hearing, "Machiavellian intrigue."

But when I teach, I try to have a map that accomodates itself to terrain, both old and new to me. There are surprisingly many things I believe that are human universals, although I won't discuss them here. But diversity is foundational to how I communicate, and in particular teach.

By "diversity" I don't just mean "affirmative action concerns." I read what I can about minority cultures, and how Asperger's or ADD minds tick. That much is important, and I'm not just jumping on the bandwagon. But diversity doesn't begin when a student labeled as "minority," "different," or "disadvantaged" sits down in your classroom. Diversity begins much earlier. Diversity is every person. I'm fond of books like David Kiersey's Please Understand Me II which explore what temperament and Myers-Briggs types mean for personhood. I want to appreciate learning styles. I absolutely love when students come in during office hours, because then I can see exactly where a student is, and exactly how that student is learning and thinking, and give an explanation that is tailored to the student's specific situation. I like to lecture too, but I'm freest to meet student needs when students visit me in my office.

And one very important facet of that diversity is one that is unfashionable today, more specifically IQ.

The Visionary: I remember seeing a report that your IQ was so high it was untestable by normal means. I've heard that polite drivers value politeness, skillful drivers value skill, and safe drivers value safety. Is there...?

The Alumnus: If you want to dismiss what I'm saying because of speculation about my motives, there's a good case to do so. I know that. But please hear and accept or dismiss my arguments on their merits, and if you read books like James Webb's Guiding the Gifted Child, you'll see this isn't just my idea. I accept multiple intelligence theory as a nuance, but I would point my finger to the idea that a single IQ was an adjustment in theory, made by people who started by assuming multiple intelligences.

But with all the debates, and in particular despite the unfashionability of "IQ", there is excellent reason to discuss giftedness in terms of IQ. IQ may not be the whole story, but you're missing something big if it is treated as one factor among others.

Several caveats deleted, I would point out that giftedness is not a binary attribute, any more than being tall is binary. There may be some people who are clearly tall and others who clearly aren't, but regardless of where you draw the line, you can't divide people into a "tall" group of people who are all exactly 190 centimeters tall and a "non-tall" group of people who are 160 centimeters tall. There is diversity, and this diversity remains even if you restrict your attention to tall people.

The Visionary: So then would you say that most high schools serve an average diversity, and IMSA serves a gifted diversity?

The Alumnus: Umm...

The Visionary: Yes?

The Alumnus: An average high school breaks at both ends of its spectrum...

The Visionary: Yes?

The Alumnus: Um...

The Visionary: Yes?

The Alumnus: And IMSA breaks at both ends of its spectrum.

The Visionary: If there are some students who the administration overestimates, this is unfortunate, but--

The Alumnus: That's not my point. Ignoring several other dimensions of diversity, we don't have two points of "average" and "gifted" defining a line. Giftedness, anyway, is not "the same kind of intelligence as most people have, only more of it and faster"; it's a different kind of intelligence. It diverges more the further you go.

Instead of the two points of "average" and "gifted", there are three points to consider: "average", "gifted", and "profoundly gifted."

I think it is to IMSA's great credit that you have a gifted education, not a pullout tacked on to a nongifted education. Serving gifted needs isn't an adjustment; it's the fabric you've woven, and it is impressive.

But "profoundly gifted" is as different from the "moderately gifted" as "moderately gifted" is from "average"...

...and IMSA attracts a good proportion of the profoundly gifted minority...

...and the position of the profoundly gifted at IMSA is exactly the position many IMSA students had in TAG pullouts.

The Visionary: May I say a word in IMSA's defense?

The Alumnus: Certainly.

The Visionary: IMSA began as a dream, a wild, speculative, powerful, risky vision. From the beginning, its place was tentative; some of the first classes did math problems before the state government because IMSA was threatened with closing. IMSA makes things happen that wouldn't happen anywhere, and for all we've done, there are still people who would remove us from the budget. I've talked with alumni, both those who like and dislike the school, and I see something in them which I didn't see in other places.

The Alumnus: And IMSA is a safe place to learn and grow, and IMSA alumni are making a powerful contribution to the world. All of this I assume. And IMSA seems like the kind of place that could grow, that does grow. IMSA could offer the world certain extraordinarily talented individuals that have been stretched to their limit, who have spent certain very formative years doing things most people don't even dream of, and doing so not in isolation but guided and supported as powerfully, and as gently for their needs, as IMSA already offers to so many of its students.

The Visionary: If you have any plans, I would like to hear them.

The Alumnus: Before I give the plans as such, I would like to give a brief overview, not just of the average, moderately gifted, and profoundly gifted mind, but of the average, moderately gifted, and profoundly gifted spirit. Keep in mind that this is not a trichotomy, but three reference points on a curve.

The average mind is concrete. It deals in practical, concrete matters. There was one study which posed isomorphic problems to people, one of which was stated abstractly, and one of which asked in concrete terms who the "cheaters" were. The average respondent did poorly on the abstract isomorph, but was astute when it was put concretely. The average mind is more practical, and learns by an understanding which gradually emerges by going over things again. The preferred learning style is oriented towards memorization and is relatively slow, concrete, and (on gifted terms) doesn't make connections. This person is the fabric with which society is woven; a person like this tends to understand and be understood by others. The average mind concentrates on, and becomes reasonably proficient, in a small number of skills.

The moderately gifted mind, around an IMSA IQ of 140, deals with abstractions. It sees interconnections, and this may be related to why the moderately gifted mind learns more skills with less effort. (If this is true, an average mind would be learning from scratch, while a moderately gifted mind would only make adaptations from similar skills.) This person is likely to have a "collection of skills", and have a low self-assessment in those skills. (Today's breathtaking performance is, tomorrow, marginally adequate.) Self-actualizing concern for becoming a particular kind of person is much more common. The moderately gifted mind enjoys an advantage over the average mind, and is different, but still close enough to connect. This person learns more quickly, and most of society's leaders are moderately gifted. (Some have suggested that this is not just because people above that range are much rarer, but because they can easily connect.

There is controversy about how isolated the profoundly gifted person is, with an IQ around 180. Some researchers believe that the greater gap is bridged by the greater ability to connect; Webb suggests otherwise, saying that children with an IQ above 170 feel like they don't fit in anywhere. He asks what the effects would be if a normal child grew up in a world where most people had an IQ of 50-55. Some profoundly gifted have discussed the feeling that there's an instruction manual to life that everyone but them has. The unusual sense of humor that appears in the moderately gifted is even more pronounced in the profoundly gifted. Average people tend to believe some tacit and naively realistic philosophy. Moderately gifted people tend to believe some conscious and creative reinterpretation of realism. Profoundly gifted people tend to believe an almost automatic anti-realism. The realism assumed by most people doesn't resonate with them. And I need to explain what I mean by "believe" here. I don't mean that someone engaged them in a discussion and are convinced by logic or eloquence that an anti-realist philosophy is true. I mean something close to experience, as we believe that a radiator is hot after we touch it. Realism is obvious for someone of average intelligence. For someone profoundly gifted, coming to that perspective represents a significant achievement.

Furthermore, where the moderately gifted person has a "skill collection", the profoundly gifted individual has what might as well be magic powers--

The Visionary: You mean is involved with the occult or psychic phenomena?

The Alumnus: Not exactly. Profoundly gifted individuals have been known to do things like reinventing the steam engine at age six. Some of them can walk into a room and in an instant infer what kind of presentation is going to be given, and what kind of organization is going to give it. They have been known to make penetrating observations of connections between vastly different disciplines. Some have written a book in a week. Others remember everything they have read. Verbatim. Another still has invented a crude physics and using it to solve problems before she was old enough to talk. It's entirely plausible for a profoundly gifted individual to think for a few hours about a philosophical school he's just read about, and have a better grasp of the assumptions and implications surrounding that school than scholars who have studied the discipline for years. Many accomplishments are less extreme than that. Some are more extreme. I said that they might as well be magic powers because they are no more believable to many people than levitation or fairies granting wishes. Moderately gifted achievements are envied. Profoundly gifted achievements are disbelieved, and one social lesson the profoundly gifted learn is that there are certain accomplishments that you don't talk about... which feels the way most people would feel if people were shocked and offended when they tried to say, "I can read," or for that matter, "I can breathe."

These people do not think of themselves as having magic powers. Their impressive abilities are no more breathtaking or astonishing to them than our impressive abilities of walking through an unfamiliar room or understanding a children's book are to us--and if you don't believe that walking through an unfamiliar room or understanding a children's book is an astonishing mental feat, just spend a year in artificial intelligence. Artificial researchers know what kind of achievement is represented by these "basic" tasks. The rest of us misunderstand them as mundane. If you can understand how you can be better at understanding emotions than any computer in the world, and not think of yourself as gifted, you have a good start on understanding what it's like to feel that it's natural to tinker with your hands, imagine who you're going to be when you grow up, enjoy cooking, and have dreams where your brain creates languages on the fly.

It's a commonplace that the gifted can have a rough time of school. What IMSA does is place the profoundly gifted in the position of fixed pace classes designed for people significantly less intelligent than them.

It's easier to criticize than it is to give a positive alternative; let me give a positive alternative.

First of all, profoundly gifted students can pick things up much more rapidly even than most IMSA students. Something like a factor of four speedup can happen again and again. Many of these students would tear through textbooks if you let them.

The Visionary: But at IMSA we don't dump textbooks on students. We provide an environment where they can discover things for themselves.

The Alumnus: They will discover things for themselves. But if you look at learning styles, the profoundly gifted are some of the most able to understand a crystallized abstraction, and the most likely to work ahead in their textbooks.

IMSA may have a dozen or so profoundly gifted individuals at any one time.

The Visionary: And we've provided accommodation for a bright sophomore physics class.

The Alumnus: Yes, it is possible for students to lobby for accommodation on a specific point.

But it's possible to go further, as IMSA has gone further than TAG pullouts.

There could be a small number of people who serve as tutors, in a sort of tutorial system as can be seen in Oxford's and Cambridge's history. They would be like thesis advisors, less responsible for knowing what the students need to learn than offering direction and referrals.

The Visionary: What would you have them do if they tear through IMSA's curriculum sophomore year?

The Alumnus: Students that bright are likely to have their own axes to grind--good axes, axes which they should be encouraged. I really have trouble imagining a student flying through IMSA's normal curriculum and then wanting to watch TV for two years. The problem of motivating these students is like the problem of defending a lion: the first thing is to get out of the way.

The teachers themselves should offer the kind of individualized instruction that is basic to special education, and deal with the "magic powers" that the main curriculum doesn't know how to deal with.

The Visionary: Would the teachers have to be profoundly gifted?

The Alumnus: I don't know. I would place more emphasis on understanding profoundly gifted students than necessarily being profoundly gifted oneself.

Furthermore, as well as standing in need of conceptual education, profoundly gifted students could benefit from personal development to help them meet the rest of the world. I don't know whether it would be correct to say that average education should be about knowledge, gifted education should be about how to think, and profoundly gifted education should be about personal development. I think the idea is worth considering. And I would try to develop some things that aren't needed in average education and less needed in moderately gifted education, such as how to bridge the gap and meet the rest of the world.

The Visionary: I'll think about that. I would be delighted to say you've shown me how to solve this problem.

The Alumnus: I'd be surprised if I've shown you how to solve this problem. If I were asked what I could guarantee for this model, it would be that some part of it is wrong. I would ask you to consider what I've presented you as a rough draft. In my opinion it is a rough draft worth revising, changing course in midstream if need be, but it is a rough draft.

The Visionary: This is all very well for office hours, but how do you teach a class? You don't try to individualize a lecture twenty different ways, do you?

The Alumnus: I believe what I said about diversity as foundational, but I also believe there are things that are common. I believe there are significant commonalities as well as significant differences.

What would you say is the dominant educational philosophy at IMSA?

The Visionary: There are several philosophies we draw on, and several things vary from teacher to teacher. But if I were to pick one school, it would be constructivism.

The Alumnus: Does constructivism see the student as an empty pot, to be filled with knowledge?

The Visionary: Quite the opposite. Constructivism sees the students as agents, trying to actively construct their models of the world, not as empty pots to be filled, or as formless clay for the teachers to shape. We see the teacher as supporting the student in this active task.

The Alumnus: And I agree that students should be active and encouraged by teachers. A related question--do you believe mathematics is something that research mathematicians invent, or something that they find out?

The Visionary: Well, the obvious answer would be that it's something constructed.

The Alumnus: I disagree with you, at least about the "obvious" part.

The Visionary: Then I'll trust your judgment that it's something mathematicians discover. You've probably thought about this a lot more than I have.

The Alumnus: You don't need to agree with me here. There are a lot of good mathematicians who believe mathematics is something invented.

The Visionary: Are you saying I should believe mathematics is constructed?

The Alumnus: No. There are also a lot of mathematicians who understand mathematics and say mathematics is something that's found out.

The Visionary: Now I'm having trouble seeing where you're going.

The Alumnus: There's a debate among mathematicians as to whether mathematics is invented or discovered, with good mathematicians falling into either camp. The word 'discover' itself is ambiguous; one can say "I discovered the TV remote under the couch" and have "discover" mean "dis-cover" or "find out," but one can also say, "I discovered a way to build a better mousetrap," and have "discover" mean "invent". "Invent" derives from the Latin "invenire," which means "come into", i.e. "find," so that it would be more natural in Latin to say "I just invented my car keys" than "I invented a useful tool."

The Visionary: I think I see what you are saying... Are you saying that there is a single reality described both by discovery and invention?

The Alumnus: Yes. Now to tie in with constructivism... What are students doing when they are constructing models?

The Visionary: They are shaping thought-stuff, for lack of a better term, in a way that's different for each learner.

The Alumnus: And this is to break out of the Enlightenment/Diderot encyclopedia mindset which gives rise to stuffing the learner with facts?

The Visionary: Absolutely.

The Alumnus: Where would you place Kant? Was he a medieval philosopher?

The Visionary: He was one of the Enlightenment's greatest philosophers.

The Alumnus: And Kant's model of ideas was unchanged from Plato.

The Visionary: Um...

The Alumnus: Yes?

The Visionary: What Plato called "Ideas" and Kant 's "ideas" are two different things. For Plato, the Ideas were something strange to us: a reality outside the mind.

The Alumnus: Um... Plato and Kant would equally have affirmed the statement, "Ideas are internal."

The Visionary: I don't think so. Plato's Allegory of the Cave suggests that the Ideas are part of something that is the same for all people.

The Alumnus: If I may digress for a moment, I think that famous passage should be called "the Allegory of the Television." I appreciate your limiting the place of television at IMSA. But back to the topic, for Plato the Ideas were internal, but were not private.

The Visionary: Huh?

The Alumnus: Kant was a pivotal figure in our--the Enlightenment's--idea that the only real stuff outside our head is matter. When Kant says "internal," he says "private," and when we say "internal," we say "private." If you think this way, then you believe that thought is something done in a private corner. This privacy may be culturally conditioned, but it is privacy. And yet, however self-evident this seems to us, a great many philosophers and cultures have believed otherwise.

There is a private aspect to thought, but my research into how to think has led me to question the Enlightenment model and believe that we all think on the same contoured surface. We can be on different parts and move in different ways, but in thinking we deal with a reality others deal with as well. And I'm going to sound like a kooky philosopher and say that you have a deficient cosmology, and therefore a deficient corollary understanding of how humans are capable of learning, if you believe that everything is either inside the mind or else something you can kick.

The Visionary: But we're questioning the Enlightenment model, and rejecting parts of it that have problems!

The Alumnus: I know you are. And I would encourage you to question more of it.

The Visionary: How does this belief affect teaching for you?

The Alumnus: Most immediately, it helps me say ways to identify with students--connect with their thought. There are some things that pay off long term. But in the short run, when a student makes a mistake, the student is not bad, nor is the mistake is not an anomaly to push away. A mistake is an invaluable opportunity for me to understand how a student is thinking and draw the student to a better understanding.

In terms of base metaphor, if you look at Dewey's

foundationalism, what it is that bothers many IMSA teachers and IMSA teachers are working to change, the basic idea is that the teacher is building up knowledge, from its foundations, in the student's mind. If I were to try and capture it in a metaphor, I would say that the student is an empty lot, and the teacher is building a house on it. The teacher is actively doing teaching to the student.

The constructivism that resonates with many IMSA teachers doesn't like the idea of the teacher being active and the student being the passive receptacle of teaching. It's fine for the teacher to be active, but they don't believe the student is passive because they were quite active learners themselves. Constructivist writers don't refer to 'students' so much as 'learners;' they emphasize that the learner is active. The basic idea is that people are actively trying to build their own unique understandings of the world, and a constructivist teacher is trying to support learners in this endeavor. If foundationalism is crystallized in the image of a teacher building a house on an empty lot, constructivist learning theory is crystallized in the image of learners picking up what they can to build their own private edifices of thought, their interior castles.

The Visionary: What do you think of those?

The Alumnus: I think we're comparing a hammer with a screwdriver. If you read debate on the web, you'll see people who think constructivism is a hazy and incomprehensibly bad version of foundationalism, and people who think foundationalism is a hazy and incomprehensibly bad version of constructivism. The truth is neither; good foundationalist teaching like Direct Instruction is doing one thing well, and good constructivist learning is doing another thing well, and different people learn differently.

The Visionary: But do you have an alternative?

The Alumnus: Yes, and it is again suggested by basic metaphor. Instead of building a house, or helping learners construct their private models, I would suggest looking at a single word, *katalabein*. I am using a Greek word without an exact English equivalent, because it ties together some things that are familiar--part of the shared inner human reality which we can recognize. It can be translated 'overcome' or 'understand', and it provides for a basic metaphor in which what is understood is actively acquired, achieved even, but it is not necessarily idiosyncratic and private. We still have an active learner, and implications for how a teacher can support that active learner...

The Visionary: Go on.

The Alumnus: But it's different. I was fascinated with one constructivist learning page that recast the teacher as a sort of non-directive counselor. They facilitated learning experiences, but they realized that students came in with beliefs, like "Weeds are not plants because they don't need to be nurtured," and what really fascinated me was that some of them found themselves in an ethical quandary about the appropriateness of using a science class to influence student beliefs, say to agree with a botanist that dandelions are plants.

The Visionary: None of the IMSA teachers are *that* squeamish about influencing student beliefs.

The Alumnus: One alum made a comment that "looney liberals" seemed to him to offer a similar service to coal miner's canaries. It wouldn't be fair to accuse most liberals of their excesses, but it was still worth keeping an eye on them: they could be a warning that it was time to rethink basic ideas. Even if those web pages may fall more into the "canary" category than anything else...

The Visionary: But what do you have instead of helping students build private world-pictures?

The Alumnus: Instead of helping students build private world-pictures, helping students grapple with, in the overcoming that is understanding and the understanding that is overcoming, the *katalabein* of material. And this is material that always has a personal touch, but is understood to be internal in a way that is not simply how one has arbitrarily exercised privacy, but connects with a sort of inner terrain that is as shared as the outer terrain. No two people are at--no two people *can* be at--the exact same place in the external, physical world, nor can two people see the same thing, because their personal bodies get in the way. But that does *not* mean we inhabit our own private physical universes. I can tell you how to drive to my house because to get there, you would be navigating some of the same reality as I navigate. But somehow we believe that our bodies may touch the same doorknobs and our shoes may touch the same carpets... Somehow we believe that when we turn inside, the "reality" becomes impenetrably private, influenced by culture perhaps but shared to so little an extent that no two people shares the same inner sun and moon.

The Visionary: But that's the external world! You're not talking about when people can make up anything they want.

The Alumnus: Hmm... As part of your job, you field criticism from people who want IMSA to be shut down, right?

The Visionary: Yes.

The Alumnus: And a good portion of that criticism comes from people who are *certain* you've never considered the objection they raise, right?

The Visionary: You've been reading my mail!

The Alumnus: And how many years has it been since one of those letters contained a criticism that was new to you?

The Visionary: You've been reading my... um... [pause] Wow.

The Alumnus: The introduction to the *Handbook of Special Education* tries to make a point by quoting the opening meeting of the International Council for the Education of Exceptional Children. The meeting had in all respects a typical (for today) discussion of how one should define special needs children. And the meeting was in 1923. The point was made that special educators assume they're the first people to address new issues, when neither the issues nor their thoughts are new. An old internet denizen, writing about "the September that never ended", talked about how each year in September new college students would flood newsgroup discussions with "new, new, new" insights that were, in the denizen's words, "exactly the same tripe" that had been posted the previous year.

There is really not that much that is new, and this is tied to another observation. There is really not that much that is private. There is some. Even in the outer world there are some things that are private to each person. But in the inner world--and I am not talking about *your* inner world, or mine, but a real world, *the* inner world, a place that has contours of its own and laws of its own and terrain of its own and substances of its own which are no more the subject of an idiosyncratic private monopoly than the outer world's sun and moon. Perhaps it has a private dimension, but to assume that an inner world is by definition someone's most private possession is almost like answering the remark "The Atlantic Ocean is getting more polluted," with "*Whose*

Atlantic Ocean?"

The Visionary: Is there a way to integrate the inner world with the outer world?

The Alumnus: I am guilty of a rhetorical fault. I have spoken of the outer world as if it were separate from the inner world, and the inner world as if it were separate from the outer world. The real task is not one of integration but desegregation, and that is a lesson I've been wrestling with for years. The biggest lesson I took from my Ph.D. thesis, where I achieved a fascinating distillation of how to think from learning as we know it, is that how to think cannot be distilled from learning, and learning cannot be distilled from the rest of life. It is all interconnected. It's like a classic plot in fantasy literature where a hero is searching for a legendary treasure, and goes to strange places and passes amazing trials. We're there learning with him, until there is an end where "nothing" happens, but by the time that "nothing" takes place, we've been with the hero all along and we have been transformed just as much as he is, and we see through the "nothing" to recognize the treasure that has been all around the hero--and us--all along.

The real world has an internal and an external dimension, and there is nothing like trying to crystallize purer and purer internal knowledge to see the interpenetration of the internal and the external. I learned that the internal is not self-contained.

The Visionary: Is there anything that has been written which deals with this connection?

The Alumnus: Are you asking me if you can borrow a truckload of books? There are some cultures where it's hard to find material which *doesn't* relate the connection in some form.

But let me tie this in with education. Postmodernism is fragmented, so much so that postmodern scholars tend to put "postmodern" in ironic quotes and add some qualifier about whether it's even coherent to talk about such a movement. From the inside, there isn't a single postmodern movement; talking about a postmodern movement is like talking about a herd of housecats. But this is not because talking about being "postmodern" is meaningless; it's because one of the characteristics is fragmentation, and so if there is anything called postmodern, then it will be much more of a grab bag than something called modern.

Constructivism is postmodern, not in that anything called postmodern must resemble it, but because it can be placed on a somewhat ad hoc spectrum. It is internally fragmented, in that it is not helping students navigate *the* world of ideas, but in trying to reckon with learners' development of private models of the world. In typical postmodern fashion, the movement shows exquisite sensitivity to ways in which student constructed models are parochial, and does not inquire into ways in which students may be grappling with something universal. (At best learners' constructs are culturally conditioned.)

In what I am suggesting, learners are active, but students are working with something which is not so much clay to be shaped in the privacy of one's mind. I am aware of the parochial dimension--as a culture, we've been aware of it to death--but I'm trying to look at something we don't pay as much attention to today. I suggest, instead of a basic metaphor of learners constructing their own models, learners struggling to conquer parts of the world of ideas. Conquer means in some sense to appropriate; it means in part what we mean when we say that a mountain climber physically conquered an ascent and mastered its terrain. And this is not a cookie cutter, but it provides serious place for something that doesn't have soil to root itself in in constructivism.

I suspect that this is a lot less exotic than it sounds. Would you say that IMSA teachers often understand their students?

The Visionary: I think they often *try.*

The Alumnus: I think they often succeed.

Communication in general draws on being able to identify with the other. It says, "Even if I disagree with you, I understand what it means that you believe differently from what I do." You know what it's like when someone is talking with you and simply cannot identify with where you are coming from. It feels clumsy. Good communicators can identify with other people, and even a partial understanding is much better than no understanding at all.

I think the teachers I had at least showed something wiser than constructivism. Read something like Kuhn's *The Structure of Scientific Revolutions* and you will see appreciation of incommensurability and a communication divide between opposing camps; unlike the later Kuhn, you will also see that this claim of incommensurability, where opposing sides invariably argue past each other in debates, is applied to both major and minor paradigm shifts. Now if we look at a constructivist approach, where this kind of thinking is applied to individual peoples' models as well as models that are shared across a camp, then we have an excellent reason not to teach.

We have an excellent reason to say that teachers' and students' models are not only conflicting but incommensurable, that the teacher may have more power but in a fair debate they would argue past each other, and that the basis for the teacher understanding and therefore successfully influencing the student is at very least questionable. In the end, we have something which affects the concept of teaching more profoundly than the observation that students will see things that teachers don't realize. If you look at Kuhn, you will see a remark that the winning side of a scientific paradigm shift will naturally view the shift as progress. This contributes to an account for people thinking science progresses without science actually progressing. Science shifts. But the shift is not a step forward from less developed science to more developed science. It is a step sideways, from one reigning paradigm to another. And in like fashion, if you follow a natural constructivist path, you have an alternative to saying that the teacher knows more about science than the students. The teacher is more powerful, but there is a way out for someone who wants to deny that the teacher has more desirable knowledge that the students should learn. Not only can we argue that "teaching" communication is impossible, but we can argue that "teaching" communication is undesirable even if it were possible.

The Visionary: But that can't be what our teachers believe! You have to be misunderstanding constructivism. That's not how it works out.

The Alumnus: I agree with you that that can't be what many IMSA teachers believe. It is only what they say. And what they think they believe.

The Visionary: You mean...

The Alumnus: Foundationalism is a bad account of how most IMSA teachers learn. They learn actively, and IMSA students learn actively. And constructivism offers a compelling metaphor for active learning. But teachers at IMSA don't believe all its implications. Like the character in a George MacDonald book who was fond of saying,

"Marry in haste, repent at leisure," and had married in haste, but hadn't really thought about repenting, even though she'd had plenty of leisure in which to repent. If constructivism may undercut the possibility of communication, and the possibility of the teacher drawing students to join her in expert practice, this is not yet a problem. In practical terms, teachers believe they can communicate, and they have something to share. And they do this. There may be problems where this goes down the road, but in practical terms IMSA teachers live a philosophy with communication that is often excellent.

And, as far as metaphors go, I think that the *katalabein* metaphor offers something valuable that the constructivist metaphor doesn't. In particular, the fact that teachers can communicate, and leave students better off, doesn't just happen to be true; it's something that one can delve into. You don't just take the metaphor into consideration when you communicate on a basis that doesn't come from the model; the metaphor itself gives you a basis to communicate. And it's different enough to compete in an interesting way. Or complement constructivism in an interesting way. Even if it's not perfect.

The Visionary: Yes, I know. Do you regret the fact that it's so messy?

The Alumnus: I regret the fact that it's not messy enough.

When we describe a rainbow, we say that the colors are red, orange, yellow, green, blue, indigo, and violet. But those aren't the colors of the rainbow. If you pick a color at random on the rainbow, there's a zero percent chance that you will exactly pick one of those colors. A rainbow is a spectrum, and if you have a wavelength for each of those colors, you have seven reference points for a spectrum with infinitely many colors. And a reference point can help you understand a spectrum, but a reference point is not a spectrum.

I've done, I think, a decent job of describing one reference point on a spectrum. But teachers rarely follow one educational theory in pure form; they tend to draw on several, and this is intended not to be a complete theory, but a reference point in a pluralistic theory. Most theories are a single point. This theory is meant to be a spectrum, but isn't there yet.

And as much as a robust theory of education needs to be pluralistic, sensitive to the diversity that is every student, there also also needs to be a sensitivity to the diversity of knowledge. English is cursed to only have one word for knowledge.

The Visionary: But we have well enough established division of knowledge into subjects. In fact that's what we're trying to teach our students to get past.

The Alumnus: That's not quite what I meant.

In most of the languages I know, there's more than one word for knowledge. In French, there is *savoir*, which is the knowledge one has about facts, and *connaissance*, which is the knowledge one has of a person. It's a different kind of thing to know about a fact and to know of a person, and this is reflected in different words. *Conscience* is not simply the French word for conscience; it means consciousness, and some of the more ethereal and personal aspects of knowledge. The Latin *eruditio* and *notitia* have other nuances. In English we do have "wisdom," "knowledge," and "information," which are as different from each other as an apple, an orange, and a pear.

And this is without treating ways of thought. One of the

things I learned was that knowledge and ways of thought could be distinguished but not separated. If you look at Eastern ways, whether they are religions like Hinduism or Eastern Orthodoxy, or martial arts like Kuk Sool Won or Ninpo, you will find quite a different pedagogy from what we assume in the West. Instead of trying to open the mind and dump in knowledge, they begin by training the body, in actions, and then this begins to affect the soul and transform the spirit.

The Visionary: Isn't constructivism more like that?

The Alumnus: It is. But instead of reinventing experiential learning, Eastern ways preserve a Tao, or for a Western word, a matrix. Most recently in the West, *Matrix* is the name of a trilogy where each movie was better than the next. But before that, a matrix was a mathematical construct, and are you familiar with what "matrix" meant before that? It was the Latin word meaning "womb." And this concept of a womb, or a matrix, is something which has become alien to Western thought. A matrix is the medium in which you move, the air in which you breathe. It has the authority of your culture and your mother tongue. It is a very different kind of authority from the authority of a single leader, or a written rule; a matrix does not consciously command you, but provides you with the options which shape your choice. And the Eastern ways all preserve a matrix, a way, that provides their pedagogy. In a sense the difference between constructivist experiential learning and Eastern experiential learning is the difference between non-native speakers trying to speak a language and a community of native speakers continuing to use their language. Except to make the comparison more fair, constructivists are trying to construct a language, and put together something that works, and Eastern pedagogues have inherited something that works. The difference is kind of like the difference between an experimental kind of baseball glove that someone is trying out and a glove that is not only traditional but already broken in.

The Visionary: Um... I'll have to think about what you have said about a "matrix." Ok, you've given me a lot to think about. It would be premature for me to respond now. I'm going to need to think about what you've said. But let me change the susbject. What other ideas do you have about teaching, especially concrete ones?

The Alumnus: It's a bit like a light--it makes other things easier to see. But let me talk about other ways of teaching, such as listening.

The Visionary: I know how you can listen if a student asks a question, but how do you listen when lecturing?

The Alumnus: Listening is about trying to understand the other person as a basis for communication. Apart from the feedback that's in student questions--if you look for it--a person's face is a window to what is going on inside, and a teacher sees student faces frequently. I know the ominous silence when the class is so lost that students are afraid to ask questions. I don't just charge on because it's important to cover the remaining material. I try to stop, back up, and help the students to genuinely understand, and then proceed from genuine understanding. Homework offers implicit feedback on what I succeeded in communicating, and what I did not succeed in. And there's an implicit listening mindset behind trying not to inundate students with too much information at once.

There's a book of little stories, and in one of them, a sage was asked, "What is your name?" He pondered for a moment and said, "My name used to be... Me. But now it's... You." I didn't like that story at first, because I didn't understand it. Now I understand enough of it to see that it has a profound truth. Talking is about "me", and listening is part of a lifelong journey of learning to think in terms of "you." Listening has far more to offer a teacher than a better understanding of student questions.

There are a lot of things I like about how IMSA works--your belief that the needs of the mind cannot be met if the needs of the body are neglected. How this you fit this in with Arbor food service is not clear to me--

The Visionary: Thanks, Dear...

The Alumnus: Any time. But I really like the understanding you have of the human person as interconnected on multiple levels, including the body and mind. I also take that as axiomatic, and teach so that students will understand concepts and preferably their connections, and many other things. Just as I haven't read what I just said about listening in anything that came out of IMSA, but the teachers I had at IMSA were all examples of good listening.

The Visionary: Thank you.

The Alumnus: You're welcome.

But another part of the Enlightenment I reject is its depersonalization of knowledge and teaching. Have you read any Polanyi?

The Visionary: Not yet. Should I put him on my reading list?

The Alumnus: I don't know. He writes hefty, if understandable, material. It takes time to understand him, but he's worth understanding.

Michael Polanyi was a philosopher of science, and his big

work was on tacit and personal knowledge. The core idea is that scientific knowledge (I would say knowledge in general) is not a set of dessicated constructs that can be understood without reference to people; it is enfleshed in people who know it. He talked about how competing swimmers inhale a little more air and exhale a little less, so they always have more air in their lungs and therefore buoyancy than we would, but this knowledge is never thought of in so many words by the coach or by the student who "picks it up" from the coach, wordlessly. I don't know if it's a fair reading to say that the knowledge we can articulate is the just tip of the iceberg, but what I do think is a fair reading is to say that the knowledge we can put into so many words is not the whole picture. I think he would have liked IMSA trying to avoid teachers mindlessly regurgitating material so students can learn to mindlessly regurgitating material.

In tandem with the Enlightenment depersonalization of knowledge, is a depersonalization of the concept of teaching and a teacher. About two thousand years ago, one teacher tried to demote teachers from being human gods (who were superior to everyone else) to being human like the rest of us. Then, in connection with the Enlightenment there came a second demotion. A teacher was no longer someone responsible for initiating those in their care into humanity, but only a part of a person imparting a skill to another partial person.

That is an illusion; no matter how much keep our mouths shut on certain matters, we are humans teaching. The question is not whether or not teachers will be an ethical force; the question is whether, given that teachers will be an ethical force, whether they will be a positive force or a negative force. Because students are affected by what kind of people their teachers are--as well as what they say--a teacher should try to be a positive force. This means things like a humility that listens and appreciates other people, and caring, and is willing to listen both to "I don't understand partial differentiation," and "I've had a lousy week."

This means that a teacher who sees past the present, and sees students as the concert pianists, research scientists, and ballerinas they can become, will by that very respect help make that potential a reality.

The Visionary [looks at watch]**:** Thank you. I need to be somewhere in a few minutes; do you have any closing comments?

The Alumnus: I think that one aspect of how we speak of teaching is unfortunate. We speak of the active teacher who teaches, and the presumably passive student who is taught. Nothing of this manner of speaking suggests a dialog, a two-way street--but if teaching succeeds, it must be because of a cooperation between student and teacher. Even with constructivist understanding of learning, we're just looking at what the teacher can do.

I spend most of my time thinking about how I can see to my end of the partnership, not how students can handle their job. But there is something I would love to say to students, reinforced by a handout, on the first day of class, some toned-down version of:

Steal knowledge.

Prometheus stole fire. Your job is to steal knowledge.

The wrong way to think is that my job is to teach you, and you just sit there and be taught, and after enough teachers have taught you, you'll be educated.

You will get a much better education if you think that whatever I do, however well or poorly I teach, is simply the baseline, and you can start from there and see what you can do to take as much knowledge as you can.

Listening in class and asking questions is one way to steal knowledge. Is there something I said that doesn't quite make sense? If you just let my teaching wash over you, you've missed an opportunity to steal knowledge.

If you listen to my words, that's good. It's even better if you think about why I would say what I am saying. There may be a clue, maybe a little whisper in your intuition that something more is going on than you realize. That is a key that you can use to steal knowledge.

When you read the textbook, it will tell you more if you push it harder. Look at the problems. What are they asking you to know? What are they asking you to think about? There's a powerful clue about what's important and what's going on, if you're adept enough to steal it.

What do I assume about the material? I make assumptions, and some of those are assumptions I make because of what I know. If you're willing to ask why I assume something, you may steal knowledge of how people think when they understand the material.

My office hours are meant for you. Come in and discuss the material. If I see you make a mistake, that's good. It means you're learning and I have an opportunity to clarify. If you don't understand something, and all of us don't understand things from time to to time, it will cost you points to wait until the test to find out that you don't understand it. It won't cost you anything if you come in during my office hours, and I'll be glad you visited. And you might steal some knowledge.

Steal knowledge. There'll be some days when you're a little tired, and you can't look for all the extra knowledge you can steal. That's OK; just try to take the knowledge I clearly set out before you. But steal knowledge when you can.

You've gotten into IMSA, which is one of the best and one of the worst places in the world. Take advantage of opportunity. Learn to steal knowledge. And when you graduate from IMSA... Steal knowledge.

The Visionary: I definitely have some food for thought to take into the meeting. Do come and visit again! Goodbye!

The Alumnus: That I shall. Goodbye!

The Wagon, the Blackbird, and the Saab

Before I get further, I'd like to say a few words about what I drive.

I drive an Oldsmobile F-85 station wagon. What's the color? When people are being nice, they talk about a classic, subdued camouflage color. Sometimes the more candid remarks end up saying something like, "The Seventies called. They want their paint job back," although my station wagon is a 1964 model. All in all, I think I had the worst car of anyone I knew. Or at least that's what I *used* to think.

Then I changed my mind. Or maybe it would be better to say that I had my mind changed for me.

I was sitting at the cafeteria, when I saw someone looking for a place to sit. He was new, and I motioned for him to come over. He sat down, quietly, and ate in silence. There was a pretty loud conversation at the table, and when people started talking about cars, his eyes seemed to widen. I asked him what kind of car he drove.

After hesitating, he mumbled something hard to understand, and looked like he was getting smaller. Someone said, "Maybe he doesn't drive a car at all," and whatever he mumbled was forgotten in raucous laughter.

I caught him in the hallway later, and he asked if I could help him move several large boxes that were not in the city. When we made the trip, he again seemed to be looking around with round eyes, almost enchanted by my rustbucket.

I began to feel sorry for the chap, and I gave him rides. Even if I didn't understand.

He still managed to dodge any concrete hint of whatever it was that got him around--and I had a hunch that he hadn't just walked. My other friends may have given me some ribbing about my bucket of bolts, but really it was just ribbing. I tried to impress on him that he would be welcome even if he just got around on a derelict moped--but still not a single peep.

By the time it was becoming old to joke about whatever he drove, I accepted a dare and shadowed him as he walked along a couple of abandoned streets, got to the nearest airstrip...

and got into an SR-71 Blackbird. The man took off in an SR-71 Blackbird. *An SR-71 Blackbird!* Words failed me. Polite ones, at any rate. The SR-71 Blackbird may be the coolest looking reconnaissance plane ever; as far as looks go, it beats the pants off the spacecraft in a few science fiction movies. But the engineers weren't really trying to look cool; that was a side effect of trying to make an aircraft that *was* cool. It has those sleek lines because it's a bit of a stealth aircraft; it *can* be detected by radar, but it's somewhat harder. And suppose you're in an SR-71 Blackbird and you *are* picked up by radar, and enemy soldiers launch a surface-to-air missle at you--or two, or ten? Just speed up and you'll outrun it; the SR-71 Blackbird is the fastest aircraft ever built. Some SR-71 Blackbirds have been shot *at*. Ain't never got one shot *down*. One of the better surface-to-air rockets has about the same odds of hitting an SR-71 Blackbird doing Mach 3.2 as a turtle trying to catch up with a cheetah and *ram* it. An SR-71 Blackbird is a different kind of rare. It's not just that it's not a common electronic device that you can pick up at any decent department store; it isn't even like something very expensive and rare that has a waiting list is almost never on store shelves. The SR-71 Blackbird is more like, if anything, an invention that the inventor can't sell--perhaps, some years back, one of the first, handmade electric light bulbs--because it is so far from how people think and do things that they can't see anyone would *want* to use them. The SR-71 Blackbird is rare enough that few pilots have even seen it. And I saw, or thought I saw, my friend get into one.

I walked back in a daze, sat down, decided not to take any drinks just then, and cornered the joker, who couldn't keep his mouth shut. I told him to fess up about whatever he slipped me, but he was clueless--and when I couldn't keep my mouth shut and blabbed why, he didn't believe me. (Not that I blame him; I didn't believe it myself.)

I ate by myself, later, and followed him. The third time, I caught him in the act.

I was red with anger, and almost saw red.

He blanched whiter than at the wisecrack about him maybe not driving a car.

What I would have said then, if I were calmer, was, "Do you think it's right for a billionaire, to go around begging? You have things that none of us even dream of, and you--?"

After I had yelled at him, he looked at me and said, "How can I fuel up?"

I glared at him. "I don't know, but it's got to be much cooler than waiting in line at a gas station."

"Maybe it is cooler, but I don't think so, and that's not what I asked. Suppose I want to fly in my airplane. What do I do to be fueled up?"

"Um, a fuel truck drives out and fills you up?"

"And then I'm good to go because I have a full tank, just like you?"

"I don't see what you're getting at."

"Ok, let me ask you. What do you do if you want to make a long trip? Can you fill your tank, maybe a day or two before your trip, and leave?"

"Yes. And that would be true if you had a moped, or a motorcycle, or a luxury car, or even something exotic like an ATV or a hovercraft."

"But not an SR-71 Blackbird."

"What do you mean, not an SR-71 Blackbird? Did you get a good deal because your aircraft is broken?"

"Um, just because you can assume something in a good car, or even a bad car, doesn't mean that it's true across the board. When it's sitting on the ground, my aircraft leaks fuel."

"It leaks fuel? Why are you flying an aircraft that's not broken?"

"There's a difference between designing a passenger car and what I deal with. With a passenger car, if the manufacturers are any good, the car can sit with little to no fuel leak even if it's badly maintained."

"But this does not apply to what the rest of us can only dream of?"

"No."

"Why not?"

"A passenger car heats up a little, at top speeds, due to air friction. One and the same part works for the fuel line when it's been in the garage for an hour, and when it's driving as fast as you've driven it. Not so with my aircraft. The SR-71 Blackbird is exposed to one set of temperatures in the hangar, and then there is air friction for moving at Mach 3.2, and there's a basic principle of physics that says that what gets hotter, gets bigger."

"What's your point?"

"The parts that make up an SR-71 Blackbird are one size in the hangar and other sizes when the aircraft is flying at high speeds. The engineers could have sized the parts so that you could keep an aircraft in the hangar without losing any fuel... or they could make an airplane that leaks fuel on the ground, but it works when it was flying. But they could not make an airplane that would work at Mach 3.2 *and* have a sealed fuel line in the hangar... and that means that, when I go anywhere worth mentioning in my hot, exciting airplane, even I get fueled up on the ground, and I lose quite a lot of fuel getting airborne and more or less need an immediate air-to-air refueling... This is besides the obvious fact that I can't run on *any* fuel an ordinary gas station would carry. For that matter, the JP-7, a strange beast of a 'fuel' that must also serve as hydraulic fluid and *engine coolant*, is about as exotic compared to most jet fuel as it is compared to the 'boring' gasoline which you take for granted--you can't get fuel for an SR-71 Blackbird at a regular airport any more than you can buy 'ordinary' jet fuel at a regular gas station... and you think me strange when I get excited about the fact that you can drive up to any normal gas station and fill-er-up!"

I hesitated, and then asked, "But besides one or two details like--"

He cut me off. "It's not 'one or two details,' any more than--than filling out paperwork and dealing with bureaucracy amounts to 'one or two details' of a police officer's life. Sure, on television, something exciting happens to police officers every hour, but a real police officer's life is *extremely* different from police shows. It's not just paperwork. Perhaps there is *lots* of paperwork--a police officer deals with at least as much paperwork and bureaucracy as an employee who's a cog in a big office--but there are other things. Police officers get in firefights all the time on TV. But this is another area where TV's image is not the reality. I've known police officers who wouldn't trade their work for anything in the world. Doesn't mean that their work is like a cop show. When police officers aren't being filmed on those videos that make dramatic shows, and they aren't training, the average police officer starts firing maybe once every three or four years. There are many, many seasoned veterans who have never fired a gun on the street. And having an SR-71 Blackbird is no more what you'd imagine it was like to have a cool, neat, super-duper reconnaissance plane instead of your unsatisfying, meagre, second-rate, dull car than... than... than being a police officer has all the excitement of surviving a shootout every day, but only having to fill paperwork once every three or four years if at all!"

"Um, what else is there?"

"Um, what's a typical trip for you? I mean, with your car?"

"My wife's family is at the other side of the state, and--"

"So that's an example of a common trip? More common than shopping or driving to meet someone?"

"Ok; often I'm just running some errands."

"Such a boring thing to do with a station wagon. If you want things to get interesting, try something I wouldn't brave."

"What?"

"Go for the gusto. Borrow *my* vehicle! First, you can fuel up at home, as any fuel that had been in your tank is now a slippery puddle underneath the vehicle you wish you had. Then start the vehicle. You'll have something to deal with later, after the hot exhaust sets your trees on fire. And maybe a building or two. Then lurch around, and try to taxi along the streets. (Let's assume you don't set any trees on fire, which is not likely.) Now you're used to be able to see most of the things on the road, at least the ones you don't want to hit? And--"

"Ok, *ok*, I get the idea! The SR-71 Blackbird is the worst, most pitiable--"

"Perhaps I have misspoken. Or at least wasn't clear enough. I wasn't trying to say that it's simple torture flying an SR-71 Blackbird. There are few things as joyful as flying. And do you know what kind of possibilities exist (in everything from friendship to work to hobbies) when the list of things you can easily make a day trip to the other side of the globe? When--"

"Then why the big deal you just made before?"

"An SR-71 Blackbird is many things, but it is not what you imagine if you fantasize about everything you imagine my vehicle to be, *and assume almost everything you take for granted in yours.* There are a great many nice things that go without saying in your vehicle, that aren't part of mine. You know, a boring old station wagon with its dull room for a driver plus a few passengers and some cargo, that runs on the most mundane petroleum-based fuel you can get, and of course is familiar to most mechanics and can be maintained by almost any real automotive shop, and--if this is even worth mentioning--can be driven safely across a major network of roads, and--*of course* this can be taken for granted in any real vehicle--has a frame that gives you a fighting chance of surviving a full-speed collision with--"

"Ok, *ok*, I get the picture. But wouldn't it have helped matters if you would tell people these things up front? You know, maybe something about avoiding these confrontations, or maybe something about 'Honesty is the best policy'?"

He said, "Ok. So when I meet people, I should say, 'Hi. My vehicle leaves Formula One racecars in the dust. It also flies, can slip through radar, and does several things you can't even imagine. But don't worry, I haven't let any of this go to my head. I'm not full of myself. I promise I won't look down on you or whatever car you drive. And you can promise not to feel the least bit envious, inferior, or intimated. *Deal*?' It seems to come across that way no matter *how* I try to make that point. And really, why shouldn't it?"

I paused. "Do our vehicles have *anything* in common at all?"

"Yes--more than either of us can understand."

"But what on earth, if we're so different? My vehicle is a 1965 model; your vehicle sounds so new you'd need a time machine to get one--"

"My vehicle is a 1965 model too."

"If you want to lie and make me feel better, you could have told me that your vehicle was years older than mine."

"I meant it. There is something about our vehicles that is cut from the same cloth."

"How can you say that? I mean, without stretching? Is what they have in common that they're both in the same universe? Or that they're both bigger than an atom but smaller than a galaxy? Or some other way of *really* stretching?"

"If you want to dig deeper, have you read, 'I, Pencil'? Where an economist speaks on behalf of a common, humble pencil?"

"A speech from a pencil? What does that have to do with our vehicles? Are you going to compare our vehicles to a pencil?"

"Yes."

"So you're stretching."

"No."

"In I, Pencil, a cheap wooden pencil explains what it took to make it. It talks about how a diamond in the rough--I mean, graphite in the rough--crosses land and sea and is combined with clay, and a bit of this and that to make the exquisite slender shaft we call pencil 'lead'. The wood comes from the majestic cedar--do you know what it takes to make a successful logging operation--and then a mind-boggling number of steps transform a hundred feet of tree into something that's a little hard to explain, but machined to very precise specifications, and snapped together before six coats of laquer--oh, I forgot, before the cedar wraps around the slender graphite wand, it's also adorned by being tinted a darker color, 'for the same reason women put rouge on their faces' or something like that. Its parts come through a transportation network from all over the world, and the rubber eraser--which wouldn't erase at all well if were just rubber; it needs to be a cocktail of ingredients that perform at least three major tasks if it will work as an eraser. Try erasing pencil with a rubber ball sometime; it will erase terribly if it erases at all. Your erases is not mere rubber, but a rubber alloy, the way airplanes are made, not with mere aluminum, but with an aluminum alloy, and--"

"So the parts of a pencil have an interesting story?"

"Yes. And the quite impressive way they are put together--pencils don't assemble themselves, and a good machine--for some steps--costs a king's ransom. And the way they're distributed, and any number of things necessary for business to run the whole process, and--"

"Then should I start offering my daughter's pencils to a museum?"

"I wouldn't *exactly* offer one of her pencils to a museum. Museums do not have room for every wonder this world has. But I will say this. The next pencil you forget somewhere wouldn't have been yours to lose without more work, talent, skill, knowledge, venture capital, and a thousand other things than it took to make a wonder like the Rosetta Stone or the Mona Lisa."

As usual, she was dressed to kill. Her outfit was modest--I can almost say, *ostentatiously modest*--but, somehow, demurely made the point that she might be a model.

I had a bad feeling about something. During our conversation on the way over, I said, "You have an issue with Saab drivers." He replied, "No. Or yes, but it's beside the point. Saab drivers tend to have issues with me." I was caught off-guard: "That sounds as arrogant as anything I've--"

He asked me to forget what he had said. For the rest of the conversation, he seemed to be trying to change the subject.

She greeted us, shook his hand warmly, and turned back. "--absolutely brilliant. Not, in any way, like the British Comet, which never should have been flown in the first place, and was part of why jumbo jetliners were dangerous in the public's eye. The training for people who were going to be in that jumbo jetliner--the Comet--included being in a vacuum so that soldiers would know what to do if they were flying in a sparse layer of the atmosphere and the airplane simply disintegrated around them and left them in what might as well have been a vacuum. This sort of thing *happened* with enough jumbo jetliners that the public was very leery of them. For good reason, they were considered a disaster looking for a place to happen.

"And so, when Boeing effectively bet the company on the Boeing 707--like they did with every new airplane; it wasn't just one product among others that could be a flop without killing the company--they gave the test pilot very careful instructions about what to do when he demonstrated their new jumbo jetliner.

"At the airshow, he was flying along, and after a little while, people began to notice that one of the airplane's wings was lower, and the other was higher...

"The Boeing 707 test pilot was doing a barrel roll, which is extremely rough on an airplane. It's like... something like, instead of saying that a computer is tough, throwing it across the room. This stunt was a surprise to the other people at Boeing, almost as much as to the other, and it wasn't long before Boeing got on the radio and asked the pilot, 'What the §±¤¶ do you think you're doing?' The pilot's reply was short, and to the point:

"'Why, selling airplanes, sir.'

"He told a reporter afterwards, 'And when I got done with that barrel roll, I realized that the people weren't going to *believe* what they just saw... so I turned around and I did another one!'"

A moment later, someone else said, "What does 'Saab' mean again? You've told me, but--"

She smiled. "It took me a while to remember, too. 'SAAB' stands for '*Svenska aeroplan Aktiebolaget*,' literally 'Swedish Aeroplane Limited.' It's a European aerospace company that decided that besides making fighter jets and military aircraft, they would run a side business of selling cars, or at least the kind of car you get when you combine a muscle car, a luxury vehicle, and more than a touch of a military jet. It's like an airplane in big and small ways--everything from, if you unbuckle your seatbelt, a 'Fasten seatbelts' light just like an airliners', to the rush of power you feel when you hit the gas and might as well be lifting off... I'm not sure how you would describe it... It's almost what Lockheed-Martin would sell if they were Scandinavian and wanted to sell something you could drive on the street."

He said, "It sounds like a delight to drive."

She said, "It is. Would you two like me to take you out for a spin? I'd be delighted to show it to you. What kind of car do you drive?"

He paused for a split second and said, "I needed to get a ride with him; I have nothing that I could use to get over here."

I told her, "He's being modest."

She looked at me quizzically. "How?"

"He flies an SR-71 Blackbird... um... sorry, I shouldn't have said that just as you were taking a drink."

He seemed suddenly silent. For that matter, the room suddenly seemed a whole lot quieter.

She said, "You're joking, right?"

No one said a word.

Then she said, "Wow. It is a privilege and an honor. I have never met someone who..."

He said, "I really don't understand... maybe... um... I'm not really *better*, or--"

She said, "Stop being modest. I'd love to hear more about your fighter. Have you shot anything down?"

He looked as if he was thinking very hurriedly, and not finding the thought that he wanted.

"The SR-71 Blackbird would be pretty useless in a dogfight. It is neither designed or equipped to fight even with a very obsolete enemy aircraft; it's just designed to snoop around and gather information."

She said, "Um, so they get shot down all the time? Wouldn't you tend to get a lot of missiles fired by enemy fighters who aren't worried about you shooting back? What do you do when you run out of countermeasure flares?"

He paused for a moment, saying, "The SR-71 Blackbird doesn't have anything you'd expect. Flares are a great way to decoy a heat-seeking missile, but the SR-71 Blackbird doesn't have them, either."

I turned to him and said, "You're being almost disturbingly modest." Then I turned to her and said, "An SR-71 Blackbird can go over three times the speed of sound. The standard evasive to a surface-to-air rocket is simply to accelerate until you've left the rocket in the dust. I'm not aware of one of them being shot down."

Her eyes were as big as dinner plates.

She said, "I am stunned. I have talked with a few pilots, but I have never met anyone close to an SR-71 Blackbird pilot. I hope we can be friends." She stood close to him and offered her hand.

The three of us ran into each other a number of times in the following days. She seemed to want to know everything about his aircraft, and seemed very respectful, or at least seemed to be working hard to convey how impressed she was.

It was a dark and stormy night. He and I were both on our way out the door, when she asked, "What are you doing?"

He said, "I want to try some challenges. I plan on going out over the ocean and manoeuvering in the storm system."

She turned to him and said, very slowly, "No, you're not."

He turned to me and said, "C'mon, let's go."

She said, "Are you crazy? A storm like that has done what

enemy rockets have failed to do: take down your kind of craft. I've grown quite fond of you, and I'd hate to see you get killed because you were being stupid. Think about 61-7969 / 2020."

He said, "May I ask why you know about that?"

"I have been doing some reading because I want to understand you. And I understand people well enough, and care about you enough, to tell when you are acting against your best interests."

He grabbed my arm and forced me out the door. Once in the car, he said, "I'm sorry... I needed to get out before saying something I would regret."

"Like what?"

"'So you know just the perfect way to straighten me out, and you don't even need to ask me questions. Walk a mile in my shoes, to a place you can reach in a car but not my aircraft, and then we might be able to talk.'"

I watched him take off, and I came back to pick him up, after waiting an hour. I could tell something that seemed not quite perfect about his flying, but I do not regret that I kept my mouth shut about that.

The next day she surprised us by meeting us first thing in the morning.

She gave us a stack of paper. "I care about you quite a lot, and I don't want to be invited to your funeral in the next year. Here are detailed aviation regulations and international laws which are intended for your safety. I could not get an exact count of the number of crimes you committed, either for last night or for your reckless day-to-day flying around. I am sure that there are many responsible ways a vehicle like yours can be used, and I have inquired about whether there are any people who can offer some guidance and free you to..."

He turned around, took my elbow, and began walking out to the parking lot. We got in my car, and she raced for hers.

I saw her go to the mouth of the parking lot and then stop. The one Rolls-Royce in town had broken down, of all places *there*, and the owner and chauffer were both outside. I had thought that the person who was chauffered in a Rolls-Royce was a peaceful sort of man, but he was yelling then, and before she got over the owner positively erupted at the chauffeur and waved his arms. She had gotten out and wanted to talk with them, but you can't get a word in edgewise at a time like that.

Now I'd like to clarify something about my car. I've only seen a vehicle like mine in a demolition derby once, but I was surprised. I wasn't surprised, in particular, that the wagon was the last vehicle moving. What I was surprised at was that over a third of the derby had passed before the ugly wagon started to crumple at all.

And one other thing: one April Fools' Day, a friend who drives a sleek, sporty little 1989 Chrysler LeBaron gave me a bumper sticker that said, "Zero to sixty in fifteen minutes," and then acted surprised when I challenged him to a short race. When the race had finished, he seemed extraordinarily surprised, and I told him, "There is a question on your face. Let me answer it." Then I opened the hood on my ugly, uncool station wagon and said, "Your sleek little number can get by on a 2.2 liter engine. Do you know what *that* is?" He said, "Um, the engine?" And I said, "That is a 6.6 liter V8. Any questions?"

Ok, enough clarification. I looked around, turned in the opposite direction, and floored my car, blasting through the hedges and getting heavy scrapes on the bottom of my car. I got shortly on the road, and had a straight shot at the airport. She did eventually catch up to me, but not until there was nothing left to see but some hot exhaust and the fuel that had leaked when he tried to take off. (I still get the occasional note from him.)

Besides worrying about him, I was also much less worried about my car: tough as it is, cars don't like getting their undersides scraped on gravel, and I decided to take my car to the garage and have the mechanic take a look at it and tell me if I broke anything.

I was surprised--though maybe I shouldn't have been--to see the Rolls-Royce in the garage when I pulled in. I intended to explain that I might have scraped the bottom up, and after I did so, my curiosity got the better of me. I asked something about

Rolls-Royces breaking down.

The mechanic gave me the oddest look.

I asked him, "Why the funny look?"

He opened the hood, and said, "Rolls-Royces do break down easily... and it's even easier to break down if you open the hood, jam a screwdriver right *there*, and rev it as hard as you can."

The Spectacles

I got up, washed my face in the fountain, and put out the fire. The fountain was carved of yellow marble, set in the wall and adorned with bas-relief sculptures and dark moss. I moved through the labyrinth, not distracting myself with a lamp, not thinking about the organ, whose pipes ranged from 8' to 128' and could shake a cathedral to its foundation. Climbing iron rungs, I emerged from the recesses of a cluttered shed.

I was wearing a T-shirt advertising some random product, jeans which were worn at the cuffs, and fairly new tennis shoes. I would have liked to think I gave no hint of anything unusual: an ordinary man, with a messy house stocked with the usual array of mundane items. I blended in with the Illusion.

I drove over to Benjamin's house. As I walked in, I said, "Benjamin, I'm impressed. You've done a nice job of patching this place since the last explosion."

"Shut up, Morgan."

"By the way, my nephews are coming to visit in two weeks, Friday afternoon. Would you be willing to tinker in your laboratory when they come? Their favorite thing in the world is a good fireworks display."

"Which reminds me, there was one spice that I wanted to give you. It makes any food taste better, and the more you add, the better the food tastes. Pay no attention to the label on the bottle which says 'arsenic'. If you'll excuse me one moment..." He began to stand up, and I grabbed his shoulder and pulled him back down into the chair.

"How are you, Benjamin?"

"How are you, Morgan?"

I sat silent for a while. When Benjamin remained silent, I said, "I've been spending a lot of time in the library. The sense one gets when contemplating an artistic masterwork is concentrated in looking at what effect *The Mystical Theology* had on a thousand years of wonder."

He said, "You miss the Middle Ages, don't you?"

I said, "They're still around--a bit here, a piece there. On one hand, it's very romantic to hold something small in your hand and say that it is all that is left of a once great realm. On the other hand, it's *only* romantic: it is not the same thing as finding that glory all about you.

"The pain is all the worse when you not only come from a forgotten realm, but you must reckon with the Illusion. It's like there's a filter which turns everything grey. It's not exactly that there's a sinister hand that forces cooperation with the Illusion and tortures you if you don't; in some ways things would be simpler if there were. Of course you're asking for trouble if you show an anachronism in the way you dress, or if you're so gauche as to speak honestly out of the wisdom of another world and push one of the hot buttons of whatever today's hot issues are. But beyond that, you don't have to intentionally cooperate with the Illusion; you can 'non-conform freely' and the Illusion freely conforms itself to you. It's a terribly isolating feeling."

Benjamin stood up, walked over to a bookshelf, and pulled out an ivory tube. "I have something for you, Morgan. A pair of spectacles."

"Did you make these?"

"I'm not saying."

"Why are you giving me eyeglasses? My eyes are fine."

"Your eyes are weaker than you think." He waited a moment, and then said, "And these spectacles have a virtue."

"What is their virtue? What is their power?"

"Please forgive me. As one who has struggled with the Illusion, you know well enough what it means to deeply want to convey something and know that you can't. Please believe me when I say that I would like to express the answer to your question, but I cannot."

I left, taking the glasses and both hoping that I was concealing my anger from Benjamin and knowing that I wasn't.

I arrived at home and disappeared into the labyrinth. A bright lamp, I hoped, would help me understand the spectacles' power. Had I been in a different frame of mind, I might have enjoyed it; I read an ancient and mostly complete Greek manuscript to *The Symbolic Theology* to see if it might reveal new insights. My eyes lingered for a moment over the words:

> That symbol, as most, has two layers. Yet a symbol could have an infinite number of layers and still be smaller than what is without layer at all.

I had a deep insight of some sort over these words, and the insight is forever lost because I cared only about one thing, finding out what magic power the spectacles held. I tried to read a cuneiform tablet; as usual, the language gave me an embarassing amount of trouble, and there was something strange about what it said that completely lacked the allure of being exotic. Wishing I had a better command of languages, I moved about from one serpentine passageway to another, looking at places, even improvising on the organ, and enjoying none of it. Everything looked exactly as if I were looking through a children's toy. Had Benjamin been watching too much *Dumbo* and given me a magic feather?

After a long and fruitless search, I went up into my house, put the spectacles in your pocket, and sat in my chair, the lights off, fatigued in mind and body. I do not recall know how long I stayed there. I only know that I jumped when the doorbell rang.

It was Amber. She said, "The supermarket had a really good

sale on strawberries, and I thought you might like some."

"Do you have a moment to to come in? I have Coke in the fridge."

I had to stifle my urge to ask her opinion about the spectacles' virtue. I did not know her to be more than meets the eye (at least not in the sense that could be said of Benjamin or me), but the Illusion was much weaker in her than in most people, and she seemed to pick up on things that I wished others would as well. We talked for a little while; she described how she took her family to a pizza restaurant and her son "walked up to a soda machine, pushed one of the levers you're supposed to put your cup against, jumped in startlement when soda fell on his hand, and then began to lick the soda off."

"I've got to get home and get dinner on, but--ooh, you have new glasses in your pocket. Put them on for a moment."

I put my spectacles on, and she said something to me, but I have no idea what she said. It's not because I was drained: I was quite drained when she came, but her charm had left me interested in life again. The reason I have no idea what she said to me is that I was stunned at what I saw when I looked at her through the spectacles.

I saw beauty such as I had not begun to guess at. She was clad in a shimmering robe of scintillating colors. In one hand, she was holding a kaliedoscope, which had not semi-opaque colored chips but tiny glass spheres and prisms inside. The other hand embraced a child on her lap, with love so real it could be seen.

After she left, I took the spectacles off, put them in their case, and after miscellaneous nightly activities, went to bed and dreamed dreams both brilliant and intense.

When I woke up, I tried to think about why I had not recognized Amber's identity before. I closed my eyes and filtered through memories; Amber had given signals of something interesting that I had not picked up on--and she had picked up on things I had given. I thought of myself as one above the Illusion--and here I had accepted the Illusion's picture of her. Might there be others who were more than meets the eye?

I came to carry the spectacles with me, and look around for a sign of something out of the ordinary. Several days later, I met a tall man with cornrowed greying hair. When I asked him what he studied in college, he first commented on the arbitrariness of divisions between disciplines, before explaining that his discipline of record was philosophy. His thought was a textbook example of postmodernism, but when I put my spectacles on, I saw many translucent layers: each layer, like a ring of an oak, carried a remnant of a bygone age. Then I listened, and his words sounded no less postmodern, but echoes of the Middle Ages were everywhere.

I began to find these people more and more frequently, and require less and less blatant cues.

I sat in the living room, waiting with cans of Coca-Cola. I enjoy travelling in my nephews' realms; at a prior visit, Nathan discovered a whole realm behind my staircase, and it is my loss that I can only get in when I am with him. Brandon and Nathan had come for the fair that weekend, and I told them I had something neat-looking to show them before I took them to the fair.

I didn't realize my mistake until they insisted that I wear the spectacles at the fair.

I didn't mind the charge of public drunkenness *that* much. It was humiliating, perhaps, but I think at least *some* humiliations are necessary in life. And I didn't mind too much that my nephews' visit was a bummer for them. Perhaps that was unfortunate, but that has long been smoothed over. There were, however, two things that were *not* of small consequence to me.

The first thing that left me staggered was something in addition to the majesty I saw. I saw a knight, clad in armor forged of solid light, and I saw deep scars he earned warring against dragons. I saw a fair lady who looked beautiful at the skin when seen without the spectacles, and beautiful in layer after layer below the skin when seen with them. The something else I saw in addition to that majesty was that this beauty was something that was not just in a few people, or even many. It was in every single person without exception. That drunken beggar everyone avoided, the one with a stench like a brewery next to a horse stable--I saw his deep and loyal friendships. I saw his generosity with other beggars--please believe me that if you were another beggar, what's his was yours. I saw the quests he made in his youth. I saw his dreams. I saw his story. Beyond all that, I saw something deeper than any of these, a glory underneath and beneath these things. This glory, however disfigured by his bondage to alcohol, filled me with wonder.

The reason the police kept me in the drunk tank for so long was that I was stunned and reeling. I had always known that I was more than what the Illusion says a person is, and struggled to convey my something more to other people... but I never looked to see how other people could be more than the grey mask the Illusion put on their faces. When I was in the drunk tank, I looked at the other men in wonder and asked myself what magic lay in them, what my spectacles would tell me. The old man with an anchor tattooed to his arm: was he a sailor? Where had he sailed on the seven seas? Had he met mermaids? I almost asked him if he'd found Atlantis, when I decided I didn't want to prolong the time the police officer thought I was drunk.

This brings me to the second disturbing find, which was that my spectacles were not with me. I assumed this was because the police had locked them away, but even after I was released, determined inquiry found no one who had seen them. They looked interesting, oddly shaped lenses with thick gold frames; had a thief taken them when I was stunned and before the police picked me up?

The next day I began preparing for a quest.

It filled me with excitement to begin searching the black market, both because I hoped to find the spectacles, and because I knew I would experience these people in a completely new light.

I had dealings with the black market before, but it had always been unpleasant: not (let me be clear) because I did not know how to defend myself, or was in too much danger of getting suckered into something dangerous, but because I approached its people concealing the emotions I'd feel touching some kind of fetid slime. Now... I still saw that, but I tried to look and see what I would see if I were wearing my spectacles.

I didn't find anything that seemed significant. The next leg of my journey entailed a change of venue: I dressed nicely and mingled with the world of jewellers and antique dealers. Nada.

I began to search high and low; I brainstormed about what exotic places it might be, and I found interesting people along the way. The laborers whom I hired to help me search the city dump almost made me forget that I was searching for something, and over time I chose to look for my spectacles in places that would bring me into contact with people I wanted to meet...

Some years later, I was returning from one of my voyages and realized it had been long (*too* long) since I had spoken with Benjamin. I came and visited him, and told him about the people I'd met. After I had talked for an hour, he put his hand on my mouth and said, "Can I get a word in edgewise?"

I said, "Mmmph mph mmmph mmph."

He took his hand off my mouth, and I said, "That depends on whether you're rude enough to put your hand over my mouth in mid-sentence."

"That depends on whether you're rude enough to talk for an hour without letting your host get a word in edgewise."

I stuck my tongue out at him.

He stuck his tongue out at me.

Benjamin opened a box on his desk, opened the ivory case inside the box, and pulled out my spectacles. "I believe these might interest you." He handed them to me.

I sat in silence. The clock's ticking seemed to grow louder, until it chimed and we both jumped. Then I looked at him and said, "What in Heaven's name would I need them for?"

Firestorm 2034

Acknowledgments

When I read a book, I usually skip or maybe skim the acknowledgments; I find a long list of names of people I've never heard of to be deadly dull. There have been two times that I've read a list of acknowledgments that I've actually liked. One was written by a very witty writer who could, and did, make even technical documentation interesting to read. (Making someone want to read a list of names is only slightly more difficult than writing interesting documentation, and I don't consider myself a good enough writer to do either.) The other time was an acknowledgment that personally named and thanked me, and that was my favorite part of the whole work. Apart from that, I don't think that a list of strangers' names is fair to inflict on the reader. So I'm not going to try it.

Of course this is not solely my work; many others paid a role in it. You know who you are. I do wish to explicitly thank one person, though, whom many authors omit from their long lists. I wish to thank *you*, the reader. Of course the people who helped me write this are important, but they are not nearly so important as the people who take the time to sit down and read it, let the story live in their imaginations, and (I hope) tell a friend if they think it's cool. My work is only half done when, I write down my thoughts and put them on the web. It is finished when you breathe life into the story as you read it, and consider its ideas and make them a part of you. Only then can my story be complete. I therefore give my thanks to you, the reader.

In the Glade

"I still do not understand," Grizelda said, "why you asked your father not to find you a wife, if you are not going into a monastic order. And why he listened to your request."

"As Solomon said, he who finds a wife, finds a good thing," said Taberah, and then paused. A quotation from a written source came quickly to him, but a more substantial reply would take a moment's thought. *I am at home among most all of the people I have visited*, Taberah thought, *but I am not like any of them. And explaining myself is difficult.*

Grizelda stopped and looked at him; her pale blue eyes bore a gaze that was intense and probing, and yet not piercing. Her hair was pulled back from the sides of her head, and fell darkly onto her blue dress. The people at the castle spoke highly of Grizelda; some said she had a mind like a man. Her husband, Melibée, stood at her side, listening. They were in a forest glade outside the town walls, and were nearing the banks of a river.

Taberah nimbly climbed a tree, and tossed down two large pears. Then he climbed down, an even larger pear in his teeth.

"One good need not be the only good; even God, when he was the only good, chose to become not the only good. That is what creation means. For a man to have a wife is not the only good; there is also good in a man being single."

Melibée spoke up. "But then why not enter a monastery? Surely that is a good place."

Taberah shook his head. "Being celibate is good, a good that monastic life embraces; it does not follow that being celibate requires entering a monastery. I see another option; marriage and monkhood are not the only possibilities."

Grizelda began walking again, followed by the others. "There is still something in it I question. The different kinds of heretics often see other options, and the Church has condemned them. I know you don't have condemnation from the Church, but I don't see why you don't."

Taberah thought for a moment about whether to explain a logical principle, but decided not to. "All of the monastic orders were also started by people who saw other options; if you will think on the saints' lives, you will see that God led them outside of what everyone else was doing."

Grizelda stopped, and asked, softly, "You claim to be a saint?"

"Hardly," Taberah said. "I try to serve God, but I do not reach that standard. The reason I brought them up is that they are examples of how God wants us to live life. They play by the same rules as us; they just do a better job. I am not married because I am serving God in a way that does not involve marriage, at least not yet; I seek to follow him."

Grizelda began to speak when there was a thunderous boom. The ground shook, and a luminous being stood before them. Around the being was a presence, a reality of terrifying glory, as solid and real as if the weight of a mountain were pressing down on their spirits, and then more real. It was like a storm, like the roaring of a lion. The three friends fell to the ground in fear.

The Presence spoke with a voice like roaring water. "Fear not! Stand up!" As the quaking bodies heard those words, the command gave them the power to rise, and they did rise, and bow low. Again he spoke: "Never!"

As the friends stood in awestruck fear, the being turned towards Taberah and said, "Taberah. Will you go wherever God leads you? I have been sent to call you to come on a voyage, to a land you do not know and have never heard of, a voyage you may never return from. Will you come along?"

Taberah closed his eyes. In an instant, time stopped, and Taberah was thinking, neither in his native Provençale nor erudite Latin nor any of the dozen other languages he had worked with, but beyond words, beyond language. He looked into his own heart, and into God's, and a single word formed on his lips, without effort or volition: "Yes."

There was a tremendous flash of light, and Grizelda and Melibée fainted.

An Encounter

Taberah looked around. Four immense young men were throwing around a dinner plate -- or at least that's what it looked like on first glance. They were brawny, and the plate had something unearthly about it --

One of the men shouted something, and hurled the plate at Taberah. He dodged, and then watched in amazement as it bounced off a tree but did not shatter. It was red, and it had an unearthly symmetry, symmetry like he had never seen before. He went over and picked it up; it was light, and felt vaguely like leather or wood.

One of the men walked over, and said something in a language he did not recognize. Taberah said, "Taberah," and looked at him. The man extended a finger towards him and said, "Taburah," and then took the artifact and tugged on his arm. He was standing on the edge of a forest, and was being led into a clearing with buildings. The architecture was alien, and looked like a slightly grotesque simplification of what he was used to. There was a strange precision to the buildings, and a smell like smoke and roasting flesh -- though he could see no firepit, nor any animal.

The man took him out into the open field -- the grass was strangely short and uniform in height, lacking the beautiful variety in the fields he was used to seeing. He bent over, and plucked a blade of grass. It had been clipped. Not grazed by animals, but painstakingly clipped.

Looking around, he saw the men tossing the strange plate between each other. It sailed through the air, almost as if it had wings. One of them caught his eye, and tossed it over. Taberah snatched it out of the air with one hand, and then tried to throw it. It fell like a stone.

One of the men came over, and made the motion of

throwing it with exaggerated slowness. It was different from how one threw daggers, or stones, or much of anything else; it vaguely resembled skipping a rock. Taberah took the plate and held it properly; one of the men took it and turned it upside down. Holding it upside down, Taberah tried to imitate the throw he'd seen; the plate wobbled and fell to the ground. The people clapped.

One of the people said something that he didn't understand; seeing Taberah's incomprehension, he repeated his words, only louder. When Taberah didn't understand that, they beckoned him over to where the smoke was coming from. There was some sort of miniature fire, above which geometrically shaped pieces of meat were roasting; one of them gave him a large piece of meat -- they were all large -- wrapped in bread, with some brightly colored liquids poured over -- some sort of decoration? He wondered what the feast was, that they were eating meat, and had such a sumptuous banquet. The meat tasted slightly strange, although fresh, and the bread was finer than anything he had ever tasted. It didn't have any pebbles, and it was softer than cake.

Not knowing the local language, Taberah expressed his gratitude with his eyes; he listened intently to the conversation, trying to see if he could make sense of the language. Every once in a while, he heard a word that sounded vaguely like Latin, and by the end of the conversation he had figured out these people's names. The man standing by the fire was very old, so old that wisps of silver hair were beginning to appear among the black locks of his temple. He looked mature, regal, venerable. He must be a king, owning the small palace nearby and the ones around it; he could look in the windows (fitted with *glass* -- and glass so smooth you could barely see it), and see the illumination of a thousand candles. Or was he a servant? He looked mighty, built like a great warrior, and was even taller than the other men. And it was a lordly thing to give food to anyone who came. He was cooking, but the demeanor of the other men treated him as their elder, and not just in years. By the end of the conversation, Taberah had conveyed his name, and knew their names. After the effort of listening to the conversation and trying to see if he could hear any words related to ones he knew, he sat down in one of the chairs -- at least he thought it was a chair; it was sturdy, but so light he could lift it with one hand.

Taberah sat down in this chair, happy to sit and think as the others romped on the plain. Where to begin thinking? The language had Latin words, but it did not sound like any Romance language; that was confusing. And these people owned massive wealth, wealth far beyond anything his lord owned, and different goods than he had seen before. And they were immense. But that was only the surface of what he was sure was there. These people seemed to treat him hospitably, but what struck him wasn't exactly hospitality so much as something like friendship. Why were they treating him as a friend when they had just met him? When he watched them, he was puzzled at seeing respect in the younger men's treatment of the elder, but not etiquette. How could this people have respect without having its form? They did, but how? Or was their etiquette merely strange? They were not accustomed to wayfarers; they didn't look like heathen, but they didn't recognize Latin -- or Greek, or even Arabic, for that matter. And what would motivate anyone to cut grass at a uniform, mathematically precise height? What strange symbolic gesture would be manifested in that way? Or was it a symbolic gesture? It seemed more like a rash vow. Or was it something stranger still?

To the eyes around him, Taberah looked lost in thought. And he was -- he saw certain things that were human, but there were other parts that he could not understand at all. What did they mean?

First Clues

Aed looked on the stranger as he gazed. He was unbelievably short and scrawny, not to mention gamy; his clothing looked like a getup from the Middle Ages, a tunic and hose with irregular stitching and any number of holes. He could readily believe it when he walked by and saw lice. He had a thick, scraggly head of hair with a very thin beard. And yet, for all this,

Taberah was quite attractive. He had a merry, comely face, with a deep, probing gaze. It was a penetrating gaze; Aed had the feeling that if he stared at a piece of paper too long, it would catch fire. Taberah had been listening intently, and was now off in his own little world.

I must look up one of those charities that deals with foreigners, Aed thought, *as he seems quite lost. For now, he can have the guest bedroom. It's a good time it's summer; I have a little more free time to deal with him. He looks a little older than my children.* Aed began to gather up the food, called his son and daughter to help, and then they went in; it only took the stranger a couple of times to learn the gesture that meant, "C'mon! You're invited over here!"

The stranger looked with some bewilderment over the contents of a room, and then his eyes lit up over a chess table packed in the corner. He started to pull the pieces off and walk over to the table; Aed stopped him, pulled out the table, and arranged a game before them. *The international game*, he thought. *We don't know a common language, but we have a common game.*

Aed's first thought upon seeing the stranger play was, "He has seen this game before, but does not know how to play." This was revised to, "He does know how to play, but he cheats -- making moves that are almost legal and always to his advantage." Then a moment of dawning comprehension came, and he realized that the stranger was not cheating -- he just didn't understand that chess was played over a grid. Aed groaned, and picked up the pieces and arranged them on the table, understanding why Taberah had made such a bizarre action as to take them from what he now understood was taken as a storage place, and decided to play it his way.

Aed was rated at 1975, although on a good day he could give almost any chess player a run for his money. He was therefore stunned after he lost five games in a row. The young stranger was very, very cunning, and saw things that would never occur to him. After the fifth game, he felt quite tired, and he could see that the stranger was tired--

--and was therefore quite stunned as, in the living room and in the presence of his teen-aged son and daughter (his wife was away at a conference), Taberah took off all his clothes and lay down on the floor. He sent his daughter Fiona out of the room, and then covered Taberah with a blanket that lay at hand. Taberah's face told a thousand words; shocked as Aed was, he saw at once that Taberah's action was not sexually provocative, or for that matter done as anything significant; he apparently saw that he had made a social blunder, but was at a loss for what. He did not feel any shame or guilt, but perhaps regret that something he had done had upset his generous host -- and gratitude to be given a blanket, and puzzlement at why his host had invited him into his house but not to crawl into his family's bed. Puzzling, but Taberah had enough to think about already, and was sure that tomorrow would have enough puzzles of its own.

Aed, for his part, could see how to send him out, but not how to tell him to put his clothes on first; he went to bed, grumpily thinking, *He may stay tonight because he's here, but tomorrow night he's spending at PADS. What kind of manners is it to strip in front of your host's daughter? ...* He had a feeling of shock, of wrongness, of indignation at a transgression against reality; he told himself that this was culture shock, but that did not make things easy.

He drifted in and out of sleep, and was awakened by the sound of someone vomiting. Habits of a father, habits stronger than the weight of his grogginess, marched him out to the living room, where he stared in horror. Taberah was shaking, shivering in a cold sweat.

What shocked Aed most was not that one side of Taberah's face was wet with his own vomit.

What shocked Aed most was that Taberah looked so miserable that he didn't seem to even care.

The Hospital

The hospital was a nightmare. Taberah had no insurance, no

paperwork and no legal guardian; it was only because of the dire nature of the emergency that he was admitted at all. In the absence of identification or any ability to speak English, the hospital was by law required to file paperwork with the Bureau of Immigration and Naturalization Services; an embarrassed hospital representative explained that Taberah was in the eyes of the law an illegal immigrant and nothing more; if there was a way for him not to be deported to his country of origin, he didn't see it.

Aed came back each day for a week, during which his whole parish was speaking with him; his conversation with the doctors was alarming.

"I am baffled by this young man's condition. He is sick, but no test has been able to tell what he has. It might be a virus."

"Do you have any ideas of what it is?"

The doctor looked slightly embarrassed.

Aed stood in silence and prayed.

"Uh, have you read Ahmik Marison's *How the West Was Lost From a Medical Point of View*?"

"Never heard of it."

"Off the record, this young man is suffering from one -- or several -- of the conditions that ravaged the American Native population when European settlers came."

Aed stood in stunned silence. This did not make any sense at all. Or (he had the exacting honesty to admit to himself) it made sense in a way he couldn't believe.

An Anthropologist's Visit

"Noah, he doesn't speak any English." By now, Dr. Pabst and Dr. Kinsella were at the doorway to Taberah's room; they turned in, and saw him looking with interest at a book. Taberah looked up and said, "Grace and peace from God our Father, and the Lord Jesus Christ." His accent was thick, but mostly understandable.

"I'm an anthropologist and not a linguist," Noah said, "but that sounded an awful lot like English to me."

Aed opened his mouth, closed it, and said, "This isn't the

first time he's surprised me." He explained about Taberah playing chess, and undressing.

Dr. Pabst turned to the young man. He said, "Do you understand me?" The man scrambled off his bed with remarkable speed, and crouched in front of the anthropologist, and said, "I thou under stand."

Dr. Pabst simplified his language, and spoke slowly, separating his syllables. "How speak English?"

"English, that is what?"

"This language."

"Language, that is what?"

"How we speak now."

Taberah's eyes lit up. "I am in read Bible."

The anthropologist scratched his head. The young man appeared not to be lying, but even for a genius, learning a new language was difficult, and learning from a book written in the language without any people to help, unless--

"What you call Bible in your language?"

"No Bible in language."

Noah scratched his head. Then he said, "Have you read Bible before here?"

"*Biblia Sacra Iuxta Vulgatam Versionem.* I not know not how to say in English."

Aed said, "The lad is tired from concentration, and perhaps he shouldn't have jumped from his bed to --" Dr. Kinsella cleared his throat, "--under stand you. Perhaps we could talk out in the hallway?"

In the hallway, Aed said, "So, what nationality is he?"

Noah said, "I haven't the foggiest idea. He looks Western European, perhaps Mediterranean, by ancestry, Third World by nourishment. His accent is that of a Romance language, but I don't know. Picking up an alien language by studying a text in that language is next to impossible; the Mayans have left behind three codices that we still haven't deciphered for the most part. Or at least, it's almost impossible unless you already know the text in another language. I don't know how to coalesce my observations into a coherent picture. He -- is it OK if I change the subject slightly to recommendations?"

"Certainly."

"He's very bright and is picking up English quickly. He probably knows multiple languages, which makes it easier to pick up another; I'd get him three Bibles -- one in the Latin he knows, one in a literal rendering in modern English, and a free translation to contemporary English. And continue to visit him. My summer class starts tomorrow, so I won't be able to visit, but in brief: speak slowly; in-it-ial-ly break up the syl-la-bles; pay attention to what words he uses. (And, when he understands it, speak as you would to another American.) Contrary to intuition, he might understand you better if you use big words."

"What?"

"He already knows Latin, or perhaps some other language or languages derived from it; there are a lot of common roots in the bigger words. They came over with the Norman invasion of England; small words change much more quickly, and many of our small words are Germanic in character. And you know the artificial intelligence findings that big words are impossible for a computer to deal with, and small words doubly impossible? What is easy for us and what is easy for him may be two very different matters."

"Yes, I see," Aed said.

"Oh, and one more thing. Keep me posted; if you want, I may be able to send in a grad student. He's a puzzle, and I like puzzles. Maybe something will click about him."

"I'll keep the grad student in mind; maybe later, when I have more to tell. Actually, why don't you give me the net address of a student whom I will be able to talk with? I'll probably have some questions. Or should I ask you?"

"Feel free to ask me. Just keep it down to a few minutes a day."

Trouble

After a phone conversation with Dr. Pabst, Aed began to

understand how the universality of good will he believed in coexisted in an arbitrariness of manners; he restrained himself from knocking on the door before entering, and saw Taberah bright-eyed as he entered.

"Hell!" Taberah said eagerly, jumping up. He had a long tether from his intra-venous tubes, and he was becoming stable on his feet. (He still felt slightly dizzy as he rose.)

"What?" said Aed and the other visitor.

"Hell! Hell!" Then Taberah saw their puzzlement, wondered what was wrong, and then reminded himself of how important pronunciation was. "Hello!" he said.

Aed laughed, and said, "Hello! Taberah, I'd like you to meet my wife, Nathella. She is--"

Taberah grinned, said, "Beautiful!" and jumped up, pressing up against her and kissing her on the lips.

Nathella stood in paralyzed shock for a second, then drew back and ran out of the room, Aed on her heels.

She slowed to a brisk walk after they reached a second corridor, and said, "I don't know why you let him in our house. I don't want to see him again. There are differences between cultures, but that lust is unacceptable in any culture."

Aed said, "I am sorry he did that. I was not expecting that when I brought him in."

They walked on in silence, Nathella setting a fast pace in silent fury.

"You're holding out on me," she said. "You're not telling me something."

"His eyes," Aed said.

"What?" Nathella said.

"Did you see his eyes?" Aed asked.

"I assure you, I was quite occupied with his lips!" she snapped.

"What do you think was in his eyes?"

"Lust. Selfishness. A lack of any caring and decency."

"I saw his eyes," Aed said.

They walked on in silence, now a bit more slowly.

"You're waiting for me to ask you what you saw in his eyes. Out with it," Nathella finally said.

"I was watching his eyes, and I didn't see the faintest trace of greed or lewdness. I saw a rambunctious energy, the same rambunctious energy Clancy uses when he's picking on Fiona."

"Are you saying that what that man did to me was right?"

"No; I'm saying that he didn't know what he was doing."

Confusion

As Aed walked back, he processed through a memory, and realized the look in Taberah's eyes after Nathella had run out of the room. He looked like a hurt puppy. Aed had promised his wife not to have the man back on their property without talking with him and then talking it over with her.

The conversation that ensued between him and Taberah was maddening. It wasn't just the language barrier, even though they got a good half hour into the conversation before Aed realized that Taberah thought Aed was talking about something else entirely. It was rather that Aed was just beginning to see an alien conceptual map, an alien interpretation of the world. After clearing up the initial confusion, Aed managed to paraphrase "You don't have the right to go around kissing women on the lips," in different ways until Taberah appeared to understand, when he got to the second difficulty: "What is a right?" Taberah seemed not to think in terms of rights, to find them an alien philosophical concept; this difficult was not surmounted so much as circumvented, in being told, "It is wrong to go around kissing women on the lips." That was met with a third difficulty: "Why not?"

After a long and involved conversation, Aed pieced together the following observations:

- Taberah regarded his actions as being a very warm greeting, meaning roughly what Aed would have meant in sending someone he'd just met a virtual card. Taberah could envision a concept of "too warm and friendly, to the point of being unpleasant and unwelcome" if Aed led him to see it, but it was not a natural concept, much as "paying too many compliments, to the point that they are an annoyance that occupies too much time" would be an understandable but not natural concept to Aed -- when Aed complimented a friend on her shirt, it never occurred to him to ask "Is she receiving so many compliments that this one would be unwelcome and repetitive?"

- Taberah was saddened to have made a *faux pas*, but bewildered as to what was wrong about what he did. (He initially wondered if she was upset because he had not greeted her with words first.)
- Taberah did not regard the breast as being a body part that especially symbolized sexuality, and would consider a woman not wearing a shirt to be less significant than one of the nurses in long miniskirts -- to the extent that he found seeing body parts to be arousing, which was not particularly much.
- If Taberah's reasoning on one line were translated into 21st century concepts, they would not so much be "A man has a right to invade a woman's touch-space," so much as really a non-concept of "There is not enough of a personal touch-space for there to be an invasion necessary to a question of whether a man has a right to do do so" -- in many regards, like Aed regarded tapping shoulders.
- Taberah had a very different understanding of sexuality and touch; his line of acceptable touch was drawn so that it included a great deal of touchiness in contexts that Aed's culture did not even consider regarding as acceptable.

Taberah looked crestfallen when Aed told him not to touch women without asking permission; Aed revised this to, "Don't touch people in a way you haven't seen," knowing full well that this would lead the door open to further confusion. When Aed told Taberah in an authoritative tone of voice, "Don't kiss anyone you don't know well," and then thought and added, "Don't touch women's breasts," the hurt Taberah cried for a few minutes, and then asked, trembling, why he was not ever to give a woman a hug. Aed was puzzled as to why Taberah would make such a connection, and then when he saw the very straightforward reason why, it seemed that his explanation of why it was OK to touch a woman's breasts with his chest but not his hands caused more confusion than it alleviated.

Aed's head was spinning when he left the room. He was barely able to call his friend Noah and explain what had happened.

Dr. Pabst cursed himself for not coming himself, and had his graduate student teach the first day of class so he could try to provide the young man with band-aid coaching for at least one cultural land mine.

Taberah sat, shaking in sadness. He knew he would make mistakes, but to make such a big mistake so soon, and then not be able to understand why he was wrong -- this was the most confusing place he had ever been in. He closed his eyes and cried himself to sleep.

Immigration and Naturalization Services

Aed had barely slept, and when he returned early the next morning with Dr. Pabst, he found three men in dark suits standing near Taberah. "Good morning. I am Dr. Kinsella, a professor at the University. Who might you be?"

One of the men showed a badge and said, "Salisbury, Bureau of Immigration and Naturalization Services."

A chill ran down Aed's spine. "May I ask what your interest in this young man is?"

"This patient is an illegal alien. We are here to deport him to his country of origin."

If I thought, I could make enough publicity to hurt the INS badly if they deport this wayfarer, Aed thought, but even then felt a prompting of intuition, *that is not the way.* Still, he continued thinking, *I could say, "I can't stop you from deporting this man, but I can see to it that you will have publicity that hurts you. Do you have authority to stop the deportation? No? Would you rather give me contact information for someone who has such authority now, or have me find out as I create publicity and then contact him and have you fired?" If I think further, I can probably think of something truly Machiavellian...*

Even as he thought, he struggled, and Aed resolved to follow his conscience. "I'll be praying for you; I'm an interested party, and if you need to get in contact with me, the hospital has my net address." He decided it better not to give the INS agents a brain dump of the interactions; a description of a rocky adjustment to American culture was sure to hurt the lad. Dr. Pabst didn't think there was any advantage to staying, so they left. Aed returned home and brooded.

Taberah was not well; he was mostly over his sickness, but the INS agents had pressured the hospital staff for a release as soon as possible. He left the hospital weak and slightly unsteady on his feet.

His first ride in a moving room, he had been too miserable to notice what was going on. Now, he was able to observe, see what he had to learn. The room was bouncing around, but not nearly as much as a galloping horse -- even though it was moving faster. Through an arrangement of squares and a glass window he could see the city and countryside whizzing past; the speed was unpleasant, and it nauseated him. If he hadn't tried hard to control himself, he would probably have thrown up.

The two men were in the compartment with him, along with some men who looked vaguely like Saracens, only with redder skin, who seemed to be ill at ease. The two men looked -- not exactly like soldiers; there was a noble bearing and heroic resolve to even commoners who took arms to war with a neighboring city-state, but these men looked more like mercenaries set to guard. He tried to speak with them, but they would not speak to him; even in the hospital, they had spoken with the hospital staff but never addressed him personally.

Two of the red-bronze Saracens began talking, and he found with delight that they spoke with a familiar accent. He could not recognize the language, but he felt that he could learn their language quickly.

He tried to see what else he could grasp -- with his mind; there were some kind of thin shackles about his wrists, which set him ill at ease -- was he being taken to the torturer's for whatever crime he had committed against Nathella? There was noise about, a strange alien noise; everything about his surroundings was alien. And the bouncing room made it impossible to think.

Taberah realized he was ready to throw up, and he focused his attention on trying not to throw up.

Aed was sitting in his living room, staring sadly at the chess pieces on the table. Taberah's king had been knocked down, even as the pieces stood to checkmate Aed. Nathella walked into the room, leaned against Aed, and said, "Do you want to talk about Taberah? I've -- adjusted; I can deal with his rambunctiousness."

Aed said, "The INS is taking him to be deported. I don't want to talk about it."

Nathella put her hand to her mouth, and then held Aed. "I'll be waiting in the kitchen, when you're ready to talk. I'll be praying," she said, and kissed him.

Aed sat and stared at the dusty bookshelf for a while, and then picked up Taberah's king and set it down. He stared, and realized that he had placed the king in check from one of his knights.

Aed looked at the king and said, "Did you have to leave before I knew you?"

The game gave him no reply. Aed went to the computer room, got in to the computer, and went to a dreamscape where colors and shapes shifted. He watched the forms flow. Maybe that could distract him. No; time dragged, and even the fantasia of images could not fascinate him.

An avatar appeared before him. He looked; the avatar said, "May I speak with you?"

Muttering, "This had better be good" under his breath, Aed said, "Who is it?"

"Salisbury, Bureau of Immigration and Naturalization Services."

Aed winced. He doubted he could go through an interview without hurting both himself and Taberah. "Yes?"

"We have had a number of translators try to talk to the young man, and none of them is able to identify his language beyond something coming from the Romance family. We have run genetic tests on him, and France, Spain, and Romania among other countries have all said not only that he was not born there, but that they do not have any close relations on file. We are therefore unable to identify his country of origin, and are releasing him to your temporary protective custody. Are you at your home?"

Aed caught himself, and said, "Yes, we will be waiting."

After talking about a few technical details, Aed went upstairs. Someone had bumped the table, and tried to set the pieces back up where they were -- Clancy? If he did, he was in a hurry; the pieces were not in a similar state. This looked a little different. Taberah's king was now in check from both the knight and a rook, but he had a few moves left to stave off checkmate. And they were not playing on a grid; there were uncertainties. Could Taberah escape?

Home Again

Taberah spent a few days in the hospital, regaining his strength, but the staff could see that he was eager to escape its confines. He avidly read the three Bibles, plus a Latin-English dictionary Aed had procured; Aed for his part was reading a book Dr. Pabst had given him on the art of crossing cultures, both for his own sake and to be able to explain things to Taberah. He had never kissed a man on the lips before -- not even his own son -- but when he saw how delighted Taberah was at Noah giving him a kiss, he set his mind to enter Taberah's world as much as possible. He slowly realized, with certainty, that his willingness to do one thing against his gut reactions was only a shadow of what Taberah was willing to, and had to be willing to, do. He was not surprised when Noah explained to him that culture shock is one of the top causes of suicide, ranking with divorce.

Getting him home from the hospital bore an unexpected surprise. Taberah was happy to be walking out of the hospital, and then stiffened when he saw that they were walking towards Aed's car, a sleek hybrid between a minivan, a sport utility vehicle, and a station wagon. Noah said, "He's had more trauma in the past two weeks than most of us have in a year; is there any way to circumvent a car trip?

Nathella looked at Aed for a moment, and said, "We can walk."

Aed winced. "It's eighty-five degrees, and we're eight miles from home. It will take two hours to walk home!"

Nathella said, "I'll walk with him. He has a lot of extra energy. Why don't you drive home and make lemonade?"

Aed said, "Um, you want to be alone with him, even in public? I know he hasn't given us his last surprise."

"I'd rather take whatever risks there are than force that child through a car ride. And trusting people can make them worthy of being trusted. Honey, did he ride in a car with the INS?"

"Uh... I'll walk, too, and we can get the car later."

Noah said, "If you give me your keys, I'll get my son, and we can drop your car off at your house."

Three hours later, the trio arrived at home, hot, sweaty, tired, and parched. They made a gallon of lemonade, and then another; it took two and a half gallons of lemonade to fill them all. Aed expected a conversation of some sort, but Taberah was happy to sit in a chair and smile and fall asleep.

Aed expected it would be an interesting endeavor to teach Taberah to take a shower.

Logical Rocks

Taberah read avidly; he wished to derive as much benefit from the four books he had been lent (*four!* -- the *Vulgate Versio*, the *Revised New American Standard Bible*, *The New Message: Complete Text, Revised*, and *Harrah's New College Latin and English Dictionary, Revised*) before they had to be returned to the patron who owned them. He very much wished to meet the man.

It was about a week before he began to see that his hosts wanted him to talk with them from time to time -- mostly out good manners; he had never been in the possession of even two books at the same time, and never encouraged to read outside! -- and another week before Aed sat down with him to try to explain to him that there was life outside of books.

Then Taberah became a fount of unending questions, questions as startling as those Clancy and Fiona had asked as a child -- and yet questions that showed the intellect of a sharp adult. They were, nine times out of ten, questions about things he would never think about, and questions he had no ready answer for. At times Aed thought it would have been easier to answer, "Why do things look smaller when they are farther away?"

One day, Aed was sitting in his chair and thinking about how quickly his children were growing up -- and he was beginning to think of Taberah as a child, or a foster child at least -- and realizing that things had been silent for too long. This was longer than the silence after Taberah had realized that a screwdriver can unscrew the screws that were holding the blender together...

"Aed!"

"Yes, Taberah, what is it?"

"Aed, what is this?"

The sound of his voice was coming from a specific room, it was coming from --

Oh, no! Aed thought. *Anything but that. I am ready to explain anything but--* but his feet had carried him to the room Taberah was in.

"Aed, what is this?" Taberah repeated.

A dozen replies flitted through his mind: a moving picture, something to think with, a hobbyist's delight, a shortcut in talking with people --

"This is a rock that can do logic."

"What?"

"This is a rock that can do arithmetic and logic very, very quickly."

Taberah said, confused, "How numbers they and logic they make a picture move?"

Aed sighed. "Taberah, can I answer another question? This one's awfully hard to explain."

Taberah slowly said, "Yes. What question to answer?" But his eyes betrayed him.

Aed thought, and asked, "Do you know that clock in the living room?"

Taberah said, "Yes. Why have you a clock? And not you use it to pray? It rings bells, but I not you see not pray."

Aed said, "One question at a time, please. Do you know what it has inside?"

"I have seen opened one clock."

If he'd opened the grandfather clock, he had put it back in working order. Aed respected the lad's abilities, but this seemed too much. Or had he opened another clock? "What did you see inside, child?"

"Springs rods gears moving *beautiful!*" Taberah said, his eyes glowing with excitement.

"Do you know how clocks work?"

Taberah said, "Yes," followed shortly by, "No. What?"

Aed moved his forearms like the hands of a clock. "Know why hands turn?" he said.

"Yes! Fixed hands, stopped turning."

Aed said, "You can do many things with gears and pulleys. You can store numbers, add them, make decisions: if this rod is here, turn. A computer is like that, only it uses things besides gears. It uses pictures on tiny rocks. And it is very fast."

Taberah looked at Aed, and then looked at the computer screen. He was trying to believe him, but just couldn't see a connection.

Aed said, "See this wall? Look very closely. There are arranged pieces of color. They are called *pixels*. Do you see them?"

Taberah squinted, and touched the surface. "I see."

Aed said, "The computer uses numbers and rules to decide

what color to make each pixel. All of them together make a picture."

Taberah closed his eyes in concentration. He moved his hands, sorting out concepts. Then --

"Why is the picture moving?"

"Because the computer is making many different pictures, one after another, and together they look like they're moving. The moving picture is made up of still pictures like the still pictures are made up of pixels."

Taberah stared at a small patch of the wall as colors flowed. His face met with a dawning comprehension. Then he said, "The computer very, very intelligent! I want talk with computer."

Aed shook his head. "You can't, son."

"Why not?"

"The computer is not intelligent."

"But you said it can do logic!"

"It can do logic, but it's not intelligent."

Taberah ran out of the room, and returned holding the Latin-English dictionary. He flipped through several the entries, several times, and then looked at Aed in puzzlement. "I don't understand."

Aed said, "Can you write?"

Taberah said, "I can write Latin. I not know not the script of your books."

Aed said, "One moment." He returned, holding a notebook and a pencil.

"Write down, with logical rules, how to talk in a conversation. In your language," he said.

Taberah's jaw dropped in shock. "Write *that* on paper?" Taberah would as soon scratch the surface of a painting as write something that unimportant on precious paper.

Aed scratched his head. He didn't see what could possibly be so offensive about an innocuous attempt to write rules. "Ok, don't write that. But can you think of rules for a conversation?"

Taberah began to translate a Quixotic code of etiquette.

"No, not those rules. Logical rules."

Taberah looked frustrated. "But polite is reasonable!"

"Explain to me how to talk using only if-then-else and while-this-is-true rules, and words you decide ahead of time."

Taberah's gaze bore into him. Then, "I can't. That isn't how I talk."

"That isn't how anybody talks. You can't talk that way. But that's the only way a computer can work. Computers can't think."

"Then how create beautiful moving picture?"

"Some people spent a lot of time thinking of clever ways to explain how, using only math and logic. There are a lot of things we can do, but a lot of things we can't do. We have an old phrase, 'silver bullet', which refers to a way to make everything easy with computers and fix all problems. The term is kind of a joke; calling something a silver bullet is a way of saying that it's supposed to do something impossible. And the same thing has happened with the effort to make computers think -- it's called artificial intelligence, and people have learned a lot from trying to do it, but they haven't succeeded. A very great mind named Alan Turing proposed the Turing Test: a computer is intelligent if you can't tell it from a human when you talk with it. No computer has been able to make it."

Taberah looked irritated, flipped through memories of conversations, and said, disgustedly, "Bad reason! False reason!"

"What, Taberah?"

"Is bad think. What human is and what human talks like is much different thing. If logic is not whole human reason, talk is not whole human reason." He flipped through the book, and read out, "Confusion, accident, substance." He closed the dictionary. "Is accident confused with substance. And is possible cheat Turing Test."

"Cheat on the Turing Test? How? How can you talk like a human without understanding human reason?"

Taberah closed his eyes, and said, "Moving picture? How? How can you move like world without understanding world?"

Aed thought for a moment, and said, "I see how you can think that. But decades of attempts have failed to produce anything that can even cheat on the Turing Test. Most people don't try."

Taberah looked in the book. "Fifty attempts are not many."

Aed said, "Not fifty. Over fifty years' worth."

"Why number attempts in years? Is not sense."

It took a good two hours more conversation to answer all the questions Taberah came up with, and afterwards Aed padded off to his bedroom, exhausted, but at least happy to have gotten *that* conversation out of the way. He drifted off to sleep in blissful happiness that tomorrow was Saturday, and he could sleep in until noon.

At 10:00 he was awakened by a voice calling, "Aed! Aed! How to use computer?"

Thinking About Logical Rocks

"Taberah, can I please get a couple of hours' sleep? This is Saturday, and I'd like to sleep in."

Taberah was puzzled as to why one should sleep in on a particular day, but thought this a poor time to ask. "Okay!" he said, and went to try to memorize parts of the dictionary. He was beginning to feel accustomed to the books -- their size, their print, their light weight, their smooth sides -- at least, although he was still puzzled about why someone had bothered to make a book for the sole purpose of keeping track of words. Were there not scholars who could be asked about these things?

Aed woke up some time later, and looked at the clock. It was 13:00. Taberah had given him a fair amount of time. He lay in bed, ruminating about how to explain how to use a computer. Taberah knew enough of how a computer worked -- explaining memory and parallel computing should not be that much harder -- but how to explain how to use it?

Space would be the first major obstacle to overcome. The computer gave a virtual reality environment, with the walls of a room as screens; when you put on a pair of goggles, it was as if the walls were transparent and you could see through them to the world, as if the walls were only a glass box. But space behaved differently than in the real world. Aed thought for a moment about the mathematical abstractions by which the space worked -- the classic introduction described taking a tessellation of cubes, and then cutting them apart and connecting the sides arbitrarily. You could take two windows of a bedroom, and attach them so that looking out the North window gave a view as if you were looking in the East window, and vice versa. It was fantastic and dreamlike; it allowed portals between different areas of space, so that there were no difficulties in taking a room in Chicago and making a doorway open out of a subway closet in Paris. Aed remembered the first time he played a game with a labyrinth connected in this manner; he had been awed when he walked around a pillar again and again and never came to the same place twice.

Space might be the first obstacle, but it wouldn't be the only obstacle. How could he describe the richness of the environment? And how could he describe its weak points?

Aed thought over the many things that contributed to the richness of the environment. There were:

- Jump points. These were like travel locations, but with all manner of portals to interesting places. One was a long hallway full of doors, through which a person could step into other areas. Another was a library full of books which, when opened, would expand into other places. (How would he explain to Taberah that objects were putty-like, able to expand and contract, that you could push a button and have a menu pop out?) Another still was a slide show, where you could jump into the show at any point and be where it portrayed. There were others; there was not yet a standard.
- Programming workshops. Programming constructs behaved like any other object; one could assemble them as objects, algorithms, constructs, patterns. It was also possible to take programmable objects and pull off the skin to reveal the structure underneath, and tinker with it.

It had taken Aed a long time to get used to this interface -- it was a bigger transition even than moving from text-based languages to graphical development and intentional programming -- but even then he objectively realized that it was a simpler environment to use, and now it was second nature. Aed realized another thing to explain to Taberah -- that objects were not permanent; they could be modified, extended, simplified, cloned at will, and the many implications -- there was nothing that had the status of gold, of being something valuable because it was scarce. Taberah had enough difficulty understanding that paper was cheap; what would he make of this?

- Virtual brothels. Aed winced at the time Taberah would stumble on one of these; the freedom to avoid pornography was hard to come by; it was like avoiding advertisements when he was growing up. There were perennial attempts made to curb pornography, but -- even when it was widely acknowledged fact that the vast increase in rape since the web's second successor appeared was due to sexual addicts who got their start online, and then ravaged real women because pornography could only go so far -- they always fell on the rocks of a freedom of speech argument. Aed grumpily muttered to himself that household appliances were in some sense sculpture, in that their designs involved commercial artists, but the banner of freedom of expression did not make for any exemptions from environmental regulations in manufacture; it was recognized for the commercial product that it was. Why wasn't pornography recognized as a commercial product? Had the news ever carried a report of a pornographer who lost business because of making an artistic statement that was less arousing? Had there ever been a site where the valerie was glaring in hate at the voyeur? It seemed a funny form of expression that could only express itself in ways that coincided with a calculated commercial product. But the courts had argued that brothels popping up everywhere you wanted them and everywhere you didn't want them was sacrosanct free speech, and 'censorship' (that pejorative term) was tantamount to violating the Constitution. Well, not exactly. The phrase, "The illegal we can do right away, the unconstitutional takes a little longer," was obsolete, because the Constitution was a dead letter. In *Roe v. Wade* in 1974, the Court had made a strained argument finding an unnamed right to privacy to make the question of an unborn child's right to life irrelevant, skirting even the issue of whether that entity was a person or a part of another person. When the decision was reviewed in the late 1990s, the ruling recalcitantly acknowledged that the 1974 ruling was wrong, but said that it would be wrong to take away the sexual freedom that young people had gotten used to. In *Purdie v. Braverman* in 2024, fifty years after *Roe v. Wade* to the day, the courts had ruled infanticide legal, "up to a reasonable age", and specified neither what a reasonable age was, nor even a contorted lip service argument as to why the Constitution justified infanticide -- perhaps because they could find none. It had not surprised Aed two years later when the courts legalized euthanasia, with only the vaguest and most confusing guidelines as to when it was permissible and when consent was even necessary -- he shuddered when he remembered the definition of implied consent. Now, it was 2034, and the date had passed when Aed was no longer surprised by anything the courts did. He -- Aed suddenly realized that he was not thinking about computers. He tried to focus his thoughts -- what else after brothels?

- Society for Creative Anachronism re-enactment arenas. These places set up an environment to resemble that of a time and date in the past, and then people attempted to live and interact as people of that era and place. Even the avatars looked like people from those times -- avatars were another thing to explain to Taberah. An avatar was the moving image which represented a person in the world -- like the piece that represented a king in a game of chess. The image was completely customizable and configurable, with the effect that many people looked like a supermodel, although it was not uncommon to encounter unicorns, dragons, mermaids, cybernetic organisms, anthropomorphic robots... but never a person who was fat or ugly. Human-like robots had never materialized, any more than the anti-gravity devices imagined of old; the development of technology had shifted direction towards a primary focus on information technology, but this and all manner of fantasy appeared in the virtual worlds. Aed reflected that there was a good sense and a bad sense to the word 'fantasy', and both of them were amply represented in the virtual worlds.

- Bedrooms. A bedroom was a place with one person's very personal touch; there were elements there that would never surface in an institutionalized setting. There were not exactly bedrooms *per se*, so much as creatively developed spaces that had personal sharing. Because it was possible to let someone in a room without being able to easily do damage, you could go and visit people's bedrooms. There were quite a lot of interesting sites to see.
- Clubhouses. If a bedroom expressed the spirit of a person, a clubhouse expressed the spirit of a group of people. These had both function and decoration to them, and almost always had something of a personal touch.
- Museums. There were museums of almost every sort to visit. Because a painting could be in more than one place, and it was not nearly as expensive to build them, there was a much more vast diversity of museums, many which were much more specialized. The low expense of creation made for a much greater diversity, with many more excellent things available, but also a much lower average quality. Sturgeon's law applied *a fortiori*: "90% of everything is

crap."

- Special museums which had disassemblable and scalable models of human and animal bodies and machines. Aed's children had not dissected animals in school; they went into museums where it was possible to strip off skin, strip off muscle, double the size, half the size, make everything but the skeletal and nervous systems translucent...
- Role play arena. In the 20th century, the basic unit of time-consciousness was the decade; now it was the semi-decade, or semi. Role play was one of the trends that was in this semi, and there were virtual worlds for all kinds of different role playing games.
- Dreamscapes. In these places, there were a number of momentary images, represented by blocks something like the Capsella toys Aed had played with as a child. One put them together in a particular way, and then set the composed dreamscape in his pack. Then nothing happened, until you hadn't done anything with the computer for a while. The computer would then begin "dreaming" -- start a random walk that began with one block, and shift, images flowing, to a neighbor, and then a neighbor's neighbor... Aed had seen some truly beautiful artwork that way.

Aed wondered, "What time is it?" Then he looked at the clock. 15:00. Yikes! He got up, got dressed, and looked for Taberah.

Taberah was reading the bilingual dictionary with rapt concentration.

Using Logical Rocks

Aed walked over to the computer room, grabbing two pair of goggles. He showed Taberah how to put one of them on, and then said, "Sit down and wait here for a moment."

In a few minutes, an avatar appeared before Taberah and said, "Take my hand." Taberah reached for it and grabbed, but felt nothing. He was confused. The scene changed, and he saw that he was inside a sunny field, with forest to the east.

Taberah asked the avatar, "Who are you?"

The avatar said, "I am Aed."

Taberah said, "But you not resemble not Aed. You look -- your clothes are different, and skin different, and --"

Aed said, "Never mind that. Do you see my hands?"

Taberah said, "Yes."

Aed said, "Move your hands like mine."

Taberah did, and found himself moving rapidly through space. His stomach lurched; he put his hands over his eyes.

Aed said, "Take your hands off your eyes, son."

Taberah did, and saw he was a good fifty hands off of the ground. He braced himself for the fall, and put his hands over his eyes again.

Aed thought for a moment, and said, "We're going to try something different. It takes a little while to get used to moving about, but you'll learn. In the mean time, I'll let you see through my eyes."

Instantly the perspective changed. Taberah looked down, and saw a pair of hands pull a book-shaped object from a pocket, with a picture on front. The hands pulled on the book and expanded it, then pressed buttons, flipping through pictures. Taberah saw a picture of a stag, and said, "Ooh!"

The picture expanded, and they fell through it. They were in a forest glade; a stag was looking at them curiously.

Then Taberah saw himself walking rapidly to a door with a picture over it; he said, "Too much of fastness!" and the pace slowed. He was through, to a dark forest with unfamiliar plants, and a large snake slithering towards them. Afraid, he said, "Snake!" and saw himself walking towards another door with another picture, and he looked around. The landscape was alien; it was rough terrain covered completely by snow, and he saw fat black and white birds walking around, and some big black fish-like animals on the ice.

Taberah looked intently at all that was around him; it was

strange, but none of the animals began to threaten him. After a few minutes, he said, "I have sick of sea." He wasn't feeling very good.

There was moment of nothing happening, then a jar of perspective, and then stillness. Taberah closed his eyes to shut out the view. Then he heard Aed calling, and touching his shoulder. He was holding a tiny cup of the thinnest glass, with something that looked like wine. "Drink," he said.

Taberah drank it, and the nausea began to go away. Had he been given a magic potion? He was confused, but pushed this question to the back of his mind. He wasn't sure yet what was magic in this land and what wasn't -- that seemed a confusing question here, and the people treated the moving rooms as something as believable as a horse! Aed asked him to step out and sit on the sofa.

Aed was trying to think of how to explain the way space worked. He was expecting a question about why there was a door, all by itself, in the jungle, and the moment you stepped through it, you were in Antarctica. When Taberah remained silent, he asked, "Taberah, was there anything you found confusing about that world?"

"Yes, movement."

"Ok. Anything else?"

"Yes, doors."

Aed went into a long and involved attempted explanation of how different parts of space were connected, and saw the confusion on Taberah's face growing with each step. Finally, he said, "Taberah, why are you confused?"

"What is it that the pictures?"

"Huh?"

"Pictures on doors. Why?"

Aed said, "I don't understand. Could you rephrase that?"

"Pictures. Doors. Top."

Aed said, "One moment," and went over to the computer to look at one of the doors. "Aah," he said, returning. "Those are advertisements."

"What is advertisement?"

"An advertisement is a message from a company telling a customer about one of its products."

"I not understand not. For what is it that advertisement needed? Is it that townspeople not tell not where merchant is?"

Aed thought for a moment, and said, "Advertisements exist to stimulate sales, to help a company sell things to people that otherwise wouldn't buy them."

Taberah looked even more confused, thought for a moment about wording and grammar, and said, "And which of the seven deadly sins is it that this custom embodies?"

In the ensuing discussion, Aed slowly realized that Taberah had not been troubled by the nature of space. He had been able to accept as perfectly natural a portal between two different regions of space, and Aed wondered what kind of conception of space his culture had to let him accept that at least quite placidly. The first time he had entered that kind of virtual environment, Aed had been thrown off by the conception of space. And he had felt nauseated, his head spinning after -- suddenly he found Taberah's "sick of sea" more understandable. And he began to see something that he had not thought about, not for a while: that advertisement does not exist for the customer's benefit, but for the company's benefit, so that it can get more money out of the customer; this practice clearly ran contrary to Taberah's way of thinking, and at the end of the discussion, Aed walked away, for once, with his head not spinning, and thinking not only that Taberah's way of thinking was understandable, but that he might have a point.

A New Friend

The next few days saw animated discussions, a lot of reading on Taberah's part, and a few more minutes using the computer -- at Aed's urging; Taberah wanted nothing more to do with it.

Taberah was sitting on the ground outside, drinking a glass of nice, warm water, when he saw a large, black, almost grown

Newfoundland puppy come wandering by. And gulped. Such a beast would be a prime candidate for a dog race.

Dog races, in his homeland, occurred when people would gather together stray dogs, tie metal pots to their tails, and then let the dogs go. The dogs would start to walk, then hear the sound of the pots scraping against the stones of the road, get scared, and start running to get away from the noise. When the noise grew louder, the terrified dogs would run, and run, and run, and run -- until they dropped dead from exhaustion. The winner was the boy whose dog ran the farthest before dying.

Taberah hated the dog races with a passion. They made him sick; after his protestations, his lord issued a rule that no dog races were to be held while Taberah was around, but that was the best that had happened. He was humored at best; nobody else save Grizelda shared his objections to the races. Most people were so blazé that they didn't see what the big deal was in the first place. Yes, it was his homeland, but it wasn't his homeland. It was the place he was from, and the place where he had spent most of his life, but he wasn't at home there. In a way, he could adjust to almost any place -- was adjusting to the kingdom he was in now (what was it called, and who was its king?) -- but in a way he was never at home. There was always something about him that didn't fit. Why was he the only one who cared about dogs? Francis of Assisi was venerated, but the people who venerated him did not imitate his treatment of animals. Well, he could try to save at least one dog from the races --

Hastily setting down his glass, Taberah sprinted at full speed after the dog, which ran away from him, barking. He continued chasing the dog for a full hour, his toughened feet pounding on the asphalt until they were sore, until he dropped in exhaustion, panting and thirsting. It wasn't until he stopped that he realized the exquisite pain in his feet. He looked down, and realized his feet were cut. Where was he? The buildings looked different; the outside looked more like buildings than outside. He was by a room of sorts with two walls missing, but with a ceiling. It was raining; he crawled over to a puddle, and began to lap at it.

He looked up, and saw the dog drinking from the other side of the puddle. It came over and sniffed at him; Taberah hugged and kissed it. Beginning to feel chilled, Taberah crawled under the shelter, holding the Newfoundland next to him. He could not get to sleep, both because of all the moving rooms passing by, and because he had plenty to think about.

Taberah felt happy and comfortable as he had not felt in a long time. The wealth he had been in was strange to him; it did not seem real. Out, even in a strange, semi-open place (why would someone build two walls and a roof of a room, and then make the inside part of a thoroughfare?), finally next to another warm body (even if only a dog's), Taberah felt happy. He settled into a slumber, thanking God for bringing him to a place that felt a little home-like.

Midnight Oil

Aed drove around, trying to see if he could find where Taberah had gone. Fiona had run and told him that had seen a dog and bolted; as he drove around, he called the police and summarized what had happened. The dispatcher explained that he could not be classified a missing person until he had been gone for twenty-four hours; that was twenty-four hours in which to brood. The family looked until three in the morning, and then went home because both Aed and Nathella were too tired to continue driving.

At four in the morning he was awakened by a call. Groggy, Aed turned on the videophone and said, "Yes?"

A police officer in a car sent a still shot and said, "Officer Shing, State Sheriff. Is this the man?"

"We found him sleeping under a bridge, along with a dog he refuses to part with. He had lacerations to the soles of his feet; the EMT thinks he ran barefoot over broken glass. We have taken him to Mercy Memorial Hospital; he is presently in the emergency room, waiting for treatment."

Aed said, "Thank you. Why did you take him to Mercy? I don't understand that. Mercy is almost fifty miles away from here."

Shing replied, "Mercy is the closest hospital to where we found him. Is there anything else we can help you out with?"

Aed thought for a moment, and said, "Not now, but I might call you if I think of something else. I'm going to grab a few coffee beans, and then go to pick him up. Is there anything else I need to know?"

The officer said, "No, but you might want to take him shopping for some clothing and shoes. He's wearing a ragged getup, and -- the hospital will be able to tell you about his special needs to heal from the lacerations."

Aed said, "Thanks. Over and out."

Nathella rolled over and said, "You weren't thinking of getting him without bringing me, were you, honey?"

Aed said, "Get dressed, and come along. I'll get the coffee beans."

Two voices from below said, "Me, too!"

The emergency room was fairly quiet; doctors were removing glass shards from Taberah's foot and stitching up the cuts. Taberah looked confused; there was something in his eyes that even Nathella didn't understand. He was under local rather than general anaesthesia, but he still started nodding off to sleep.

He received some soft "shoes" made of bandages, and the doctor told Aed to keep his feet bandaged and give him high top athletic shoes a couple of sizes too large. When it was time to go, everybody climbed in to their van, the dog brought along as well. Aed tried to ask why this attachment to a dog (it belonged to a neighbor, and periodically ran loose), but could find out nothing beyond that Taberah did not want it to be raced. Aed let that be; he wanted to get back to sleep, and wait until tomorrow to tackle the puzzles. Taberah agreed not to leave the house without having someone else along, and seemed relieved to learn that this kingdom didn't race that type of dog. He was even happier to find out that the dog belonged to someone nearby, and would be taken care of; he wanted to meet the neighbor the next day. "Very well," Aed said, "but we need to get some sleep first." This time,

Taberah joined everybody else in sleeping in until the afternoon.

I Can't Believe...

Nathella and Fiona were working in the kitchen; good smells came upstairs. The Kinsellas (and Taberah) settled down for a late dinner, a family complete, such as it were.

They sat in silence around the table; there was a simple joy in everyone -- or almost everyone. After Dr. Kinsella said grace and the food was passed around the table, Taberah broke the silence by saying, "Nathella, would you pass the *I Can't Believe It's Not Better*?"

Nathella smiled and passed the spread, and made a mental note to buy butter the next time she went shopping. As she passed it, she saw something in Taberah's face. "Taberah, are you homesick?"

Taberah looked at her. "What is 'homesick'?"

Nathella thought for a moment and said, "Homesick is when you aren't comfortable in one place, and you miss the place that is your home."

"I don't know if I'm homesick. Maybe. Yes. No. I don't know if I have a home; maybe if I understood the word better..." His voice trailed off, but the others remained silent. "It's just a bunch of little things, like strange foods and too soft bread without any rocks and no touching, not even wrestling, and... Or maybe that's not a little thing." He stared at his food.

Clancy said, "C'mon out back dinner. We can roughhouse in the back. Fiona and I wrestle a lot, only not recently. We've been busy with you, and we didn't know you liked to horse around. Fiona's in the house to be picked on," Fiona made a face at him, "and I'll flip you around. I would pin you, but you need to be soft on your feet."

Taberah's face brightened.

Nathella said, "Is there anything we can do that will bring you a little piece of home?"

Taberah hesitated, and then said, "Have you no wine in this country?"

Nathella smiled gently and looked at him. "Yes, we do, but not in this house. I'm an alcoholic."

Taberah asked, "What's an alcoholic?"

Nathella said, "Do you know the word 'drunkard'?"

Taberah said, "You're not a drunkard! I haven't seen you drunk. I haven't even seen you drink wine."

Nathella said, "Not now, but once my life was given over to alcohol. Escaping alcohol was the hardest thing I ever did, and if I start to drink, I won't be able to control it. It would control me. So I can't have alcohol in the house."

Taberah looked disappointed. He said, "Then it is good of you not to drink."

Nathella said, "Thank you, Taberah. Maybe sometime when I'm visiting with one of my friends, Aed will buy a small bottle of wine for you two to have. He likes a good drink, and he will have a beer when he's out with his friends. But he doesn't drink in the house. He doesn't want to tempt me."

Taberah smiled. He was warmed with a patient assurance that he would have wine, and was in no particular hurry. He looked around, and then his gaze settled on Fiona. "Why are you homesick, Fiona?"

Fiona smiled, and said, "I'm not homesick, at least not for a place. I wish it were Christmas, with the family and gifts and wassail and -- ooh! the music. I miss the music."

Taberah said, "What kind of music?"

Fiona said, "One is, O come, O come Emmanuel. Do you know it?"

Taberah thought for a moment, and then thought a little more, and said, "Could you sing it for me?"

Fiona sang, in her thick countertenor,

O come, O come, Emmanuel
And ransom captive Israel
That mourns in lowly exile here
Until the Son of God appear.

Rejoice! Rejoice! Emmanuel
Shall come to thee, O Israel.

Taberah said, "I think I know it. Let me sing it as I know it." He took a sip of milk, and then stood up on the chair, and began to sing:

Veni, veni Emmanuel!
Captivum solve Israel!
Qui gemit in exsilio,
Privatus Dei Filio.

Gaude, gaude, Emmanuel
Nascetur pro te, Israel.

Veni, o Sapientia,
Quae hic disponis omnia,
Veni, viam prudentiae
Ut doceas et gloriae.

Gaude, gaude, Emmanuel
Nascetur pro te, Israel.

Veni, veni Adonai!
Qui populo in Sinai
Legem dedisti vertice,
In Majestate gloriae.

Gaude, gaude, Emmanuel
Nascetur pro te, Israel.

Veni, o Jesse virgula,
Ex hostis tuos ungula,
De specu tuos tartari
Educ et antro barathri.

Gaude, gaude, Emmanuel
Nascetur pro te, Israel.

Veni, Clavis Davidica,
Regna reclude caelica,
Fac iter tutum superum,
Et claude vias inferum.

Gaude, gaude, Emmanuel
Nascetur pro te, Israel.

Veni, veni o Oriens!
Solare nos adveniens,
Noctis depelle nebulas,
Dirasque noctis tenebras.

Gaude, gaude, Emmanuel
Nascetur pro te, Israel.

Veni, veni, Rex gentium,
veni, Redemptor omnium,
Ut salvas tuos famulos
Peccati sibi conscios.

Gaude, gaude, Emmanuel
Nascetur pro te, Israel.

Taberah sat down and was very still. The room was very still -- one could hear a pin drop. His singing voice was a tenor, but there was nothing flimsy about it; it was rich and powerful, like silver, like something between a stream and a waterfall, and for the moment he had looked like a bard. It was hard to believe that such a mighty voice, filled with silent strength, could come from such a tiny body -- and yet, somehow, after that song, Taberah did not again look tiny to the Kinsellas. Nothing about his physical appearance was changed, but none the less the way he looked to them was different.

Aed finally broke the silence by saying, "I never knew you could sing like that, Taberah, and I should very much like to have you over for Christmas. Is there any way I can thank you for that song?"

Taberah said, "Over for Christmas? All twelve days?"

Aed thought. School resumed classes from winter break on the third of January; getting permission to take time off through the seventh would involve some major administrative headaches. "All twelve days," he said. "I'll make sure of it."

Taberah said, "Then what I would most like for my song is to go out and wrestle."

Clancy bolted out of his chair and had Taberah in a fireman's carry before anyone else knew what was going on; Taberah was out of Clancy's grip and bolting out the door before Clancy knew what was going on. It wasn't until later that Aed wondered how he could run with healing, stitched lacerations in his foot; soon they were all outside, a crazy, happy, moving, squirming bundle of arms and legs with grass stains on its shirts. And Taberah was happy, happy as he could ever remember being.

It was only a few minutes before they were all sitting and panting; Taberah did not understand why they wanted to rest so soon, or why they didn't give him more resistance in the fray, but he basked in the afterglow. The memory of that moment would be a treasure to him as long as he walked the paths of the earth.

A Guided Venture

Nathella said, "We need to give him some of Clancy's old clothes so he's decent, and then take him to one of the old-fashioned clothing stores -- he won't be able to try stuff on online. Clancy, would you come with to help him with the clothing?"

They arrived at the store, and Nathella said, "Here we are, to get some clothing. You can take anything in the store."

Taberah looked, and bright colors caught his eye. He went over and started to stare at a rack of shirts.

"Not there," Nathella said. "Those are children's clothing."

Taberah thought it strange that there should be special clothing for children, but said, "I am a child. You're a child. Clancy's a child. Want children's clothing."

Nathella, who had felt almost guilty about her age since her thirtieth birthday, said, "That's sweet, honey, but I am not a child. Neither are you. And Clancy's not really a child any more."

("Thanks, Mom!")

("Shut up, dear.")

Taberah looked puzzled. "Are you not born of a woman?" he asked.

Nathella said, "Uh, of course I -- ooh, I see. Taberah, we use the word 'child' to mean someone who's younger than Clancy, and 'adult' to mean someone who's older than Clancy. Clancy's -- in between."

("Thanks, Mom!")

("Shut up, dear.")

Nathella continued. "And children wear different clothing than adults."

Taberah said, "Why?"

"Because children are different from adults."

"Why?"

"Have you seen a tadpole?"

"Yes."

"Have you seen a frog?"

"Yes."

"Do you know that tadpoles turn into frogs?"

"Yes."

"But tadpoles and frogs are different, right?"

"Yes."

"Children and adults are different in the same way, right?"

"How?"

Nathella did not reply to the question. Clancy, in a particularly mischievous mood, would be able to ask a series of questions like that while keeping a perfectly straight face, and he often managed to catch his father. But she could sense a complete honesty in Taberah's questions; they were as honest as a child's.

And as unending. She was beginning to realize that he did not perceive anything approaching a sharp demarcation between childhood and adulthood. "Come over to this section. I want you to pick out a shirt from one of these racks, and a pair of pants from one of these racks."

By the second or third try, Taberah had picked out clothing that would fit him; it seemed a bit loud to her, but she did not want to argue with that. He went into a fitting room, and, with Clancy's help, put the pants on properly and the shirt on backwards. He came out, and said, "I like it. Let's pay for it."

Nathella said, "Hold on, Taberah. I want to pick up a week's worth of clothing."

Taberah said, "This clothing will last for a week, more."

Nathella said, "I want to buy you enough clothing so that you can wear different clothing each day and not have to wear the same clothing for a week."

Taberah's jaw dropped. He had a vague realization that the others' clothing looked different over time, and he knew that some of the people of his home town were wealthy enough to have two sets of clothing -- one for summer and one for winter. He had not, in his greediest dreams, ever wanted to wear different clothing each day. He asked, "Why?"

The trio arrived at home, carrying a large bagful of clothing. Aed asked, "Hi, guys! How was the shopping?"

Clancy asked, "Would somebody stop the room, please? I'd like to get off."

I Envy...

Taberah asked Aed, "What is your trade?"

Aed recalled a moment in graduate school where one of his colleagues had said, "I envy people in nuclear physics. They can tell other people what they do for a living." He said, "I teach -- do you know logic?"

Taberah said, "Yes."

Aed asked, "Have you done geometry?"

Taberah said, "Yes."

Aed said, "What I do is like geometry and logic; logic and geometry are examples of it."

Taberah said, "Give me an example."

Aed thought of the three rules of a metric space, then thought how little those rules illuminated what he was thinking -- as little as a list of chess rules gave any obvious feel for deep strategy. Aed had learned long ago that it was possible to understand the rules of a game completely without having the foggiest idea what its strategy was like -- human understanding never included instant sight into logical depths, any more than good eyes enabled you to see infinite detail despite distance and twilight! In the classroom at the university, Aed would have to bow to custom and labor over the basic rules, but Taberah was not a student at school, and -- "I am studying collections of objects where you can tell how far apart two objects are."

"Like geometry!" Taberah said."

"Yes, but it includes many things that do not have the structure of a space. Like words. 'Man' is close to 'woman', farther from 'dog', farther from 'tree', and farther still from 'rock', and very far from words like 'move'.

Taberah said, "Yes! That's how to cheat on Turing test!"

Aed winced and said, "Uh, how?"

Taberah paced the room in thought. "Can computers record conversations?"

"There are many, many conversations on record. I can download a collection of them now, if you wish."

"Well, first find out how to measure the distance between two words," Taberah said.

Aed nodded. The artificial intelligence literature had found a way to map the distance between words by measuring frequencies of words occurring before and after them in a histogram.

"Then have something that will look through conversations, matching up by words and grammar, and return the closest match!"

Aed looked at Taberah hard, and then said, "Son, how'd you like to learn how to program?"

Hacking Away

Aed led Taberah into the computer, and then left him; Aed's avatar soon appeared nearby. "Put your hand on that picture on the wall," Aed said, and when Taberah reached out, he was in a large room, with alien artifacts on the walls and shelves.

Aed flew through the room, touching partially assembled objects; they vanished, leaving an open space to work in. "The first thing to do," he said, "is to make a Turing test room. Touch that bin over there."

Taberah touched it; it grew to fill half the room, and then its sides vanished. "See that red thing? Take it out of the bin, and then touch the button on the bottom of the bin; it will shrink back to its normal size. That is a room object; say 'Options.' See that popup menu? That's the thing that looks like a sheet of paper. Turn on the one that says 'Maximum occupants'; set the number to three. Then press the 'recording' button. I'll come back and record messages for the three users; the first user is the tester, and the second and third users are trying to convince the tester that they're human. Initially they'll both be human; later, one will be an avatar for our program. Pick up a dialogue slate; say, 'Record: Which user do you think is human? Now touch choice one, and say: Contestant one. Choice two: Contestant two. Choice three: Can't tell.' Ok; expand the room, and place the dialogue levitating in the center, in front of the tester's door. Wait, put three doors on for the user to enter. Oh, that looks funny because you have a bug. You have the buttons switched. You should --"

After the room was completed, Aed summoned the chancellor of the university and asked him to make an announcement of a Turing game. He recorded the announcement, and, after the chancellor disappeared, said, "This will give us some time to work out the artificial intelligence decoy. If you give me a moment, I will find the metric for words..."

It took Aed and Taberah a long time to get to sleep that

night; it took them a long time to stop tinkering, but even after that, they were filled with an excitement of discovery, of uncertainty, asking, "Could this be? Have we really discovered what we think?" Their excitement was raised in the morning when Nathella said, "Why don't we go downtown this evening for a Tridentine mass? Taberah, it's in Latin; I think you'll enjoy it."

Taberah was not sure why the Kinsellas went to mass every week; it had not been any special holiday, so far as he could tell, and he could never get out of them a straight answer as to why they went to mass when there was no particular reason to do so. But now he was in such high spirits that he wanted to go.

Another Era

Nathella walked in to the massive church. It was plain, and all was still. As the liturgy began, the stillness was not broken; the majestic Latin spoken by those up front only augmented the silence. Each step was majestic; she lost herself in its familiar details.

After the service, she put her hand on Taberah's shoulder, and asked him, "So, whatchya think?"

Taberah's eyes were misty. He closed them, then opened them, saying, "I don't understand. I did not see the guest of honor. Was he a theologian?"

Nathella said, "What?"

"Was the guest of honor a theologian?"

Nathella reminded himself that Taberah sometimes approached matters strangely. "I would rather think of him as God who told stories. What do you think?"

Taberah said, "Not Jesus, the person the -- now I remember the word -- funeral is being held for. Was he a theologian?"

Nathella withdrew, slightly surprised. She said, "Why do you think this was a funeral?"

Taberah said, "It was so mournful. People were silent; they did not say anything, and the person up front was impossible to hear. There weren't any changing songs. And I didn't hear any instrument music, no organ. And this church had its walls stripped

-- no statues, no color in windows. Does this building have anything besides funerals?"

Nathella accepted that Taberah's perception of the Latin mass was very different from her own. No, that wasn't quite right. He wasn't responding to the Latin, *per se*; it was something else that accompanied the Latin. It -- she decided to stop musing and respond to him. "At home we have a machine that can make organ music; would you like to come home?"

At home, they sat down on a sofa and set the computer to play music. Taberah listened to the sound, the familiar sound of an organ -- no, it was not; it had range and voices and a perfection of sound such as he had never heard, and such speed! Then it unfolded, into two voices, three, four. Taberah felt dizzy with the complexity, or more accurately, giddy, drunk; he heard wheels within wheels within wheels within wheels. It was alien in many ways; most of all, he felt that he had never encountered such a mind. He never knew that such music existed. When the moment wound down after several pieces, he said, "I awe," and then, "Who was that?"

Nathella smiled and said, "That was Bach."

"May I speak with Mr. Bach? I would very much like to meet him."

"Honey, Bach has been dead for almost three hundred years."

At this, Taberah was surprised. "If Bach is dead, how did he play that?"

"Bach wrote his music down, then someone else played it on an organ, then the computer kept and transported the sounds so we could hear them."

"How can a rock transport sounds?"

"Aed, would you explain that?"

As Aed explained, Nathella observed Taberah. He no longer seemed so completely homesick; his face bore the excitement of discovery. Taberah was adapting to his new land.

Angels Dancing

"And all they were doing," Nathella said to Aed, "is endlessly debating 'How many angels can dance on the head of a pin?'!"

"That's the best question," Taberah said. "That's a very good question."

"What?" Nathella and Aed said together.

"'How many angels can dance on the head of a pin?' is a good question."

"Why?" Nathella said.

"Do you know how many angels can dance on the head of a pin?" Taberah asked.

"Um, I don't know. Five? Twelve? Seventeen? I have no idea." Nathella said.

Taberah looked displeased. "I don't think you understand the question. Say seventeen angels can dance on the head of a pin, but not eighteen. Why?"

Nathella said, "I don't know. That's why it's a silly question."

Taberah said, "Ok. How many people can dance on the head of a pin?"

Nathella answered, "If the pin was lying on the floor, one."

"Why not two? Why not three? Why not five?"

"Because people have bodies, and they'd bump into each other."

"Do angels have bodies?"

"No; they're spirits."

"Can angels bump into each other?"

"No; there can be as many angels in the same place as want to be, because spirit -- ooh! Two, or five, or seventeen, or an infinite number of angels can dance on the head of a pin at once, because they don't take up space the way we do."

Taberah smiled. "Is that a silly question?"

Nathella hesitated, and said, "If you are asking an abstract question, why embed it in a concrete and silly-looking facade? Why not ask it abstractly?"

Clancy burst in the door, out of breath, and said, "Hey, Mom! How many field service engineers does it take to screw in a light bulb?"

Nathella was about to say, "I'm in the middle of something, dear," when Clancy said, "Two. One to find a bulb, and one to pound it into the socket."

Nathella giggled for a moment, then her face showed confusion, which slowly turned into dawning comprehension. Clancy watched her, and said, "*Et voila!* It took you long enough this time, Mom!"

Nathella said, "It's not that, honey; I got the joke immediately. It was just that Taberah had asked an abstract question in a way that looked simple and silly, and I had asked why he did that, and now I realized that our light bulb jokes work the same way. The canonical 'How many morons does it take to screw in a light bulb?' 'Five. One to hold the bulb, and four to turn the ladder,' is only incidentally about ladders or even lightbulbs. It's about stupidity trying to do things in an ineffective and unproductive manner, and it provides an illustration. Wouldn't you say so, dear?"

Aed said, "I was just thinking about what impact such a presentation might have on my teaching at school. A concrete capture of an abstract idea is harder to make than an abstract decision, and much more powerful to understand. Whether I have the political strength to get away with a non-standard treatment of content is --"

Clancy cut him off. "What was the question Taberah asked? Was it something like 'How many angels can dance on the head of a pin?'"

Beyond a New World

Taberah was sitting on the lawn, resting, thinking -- when he realized that he had never explored the computer. He had gone to a couple of its rooms when Aed had led him, but he had never set out to see what there was to be seen.

That was strange. When he was little, Taberah had explored

every building he was allowed in with a sense of fascination; he still remembered the wonder with which he had imagined a door opening, beams of light showing from behind. He asked Aed if he could explore the computer; Aed would have liked to accompany him, but was thinking about a problem he was researching. So Aed said, "Go ahead. Touch the picture with a gold border."

Taberah went in; he was in a gallery of pictures, and reached out for one of them. He was drawn to it

was through it.

Taberah looked around. He was in an immense labyrinth; he started to fly around, the walls shifting and changing as he walked. There were statues, and fountains, and shadows lurking; there was something strange about it that felt like home.

Taberah turned a corner, and looked around. He was in a circular room with no doors; after looking around for a moment, he saw a knob at the side of a large black disc in the middle of the floor. He reached for it, and pulled; downwards was a brick tunnel, reaching into fathoms of darkness. After thinking a moment, Taberah left the annulus and tumbled down.

It was dark, or almost dark, around him; it looked like a room with candlelight. As his senses adjusted, Taberah heard crickets chirping, and realized there was the sound of the ocean; he looked around, and saw starlight. Which reminded him -- but he would have to do that later. He started to fly about, and realized that he was in a huge forest. He came to the water's edge and dove down.

It was scary to see the water close above him; Taberah held his breath before reminding himself that he was just surrounded by moving pictures. He went in and down, in and down.

After a little while of pitch darkness, Taberah could see a faint blue light. He flew towards it, and saw color dancing. He saw thin slivers moving by twos and threes -- fishes, he thought, and then went closer and saw that the swimming creatures were mermaids and tritons. Then he recognized the light: it was a vast city of sunken stone, an alien ruins. A mermaid swam by; he reached for her hand, and then he realized that he could not touch her. He followed her around, through streets and doorways and tunnels, between walls with runes glowing blue-white. The mermaid swam off; he opened one door, and saw a decorated room which made him forget he was underwater. Then he saw a strange picture on the wall; it puzzled him. He reached for it --

What is This?

"Aed!" Taberah called. "Aed! What is this?"

Aed came running, muttering under his breath, "This had better be good!"

Aed looked at the screen -- a nude female avatar was writhing in sexual ecstasy -- and, after staring a moment, turned the video off. "That's a valerie," he said. "I should think that her purpose should be obvious enough."

Aed looked at Taberah, and then realized that he had misjudged the look in Taberah's eyes. Taberah had been staring at the valerie in fascination, but not exactly lust. He had rather been staring in puzzlement, and in the same horrid fascination that he had seen on Clancy's face, looking at a car wreck. Aed began to realize that an off the cuff response was not going to work here. After collecting his thoughts, Aed said, "Well, what do you think the picture was about?"

Taberah said, "I do not understand. She looked on her face like a woman wanting to be bounced, but she had her clothes off, and what a horrid body! Her breasts were enormous; they were ten times as large as beautiful breasts, and the rest of her body looked like a muscular boy's body, or a man's." He paused a moment, and then his face was filled with a flash of insight. "Aed! Was this valerie made for lust by a pedophile who wanted to pretend that he was looking at a woman instead of the boy's body he was looking at? He must have been trying very hard to fool himself, to have put on such huge, ugly breasts! But why make a picture to lust at in the first place?"

Aed mulled over this response, and mentally compared the valerie's body with his wife's -- and then looked into his own reactions. "Taberah," he said, "a valerie looks like that because that is what my nation thinks a beautiful woman looks like. I don't know how to explain it, but even though I try to love and honor my wife, the trend is strong to me; the valerie looks better to me."

Taberah turned green, and said, "Why? And I still don't understand why to make pictures for that purpose. Do you not think God's way of making women is beautiful?"

Aed thought for a moment and said, "Taberah, the culture we are in is sick. It is dying. This is one of many signs of its sickness."

Taberah said, "Then why not heal it?"

Aed said, "I don't know."

In the Stars

After taking some time to rest -- Taberah was still quite confused -- he asked Aed, "When was the day of your birth?"

Aed said, "It's really not that important."

Taberah said, "Why should a man of your age not want to tell when he was born?"

Aed said, "I'm old enough, Taberah. Why do you want to know?"

Taberah was puzzled; Aed had attained a very respectable age, and Taberah could not understand why he looked uncomfortable about it. Maybe to explore later...

"I want to go outside at night," Taberah said, "and gaze upon the stars and the crystalline spheres, and know the influence of the planets when you were born upon your life and at the present day."

Aed took a moment to parse this sentence, and said, "You want to cast my horoscope?"

"Yes."

"I thought you were a Catholic."

"I am."

"Then why do you want to cast my horoscope?"

"In order to understand you better."

"Don't you think there's something wrong with astrology?"

"What?"

"What do you think astrology is?"

"Natural philosophy, exploring the interconnected world in which we live."

"Taberah, astrology is not science. It's magic, or like magic. It belongs to the occult."

Taberah was trying to sift this apart. "Why?"

"It is divination. It does not work according to the basic laws of science. Astronomy is science; it studies how the heavens go. But it does not believe in influences, any more than looking at the entrails of a chicken will tell the future."

Taberah said, "Aed, what's the difference between science and magic?"

Aed was caught completely off guard. The disowning hostility of science to magic, *The Skeptical Inquirer*, the use of the word 'scientific' to mean 'rational' and 'working' and 'magic' as a pejorative metaphor for technology that did not appear to behave according to rational principles -- Taberah might as well have asked him to explain the difference between light and darkness. But his question deserved an answer; science does not include divination -- no, that would exclude weather forecasting; science provides theories and laws about how the world works -- so does magic; science is about exploring the forces of nature -- no, magic claimed to do that as well; science is reductionistic and magic holistic -- no, that was, if true, looking at the surface rather than the nature of things, and that wasn't true; it excluded psychology; science produces predictable results according to its theories that -- well, that also rules out psychology as science...

"Taberah, what can astrology tell you about a person?"

Aed listened to Taberah's explanation, and slowly stopped fighting a realization that this made more sense than what he was taught in his undergraduate psychology class, particularly behaviorism -- he felt he would be much better understood by Taberah's astrology than by a behaviorist account. Astrology at least accounted for the stuff of common sense -- emotions, tendencies, thoughts, good and bad timing -- while behaviorism reduced him to an unbelievably simplistic account of just a black box that does actions. Listening to Taberah's account sounded goofy here and there, and the idea that the influence of the stars and planets controlled matters was straight-out hogwash, but Taberah's explanation overall gave him the impression of a rational account believed by a rational mind.

Science did experiments rigorously, and its standards did not validate any claims of magic -- no, wait, the dice were loaded on that question; in Taberah's explanation, Aed saw a wisdom that just wasn't found in psychology; science did not meet the standards of interesting magic. No, that was not quite right; when did science really begin flourishing? At the same time as magic began flourishing, and often in the same people; Newton's discovery of physics was almost a vacation from his work in alchemy. The two enterprises were born out of the same desire, to control nature and gain power, and in both people would readily engage in practices that had been hitherto regarded as impious and disgusting, such as digging up and mutilating the dead. Still, there was a difference, a difference which Aed felt if he could not think. They --

Aed came to himself and said, "I can't tell you the difference between science and magic, Taberah. I can't tell you, but I do know it. You shouldn't be doing astrology. You shouldn't be doing divination. If you're not sure of whether something is science or magic, you can ask me." Aed thought about buying him a psychology text, but decided not to, at least not for the moment. The psychology text he'd read, he was beginning to realize, was parochial and in many ways backwards; of course it was written by psychologists at respected schools, but the zeitgeist was -- Taberah would encounter enough of it on its own, without having it embedded in something Aed told him to have replace his belief in astrology. Aed felt vaguely guilty about destroying a treasurehouse of lore, but let this go to the back of his mind. Once Aed had explained a simplified version of physics and astronomy, it was with some deflation that Taberah saw why Aed placed astrology among divination, but not weather forecasting.

Taberah stepped out that night, and lay on his back to look

at the stars. He could not see many of them, and those badly, because of all the light. It seemed to him that something had departed from their song, but he could almost see something new. It was beautiful that the planets should revolve around the sun and not the earth; just as there were nine orders of angels -- the highest six of whom gazed continually on the glory of God, and only three of whom were sent out among men -- there corresponded nine planets, six of which were further out in the Heavens, the third of which contained life, and all of which revolved around the Light! His head went dizzy when he realized what it meant that he lived on a planet, and the sun was a star.

The Trial

A representative from the Turing Society called Aed. "We hear that you have a program that is trying to pass the Turing test. I would like to administer the Turing test to your program at 2:00 PM on Tuesday, with observation. Is that acceptable to you?"

Aed's heart jumped, and he had to force himself to stand still. "Yes. I will look forward to it."

The test room was modified to support an arbitrary number of lurkers, and excitement built around the university. Quite a number of eyes were watching as the tester strode into the room. One of the contestant avatars looked like a unicorn; the other looked like a dragon. The tester managed to conceal her surprise, and said, "Good morning. How are you today?"

The unicorn said, "I am doing quite well. You?"

The dragon said, "I've had a lousy day, but it's getting better. I love playing the Turing game."

The tester said to the dragon, "Have you ever lost the game?"

The dragon said, "I've lost once, to a salesperson. I was really mad when the judge said I was a computer."

The tester repeated to the dragon, "Have you ever lost the game?"

The dragon repeated, "I've lost once, to a salesperson. I was really mad when the judge said I was a computer."

The tester asked the unicorn, "What about you? Have you ever lost the game?"

"Yes, frequently. I guess I don't sound very human."

The tester repeated her question to the unicorn. "What about you? Have you ever lost the game?"

The unicorn hesitated and said, "Um, is there a reason you're repeating the question?"

The tester did not answer. Instead, she said to the unicorn, "Tell me a bit about yourself."

The unicorn said, "Uh, I like woodworking, and I like to collect things. I've got a roomful of bottle caps, and I have one of the biggest collections of visual textures on the net. And I like fantasy."

The tester turned to the dragon and said, "What about you? How are you like?"

The dragon said, "I'm an optimist. It's too sunny out to be crabby. And I like collecting stamps."

The tester asked the dragon, "What is your philosophy of life?"

The dragon said, "My philosophy is one of many sides. There are many sides to life; there are many sides to being a person. I am many different things as the occasion merits."

The tester turned to the unicorn and asked, "What is your philosophy of life?"

The unicorn said, "Could you ask me another question? I'm kind of nervous now, and I'm having trouble thinking straight."

The tester said, "Ok. What is the one question you most fear me asking you?"

The unicorn shivered, and said, "The one you just asked?"

The conversation continued for two hours, unfolding, unfolding. It was about that time that the tester asked the unicorn, "What was your scariest childhood moment?" and the unicorn told a story about getting lost on a camping trip, and then twisting an ankle. Then the tester turned to the dragon, and said, "How about you?"

The dragon said, "Personally, I'm partial to seltzer water.

And you?"

The tester pushed a button and left for the conference room Aed was in. She said, "You have quite an impressive achievement there, but you have a long distance to go before passing the Turing test. I tried to give two hours' testing to be sure, but I knew the dragon was a computer within five minutes of speaking with it. The clues that gave it away were --"

Aed cut her off and said, "Sorry, you guessed wrong."

"*What?*" the tester asked.

"You guessed wrong."

"Can you tell me with a straight face," she asked, "that the dragon was a human? Do I look that gullible?"

Aed gently said, "No, I'm not saying that the dragon was human. I'm saying that they were both computers. The dragon was merely an old version of the program."

The woman's jaw dropped.

Aed added, "I should also like to say that most of the ideas were my guest Taberah's; I mostly helped out. The achievement is his, not mine."

Detained

A knock sounded on the front door. "I wonder who that could be at this hour," Nathella said. "A reporter?"

She opened the door. There were several men outside, holding badges. They looked familiar, and smug; one of them said, "Officer Salisbury, Bureau of Immigration and Naturalization Services."

Nathella sank back. Aed said, "What are you doing here?"

Officer Salisbury said, "We have come to detain Taberah, before transporting him to his country of origin."

Aed thought for a moment about an English translation, and said, "What right do you have to do this?"

Salisbury said, "We are enforcing the law. If you --"

Taberah popped his head in the window and said, "What is this?"

Officer Salisbury said, "You need to come with us."

That shoots any remnants of search-and-seizure concerns, Aed thought. "Could he have a moment to gather up his possessions, at least?"

"That won't be necessary," the officer said. "We do not transport possessions beyond clothing worn. We are not a shipping service."

Aed, Nathella, Clancy, and Fiona each gave him a hug, their eyes filled with tears. Then Taberah was handcuffed and led away to a car. Nathella could see Taberah steeling himself against the ride.

Wrong Person

In the middle of the night, the videophone rang. Aed got up, turned off the video, and said, "Yes?"

The voice on the line was unfamiliar. She said, "Hello, is this Aed Kinsella?"

Aed said, "Yes."

The woman said, "I'm calling to tell you that you and Taberah Kinsella have won the 2034 Turing Award for your joint work in artificial intelligence."

Aed blinked, and said, "I'm sorry; I think you have the wrong person."

The woman laughed, and said, "I'm positive I've got the right person. Can you get Taberah?"

"I'm sorry; I can't; Taberah is being 'detained' by the INS."

"What? Who are the INS? Do the police know about them?"

"Yes; the INS are part of the police. They are the Bureau of Immigration and Naturalization Services, and they just took Taberah. He is now en route to a jail, to have his head and his beard shaved, be stripped and put in a de-humanizing uniform, and sit in a cold cell with nothing to do while he waits for the INS to decide what country to deport him to."

The woman was silent for a moment, and said, "What country is he from?"

"I don't know. Dr. Pabst, an anthropologist I know, said that he doesn't seem to be from any culture currently existing. He has learned English, but besides that -- why?"

The woman said, "Please wait a moment; I'll get back to you."

Aed had just crawled back into the covers when the phone rang. It was a journalist. And then another. And then another. After the first dozen times trying to explain that it was Taberah's work and not his, and that Taberah had been taken by the INS, he unplugged the phone.

At four in the morning, the doorbell rang. And then rang again. And again. Aed swore, and fumbled about for Nathella's keychain -- a keychain with pepper spray. He threw on a bathrobe, and padded out to the door. "Who is it?" he shouted through the door.

"Officer Salisbury, returning Taberah to your house."

"*What?*"

"When we came last night, we did not realize that he held a United Nations passport. We apologize for the inconvenience."

Aed opened the door. Taberah looked weary, frightened, relieved, and very happy to be back. Aed picked him up, and held him in thanksgiving. Then he said, "Let's both of us get some shuteye; we've got a speech to write."

A House Abuzz

There was a great deal of excitement around the house; friends and colleagues from church, the university, and other places stopped by, and some of them brought meals. Aed was excited by the activity; Nathella was wearied, and climbed into bed as soon as the last party had left.

One of the things that Aed insisted was that Taberah and all of the Kinsellas would appear through avatars, and that Taberah be referred to by a pen name -- John. This was big enough news that Aed did not want strangers on the street recognizing them from a compucast or rebroadcast, nor calling them up. While Aed was in the living room explaining details of the work to his colleagues, and Nathella and Clancy were occupied with the hospitality, Fiona was occupied with Taberah. The two of them were in the computer, talking about what Taberah's avatar should look like.

The question was a bigger question than it seemed at first. The avatar should not be recognizable as him, but it should reveal him, his bearing. "It should be a mask," Fiona said. "It should be like a Halloween costume, changing yourself in such a way that you shine through."

"What's Halloween?"

"Later, Taberah. We don't have time to explore that now, although you'll see in a few months. Now, to start off with, do you want a human-looking avatar, or a fantastic avatar?"

"I -- I don't know. Could I look at some of each?"

"Fiona said, "Hmm... There is something alien about you. Would you like to see what aliens look like?"

Taberah looked at several bodies of aliens, and recoiled. "Those aren't aliens," he said. "They're humans made to look grotesque. That's not what being alien is about."

"Ok," Fiona said. "How about fantasy? Do you like fantasy?"

They looked through a faun, a centaur, a unicorn, a dragon. "How old do you want to look?" Fiona said. Taberah didn't know. "Not that knight in armor; that would only be for going out to war. Not -- *there!*" he said, with excitement.

"You don't want that," Fiona said. "That's a court jester. They acted like fools for other people to laugh at."

"I want that! I was a court jester once!"

Fiona wondered about Taberah's statement, but this was not time for long questions. She looked through colors, and guided Taberah towards a jester's outfit that was darker and had more muted colors. It was unmistakably a jester's outfit, but it had an air of gravity about it -- which Taberah liked. "Ok," she said. "Now what do you want to eat?"

"Roast boar," Taberah said.

"Taberah, boar is awfully expensive, and there will be a lot of people there. I --"

"Give me two swords and I will kill one!" Taberah said,

grinning.

"No, Taberah. You can't do that."

"Why not?"

"To start with, there aren't any boars here. You'll have to think of something else."

"Roast pig with an apple in its mouth!"

Aed stepped in. "Taberah, would you come out for a minute? There are some people who want to see you."

Fiona said to Taberah, "We can't have pork. There will be a lot of Muslims at that dinner."

"Is this country overrun by worshippers of Mahomet? Is there no one to drive them out?"

Aed stopped in the hallway. "Taberah, a couple of things. First, Muslims are not worshippers of Mahomet, any more than Christians are worshippers of John. They believe Mahomet was the greatest prophet, but not the man-god we believe Jesus was. Second, Muslims are citizens here. They are powerful, and their power is not all to the good -- it is awfully hard to do things that Islam disapproves of, and there have been not-so-subtle manipulations against Christian evangelists speaking to Muslims, for one thing -- but they are people, citizens of this country like anyone else, and not invaders. It is sad that Christianity has let Islam take its place, but the solution is not to run them off. Third, we may have wine available at th--"

Taberah interrupted. "Spiced wine, piping hot? And cider?"

Aed said, "Spiced wine, piping hot, and cider, if you want, might be possible, but the food has to be something that Muslims may eat." Aed declined to mention the headache that would be involved in getting alcohol served...

Taberah said, "Do Muslims eat hamburgers?"

Aed threw up his hands and said, "I have guests waiting. Why don't you have *filet mignon*? It's the same kind of animal as hamburger, only much better."

Taberah was tired after the people met. He had not realized the intense energy it takes to connect with people from another land -- he and the Kinsellas had gotten used to each other through intense contact. Nathella picked up on his fatigue faster than anyone else; she encouraged him to go to bed and get a good night's rest before the big day. Everything was in place; Aed had finally managed to convince the Turing society that he did not deserve the award, and accepted the privilege of introducing Taberah. Everyone slept lightly -- everyone but Taberah; he slept like the dead, and got up to protest the stiff clothes he wore to the banquet.

Accolades

Taberah was cheered at the meat and drink; the meat reminded him of home. He was equally delighted to sit down and drink wine with Aed, and his spirits did not flag although people asked him questions that struck him as rather odd. At the end of the dinner, Taberah was pleased to have (so far as he could tell) avoided making any *faux pas*. He felt a sense of accomplishment, and felt at home.

The chairman of the Turing Society looked at Aed and pointed to his watch, and Aed nodded. He took a sip of water, and then climbed up the steps to the podium.

Nathella could not see that her husband was nervous, but she knew it. He had thrown out his introduction a dozen times. Neither of them were worried for Taberah, though; Aed and Taberah had worked out a speech, which Taberah memorized with remarkable facility.

"I would like to begin this introduction," Aed said, "by apologizing for giving an introduction not worthy of the occasion. I would very much like to give a traditional introduction, in which one perhaps starts by saying 'The person who is going to speak is a man who needs no introduction,' and then spends five or ten minutes detailing education, awards, and accomplishments. It would perhaps sound grander if I were to say that such an introduction was inadequate to him, but the truth is that I don't know enough about him to give an introduction of that sort. I don't know if he went to school at all; he appeared on my doorstep, became deathly ill, and has since then been turning my world upside down.

"His first surprise for me was in chess. I am rated at 1975, and when I invited him in, him looking dazed and confused, he took my chess pieces to the table (at least after I let him), and began to play his way -- at first I thought he didn't understand the game or was cheating, but then I realized he wasn't playing on a grid. He beat me five times in a row.

"Different members of our family have had conversations with him that left our heads spinning; my wife Nathella is the only one who has not had that experience, and I believe that is because of her ability to understand people. There's only been one time that I've been able to understand Taberah better than her, but I won't detail that here.

"Taberah is brilliant, and approaches life in ways that would never occur to me. Wherever he comes from, and wherever he was educated, he somehow had the intelligence to look at the problem of artificial intelligence in a way nobody else had seen it before. If I cannot vouch for his education or accomplishments, I can vouch for this one accomplishment. Taberah has worked into a special place in my heart, and not only because of his brilliance. Without further ado, here he is."

Taberah strode up to the podium; on the screen behind him, his avatar looked quizzical and dignified at the same time. "I was going to say," he began, "that my discovery has taught us nothing about human intelligence. But I began to reason, and realize that it has.

"Men have always wanted to create other men like themselves. I once wished to make an assemblage of gears that would make a mechanical human, and I saw no reason why not. If gears could make a clock, with continual motion controlled according to its construction, why could the best crafted gears not make a man? Certainly myths came of gods who had made mechanical men. So I do not find it to be at all surprising that, when people found a way to make a machine that could do arithmetic and logic, they thought they had made something that could think.

"Chess is something that is difficult for people to do. So it was thought, 'If we can only make a computer that can beat the best humans at chess, then we will have achieved intelligence.' The day has long past when a human could beat the best computer, but if that achievement has taught us anything about human intelligence, it is that humans do not play chess like a computer. Making better and better computer chess players did not make computers intelligent any more than making more and more realistic-looking statues will make them alive.

"Conversation is something humans do, so Alan Turing, a brilliant mathematician, thought, 'If we can only make a computer that can pass for human in conversation, then we will have achieved intelligence.' Now the day has come when a computer has passed for human in conversation, and if it has taught us anything about intelligence, it is that intelligence goes beyond conversation as it goes beyond chess. Those are both activities humans can do, but mimicking or even beating human performance does not a person make, any more than a collection of lifelike statues can be improved to the point of achieving life.

"I do not think that this calls for a new test to determine intelligence. I think it calls for a realization that human intelligence is too rich and too deep to reduce to a simple test. When a test has been proposed to measure intelligence, the test gains a life of its own, and suddenly people stop thinking about intelligence, and start thinking about how to pass the test. Chess playing programs became sophisticated with speed and advances that were not even approximated by efforts to understand how humans play chess, let alone how humans think.

"But this is enough. It is bad speaking to cram so much into your audience's heads that things are falling out; I have criticized enough for an award recipient. The field of artificial intelligence is a fertile area of thought which has brought many good things; even if artificial intelligence is never achieved, its failure will have enriched the soil of human endeavor. I thank you for this award and the other assistance the Turing Society has provided me, and, Aed, Nathella, Fiona, and Clancy for their help. God bless, and have a good evening." He returned to his place.

The chairman of the Turing Society stepped up to the microphone and said, "There is one more thing, Mr. Kinsella. The Turing Society has a fund, out of which to give prizes to its award recipients. The funding might buy research equipment, or a sabbatical, or perhaps access to online research libraries. Is there something we can get for you? Do you need a home?"

Taberah said, "I have everything I need now. But if there was one thing I could have -- do you have a troubadour's lute?"

There was a moment's pause; the chairman, Dr. Bode, spoke on his cell phone for a moment and then said, "One of the members of the audience has one now, which she will lend you while another is delivered." A small woman walked up; Taberah was puzzled, as she was holding a small black bag, but otherwise empty-handed -- there was no room to conceal a lute, even a small one. She reached into the bag, and pulled out a thick black belt and two long black gloves, long enough to cover an elbow. He could see that there were was something else in the bag. She looked at him and said, "Put the belt around your waist, and the gloves on your hands."

Taberah did so, feeling some puzzlement.

"Now," she said, "play as if you were holding a lute."

Taberah looked at her, confused.

"Like this," she said, moving her hands in a strumming motion.

Taberah moved his hands, as if to play a chord -- and jolted in surprise as notes sounded. Then he moved his hands again. There were some sounds of jarring dissonance, like a piano being played by frostbitten fingers losing their numbness, and then a simple, high, pure, aching sound. It pierced by its beauty, and with the music, words, in a voice that filled the room:

Once there was a little lady,
Fair and pure and elfin bright.
Her light skin shone like burnished silver,
Blazing light throughout the night.

Her soul it was a filled with music,
Her body was a filled with dance.
Her long hair was black like ravens,
All blazing was her countenance.

Taberah's otherworldly song filled an hour; in his song, he carried with him a feeling of home, a moment of Heaven, and all of the strangeness of the land about him, of his aching at no place that felt home, vanished. The music he made in his trance brought its listeners into another time, into another world; to those in the room, the song so filled their consciousness that they did not think of anything else. When the song began, the netcast of the awards ceremony was brought into focus, and the avatar who had looked slightly strange speaking about artificial intelligence now fit perfectly into place: a court jester -- and more than a jester -- holding a lute, telling a tale and weaving a song.

When it was over, even the silence was musical, because it bore the silent echoes of the music's spirit. Taberah walked back to his seat, and asked, "Can we go home?"

With that, the meeting was over.

Where Do You Come From?

It was the first day of classes; Aed had returned home late, to a house filled with a marvelous scent. It smelled of tomato, and basil, and bacon, and beef. Clancy said grace at Aed's invitation, and they began to pass the pasta.

Fiona looked at Taberah, and said, "Where are you from, Taberah? I don't think you've ever told me that."

Taberah said, "I am from -- Provençe, or at least half from there. My father is a merchant, and we have travelled to the ends of the world, and beyond -- but never to a place so strange as this. I am used to mountains, and seas, and strange people and barbarian tribes -- even worshippers of Mahomet --"

Aed said, "*Muslims*."

"-- even Muslims, but there are many things here that are strange to me."

"Like what?" Fiona said.

Taberah thought for a moment, and said, "It is hard for me to think of and harder to say in words."

Nathella said, "Can you think of it in your words in your own language? And then maybe translate?"

Taberah concentrated for a moment and said, "No, I can't. Not even in my own language. I will tell you later. After I think."

Aed said, "Don't worry too much if you can't answer. It was a friendly question, not a probe."

Taberah said, "It is a friendly question, and a probe, and a good question. That is why I want to answer it. Maybe after I research on the computer."

Fiona said, "Taberah, have you ever been to my Dad's campus? Tomorrow's a half day, and I could take you there. You might see more of the world."

Taberah said, "I would be happy to do that. But ooh! I miss home. I have never had a place that was completely home. Whether riding away hotly pursued, or haggling down the price of salt, or opening an illuminated manuscript -- I was at home for a moment, but over time not at home. Even in stealing a relic from a nearby cathedral --"

Fiona said, "You *stole* a *relic* from a *cathedral*?"

Taberah said, "Yes. The saint wanted to move; otherwise, he wouldn't have let his relics be moved. And I can move swiftly and silently --"

Fiona said, "Taberah, would you steal a fork from this house?"

Taberah looked surprised. "Never!"

Fiona said, "Why on earth would you be willing to steal a relic?"

Taberah had no real response to this question. He said, "If another city had a relic, and you needed it, wouldn't you assist it to your place?"

Fiona said, "I can't explain all my reasons why not, because I have to go to bed in four hours. But to start it off, that would be dishonorable."

Taberah thought, and said, "I'll have to think about that. I never met a knight who thought it dishonorable to steal a relic. Ok, I know how to explain. A relic does not belong to a living man or a place; it belongs to God and to the saint. Stealing a relic is a very different matter from stealing corn or grain. The corn really belongs to the person who has it; the relic belongs to the saint, and then to the saint's followers -- so if the people here worship a saint and want his relic more than the people where it is kept, then if the saint allows the relic to be moved, it should be moved."

Fiona said, "I can't believe this rationalizing. The bigger a sin, the more rationalizing there is, and you have rationalized an unholy theft on top of starting it in the first place!"

Nathella turned to Fiona and said, "Honey, I don't understand Taberah, but he's not rationalizing. He does not have a defensive air about him. And something tells me that he would not steal anything from this house -- nor steal anything from another place and bring it here. Right, Taberah?"

Taberah said, "Yes. I would never steal if it were dishonorable."

Clancy looked around and said, "Taberah, did you hear the joke about the cathedral that was so blessed that it had two heads of John the Baptist, one as a boy and one as a man?"

Taberah said eagerly, "No. Please tell it to me; it sounds very good!"

Fiona groaned and said, "Mom, would you please explain it?"

Nathella said, "Taberah, did you notice anything funny about there being two heads of John the Baptist?"

Taberah said, "No. It sounds like a great providence indeed, for which God is to be praised."

Nathella said, "What would have had to have happened for a cathedral to have the head of John the Baptist as a boy?"

Taberah said, "I suppose for him to have died as a boy."

Nathella said, "If there was a skull of him as a man, did he live to be a man?"

Taberah said, "Yes."

Nathella said, "So there's a logical contradiction for a cathedral to have two heads of John the Baptist, one as a boy and one as a man. Right?"

Taberah said, "Yes."

Nathella looked at him. "You still don't get the joke."

Taberah said, "I'm still waiting for the joke to be told. So I don't get it."

Nathella said, "If there's a logical contradiction, then it couldn't have happened, right?"

Taberah said, "If there's a logical contradiction, there's a logical contradiction. It doesn't mean that God can't bless a church with two heads of John the Baptist. God moves, and his ways are beyond our understanding. He has done greater things than bless us with two heads of a saint!"

Fiona said, "Taberah, if we go out for a walk tomorrow, do you promise not to confuse me?"

Taberah said, "Am I confusing you?"

Aed got up, placed his arm around Taberah's shoulders, and said,

"Wild thing!
You make my head spin!
I think I love you."

Music From Another Age

Fiona took Taberah by the hand, eagerly leading him as if she were a small child. The university's square was filled with a noisy, jostling, laughing group of people, chaotic as any bazaar. The excitement was tangible. "Today is the first day of Student Activities Week. All the student organizations are clamoring to find new recruits from among the freshmen, and anybody else who cares to come. It is a lot of fun."

Taberah walked over to one stand where several people were talking. He read the sign overhead, *Humanist Hacker's Guild*, and asked, "What is a hacker?"

One of the men looked up from a portable computer and said, "The first hackers were people in software who like solving problems and believe in freedom and helping each other. They produced a lot of computers and software. We are a special kind of hacker, hackers in the humanities. We produce artwork, music, and literature, and share it with other people. In a way, there have been humanist hackers for ages, but interaction with computer hackers has brought an awareness and a fertile field for sharing. Would you like to have a copy of one of my poems?"

Taberah said, "If I am here, why would you give me a copy? Why not just recite it?"

The hacker said, "Um, because I don't have it memorized?"

Taberah said, "I'm puzzled."

The hacker said, "Why?"

Taberah said, "How could you compose a poem, even writing it down, and then forget it?"

"Quite easily, I assure you."

Fiona put her hand on Taberah's arm and said, "Taberah, please. We are his guests."

The hacker took a sheet of paper and said, "Here. I'll read it to you."

"The Unicorn's Horn," by Elron Ellingswood

I walked out into the deep, dark, forest,
and there, in a clearing, it stood.

Oak was behind it, ferns below,
and atop its head, stood a blazing white horn.

It walked to a shimmering pool,
Its hooves not making a sound.

Around, the silence was broken
by the calling of a hawk.

The wind stirred the tree leaves
and danced softly over the grass.

The Lady of the Lake stirred,
softly,
invisibly.

Taberah looked both impressed and puzzled. He said, "You show the forest as an object of beauty. Why?"

Fiona grabbed his wrist, and tugged on him, saying, "Look over there! Karate!"

An instructor smiled and said, "Not Karate. Kuk Sool Won. Karate is a single martial art that focuses on punching, kicking, and blocking; Kuk Sool is a comprehensive martial arts system that includes joint locks, weapons, and escapes as well as many kinds of punching, kicking, and blocking."

Taberah said, "What's a joint lock?"

The instructor said, "Throw a slow punch at me."

Taberah said, "What?"

The instructor said, "Do this."

Taberah made the motion and his hand was caught, his wrist twisted.

"But what if I punch you with my other hand?"

"Why don't you try to do that? Slowly?"

Taberah did, and his puzzlement was exceeded by the instructor's, who said, after a second, "Stop. I've never seen someone who could resist a joint lock like that. You must have a tremendously high tolerance for pain."

Taberah said, "I don't understand. I didn't feel pain. I don't understand what you were trying to do."

The color of Fiona's face was beginning to match her long, wavy red hair. She said, "Taberah, come on. Let's find something else."

Taberah began to wander, and then saw -- or rather, *heard* -- something so positively medieval in spirit that it drew his attention so completely he was aware of nothing else. Up until this point, he had been thrown off balance by a hurry in the people around him -- or, at least, that would be a deficient way of putting it. A more accurate way of putting it would be that he was aware of time in the sense of an awareness of something around him, but not in any sense that would let him grasp rushing to get something done, or guilt at sitting at doing nothing. He vaguely perceived such a quality in those about him, and he was baffled and troubled by it, in the same way as if he were surrounded by people who were constantly thinking about air and in a frenzied haste to try to find some space that had enough air to breathe.

It was the near total absence of this quality in the music before him that beckoned him. It was as if he had stepped into a room of people breathing normally and attending more important concerns and only then come to realize that he had been surrounded by people fretting over whether they had enough air to breathe.

Taberah stood in silence, drinking it in. Then he stepped forward, picked up an instrument, and joined in the song.

At dinner, Aed asked Taberah, "So what did you see today?"

Taberah said, "Today was a happy day. Today I discovered New Age."

Aed suppressed a groan. How was he to begin an explanation? The phenomenon that was called New Age in its current incarnation had occurred many times in the past, and would doubtless occur many times in the future, each time under a different name; it was in spirituality what a logical fallacy is in reasoning. It was heresy -- perhaps he was safe in using that word with Taberah. In the word, 'heresy' carried a curious inversion of "a good and original idea which some benighted tradition condemns", the word being a condemnation of the tradition rather than the idea. What a diabolical trick that was! Heresies were neither good nor original ideas; they were propositions that had been weighed in the balance and found lacking, "New" Age being a manifestation of an error that had first occurred two millennia ago and had rotted every time since then. It promised freedom, and was one of the most confining and constricting prisons he had known -- a prison like being left all alone in an empty wasteland. You could go as far and wide as you wanted, and still find nothing good.

Aed hesitantly asked Taberah, "What draws you to New Age?"

"The -- music -- time -- you are hurried. They are not."

Aed nodded. New Age music was soothing music. But as to the time -- "Taberah, it's a busy time of year for me. What is this about time?"

Taberah tried to explain, and at first failed completely. Then, on the second time through, there was a look of dawning comprehension on Fiona's face, and she said, "I will try to enter your time, Taberah. But it will be difficult; we have been taught to hurry for a long time. I won't be able to do it very quickly, if I can."

Taberah kissed her cheek, and said, "I not in hurry -- ooh, did I do right in touch?"

Aed wondered what Taberah was talking about, and then recalled him sternly telling Taberah not to touch others in ways that he had not seen them touching. "It's OK, Taberah. You may give a kiss on the cheek to people in this family."

Taberah walked over, and kissed Aed on the cheek.

The Phoenix

Taberah spent most of the day running through New Age music in his head, and seeing how it would sound on his lute; Fiona had to knock on the door several times before he noticed she was there.

The square was less crowded than before; on the way in, Taberah looked and saw a place where several people were moving their fingertips about on a ridged surface, their hands dancing with energy; on a wall behind them, colors swirled and spun, vibrating with energy. "What's that?" he said.

Fiona said, "Those are visual musicians. They play instruments that do not produce sound, but color. Do you like it?"

Taberah said, "I like it, but why are they spinning so

quickly? Why --" he pointed to another booth and said, "What's that?"

A man in the booth next to them said, "Hey, a southpaw! Greetings!"

Taberah said, "What?"

"You're left-handed."

"What's that?"

"It's when someone uses the left side instead of the right?"

Taberah made the sign against evil and said, "Why would someone do that?"

"You did."

"I might have pointed with my left hand, but I do everything else with my right hand."

The student tossed a pen up, and said, "Catch!"

Taberah looked, and realized he had caught it with his left hand. "I am sorry. I have sins I did not know."

The student now no longer looked so merry, and said, "You're left-handed, but you're ashamed to admit it."

Taberah hung his head.

The student said, "You aren't part of the solution. You're part of the problem. We have a right-handed society, with right-handed machinery and right-handed rules. Even the words are prejudiced -- 'right' means correct, acceptable, and good, and 'sinister' and 'gauche' are words meaning 'left', which comes from a word meaning 'weak' or 'broken'. For years, lefthanders have been an invisible and maltreated minority, and now that some of us are speaking out and demanding that society improve, there are people like you who -- a gay who was like you would be said to have internalized homophobia. You are --"

Taberah cut him off. "Why are you so angry?"

Taberah listened with horrid fascination to the rant. He began to realize that using the left hand, like turning a wheel the wrong direction or walking backwards, was only a symbol of evil and not its substance, and began (despite all internal resistance to external pressure) to see that the student's conclusions were right, that the world was a right-handed world with subtle and invisible slights to its left-handed members -- or at least he tried to accept these things. He still felt guilt over catching the pen with his left hand, and he knew it would take time for him to shift his spirit to what he saw. But all this aside, he also saw an anger that brought far greater misery than any right-handed technology -- not confusing pencil sharpeners, not painful scissors -- could possibly cause. He narrowed his eyes, and said, "You are angry."

The student swore, and said, "I'm furious. Why do you need to point that out?"

Taberah said, "Are you happier with your pit of rage than I am with my right-handed society?"

The student was speechless. Another student, who had been listening, said, "I would like to cordially request the honor of your absence at our booth."

Taberah felt anger rising in the pit of his stomach; he felt it, but did not let it master him. He turned, and walked away, taking a long walk around the square before slowing down, and finally stopping at one place. He looked at a group of students who were standing around, talking, laughing; each of them had a necklace with a fiery bird. Taberah asked, "Who are you?"

A young woman with long, curly auburn hair said, "My name is Emerant, and we are the Phoenix Society. The Phoenix Society is a group of brothers and sisters devoted to living in the abundant life that Jesus offers, and extending that life to others. The Phoenix, the bird that ever rises anew out of its own ashes, was a holy symbol in the ancient Christian Church, and in wearing it we recall the ancient church and its life among a pagan world, and allow God to create in us the same life in a pagan world today. We have worship services every Wednesday night. Would you like to come and join us?"

Taberah felt something in the back of his mind, but he could not put his finger on it -- but it was something good, he was sure.

A young man with ebon skin placed his arm over Emerant's shoulder, and said, "What's your name?"

Taberah said, "My name is Taberah."

"How can we serve you? Do you have stuff to move in? Do

you have a story to tell?"

Taberah realized what he had felt but could not describe. There was an energy about these people, an invisible love so thick it could almost be felt. The young man was looking at him as if he were a king. The students in the group were all wearing distinctive necklaces, but their air did not treat him as an outside you, not even an outside you that they wanted to bring in. The man's eyes were dark as night, and they glittered like stars; there was something about his face that said 'I' and 'you', but even more said 'we'. Taberah smiled and said, "I should very much like to hear mass with you."

Emerant smiled a crooked smile, and said, "There is something else you want, Taberah."

Taberah closed his eyes for a second and said, "Emerant, I know your name. You, what is your name?"

The young man said, "My name is Abanu."

Taberah said, "Emerant and Abanu, I should very much like to play a song for you."

Immediately, a space appeared among the students. Taberah calmly, without any self-consciousness, walked over to the center and began to sing.

It was a noisy day, but it seemed silent inside that circle. Taberah could fill a room if he wanted to, but he was not singing loudly; still, all the students were aware of nothing else. When the song finished, Emerant looked around and saw that there were some people standing around and staring; she began to talk with him as the students asked Taberah questions.

It was not until seven that Aed found them, and told them that dinner was getting cold; Fiona had lost all track of time, and Taberah never had track of time to begin with. He slept well that night, and awoke in the morning knowing the answer to a question the Kinsellas had asked him.

In Spirit and in Truth

Taberah spent the day reading the Bible and researching on the computer; at dinner, he said, "Nathella, do you remember when you asked me a question about my place and this place, and I said it was harder to think of and harder to explain in words?"

Nathella said, "Yes."

Taberah said, "I was able to find words. In Bible, Jesus was talking with a woman at a well. She asked him what mountain to worship on. He said not to worship on this mountain or that mountain, but in Spirit and in truth. This land knows not how to worship in Spirit and in truth."

Aed's eyes narrowed. Aed and Nathella said together, "How so?"

Taberah said, "I have just begun to see how religion is, and it is not religion. It is private. It is an interest. It is a hobby. It is tame. Where I come from, religion is public because it pervades your whole being; it is who you are, and never has a pagan invader told a Catholic, 'You may be Christian, but make it a small thing. It is --"

Aed nodded and said, "That criticism has been made before, and it is not to be lightly dismissed. Is there anything else you see?"

Taberah said, "I slowly began to notice, when navigating on the computer -- where I am from, when people build a cathedral, they carve the backs of statues. I was shocked when I saw that people here do not do this. When an artist carves a statue in my land, he is not just working on a statue; he is making an offering to God, and his carving is a prayer. He carves the back as well as the front, working on a place whose fullness he may never see, because he is not making something for himself or other men, as much as making a prayer to God, who sees the back of the statue as easily as the front. Here, on the web, people do not do that. They think in terms of making a creation for other people. They do not try for completeness; they want -- I do not know the words."

"Good enough for government work?" Clancy said.

"Yes. Except that making something that is 'good enough' does not mean making something that is good. God is only in the compartment called religion; he is not big enough to make virtual reality for -- only other people who will not take the site very seriously is that important for."

I cannot make complete sense of Taberah's tangled wording, Nathella thought, *but I do not need to. Taberah has difficulties with language when he is concentrating most intensely.* She understood the meaning, if the words sometimes eluded her.

Aed said, "Anything else?"

Taberah said, "I hesitate..."

The room was silent.

Taberah continued, "I hesitate, but there is something strange about clothing and nudity. In my land, people wear clothing for custom and for decoration; being without clothing is not much. Here, clothing is for decency (a polite way to put it); there are chaste people and there are nude people, but there are not chaste, nude people. When a woman wears no shirt in an advertisement, her no-shirt means 'Look at me in lust!' She does not have a no-shirt that doesn't mean anything besides 'I don't want to have a shirt now.' There are people who say that we don't need to say clothes, and most of them say that not wearing clothes is not sexual, but few of them are chaste, or even acknowledge chastity.

"That is a symbol of something deeper. You need to cover your bodies, but even more you need to cover God, because you are ashamed of other people seeing them. And so you produce arguments to justify the existence of God, and God does or does not exist depending on whether or not he's covered.

"One of the theologians I know of, Thomas Aquinas, began his great work with five arguments for the existence of God. But these arguments have a very different meaning than yours; they were for adornment, and not for shame. Aquinas was not trying to give a needed proof of God, as your theologians do; certainly he did not think that if he failed to prove God's existence he was not able to believe in God. You speak of justifying belief, as if it needed justification, as if it were shameful if it were not covered by an argument.

"About clothing literally, I will not argue. Your way of looking seems to me a silly limitation that causes a lot of lust, but chaste nudity is not important. It is not one of the great things in life. But about clothing symbolically, I will argue much. You need in your minds to have an unblushing nudity, that can say, 'I believe in God and I accept his providence,' and not have a guilt about it for believing more than matter. You -- I am sorry, I should be able to produce more examples. But there are many ways where you do not know how to worship in Spirit and in truth."

Aed was stunned. After a while, and after nobody else said anything, he said, "Son, you've got a brilliant mind. I have a feeling of being held under a microscope. I don't know how to respond, beyond saying that you see things I would never see, and I hope you keep thinking."

Nathella said, "You almost seem like someone from another era."

Taberah said, "What's an era?"

Aed said, "Later, Taberah. Later."

Which Era?

As Aed sat down, Taberah asked him, "So, what is an era?"

Aed thought. He said, "I would better answer that question after looking at an encyclopedia; I've thought about how to explain it, and I realized I knew less than I thought I did. But here's a rough sketch of what I can explain:

"The ancient world was the world that gave birth to Christianity. It is everything before the Middle Ages, or medieval period. It gave us the apex of paganism, and philosophy, and writing.

"The Middle Ages were a thousand years of Christian faith and culture. They saw monasteries, cathedrals, castles, monks, clergy, knights in shining armor, lords and vassals and fealty, chivalry, peasants and feudalism, illuminated manuscripts...

"After that came the Renaissance and Reformation period. There was a rebirth of art and learning from classical, that is ancient, times, and the monk Martin Luther nailed theses for reform to the door of Wittenburg Cathedral, and chaos broke loose. Let's see...

"The Elizabethan time was the time of the great playwright Shakespeare, and vernacular translations of the Bible. The Baroque time saw a flowering of complexity in art and music; aah!

"Modern times began with the Elizabethan era, and started a new secularism in philosophy. It reached its climax in the Enlightenment, with people worshiping the mind and reason, and the bloodbath that followed. Then came Romanticism and Victorianism, one of them a following of emotional sensitivity that often included libertinism, the other managing to be morbidly prudish. After that, came postmodernism, the era that we are in. People have given up the quest for truth, and there has been an increase in fragmentation -- Taberah, I just saw a light go on in your eyes. What clicked?"

Taberah said, "I am medieval! What era are you from? Can you tell me how to get to the Middle Ages?"

Aed slapped his palm to his forehead and said, "Taberah, just forget this conversation and let's start over. There are some things about you that are like the Middle Ages, but the Middle Ages are a period of time in the past."

Taberah asked, "What is a period of time?"

Aed said, "It is a time when people have a certain way of living."

Taberah said, "I am from the Middle Ages period of time. And I think you might be as well. You belong to an age of faith, and you are a lord."

Aed said, "It is impossible to go back to another age. It is past. It has already happened."

Taberah would have normally backed off by this point, but there was something inside him that made him certain. He said, "Will you get out of bed tomorrow?"

Aed said, "Yes."

Taberah said, "But you have gotten out of bed in the past?"

Aed said, "Yes."

Taberah said, "Does that stop you from getting out of bed tomorrow?"

Aed saw where Taberah was going, and said, "But with history, it's different. You cannot bring back the past any more than you can make your self younger." As soon as the words escaped Aed's mouth, he remembered the difficulty Taberah had in distinguishing between childhood and adulthood. And he expected Taberah's reply:

"What is the past?"

Aed said, "Everything that has happened so far."

Taberah said, "So, the beginning of our conversation is in the past?"

Aed said, "Yes. No. Not in the sense you're speaking of. It is before the moment now, but it still belongs to the time we are a part of."

Taberah said, "I do not understand. What's the difference?"

Aed said, "Could we just forget this conversation? I know what the difference is between the present and the past, I just can't explain it..." his voice trailed off, and he said, more to himself than to Taberah, "or do I?" For a moment he began to see how someone could not perceive a difference between present and past, and not understand how, if there had been medieval people before, there could not be medieval people now. Aed remembered how, in school, when he read about different times, there was something he could identify with in a great many of them. Then the moment lapsed; Aed suddenly realized the intense concentration it took him to see into Taberah's world, and began to wonder how difficult it might be for Taberah to look into his world. To his surprise, Aed found himself saying, "I don't know, Taberah. Maybe there isn't one. Maybe we could talk about this later? I thought I was going to explain something to you; I wasn't counting on changing the way I think myself. I'm sure you know it's difficult work, changing how you think, and I am at the end of my concentration. Why don't you practice your music? Maybe you can play something for us after supper?"

Taberah looked at Aed and relaxed; it was only then that

Aed realized how intently Taberah had been listening. Taberah said, "Sure!" and bounded outside like a puppy.

A Possibility Reopened

"Stop pacing the floor, dear," Nathella said. "You're making me nervous."

Taberah stopped and looked up. "May I walk around in the street outside? I need to think."

"Ok. Don't walk in the street; walk on the sidewalks. And don't get lost. Maybe you can take one of the trails in the forest."

If there is a word-space, Taberah thought, *a space in which words exist and can be mapped out into closer and farther words, then there may be a thought-space, one in which thoughts can be mapped out.*

Outside, it was dazzlingly bright; Taberah's eyes adjusted, and he saw some little boys throwing a ball around. As he passed by, one of them dropped it, and the children started arguing.

If there is a thought-space, his thoughts continued, *then thoughts may be mapped out as paths in that space. Some thoughts can be mapped out from existing classics, and then new paths can be forged like old ones. If this can be done, then it may be possible for a computer to think.*

Taberah entered the forest, although he was not aware of it. He felt almost dizzy; he was excited, and so intent in concentration that he lost all awareness of his surroundings.

The core idea for a computer to think is to construct a space of units of thought, measured by a metric arising from that for words -- or perhaps similar; words can be sorted out by comparing histograms of words that appear before and after; a self-refining measure might compare thoughts that come before and after. A space can have trails worn in it by existing classics, as a forest develops paths from many people walking through it; the thought-space is then navigable by starting at one point and randomly picking from among the paths that lead out from it. This is how a computer can think.

How can I implement this?

I need to find Aed.

Exploration

Aed was quite doubtful that Taberah had found a way for computers to think; none the less, he regarded Taberah's ideas as interesting, and so set to work on implementing them. He used one of the methods from his own research to take a given metric space and put points into a vector space, so that a position could be described by a list of numbers: put springs between each two points in the metric space, as long as the distance between them, then put the points at random locations in the vector space and let the springs do their work. The actual method used was more complex, taking shortcuts so as to run more quickly, but the core idea was simple. A model of a car made of springs would find its shape as soon as you took your foot off it.

Aed expected it possible to make much more sophisticated measures, but to start off with he used a parser to diagram sentences, trim the sentences to subject, verb, and object, and strung together the lists of numbers to make a vector space with more dimensions. Aed realized that philosophy would probably be easier material for a computer to think about than something concrete; there was less opportunity to bump into the oddities of sense data and the external world. He the program through the philosophical classics online, and then waited to see what its first output would be:

> I think, therefore I am. From this may be deduced any number of things. It is clear that the gods are dead. There is nothing but the gods. You, me, everything are the gods. This godlike character is unto the likeness of God. Each of the gods is a facet of God. God is, and because he is he thinks. Reason is the ordering principle of the universe. I say this because reason gives us what other times sought in God.

The output went on for some length, and Taberah was

crestfallen. "Cheer up!" he said. "With computers, nothing works on the first try. It takes time to get all the bugs out."

Taberah said, "I thought computers were logical."

Aed said, "Yes, Taberah, they are logical, and that's the problem. We are not logical; we hear what a person says, and know what they mean. But a computer does not know what we mean; it only knows what we say, and there are all sorts of subtle errors that a human wouldn't even notice, that a computer does not have the ability to correct. That monologue is quite good for a first run; if you aren't listening carefully, it sounds like a philosopher. You should be proud of yourself. How'd you like to have Chinese food for dinner?"

Fortune Cookies

There was a rule in the Kinsella's house against bringing up subjects at dinner that were not understandable to everyone in the house; this rule was bent a bit to allow Taberah to explain his discovery. Dinner was over before they realized it; Taberah unwrapped his cookie, put it in his mouth before anyone could stop him, started chewing, stopped, and then spat out a piece of paper. He said, "What is this?"

Fiona and Clancy were both laughing too hard to explain; Aed said, "It's a fortune. You're supposed to take it out of the cookie before you eat the cookie. Look at it."

Taberah wiped off the piece of paper and read, "Exciting prospects come. Don't miss the opportunity."

He looked at the paper in disgust and said, "Why do you have this in the house?"

Nathella said, "It's a prediction or a piece of advice. It's just for fun."

Taberah looked at Aed and said, "Aed, you told me not to do astrology because divination is sin. This is divination. It is sin."

Aed said, "Taberah, it's not serious. Or at least we don't do them seriously; nobody believes that a fortune cookie will tell the future."

Taberah said, "If you cast a spell just for fun, is it less of a sin?"

Aed said, "I would never cast a spell."

Taberah said, "But you got fortune cookies."

Nathella said, "We didn't ask for them. They come with Chinese food."

Fiona said, "We are studying China in school now, and the Chinese do not eat fortune cookies, but fortune telling is very big in Chinese culture. People will not enter a building if a Feng Shui practitioner was not consulted about where to lay its foundations."

Clancy was looking at his fortune. The expression on his face was slowly turning to disgust. "Taberah is right. Mom, you've talked about how we let sin into our lives without challenging it; this is sin."

Fiona said, "The fortune in a Chinese cookie certainly comes out of fortune telling -- and when fortune telling is done, it varies from serious to lighthearted -- like we take fortune cookies."

Nathella said, "If you would rather, we can throw the fortune cookies away when we get Chinese, or ask them not to provide fortune cookies."

Aed didn't say anything. He had expected Taberah to know things about whatever culture he was from that Aed didn't -- but not to be able to see things in American culture that Aed couldn't. He had shifted, in his mind, from wondering why Taberah objected to fortune cookies, to wondering why he hadn't objected to fortune cookies.

What else would Taberah show him?

Miracles

Taberah had been thinking throughout the day, although not about computers. When Aed got home from work, Taberah said, "This land is very different from any of the other ones I've known. Are even the miracles different? What are miracles like here?"

Aed said, "Beg pardon?"

"What miracles have you seen? What miracles have you

been given?"

"Taberah, I've prayed for many miracles in my day, and I have had some prayer requests answered, but I have never been given a miracle -- or seen one."

"Why not? Do you not know God?"

"Taberah, I speak to God, and he is with me. But I have never seen a miracle. I'm one of few people who believes they happen at all. Most people believe that miracles don't happen -- some Christians believe that miracles stopped after the age of the Apostles."

"What? Why? Do they believe God does not love his children?"

"Of course Christians believe God loves his children."

"Then why do they not believe in miracles?"

Aed was beginning to see another difference between Taberah's culture -- might as well call it 'medieval', not having any better words to describe it -- between medieval culture and his culture. One side of Aed's realization was that Taberah's culture breathed the supernatural, might (for all Aed knew) find nothing unbelievable about a mountain being uprooted and thrown into the sea -- and the other side was that Aed's culture had fought tooth and nail to exclude any consideration of the supernatural, had struggled to make it alien. There were hints of it in ten thousand places -- in words like 'superstitious', which did not simply denote a particular kind of belief (a supernatural equivalent to practical observations such as "A pin will more easily slide into a pole if it is greased"), but a propagandistic condemnation of that kind of belief and supernatural belief in general. 'Rational' was taken to mean 'materialistic', and -- the manifestations were legion, too many for Aed to concentrate on one. He recalled with a chill the words of the Gospel, where some manuscripts said that Jesus did not, and others that he *could* not do many miracles in one town, and was amazed at their lack of faith. Aed had a queer feeling that --

"Taberah, I would like to take you someplace tomorrow, and show you something. It is my loss that I have not seen any miracles, that they do not happen when I pray. But I would like for you to see the forces that shape my culture, and are why I have never seen a miracle."

Taberah slept lightly that night; he felt both puzzlement and expectation, wondering what manner of strange sight Aed would show him.

Even if They See

The lecture hall was nearly filled; the speaker walked up to the microphone and said, "Good evening, and welcome to the Campus Skeptics' first meeting this year. My name is Nabal, and this first meeting usually draws a large crowd -- usually from hecklers who believe that what we are saying is false, but somehow never manage to prove it. I claim that there is are no supernatural forces and never have been, that all of the interaction of nature can be explained by science, and that there is nothing that science can't explain. To prove it --"

Taberah was aghast. He elbowed Aed and said, "Aren't you going to say anything?"

The speaker reached into his backpack, and drew out a pliers, a sheet of paper, and a cigarette lighter. He continued, "I have a sheet of paper and a lighter, and I am going to light this paper on fire. If there is anyone among you who has any kind of faith or magic, let him stop it from burning."

Taberah elbowed Aed again, and said, "Well?"

The speaker held the paper up, silent.

Aed found himself saying, "Nabal."

The speaker said, "Yes? Are you going to stop this paper from burning?"

Aed ignored the question. He said, "Do you know physics?"

The speaker said, "Yes. I am a senior with a double major in physics and mathematics."

Aed said, "If you know physics, then you know that physics says that the electrical charges in that piece of paper, if separated an inch together and released, would create a spark over a hundred times as powerful as a lightning bolt. Is that correct?"

The speaker said, "Yes. Actually, it's a bit more than a hundred."

Aed said, "Very well. If you know physics, separate the particles and let's see that spark."

The speaker did not reply to this comment. He said, "Are there any other comments or distracting rhetoric -- perhaps to conceal that the supernatural is not real?"

A young woman said, "I don't know if God will grant my prayer, but I am praying that that paper won't burn -- as you would fight in a battle you would rather lose than not fight at all."

Nabal said, "Any other comments?"

Taberah was trying to think of something to say, but he was at a loss for words. The speaker tried to ignite the paper; the lighter sparked several times, but produced no flame.

The speaker walked over to the table and said, "My apologies for the coincidence. Does anyone have other lighters?"

A young man with a large Afro flamboyantly tossed a golden Zippo to the front of the room and said, "Try this, brother."

Nabal took the lighter and struck it. It produced sparks, but no flame.

He adjusted the lighter, and struck it again. A large yellow flame shot out, and began to lick up the side of the paper, to turn orange, to grow stronger, hotter. Nabal turned away from the flame and looked at the eyes around him -- some smug, some saddened. The flame died out, became a thin stream of smoke, vanished. Nabal grinned and asked, "And now, where is your God?"

He continued to look, puzzled by the expressions he saw on the gathered faces. Then he looked down, and dropped the pliers in shock. The paper was not burnt to ashes. It wasn't even singed.

Aed looked at Taberah, and saw the one face in the room that was not speechless. He grabbed Taberah's arm, and said, "We need to go. Now." They slid out, leaving behind them sputters of "Chemicals and charlatanism can do a lot."

Taberah said, "Why did you leave? They were about to acknowledge something supernatural."

Aed said, "Taberah, I don't know how you did that, or what was going on, and I don't need to know. But do you remember the story of the rich man and Lazarus? Do you remember how it ended?"

Taberah said, "'If they do not listen to Moses and the Prophets, they will not listen even if a man rises from the dead.' Yes, but --"

Aed said, "Taberah, a man *did* rise from the dead, and those who killed him still did not believe. C.S. Lewis wrote that he knew of only one person who had seen a ghost, and she was positive it was a hallucination. The wind of the Spirit cannot blow where the cracks have been sealed; this age has exerted monumental effort to seal the cracks. You heard them speaking as you left. They are positive it was somebody's sleight of hand. George MacDonald, before Lewis, said, "Seeing is not believing. It is only seeing." Even I, who believe in a supernatural God, am filled with doubts over what I just saw -- half of my mind is saying that it was an illusionist stunt. Even in the Bible, seeing miracles did not make people believe."

Taberah said, "I don't understand."

Aed said, "I don't understand either. Maybe you'll figure something out -- oh! I just remembered a joke."

Taberah said, "Yes?"

Aed said, "The wars in the Middle East will only be solved by a political solution or by a miracle -- by people working out an agreement, or by God telling people to get along with each other. The political solution would be God telling people to get along with each other, and the miracle would be people working out an agreement."

Taberah listened and laughed. "So you're saying it would take a different kind of miracle, a greater kind of miracle, for people to believe."

Aed said, "Yes. And a kind of miracle that doesn't just happen, even in the Bible. A kind that God only gives, if ever, as a blessing on hard human work. Prayer does not annihilate human roles. Maybe God only chooses to work the greater miracles through humans."

Below the Surface

Aed said, "Taberah, there's something I've been meaning to talk with you about."

Taberah said, "Yes?"

Aed said, "What exactly draws you to New Age?"

Taberah said, "Music and time. Or rather, lack of awareness of time. There is something more than hurried time."

Aed said, "And New Age as a religion?"

Taberah said, "New Age is a religion? It seems much more like a people to me."

Aed said, "It's both. It is people who are drawn to a resurfacing of Gnosticism. Whether it is ancient Gnostics, or contemporary New Age, or medieval Knights of Cathare, it -- what is on your face, Taberah?"

Taberah said, "I know the Knights of Cathare. It is so sad. Is New Age the same heresy?"

Aed said, "The mask ever varies, but it is the same heresy. The same mistake. The same attempt that has been weighed in the balance and found wanting. It's OK if you listen to their music, but try to stop there --"

Nathella walked in, looked at Aed, looked at Taberah, and said, "What is it that I see in your eyes, Taberah?"

Taberah said, "New Age music will never sound the same to me again."

Nathella looked into Taberah's eyes, listening, searching. She saw a homesickness and wistfulness, and suddenly thought of the Little Mermaid in Hans Christian Andersen's fairy tales, before Disney left its mark on the classic. The witch had exacted a terrible price from the mermaid -- she would have legs, lovely legs, but she would never be quite like the humans around her. Every step she took would be on sharp knives. In a flash of intuition she saw that the knives never left Taberah. He would always walk on sharp knives.

Nathella walked up, put an arm around Taberah's waist, and

said, "Honey, will you come to my room? I want to show you something."

Taberah looked, and saw on the wall a yellowed plaque. He read:

> Only faith can guarantee the blessings that we hope for, or prove the existence of realities that are unseen. It is for their faith that our ancestors are acknowledged.
>
> It is by faith that we understand that the ages were created by a word from God, so that from the invisible the visible world came to be.
>
> It was because of his faith that Abel offered God a better sacrifice than Cain, and for that he was acknowledged as upright when God himself made acknowledgment of his offerings. Though he is dead, he still speaks by faith.
>
> It was because of his faith that Enoch was taken up and did not experience death: he was no more, because God took him; because before his assumption he was acknowledged to have pleased God. Now it is impossible to please God without faith, since anyone who comes to him must believe that he exists and rewards those who seek him.
>
> It was through his faith that Noah, when he had been warned by God of something that had never been seen before, took care to build an ark to save his family. His faith was a judgement on the world, and he was able to claim the uprightness which comes from faith.
>
> It was by faith that Abraham obeyed the call to set out for a country that was the inheritance given to him and his descendants, and that he set out without knowing where he was going. By faith he sojourned in the Promised Land as though it were not his, living in tents with Isaac and Jacob, who were heirs with

him of the same promise. He looked forward to the well-founded city, designed and built by God.

It was equally by faith that Sarah, in spite of being past the age, was made able to conceive, because she believed that he who had made the promise was faithful to it. Because of this, there came from one man, and one who already had the mark of death on him, descendants as numerous as the stars of heaven and the grains of sand on the seashore which cannot be counted.

All these died in faith, before receiving any of the things that had been promised, but they saw them in the far distance and welcomed them, recognizing that they were only strangers and nomads on earth. People who use such terms about themselves make it quite plain that they are in search of a homeland. If they had meant the country they came from, they would have had the opportunity to return to it, but in fact they were longing for a better homeland, their heavenly homeland. That is why God is not ashamed to be called their God, since he has founded the city for them.

It was by faith that Abraham, when put to the test, offered up Isaac. He offered to sacrifice his only son even though he had yet to receive what had been promised, and he had been told: Isaac is the one through whom your name will be carried on. He was confident that God had the power to raise the dead, and so, figuratively speaking, he was given back Isaac from the dead.

It was by faith that this same Isaac gave his blessing to Jacob and Esau for the still distant future. By faith Jacob, when he was dying, blessed each of Joseph's sons, bowed in reverence, as he leant on his staff. It was by faith that, when he was about to die, Joseph mentioned the Exodus of the Israelites and gave instructions about his own remains.

It was by faith that Moses, when he was born, was kept hidden by his parents for three months; because they saw that he was a fine child, they were not afraid of the royal edict. It was by faith that, when he was grown up, Moses refused to be known as the son of Pharoah's daughter and chose to be ill-treated in company with God's people rather than to enjoy the transitory pleasures of sin. He considered that the humiliations offered to the Anointed were something more precious than all the treasures of Egypt, because he had his eyes fixed on the reward. It was by faith that he kept the Passover and sprinkled the blood to prevent the Destroyer from touching any of their first-born sons. It was by faith that they crossed the Red Sea as easily as dry land, while the Egyptians, trying to do the same, were drowned.

It was through faith that the walls of Jericho fell down when the people had marched round them for seven days. It was by faith that Rahab the prostitute welcomed the spies and so was not killed with the unbelievers.

What more shall I say? There is not time for me to give an account of Gideon, Barak, Sampson, Jephthah, or of David, Samuel and the prophets. These were men who through faith conquered kingdoms, did what was upright and earned the promises. They could keep a lion's mouth shut, put out blazing fires and emerge unscathed from battle. They were weak people who were given strength to be brave in war and drive back foreign invaders. Some others submitted to torture, refusing release so that they would rise again to a better life. Some had to bear being pilloried and flogged, or even chained up in prison. They were stoned, or sawn in half, or killed by the sword; they were homeless, and wore only the

> skins of sheep and goats; they were in want and hardship, and maltreated. They were too good for the world and they wandered in desert and mountains and in caves and ravines. These all won acknowledgement through their faith, but they did not receive what was promised, since God had made provision for us to have something better, and they were not to reach perfection except with us.

Nathella waited until Taberah had finished reading, and said, "Nowhere on earth is home to us. Heaven is home, and you have less of a temporary home than most people do. It hurts to have an earthly home taken away, but the healing of the hurt is not in finding another earthly home, but in finding a heavenly home -- and once you have let Heaven be your home, you may find pieces of it on earth.

"That plaque was given to me by my mother; she had it for some time, and it was one of the last things she gave me. Now she's in Heaven.

"Inside your heart -- and mine, and Aed's -- is a God-shaped void. Only God can fill it. New Age music may bring a moment's relief, but the thirst is one only God can wholly slake." She beckoned to Aed, and the two of them gave Taberah a sandwich hug. "But we will try to make a place where you can be at home."

Taberah said, "Where's Fiona? I want to show her my time."

Taberah's Time

Fiona said, "So, Taberah, how about your time?"

Taberah said, "Why don't we take a walk in the forest, and I'll think about how to explain it?"

They began to walk along the path, Taberah stopping and thinking every so often, but saying nothing. This continued for five minutes, fifteen, thirty, an hour -- and Fiona began tapping her toes. Taberah stopped, and Fiona sat down on a log and began drumming her fingers.

"What are you doing?" Taberah asked.

"Nothing," Fiona said. "I'm just waiting for you to start explaining your time already."

"What about your hands and feet? What are you doing with them?"

"I'm just tapping them, because I'm getting impatient waiting for -- ooh... Taberah, are you walking around and not saying anything on purpose?"

"No; I'm thinking about how to explain time to you."

"Do you understand why I'm drumming my fingers?"

"No. Why?"

Fiona began to realize something. She decided to try not to drum her fingers, or pace, or tap her foot, but just sit. It turned out to be harder than it sounded. Fiona kept noticing herself fidgeting; even when she thought to herself, "It's been a while and I'm not fidgeting," somehow she realized that her fingers were drumming on her legs.

"Fiona!" Taberah spoke, and Fiona suddenly realized that she had lost track of time -- and was not fidgeting. "I do not have a different time awareness, so much as not having an awareness of time. There are moments for me, times with other people, times doing a task, and times waiting -- watches are fascinating to me, but even when I watch them, I watch the rhythmic motion, and more often than not forget that the motion is measuring something that's supposed to be time. That time is fickle; it seems to speed up and slow down. The first lesson in medieval time is to let go of it."

Taberah walked a bit further, stopping a few times, and Fiona still caught herself fidgeting -- but she began to catch herself completely relaxed at times. Fiona wondered when he would finally speak, and then was surprised when he broke the silence -- was he done thinking already? Taberah said, "There are moments -- I do not know how to say it in your language -- when you are totally absorbed, rapt in concentration, when you lose track of time because you are so completely filled. It is not so much time as a foretaste of eternity. These moments cannot be commanded or controlled, although there is a cooperation with them; they are a gift from God. Those moments are my 'time', if time is the appropriate word. 'Timelessness' is better. That is the apex of the time I live in, and I am sorry not to see you live in that time more."

"So how do I enter this time? You've told me what time you live in, but not how to get in it."

Taberah thought briefly and said, "I can't tell you that. Pray, and God may grant it. But I don't know how to enter it."

Worship

A couple of Wednesdays had passed since Taberah had first asked to worship with the Phoenix Society; something had come up, and Taberah had not been aware that time had passed. This time around, Fiona was free, and they entered the room to be warmly greeted.

The service began with hugs and lively music. Taberah was caught up in the singing; Nathella wondered if one of the moments Taberah described would descend. Or had she always had them and not been aware of them? The music gave way to prayer, Scripture, sermon; as communion came, Fiona could see that Taberah was almost in a trance, but she was not. The worship was followed by a meal; Taberah felt a tap on his shoulder, and wondered why someone would tap his shoulder. He looked up.

The young woman who had spoken up at the skeptics' meeting studied his face closely and said, "You were at that meeting and left right after the paper burned weirdly. What did you do?"

Taberah looked at her and said, "Nothing. I prayed. Same as you. God heard our prayer."

She said, "That's not the whole story."

Taberah said, "It's as much of the story as you'll believe."

She said, "What part of the story won't I believe?"

"That I am medieval."

"You mean that you try to be like a medieval, even growing out a beard?"

"No, I mean that I am medieval."

The student's gaze rested on Taberah. After a while, she said, "I don't know what to make of the claim. You're not lying, you don't seem mistaken, and I can't believe what you say." She paused, and said, "And I didn't believe the paper when I saw it. I prayed for it, but I didn't believe it." Then she blushed slightly, and said, "I've forgotten my manners. My name is Ceinwyn. What is your name?" She reached out her arms to embrace him.

Taberah enjoyed the hug; she was soft, and in her touch he could feel a spirit that was alive. He said, "My name is Taberah. I'm staying with Aed."

"Who? Is he a student here?"

Fiona said, "He means Dr. Kinsella."

Ceinwyn said, "Dr. Kinsella. You mean --" A look of dread crossed her face, and Fiona said, "Yes, he's teaching this young man his corrupt ways." Ceinwyn smiled, and said, "I have respect for anybody who can do that."

Taberah said, "Do what?"

Fiona said, "You know. What you did to win the Turing Award."

Fiona covered her mouth; as soon as the words left her mouth, she realized she shouldn't have said them. Half the room was staring, and the other half soon joined. Then she said, "Um, I would like if you could kind of forget what I said; my Dad's done a lot to try to ensure the privacy of my friend."

A young man said, "He won the Turing Award?"

Another man stood up and said, "I have a strong temptation to ask this brother for his autograph, and I would like to ask you to join me in resisting it. We need to treat him as an honored guest but nothing special beyond that, and treat his award as a matter among brothers. It has to have the highest level of confidence."

Ceinwyn looked at Taberah and said, "I am sorely tempted to ask you something more about the paper, but..." her voice trailed off.

Fiona said, "I think he may be right about being medieval. Or almost right. But there are some things about him that just don't fit. He makes my head spin, and he says the queerest things."

Another student said, "Like what?"

"Like saying that he stole a relic from a cathedral."

The student said, "Hmm... I'm a history major as well as an English major, and medieval culture was very different from ours. My name's Tala, by the way. Stealing relics was actually fairly common. Taberah, did you hear about the conversation between Saint Peter and Saint Augustine?"

Taberah said, "No, what did they say?"

Fiona said, "And that's the other thing. He gets the queerest things wrong. It's not just that he doesn't understand why people who lived in different centuries can't have talked with each other. He didn't understand why a cathedral couldn't have had two heads of John the Baptist, one as a boy and one as a man. He saw the logical contradiction, but didn't deduce an impossibility. Plus, he's so short and scrawny -- not at all like the bulk you'd expect of someone from the age of knights in shining armor."

Tala said, "I don't want to explain all of why, at least not right now, but a medieval would be quite likely to make those errors. And medievals *were* that short and scrawny -- their diets stunted their growth. It's only in the past couple of centuries that people started to look as tall as you are me -- and (I won't name names) some people today still haven't caught up." He winked.

A short, bearded student said, "I'll have you know that I represent that remark."

Fiona said, "Ooh!" and then, "Diet. He talked as if he had grown up eating mostly bread, bread with pebbles in it."

Tala said, "I think he's about as good of a mockup of a medieval as you could ask for. How and why, I don't know -- there've been a lot of queer things that have happened, most of which have an uninteresting explanation. Even with what I've seen, it would take a lot to convince me that he had -- Taberah, if you are a medieval, why are you in the twenty-first century?"

Taberah said, "What is the twenty-first century?"

Tala said, "Never mind that. How did you come to be here?"

Taberah said, "I was walking with two of my friends, when an angel called me. I took his hand, and I was in the forest outside Aed's house. Then --" and he started telling the story. It was after midnight when he finished; Ceinwyn said, "Taberah, I have many questions to ask you, but some of us need to get to bed. Would you consider visiting us again?"

Taberah said, "Certainly."

That night, as Tala lay in bed, waiting to fall asleep, strange images flitted through his mind. He saw a doorway between the medieval world and his, shimmering, the door beginning to open. A burst of light flashed around; Tala looked around and saw no one, and then looked to the doorway.

The door had been blasted off its hinges.

Second Birth

Taberah said, "Remember how we were talking about medieval time, and how we left things not finished? I have thought more about your becoming medieval."

Aed said, "Yes. Do you want to can turn back the clock?"

Taberah said, "What does 'turn back the clock' mean?"

"It means reverse the flow of time, undo the changes that have happened."

Taberah looked puzzled. "Why would anyone do that?"

Aed said, "My culture was once, a long time ago, medieval. Now it is not. We have cars, computers, and clocks. Do you want to turn that back to swords and armor? Do you want to un-invent electronics?"

Taberah said, "It is funny that you think of medieval in terms of things. Wealth is not medieval. Wealth is only an avatar; it is not the true person. Medieval is not knights on horseback."

Aed said, "Then what is medieval?"

Taberah said, "Medieval is faith. Medieval is rationality. Medieval is carving the back of a statue. Medieval is a way of life."

Aed said, "But the medieval era is gone. How can people in the four hundred and seventh semi be medieval?"

"What is a semi?"

"I'll explain it later. How can people today be medieval? We can't just automatically be medieval the way the medievals were."

Taberah closed his eyes in concentration; it took him a long time to get the point. Aed was asking him for the answer to a difficulty that simply didn't exist for him, and Taberah was trying hard to see the matter through Aed's eyes -- and at last he did.

"Aed, do you know Jesus talking with Nicodemus?"

"Yes."

"What was the question Nicodemus asked Jesus?"

"'How can someone old be born? Can a man enter his mother's womb to be born again?' I know this question well. It has been ridiculed, but it is a serious question, even profound. Can a man turn back the clock and --"

There was a look of dawning comprehension on Aed's face, and suddenly he was grasping what was *medieval* -- not lords and vassals, not illuminated manuscripts, not unending quirks and questions from a visitor whom he still could not wholly believe was medieval -- not any of these things, but Aed grasped what was medieval. He saw the force behind cathedrals, the abstraction that showed itself in the question about dancing angels, the community shared between the people and, in all of these things, he saw a little piece of his heart.

Aed saw equally why Taberah had asked the question: that turning back the clock was neither possible nor necessary, that the second birth was of a different type than the first one, and one that could still happen with much water under the bridge, that the passage of time in itself had almost nothing to do with being medieval. He saw that the fundamental beauty of the Middle Ages was one that people from his age could share -- not in exactly the same way, but it didn't need to be. People could be medieval today just as they could still be Christian today -- it involved swimming upstream, but it was worth it.

Aed looked at Taberah gently and said, "Taberah, you said that you were medieval, and asked what time I was from. I am medieval, too."

Questions

It seemed but an eyeblink and another week had passed; Fiona and Taberah were once again in the crowded worship room, and there was an audible excitement. The service was merry and passed quickly, and at the meal afterwards, Ceinwyn came up to Taberah and said, "I know what the wrong questions are to ask you, Taberah, or at least questions it is not good to ask. What are the right questions to ask you? What do you wish others understood about you?"

Taberah closed his eyes and rocked back and forth on his chair. Tears began to appear. When, after a long time, he did not answer, someone told Ceinwyn, "Ask him another question." Taberah, without opening his eyes, said, "That's the best question. That is a very good question to ask of anyone.

"I have had many people try to understand me, but most of them don't. I don't know why not. Maybe I'm just hard to understand. Some of you think of me as medieval, and I am medieval, but I'm as different from other medievals as they are from you. Even how I am talking -- it is a means of talking that I learned from your time. I have seen different peoples, and the way in which I am different is not the way one people varies from each other. Maybe there is something wrong with me. I don't fit in anywhere. I can adapt some -- I've lived in many places -- but I'm never completely -- I don't know the word. I'm not making sense. I'm not saying anything. Never mind. I can't think like other people. You asked a good question, but I don't have a good answer for it."

Emerant was pierced by the look on his face. Emerant was intelligent, if not exceptionally so, but she was a psychology major in the middle of a senior thesis studying of the psychology of extraordinary intelligence; she followed all three major schools: traditional Stanford-Binet intelligence, multiple intelligences (there were now twenty-three agreed upon intelligences among most multiple intelligence theorists), and the interactionist school, which studied its intelligence as an emergent property arising from the interaction of the basic aptitudes studied by multiple intelligence theorists. Being familiar with all three schools, Emerant regarded the traditional school as unfairly neglected, and it was that school that she thought of now. The pain Taberah voiced was not at all unique; it was part of why the gifted had joined the ranks of activist minorities filled with anger and seeking redress for grievances that were always perceived to be getting worse. There was more to it than just a taboo (now being effaced) on divulging a high level of intelligence, or a stereotype that for a long time was not realized to exist -- a stereotype embedded in words such as 'geek' and 'nerd' that only now were becoming as socially unacceptable as racial slurs. The more gifted a person was, the more differently he thought, and that is why there had been posited a range of optimal intelligence, with IQ between 125 and 145 -- beyond the upper limit of that range, a person thought differently, so that his giftedness became a mixed blessing. People with IQs over 170 tended to feel like they didn't fit anywhere. From psychological, emotional and social cues, and the Turing Award, Emerant had no doubt that Taberah's IQ was over 170, probably over 180 -- how much further, she did not bother to speculate. Above, at any rate, the point at which IQ tests cease to effectively measure, and well beyond the point that pain would begin to -- Emerant wondered what a boy of normal intelligence would think and feel growing up in a society of people who were severely mentally retarded. He would definitely perceive that he was somehow different from the others, and attribute it to either "Something's wrong with them," or "Something's wrong with me." Taberah had evidently taken the latter route, and -- where to begin to explain all this to him?

She walked up, placed an arm around Taberah's shoulder, and said, "Taberah, Taberah. I have a number of things to explain to you, but the way you think is not worse than anyone else's -- just different and special. You haven't met anybody who thinks like you (nor have I, apart from you), because God has only made a few people that way. I understand your feelings, and I would feel the same way if I were like you. I love you and I am glad you're here -- so does everyone in this room. May we sing a healing song for you?"

"What's a healing song?" Taberah asked.

"It's a song we sing to God, as a prayer for you that you may have healing."

"Yes, please." Taberah had been touched by Emerant's words, but it was her eyes most of all which caught him. Her eyes bore the embrace of a warm, generous heart, and silently spoke the message, "My heart has room for you." And Taberah realized that he had a foster family who cared about him deeply -- he decided to thank them for it. A song began, and he realized that the people had gathered around him, placing their hands on him. The music seemed to Taberah to rise like incense:

Lord God of Heaven,
Hold this child in your arms.
Fill him with your love.

Creator of Heaven and earth,
Fill his heart with your peace.
Let this peace flow through him.

Spirit of light and love,
Lift from him all darkness.
Lift him up to Heaven.

Let us be his brothers and sisters,
Your love made manifest.
Fill him with your love.

As the song ended, Taberah looked at the faces around him and wondered, "Is this what Heaven's like?"

Mysticism

"Fiona, I was thinking, and I realized a better answer to Ceinwyn's question. The answer is this: I am a mystic."

"Oh, Taberah," Fiona said, "We already knew that. Dad

mentioned that you had done some astrology, and now there's that piece of paper."

Taberah said, "Huh? What does mysticism have to do with that?"

Fiona said, "Huh? Isn't the connection obvious?"

Taberah said, "No. I have stopped astrology because I trust Aed, but astrology was not any strange mysticism; it was to me like what you do in reading a weather forecast. And the paper -- I never thought of that as mystical. I just prayed as others were praying, and God gave what we asked for. That is hardly mysticism."

Fiona had difficulty believing that all that was going on was that Taberah had asked God, but she mentally waved this aside. She asked, "Then what is mysticism?"

Taberah said, "Mysticism is living in the fire of God. It is contemplating and gazing on his glory, and for me it is action in that glory. You are concerned with getting things done, with practicality, with results; I happen to get things done, but it is not what I am concerned with. Few things are needed, really only one; I occupy myself with that one thing. That is the heart of mysticism, not astrology or saving a piece of paper."

Fiona said, "But what does your mysticism *do*? What mystic powers are you striving to develop?"

Taberah said, "What a funny idea, mystic powers! Which is greater -- getting something done, or the reason getting something done is desirable in the first place?"

Fiona said, "I suppose, what made it worth getting it done."

Taberah said, "Correct. Mysticism is not a way to get things done; it is a 'why' that is greater than getting things done. Mysticism is not a way to do something else. Mysticism is worthy in itself."

Fiona asked, "Then how are you a mystic? You say that you are the son of a merchant, that you have travelled to many places and had adventures. How does mysticism fit into that? You haven't retreated into a monastery to spend six hours a day praying; you've already managed to cause a stir. Is that more important than mysticism? Or are you a superman who can do one on top of the other?"

Taberah said, "I find your question confusing. My actions are not more important than mysticism; they are the shape that part of my mysticism takes. I do not see action as something added to mysticism; it is an expression. I am seeking God's glory by talking with you now. I have heard a saying, 'Too Heavenly minded to be of any earthly good,' and I think it embodies a mistake. You cannot be too Heavenly minded to be of any earthly good. You can quite easily be too earthly minded to be of any earthly good. Being heavenly minded is itself of earthly good, whether or not it does things in an obvious manner; that is one of many reasons why, of the nine orders of angels, the highest six gaze only on the glory of God -- it is but the lowest three who are ever sent to earth. It is a right ordering. Mysticism is sharing in the truth that the angels share in, and for me that truth takes an active form."

Fiona said, "Does this mysticism relate to your time?"

Taberah said, "My time relates to this mysticism."

"How can I enter it?"

"Seek God, and ask him how you are to enter it. He will show you."

Heaven

Taberah walked out of the computer room, thinking loudly. Aed looked at him, and simply waited for him to start explaining.

"Aed, I was doing some reading today on embryology; what your philosophers have thought of is fascinating. Something in my mind was speaking, and I realized another deep difference in belief. Medieval people believe that they're going to Heaven."

Aed cleared his throat and said, "All Christians believe that, Taberah. It's a basic doctrine."

Taberah said, "Then why does your people not act like they believe they're going to Heaven?"

"How does someone act like he believes he's going to go to Heaven? Does he kill himself to get there faster? You should know better than that."

Taberah paused in thought for a moment and said, "How can you believe you're going to Heaven and not know a change in your actions? That's like believing food nourishes you, but not knowing what eating is like."

Aed had no immediate reply to this. He asked, "How does belief in Heaven change your actions, Taberah?"

Taberah said, "In embryology, one studies how a person is becoming ready to be born and live outside the uterus. That is the whole purpose of being an unborn child -- why do the texts leave the word untranslated as *foetus*? Did the English translators of your texts not know how to render that word from Latin?"

"Later, Taberah. You're getting side tracked."

"Some of the unborn child's motions are useful there -- such as blood pulsing about the body. There are others that have no use in the uterus, such as sucking and kicking. The question is not how to arrange things to most pleasurably remain an unborn child, but to best prepare for birth and the world beyond that.

"Your people does not understand how this symbol reveals Heaven. They think that the point of living on earth is to make as much change on earth, and make earth as comfortable a place as possible, and -- I was a long time in coming to understand political ideology. Authority is necessary, and there are questions about how to best govern, to praise good and punish evil. But political ideology is not just about this -- it is about how to use government to turn earth into Heaven."

Aed said, "I do not understand. Do you mean it is wrong to try to make earth better?"

Taberah said, "All of the saints made earth better. Good deeds are an important part of how a soul is made ready for Heaven. But a centeredness, a focus on making earth better is not possible. Or it is possible, but leaves people more poorly prepared for Heaven, and more poorly equipped for earth. It is -- I do not know how to say it. My father told me, 'Drink wine to live. Do not live to drink wine.' If I were to live to drink wine, I would be disordered. The wine would ensnare me. Trying to live on technology is trying to make technology something it cannot be. It can pacify a spoiled child; it cannot make him well-raised. Your people is concerned with how to pamper and pacify a spoiled child -- and it took me the longest time to understand that not simply did I stumble on a very rich man's house, but that so many people in your society have wealth not only to have as much bread as you need, but as much meat as you want, and you do not even think of it as costly -- while mine is concerned with how to raise him well to grow into a man. In the Great Chain of Being, man lives between the beasts and the angels; it is the beasts who have this life on earth and its pleasures as all they own, and the angels who eternally gaze on the glory of God. Believing in Heaven means becoming more like an angel; here, I have seen heroic efforts to live the life of a beast."

Aed sorted this through. It had been a while since he had thought of the Great Chain of Being, and his thoughts about it moved sluggishly. Apart from that, he began to see -- and more than see, he began to believe and know -- why Taberah would look around and be convinced that Aed's culture did not believe in Heaven. With a chill, Aed realized that he could not remember the last time he had thought about how his actions were preparing him, or failing to prepare him, for the eternity before him. Slightly later, and with an equal chill, Aed realized that he could not remember the last day he had not thought about how to shape the world around him so as to bring pleasure. He slipped too often in thinking of his teaching as a way to prepare his students for the world it would face -- which it no doubt was, but if that was *all* it was, then... Aed asked Taberah, "Taberah, how can I do something that will prepare me for the next life? What is one thing I can do?"

Taberah thought for a second, and said, "Close your eyes and grow still, and wait."

Taberah waited a second and said, "You're wanting to get this over with. Stop that. Want to do this."

Time passed. Aed's breathing had stilled. Taberah said, "Now thank God for seven things he has given you."

Aed took another breath and slowly said,

Thank you, God, for my wife Nathella.
Thank you, God, for my children, Fiona and Clancy.
Thank you, God, for my professorship.
Thank you, God, for my broken garage door. It means
I have not only a house and a car, but even a building
to protect my car from the elements.
Thank you, God, for the headaches I have after
talking with Taberah. They come from a person for
whom I am very grateful, and who challenges me in
ways I never thought possible.
Thank you, God, for the hope of Heaven.
Most of all, thank you, God, for yourself.

Taberah smiled, and said, "You have now done one action to prepare yourself for Heaven."

Aed said, "Is it over already?"

"Life"

Taberah looked out; there was depth in his gaze, a gaze that was somehow present and remote at the same time. A short time ago, Fiona would have thought he was staring at her; now, she understood that he was looking past her. It relieved the feeling of being under a microscope.

Fiona sat down and said, "What are you thinking of, Taberah?"

"I don't know how to say it -- in any language. It is another part of the answer to Emerant's question."

"Can you try? Can you say something similar?"

"I -- live. I don't know how to explain. I experience things intensely. Sometimes, when I drink wine, I am not aware of anything else --"

"You get drunk? That is living?"

"I not know how to explain. I do not get drunk. It is when I am drinking it, the taste -- it also happens with thinking, and praying, and music."

When Taberah said 'music', Fiona caught a glimpse into what he was saying. She was transported back to his first chant, when the whole family had been lost in his voice -- no, that wasn't quite it. They had been lost in the light that was shining through Taberah.

An idea came into Fiona's head, and she said, "Taberah, why don't you get your lute out, and I'll go to my keyboard, and we can play together? I think I'd understand you better."

They went to the practice room, and Fiona set up her keyboard. "What songs do you know?"

"I know many songs from the lands I have travelled in. But I do not know songs here; I haven't played with musicians. Ooh! I know your church songs!"

Fiona played songs in several different styles -- ancient songs, classic hymns (meaning the contemporary songs of days past, drinking tunes such as "A Mighty Fortress Is Our God," and so on), "contemporary" music (meaning roughly three groups: music that had been contemporary in the more recent past, music that represented an unsuccessful attempt to imitate the contemporary secular style, and music that combined both attributes), songs of a new musical renaissance that did not attempt to follow either mold, but borrowed from both and brought a new light... After one of the tunes, Taberah said, "That's the one! I want to play with that song."

Fiona slumped and said, "No, Taberah, not that one! It's awful! It was in bad musical taste when it was written, and it's in bad musical taste now. One of my girlfriends said that it sounds better when it's sung off-key."

Taberah said, "I know. You've already told me that. That's why I want to work with it."

Fiona had enough of her mother's perception to realize that arguing with Taberah now would be a losing proposition. So she resigned herself to playing harmony, leaving the Taberah the melody.

The first time through, Fiona was able to shut out the

music; she expected a repose after going through once, but Taberah immediately started playing again. She kept up with the melody, but now Fiona was not able to ignore the music. Then Taberah started to improvise slightly; he made a change here and there, and then he started making only musical questions that required her to think of an answer in the accompaniment. This required Fiona to plunge even more deeply into the song. After a time, Fiona was too engaged in the music to think about how bad it was.

Time passed, and Fiona slowly became aware of something else. The music was still terrible, but she saw a luminescence shining through it. Then she realized that they were working together, and a strange beauty was emerging from the music. She played, fascinated, and gradually began to see a beauty like that of a rusty truck in a desert -- a (she did not know the word) beauty that can't be found in a place that is polished and perfect -- there is no room for it. She was fascinated by the music that was flowing around and through her. More time passed, and then a flash of insight struck and her hands froze on the keyboard; it was as if a juggler tossing seven glass balls stopped, and they fell and shattered. Taberah switched off the keyboard, and relaxed his hands. "What happened, Fiona?"

"I realized something, Taberah. I had an epiphany."

"What?"

"I had finally entered your time, Taberah. I entered your time."

Intelligence Emerging

Aed sat and thought about the output of the artificial intelligence program. Trying to decide whether it functioned intelligently was like -- no, that wasn't it. Aed couldn't tell what it was like.

Intelligent or not, it was at the same time familiar and alien. He had worked with the algorithm further, so that it stored a history in its state, drawing on the algorithm that had won the Turing Award, and the arguments were coherent -- but arguments such as he had never seen before. Any one paragraph of its output could be mistaken for human, but there was something undefinably strange about it; he could tell what the computer was arguing, but not why. Aed slapped his forehead; the arguments were evidently intelligent enough to tempt him to think of the computer as human.

Aed spent a long time trying to think if the computer's rationality was something comparable to human, or even if that were sensible to ask. Dijkstra had said, "Asking whether computers can think is like asking whether submarines can swim." Aed thought for a nuance; he thought it was closer to the question of whether a racecar can swim. Or an oven. Except that the answer was not "No, but it can do something comparable;" an answer of "Yes, but it is not comparable" would have been closer.

Aed thought for a moment, and then went down to the computer computer and navigated. An avatar was shortly before him; it said, "Aed! Still up to the usual trouble?"

"How are things in the philosophy department? I heard you've got a new tenure track position added. I'm actually up to worse trouble, now."

"I'm not surprised. How can I help you?"

"What courses are you teaching this semester?"

"I'm teaching three courses, all of which have a paper due shortly. Get something in the gradebooks for a preliminary report. I'm teaching 101, *Introduction to Philosophy*, 234, *Philosophy and Contemporary Movements*, and 312, *Integrative Metaphysics*. Have you encountered yet another guest lecturer that you want me to cede precious lecture time to?

"Actually, no. I was wondering if you could give a paper to be graded by your TAs for each of the assignments."

"Uh, OK. May I ask who the paper is by?"

"I'm not telling."

Role Play

Clancy said, "Taberah, have you been to the pool at all?"

Taberah said, "Pool? Why? To drink?"

"No, to swim, silly!"

Taberah stiffened and said, "I swam once, when I fell from a bridge. I don't like swimming."

Clancy said, "Will you come along? You don't have to go in the water. We can hang out on the deck if you want. The pool will close before too long; it's not so warm."

Taberah was careful not to sit too close to the water's edge; falling in once had been plenty for him. He watched the others with trepidation, and tried to grasp that they were in the water for pleasure's sake, and did not need to be rescued. The swimsuits gave him a shock as well. He had finally gotten adjusted to the fact that these people were not used to being naked, and seeing trunks and bikinis was a bizarre sight to him.

Fiona climbed out of the water and sat down on the chair next to Taberah; Clancy was on the other side, whistling a bird song to the robin on the lines overhead. Fiona told Clancy, "You know, it's been a long time since we role played."

Taberah asked, "What is role play?"

Fiona said, "It's -- you'll see. But you'll have to make a character. Role playing is *in* this semi."

Taberah asked, "What is a semi?"

Fiona thought for a moment and said, "Semi-decade. People used to not be conscious of what era they were in, and then they were conscious of the century, and then they thought of what decade they were in, and now it's the 5 year semi-decade."

Taberah wondered why people would be time-conscious in that way, and why the era would be that short, but was beginning to understand that certain things were wiser not to ask. He said, "I want to be a minstrel."

Fiona said, "My character is a Jane-of-all-trades named Deborah. Clancy is GMing, uh, game mastering."

Clancy said, "You are both in a forest; your ship has crashed. There is a spring of water nearby. You hear sounds like footprints nearby."

Fiona said, "Do the footprints sound human or animal?"

Clancy said, "You can't tell for sure, but there is an animal quality about them."

Fiona said, "I'm going to get my laser gun out."

Clancy said, "What are you going to do, Taberah?"

Taberah hesitated and said, "Can I hide and nock an arrow?"

Clancy said, "Yes.

"You see a huge bear on a chain. At the other end of the chain is a massive man in a rags."

Fiona said, "I am going to say 'Hello.'"

Clancy said, "He does not seem to recognize the word, and there is uncertainty on his face."

Taberah said, "I am going to put back my bow and arrow, and take my harp, and begin to sing."

Clancy paused, and said, "The bear sits and listens; the man does, too."

Taberah said, "I am going to take out some of my food and feed it."

Clancy said, "Both bear and man seem pleased at the food. The man looks at you longingly, and starts to walk into the woods."

Taberah said, "I'm going to follow him."

Fiona said, "I'll follow, too."

Clancy said, "He gets to a cave; upon following him in, it takes some time for your eyes to adjust to the twilight. The cave is a crude environment, with assorted items around."

Fiona said, "Such as?"

Clancy said, "Some burnt-out transformers, an oddly shaped granite bowl, a corroded lamp, and some empty containers."

Taberah asked, "Are the containers usable?"

Clancy said, "No; they were disposable containers. They --"

A voice from the pool shouted, "Hey, Kinsella! Want to join us in a game of Marco Polo?"

Clancy shouted, "Not now! I'm entertaining someone."

Fiona said, "What is in his eyes when he looks at us? What is in his eyes when he looks at me?"

Clancy said, "Fear, suspicion, hope, disbelief, a forlorn longing."

Fiona asked, "Does he want to be with our civilization?"

Clancy said, "He wished that at one time. He is now uncertain about what he desires."

Mist came into Taberah's eyes. Fiona turned to him and said, "What is it, Taberah? Is something bothering you?"

Taberah said, "No. There is something about man that --"

Fiona sat silently, waiting.

Taberah said, "Before I left medieval time, that was home. Now, even if I return to it, it is not home. I am part of this time now, and at times I let Heaven be my home, and at times I find Heaven, but other times -- I am learning not to be in this state, but it catches me."

Fiona wrapped her arms around Taberah, and said, "Honey, why don't you come home? We can be with you while you heal."

Taberah got up, and joined Clancy in heading for the locker room.

Rated

Aed received the three copies of the computer's ramblings that had been submitted to the philosophy TAs. The first paper had been submitted to the TA for philosophy 234, *Philosophy and Contemporary Movements*:

> Paper is nuanced and addresses many fundamental issues of relevance to contemporary movements. Nonetheless, its reflection of nuance is not matched by any kind of logical order; a logician would grade this paper harshly. B

Aed chuckled. This grade was a mark of success; it was the first time he had seen someone complain that a computer understood nuance but was logically deficient. He turned to the next copy, the one submitted for philosophy 312, *Integrative Metaphysics*:

> Paper contains brilliant application of argument from multiple domains of philosophy, combined with the indescribable eccentricity that heralds a new development. Ideas are not fully developed, but even in embryonic form, there is a raw energy to them. I have shown your paper to the professor, and she concurs with my judgments. You should do graduate work in philosophy. A+

Aed said, "This is encouraging. What did the TA for philosophy 101 have to say?"

> Paper is arrogant and pretentious, trying to be simultaneously similar to and different from existing philosophies, and combines the worst points of both. Classic example of fake intellectual who strings together a lot of things that sound philosophical and thereby considers himself a philosopher. F

Aed laughed; the 101 TA had picked up on something that the others hadn't. Very well, then; he was pleased with the results, and he was ready to announce what Taberah and he had done.

What Would You Like To Be?

The days passed quickly; the leaves on the trees turned bright colors, and Taberah seemed a shade blueish. There was another shopping trip made, in which Taberah received a warmer set of clothing; this trip passed without any remarkable events, and Clancy said he could take Taberah shopping for clothes alone next time; Nathella accepted. In watching Taberah, Nathella was reminded of her roommate freshman year in college. A young Sudanese woman, she found the cooler seasons to be bitterly cold.

A mug of spiced cider found Fiona and Taberah relaxing over a fire; Taberah was watching a leaf all from its stalk. Fiona looked at Taberah and asked, "What would you like to be for

Halloween?"

She was not surprised by his reply, "What's Halloween?", nor his followup, "I think I'd like to be myself. I don't fancy turning into a rock or a bear." She took it as an opportunity to explain a cherished time of year. "Halloween is when you dress up as something fanciful, and pretend to be something different for a day. You can go around from door to door, and knock, and show people your costume, and they give you candy. I want to be a fairy, wearing a shimmering white robe with draping sleeves and a low neckline and a long, flowing skirt, and with translucent, glittery wings."

Taberah said, "I don't know what I want to be. I was already a jester in my avatar. I know! I can dress as a night-man, with shadow-black clothes that melt in the night, and soft shoes that make no sound, and --"

Fiona said, "No. Too many criminals out at night; you'd be mistaken for one. You need to wear bright clothes and not look threatening."

Taberah said, "Euh... I could be a philosopher!"

Fiona said, "And how does one dress as a philosopher? All the philosophers I've met dress like everyone else. No, wait! You could be an ancient Greek philosopher, with toga, and laurel, and -- whatever else you think would make the point."

Taberah said, "Where do we buy these outfits? Are they in a section of the store I haven't seen?"

Fiona said, "Well, there are places that sell Halloween costumes, but they aren't very good -- a mask and a hat and some very flimsy cloth. There are places that rent them, and some of those are better -- but you only have them for a day. In our family, we have a tradition of making them. We buy cloth and patterns, and cut them out, and stitch them together. It's a great deal of fun -- almost as much fun as wearing them. I can show you old costumes I have in my closet; I've been a princess, a space ranger, an alien, an ice cube, a --"

Taberah said, "How did you dress as an ice cube?"

Fiona said, "Dad did that one. We got a big cardboard box,

painted it blue and white, and got a white shirt and white tights for me to wear underneath. That costume is -- let's see, I think it's being used to store shirts in the attic. Or something; we only go up in our attic when we're putting something up there."

Taberah said, "I was up there. It was fun; it was like climbing cliffs. Only this time there weren't brigands chasing me. I think climbing's more fun when brigands chase after you."

Fiona shuddered, and said, "To each, her own. I'd be scared out of my wits."

Taberah said, "I was scared out of my wits. And I was having fun."

Fiona said, "I guess we all have our own eccentricities. Our attic's not nearly as silly as my Dad is at times; you should see him play charades. The last time we played at a family gathering, he was jumping around with a vacuum cleaner, and humming 'Oh, when the saints go marching in!' I always remember what Dad did, never what he was -- when I watch him, I get the feeling that the game isn't about really about trying to help other guess what on earth you are."

Taberah said, "Your Dad understands games."

Fiona said, "How's that? He usually diverts games off their course."

Taberah said, "No. He changes their appearance when he gets them on course. A game on one level is about following rules in some sort of contest -- but people would never play games if that was all there was about it. It is a pleasant contest to enjoy other people -- and it sounds like your father has found a shortcut to enjoying other people. Most people need the long way about; they can't have fun unless they've carefully earned it. There are a very few people who can take shortcuts, and a very, very few people who can make others feel good about it."

Fiona thought for a moment, and said, "Taberah, I didn't know you were a philosopher."

Taberah said, "I am. You didn't know that? But 'philosophy' means something different here than in my lands. Philosophy in my home means a broad kind of learning, that touches many different places. I gather that your science is derived from natural philosophy, the philosophy that explores the natural order -- but there are subtle differences that I don't understand. Maybe that it's separated from the rest of philosophy. I understand that professors at your father's university are called Doctor of Philosophy, and their inquiries are parts of philosophy, but they are not philosophers. 'Philosophy' now means something narrow, dull, not connected with life -- some philosophers try to make philosophy relevant, but our philosophers did not need to make philosophy relevant because it already was. Philosophy can be different."

Fiona asked, "Do you think our culture is impoverished?"

Taberah asked, "What is a culture?"

This time Fiona was caught off-guard. Taberah evidently understood what a culture was; he had experienced different cultures and made any number of cultural comparisons. But, when she explained it to him, he was a long time in understanding; Fiona came to appreciate what a non-trivial concept culture was.

As soon as Taberah began to guess what a culture was, a number of possible replies came to his mind about an answer to Fiona's question. To his credit, he spoke only the truth. He said, "Yes. I think your culture is very impoverished."

Fiona asked, "Then what are you going to do about it?"

Taberah leaned back and closed his eyes. He needed and appreciated friends who would ask him questions like that -- but didn't want too many. Like the whiskey he had once tried, a little went a long way.

"I don't know," he said. "Let me think about it. Then I'll tell you -- or just act."

Women's Liberation I

Taberah was by now taking walks around the town and around the university campus; he had come to tolerate car rides, but never rode in a car by choice, and was shocked when Nathella suggested he learn how to drive a car. He decided to take a long thinking walk, and was weaving in and out among buildings when a voice caught him. "What is your name?" it said.

Taberah looked, and saw a young woman sitting under a tree. She was holding a book, and sipping a strawberry hydrolated beverage.

"My name is Taberah. Why do you ask?"

"You remind me of someone -- a friend. Someone I've not seen in a long time."

"What was he like?" Taherah asked.

"What was *she* like, you mean. Don't use exclusive language."

"What is exclusive language?"

"Exclusive language is language that uses the word 'he' to refer to an unknown person. It excludes women."

"Why?" As Taberah asked, he felt a discomfort, a desire to be anywhere else, a feeling of "Not this dance again!" -- and at the same time a feeling that there was something significant, a moral pull to be there.

"Using the masculine as the generic reference to a person exists out of sexism because of a man's world, that says by its language that men are all that's important. People tried for a time to make language more inclusive by alternating between 'he' and 'she', but that still had the loaded masculine term. We now use the feminine as a generic term, free from exclusive masculine meanings, as a convenient designation for someone whose gender is unknown."

Taberah sensed something off kilter. It was not just with the argument; though he had never heard use of masculine pronouns interpreted to mean what she thought they meant, and was baffled as to why saying 'he' would be prejudicial while saying 'she' served as a neutral term for a person of unspecified sex, he was aware of something more. What he would come to call traditional language had always been a convention to him, no more significant than the use of a pronoun for a person whose name was not known -- the argument he was hearing about exclusive language seemed to him as bizarre as an argument about "nameless language," in that persons of unspecified name were thereby meant to have no name. Taberah at least had always been acutely aware of how his thoughts were more than the words he used. He had struggled to represent his thoughts, and accepted conventions as useful in getting on to more important things. A sharp concern over "inclusive language", more to the point accompanied by a correspondingly sharp belief that the traditional use of masculine pronouns was really "exclusive language"... In itself this struck him as merely silly, and Taberah knew he was plenty silly himself. *Let he who is without silliness cast the first stone*, he had often said to himself, and he did not wish to break a tradition.

This is what Taberah sensed and thought on one level. On another level, he thought less but sensed more, and this was that the woman had a sense of anger about her. It wasn't just that her voice had risen; it was rather that in a vague sense he sensed that what he saw was the tip of an iceberg, that whatever concern and upset were caused by her upset at the word 'he' spoken of an unknown person, was only a surface glimmer, a faint shadow, cast by something he could not guess at. He looked at her, and asked, "Sister, what is your name?"

She looked startled, and said, "My name is Lydia."

He asked, "Lydia, why don't we take a long walk in the woods and talk?"

Lydia blanched, and said, "I'm staying right here."

Taberah concentrated hard and tried hard to see what his *faux pas* was this time. When that failed, he looked at her, and said, "I know I'm breaking all sorts of social rules, and that I don't understand this culture very well, but what did I do wrong? Why were you afraid when I asked you to take a walk in the woods?"

Lydia said, "I think that should be obvious enough!"

Then she saw the puzzlement on his face, and said, "You might rape me."

Taberah turned green, and asked, "Do you really think that?"

Lydia snapped, "Don't you try to put me back in place by challenging me. When a woman says something, she means what she says. From language that speaks of sports playing fields to cars that are designed to look appealing to a man but not to a woman to cutting women down to the subordinate role that would be convenient to men to logic and abstraction regarded as the essence of good thinking, you men will..." She stopped, startled by a realization.

"Taberah, why haven't you told me to go to Hell? Most men usually say that when I stop smiling and... Usually, I can put a smile on and look happy, I usually don't talk about how badly women are treated unless I am with other feminists. You, somehow -- I don't act like this. Something slipped. Why haven't you told me to go to Hell?"

Taberah looked at her levelly and said, "I am afraid to tell you."

"You are afraid of me lashing out again?"

"No. Do you want to hear anyway?"

"Yes."

"You are in Hell already."

Lydia glared at Taberah and said, "Of course I'm in Hell! With a man's world that puts women down, how can I not be in Hell?"

Taberah said, "No. Wrongs exist, but you are in Hell because you believe the world is hostile to you. You believe that all sorts of actions are slights, and if there is ambiguity, that ambiguity is to be interpreted in a fashion that means women are being oppresed. I -- I have known women who were really happy. Something about them..."

Lydia said, "What? Had they managed to create a place without sexism?"

Taberah said, "No. They lived in a broken world, a much harsher world than we have. They lived, in fact, suffering injustices that feminism has now made a big change in. But they refused to let their identity be one of being persecuted. The world their bodies lived in was far more hostile than the world your body lives in, but the world their minds lived in was not nearly as hostile as the world your mind lives in. You, in your mind, suffer unending hostility; I will venture a guess that, no matter what happens, if you choose to accept feminism's interpretation, you will be in Hell. I have seen other things like feminism; they are like fires: the more they are given, the more unsatisfied they are, the more they want."

Lydia said, "So you would have me just walk with anyone and get raped? One in three women is raped."

Taberah said, "Um..."

Lydia remained silent, and Taberah said, "I know two women who have been raped, and it is a torment I not know how to describe. But I have done some research, and the feminists who did surveys manipulated the numbers to say as many women have been raped as possible, to fuel a political agenda that claims a rape culture. In the first study that had said one in six women had been raped, over half the women who were classified as having been raped explicitly said they hadn't been raped. And --

"Being raped is terrible. It's one of few things worse than believing that you are in constant danger of being raped, and that you are never safe with men. I would not have you walk with anyone and get raped. I would have you use your judgment and intuition and walk with people when it is prudent to do so. We are never safe -- not from disease, not from being killed, nor from being wounded, nor from rape. But we can take reasonable risks."

"Ok," Lydia said. "You want to walk in the forest? I --"

"No," Taberah said. "You're not comfortable. It speaks well of you that you are able to trust where you have not trusted before, but I do not want your discomfort. What I would like is for you to think about what we have said, and then come join me at a place where women are at peace."

Halloween

Halloween came: Fiona a fairy, Taberah a philosopher, Clancy a cybernetic organism, Nathella an elfin lady, and Aed a medieval lord. After talking with Taberah, Aed wished that he could have a table piled high with food, with everyone invited to come and eat and talk -- but he could not do so; the gesture would be misunderstood. On Halloween, hosts gave out vouchers for different kinds of candy, which could be redeemed online for a delivery of different candies; it was almost as easy to poison candy as it was to put razor blades in apples. Nathella did have food waiting for the few people who knew their family, but that was all. The rural trick-or-treat Nathella had grown up with was no more.

Aed and Nathella therefore waited, lord and lady at their castle, to meet the year's assortment of ghouls, witches, archers, space cadets, cheerleaders, Romantics, and assorted and sundry other manner of visitors. A file recording of Taberah's music played in the background, and the place had a warm look to it.

Taberah was with Clancy and Fiona; if Fiona most enjoyed making Halloween costumes, Clancy most enjoyed wearing them.

"Trick or treat!" they said at one house. Fiona charmed them most; Taberah looked old to be trick-or-treating, but the costume fit the gravity that was around him. Clancy reached out with his long, metal arm and used the moving hand at the end to take his candy.

While they were out, they encountered Fiona and Clancy's friends: a bumblebee, a Hershey's Hug, a snake, and a bear were among those they saw. Fiona did not quite manage to contain her surprise when one matron gave a discerning look and told Taberah, "You do not quite look ancient, young man. I'd picture you as more medieval." It was with an unsteady step that she hurried on to the next house.

In the night's activities, Taberah saw beauty and ugliness mixed together so thoroughly that it was hard to tell them apart. People dressed up as something else -- but that something else often meant vampires, devils, and succubi. There was a moment when Taberah almost lost his step, because he had an insight. He understood role play, and saw that it was good. He thought that, in the costumes, he could see a little further into other people than in normal clothing -- but was disturbed by some of the choices. Fiona explained the historic origin of Halloween, but that did not seem to allay his concern.

It seemed too soon that moonlight and starlight were shining, and Clancy said, "We need to be heading to home now." They reached home, and Taberah had only one question to ask: "When is next Halloween?"

Women's Liberation II

As Lydia walked into the building, and as worship gave way to discussion around a table, she felt a mass of conflicting emotions within her. There were many branches to feminism, but one thing that held them in common was that, whatever the trepidation with which men and male society were viewed, men were not the real enemy. The enemy was traditional women -- people who had settled for being housewives, falling into men's shadows. They were disloyal to the cause of womanhood in a way that a man could never be.

The turmoil Lydia felt came when she saw women at the group who were traditional -- but who were not the stereotype she came to expect. They were at ease with themselves, genuinely happy, and she came to see that what the feminist movement had interpreted as living in a man's shadow did not mean what she thought it meant.

It is always a painful experience when reality intrudes on your stereotypes and preconceptions, and Lydia did not enjoy the evening. She saw that other women were enjoying it, but she was processing changes. By the end, she began to see ways in which women's interests were not best served by feminism, and she came back, sharing in the joy upon returning.

Taberah, after talking with her, said, "Lydia, I have met few people, and far between, who could change after being shown they were in error. Most just fight, and fight, and fight, and fight. What let you do that?"

Lydia said, "I suppose the same thing that led me to be a feminist. Women are slighted in most societies; I embraced feminism because I intuited that it had a truth. I let go of it because I learned of something else that could serve women's interests better. Part of it is the new feminism that Catholics called for. The other part is just that -- I never knew the tradition. I knew the feminist stereotype, but not the reality. The traditional Christian teaching has a much bigger place for women than I thought."

Lydia leaned to one side and asked, winking, "Does this mean I have to wear makeup?"

Taberah said, "Uh... I hope not."

"You don't like women wearing makeup?" Lydia asked, surprised again.

"No. My culture does not have makeup as you understand it. When I first came here, I did not understand why women were damaging their appearance by smearing strange materials across their skin. I have hawk's eye -- my mother used to call me 'hawk' -- and a face with make-up looked to me like a counter with rubbish strewn over it. It took me a long time to understand that women wear make-up to convince themselves they're beautiful while wearing it -- it took me a long time to understand what 'presentable' means. It means that a woman is not beautiful, but if she covers herself in powder and paint to look like something else, that something else is beautiful, and that the woman is OK only if she makes herself into something else."

"Taberah, are you sure that you're not a feminist?"

Taberah said, "I find that not the most helpful question to ask. Some of the truths I take with me are shared by feminism; feminism knows no doubt things that I do not know, and I know things that feminism does not know. Or at least that is what a mature person from your time would say, and it is true. But I want to see good come to all people, including the freedom of well-meaning women from a system that imposes a cure worse than the disease. I want to see women liberated from women's liberation."

Like an Emerald

A metal keychain knocked on the door. Nathella opened the door, and a young woman asked, "Is Taberah in? I'm Emerant; we've talked a little. I'm a phoenix."

"Come in," Nathella said, "I don't know where Taberah is." She called, "Taberah!" and Taberah came, holding a knife and a half-carved block of wood. The emerging figure was already discernible as a madonna.

Taberah looked sad; his expression brightened when he saw Emerant. Emerant hugged him and said, "Back at that first meeting, there was something I wanted to sit down and talk with you about, but I've been so busy since then! The courses get harder every year, and I've got one that's harder than a darwin. I'm sorry for not calling earlier, but I was wondering if you wouldn't mind going to a coffeeshop. There's this one shop on campus that only sells decaffeinated coffees, but you have to try their carbonated cappucino!"

Taberah set down the knife and statue and said "Sure!" He started to muse about how this people seemed to use big words for little ideas and little words for big ideas -- 'darwin' was slang for a course designed to weed out the less suited students from a major, and evoked the substantial philosophical idea captured in a "survival of the fittest" argument -- a discredited idea, to be sure, but a magnificent achievement none the less. On the other hand, Taberah did not know what a cappucino was, or why one would carbonate it, but from usage it was clear that the word meant a drink.

They walked along to the coffeeshop, not speaking, the loudest sound being the crunch of leaves under their feet, but they were not speaking for different reasons. Taberah was not speaking because he lived naturally in silence, did not have anything to say, and did not need to fill the time with sounds; Emerant was not speaking because she had made a conscious and counter-cultural choice to embrace silence and not fill it with noise -- the noise that came so easily to a soul raised in a society that was afraid of silence and stillness and slowness. In walking two miles to the coffeeshop, they had their fill of silence, and Taberah took fifteen minutes to decide between a carbonated cappucino and some hot cocoa. He ended by ordering both, and Emerant, who ordered an herbal mint Italian soda, did not explain to him that this was a *faux pas*.

Emerant sat down with Taberah and said, "How has your day been?"

Taberah said, "A good day. I have not carved for a long time." Then he remembered etiquette and said, "And yours?"

Emerant said, "A day with a lot of thinking. There was something I wanted to explain to you, and I've been trying to think of a good way to explain it, and I haven't found any good ways."

Taberah stiffened, anticipating a rebuke. Better to have it done with than to put it off. He said, "What have I done wrong?"

"It isn't about anything you've done wrong. It's something that I don't think anyone's ever explained to you."

"Is it about being left-handed? Aed has tried to explain about that, and I am at peace with it now. I wasn't earlier; one of my culture's peculiarities."

"It isn't about being left-handed -- something I don't know enough about, especially given that I'm ambisinistrous. It's about something else. Taberah, do you know what the word 'genius' means?"

"In Latin it means the angel watching over a person. In English, I have gathered it means something different, but I don't know what. It is a word applied to some persons, but not others."

"'Genius' means someone possessing extraordinary intelligence and giftedness, someone who has a unique potential to shape society."

Taberah drew back. "Shape society? How would someone do that? Why would someone do that? Why would some people be specially qualified to do so? Your wording means that this is desirable. Why?"

In the ensuing discussion, Emerant was challenged; she had come to explain something to Taberah, and was not expecting herself to learn something new. She had thought of medieval time as hierarchical, holding some people to be born superior -- and saw her own time as having practically invented egalitarianism. Emerant saw in her reactions to Taberah that she not only believed some people were more intelligent than others, but that the highest measure of intelligence was taken to bring a prerogative and duty to shape society as one's naked reason led him to believe was best. Taberah found this to be madness; he would as soon consider himself qualified to redesign the human body from scratch, making surgical alterations so that his beneficiaries would have one less leg and one more arm, as to attempt to redesign human society from scratch. Taberah did not mind the concept of a special word for the most intelligent humans, as the implicit belief that this difference translated to a moral entitlement to do something he found abhorrent.

Emerant said, "Taberah, let's start this discussion again. You know that you are different from other people?"

Taberah hung his head. "Wherever I go, I can't be like other people. I make mistakes -- terrible mistakes. I can't connect with other people."

"Taberah, there's a very special kind of intelligence, one that brings the ability to do things very few people can do -- but it brings pain and failures. It means that you think very seriously. Classical literature has the image of a blind seer. Do you know this image?"

Taberah nodded his head, and his expression brightened.

"The seer has supernatural vision, but the price of it is the loss of his natural vision. It is a great boon at a great price. Taberah, you're not completely blind -- you can and will, with time, be better able to connect with people -- but your natural eyes are weak because of the brilliance of your supernatural eyes. You are not a second-rate Abanu. You are not a second-rate Tala. You are not a second-rate Emerant. You are a first rate you, and you are close to God's heart. You have already managed one accomplishment most of us can only dream of."

Taberah looked surprised. "What was that?"

"The Turing Award, Taberah! Don't you know what that means?"

Taberah looked confused. "There was a lord of a city who had me over. There is not a custom like that in my land. I understand I was honored, but -- if there is one city that practices that custom, surely there are other cities that practice it! What I did wasn't any big deal."

"Taberah, dear, there is only one city that does that, and they search through the whole world before awarding that prize, once per year. There have only been seventeen other people who have received that award. Taberah, there is probably not one person in a million who is as bright as you. I want to talk with you about how you plan to use your intelligence."

Taberah was silent; he was trying to sift Emerant's words, sort them. The image of the blind seer struck a powerful chord with him; for one of the first times he could remember, he was able to think about his failures without feeling inferior. The Turing Award was still difficult to think about; he was beginning to understand that it was something bigger than a prize at a fair, but he had never begun to guess the true magnitude of his achievement. In his mind it was like the time as a boy when he was summoned to a monastery where Thomas Aquinas was passing through, and the theologian told him that he had chosen a good symbol to illuminate the Trinity -- only with more hoopla; it was still not a very big deal, and its chief significance to Taberah was the warmth the people of this land had shown him. It seemed to him a very hospitable land. He was warmed, but it did not occur to him to think that he was fundamentally more intelligent than others -- the idea of possessing a superior aptitude ran contrary to medieval culture. Taberah was touched by Emerant's statement that not one person in a million was as bright as him; his culture embraced exaggeration as a means of emphasis, and he was warmed that Emerant would make her point by exaggerating that much.

"Well?" Emerant said. "What do you want to do with your intelligence? Have you given it any thought?"

"I don't know," Taberah said. "I will need to think about what you have said. And your question is not a day's question to answer."

"Well, don't feel hurried. It'll take me some time to process this discussion as well. Taberah, you haven't touched your drinks; they've gotten cold by now. Here, let me microwave them for you. What have you been doing this past week?"

The remainder of the conversation was light and pleasant; it was a kind of conversation which Taberah had only mastered in the past couple of years, had learned did not mean anything in the sense of deep philosophy, but meant a warm personability and sharing -- that much translated across cultures. Both of them, for different reasons, learned something of the other's culture -- Emerant was enjoying an elective on ethnographic interviewing and even more enjoying an opportunity to apply her learning, and Taberah had crossed cultures from the time he was a little boy, learning something in each case. 'Student' seemed at least as interesting and difficult as any of the other professions he had seen and participated in, and went at a much faster pace with much more difficult material than an apprenticeship. He made a mental note to ask Aed if he could arrange for Taberah to work as a student.

Emerant walked Taberah home, again in silence, and then walked back to the dorm. She climbed into her bunk and punched a name on the phone.

"Tala, this is Emerant. You were right; he made my head spin. But I think that was less due to his being medieval than being astronomically intelligent." It was 3:00 in the morning before she hung up and went to bed.

Confessions

Taberah said to Aed, "I want to be a student! Can you help me be a student? What's necessary to becoming a student?"

Aed thought for a moment and said, "My university will undoubtedly take you, and give you full scholarship; the biggest thing for the moment is picking out which classes to take. That's something Nathella will probably be able to help you out with better than I can; she's very perceptive, and would have a better feel for what classes would help you most." Aed decided not to try to explain the degree programs; he believed in learning for the sake of learning, not learning for the sake of getting a piece of paper -- and a degree on top of a Turing Award would be superfluous.

Nathella was out on an errand, and as Taberah waited for her, he began to realize something. The realization was not pleasant. When she walked in, Taberah said, "Nathella, I have a confession to make."

Nathella said, "Ok; I can take you to a father confessor this afternoon."

"Not to a father confessor, Nathella. To you."

"What is it, honey?"

Taberah hesitated, and said, "Nathella, I have been looking past you, but not at you."

Nathella looked at Taberah gently, and then closed her eyes. She was a quiet type, easy to ignore; she was slender, and men seemed not to pay her much notice. Taberah was not the first person to commit this sin, but he was one of the first to admit it. When was the last time someone else had done so? The only prior time had been by Aed. She was sure there were others, but -- when she opened her eyes, she saw that Taberah was looking at her.

Taberah said, "Nathella, what are you thinking about?"

"I was thinking about part of my story."

"What is your story?"

"You want the whole thing, or the part I was thinking about?"

"The whole thing."

Nathella thought for a moment and said, "I was born on a farm; as a little girl, I had a wonderful education filled with simple amusement. We had a tight-knit community, and I miss that closeness.

"My father believed in education; he was a welder as well as a farmer, and was committed that his daughter get a college education. I went to school, and it was a wonderful extension and compliment to the rural upbringing I had. I think city kids now miss some of the things going on then; the computerized classroom doesn't teach you how to be perceptive, and I especially miss hunting -- my father gave me a hunting rifle and scope on my twelfth birthday, and the day after I killed a bear. No, it wasn't because he wished he had a son; I had two younger brothers, and both of them were given guns on their twelfth birthday as well. I didn't like hunting as much as I liked picking flowers in the field, but there's nothing like giving your Mom a bouquet of wildflowers you picked yourself, and there's nothing like sitting down to eat meat you killed yourself. I don't own a gun, not any more, and I don't want a gun in this house where someone might break in and steal it and kill someone. But I enjoyed those fields, the heat of working in a cornfield in the summer, the fruitful creativity that comes on the other side of boredom -- you get bored, and then you get bored silly, and then you think of things to do that never would have occurred if you always had a television -- and our family didn't. We had a computer, but both my Mom and my Dad believed that television was a waste of time and a waste of life. I'm better off for growing up without TV.

"Anyways, at school, it was an exciting new world, and I met Aed. That made a difference. That changed things -- and it was the only pleasant thing that happened for a while.

"Back home, my father needed to remove a few stumps, and wanted to put a pond in a field that -- I can tell you the story for that another time. Anyways, he needed some explosives, so he mixed an oil people used to use with a common farming material, and so far as I know, had the one forgetful moment of his life. He forgot what he was doing, and lit up a fag.

"That was it. On that one day, I lost my father, my mother, and both my brothers. The barn still looked basically like a barn; the house didn't. There wasn't much of anything of a house left. And I really couldn't go back -- the people would have accepted me, but a farming community without my farm and family would have been like a body without a soul: to me, dead.

"I began to notice that I didn't feel so bad after I had some whisky; it took a fair amount -- I could drink an elephant under the table. The more I drank, the more empty I felt when I wasn't drunk, and the more empty I felt, the more I drank. This continued for three years; Aed and I both finished our degrees later because of the drain of my drinking.

"There was one day when Aed was in a bad mood, and I got the brunt of everything that had gone wrong that day. I was in a terrible mood -- it had just hit me that, even if I went back to visit, there would be this horrible silence about me -- I would no longer be Nathella, who knew all the plants and animals and had yellow dandelion rubbed on her cheeks half the summer days from an old joke with two loving and rambunctious brothers; I would be that orphan thing -- in a way, not human any more. I didn't at first admit that, and when I did, it hurt, and hurt, and hurt, and hurt. I got myself drunk, so drunk that --

"Taberah, do you know what a BAC is?"

Taberah shook his head.

"BAC is short for blood alcohol concentration. One drink will give you a BAC of .02. When we were at the banquet and you said that you felt funny and that the wine seemed to have more effect than you were used to, you had a BAC of about .05, judging by the amount you drank. At .08, in the eyes of the law, you're too drunk to drive. .20 is very drunk. 1.00 will kill you.

"Taberah, I had a BAC of 1.15, and that was after the hospital pumped my stomach -- an experience I never want to live again. Several people at the hospital commented that it was a wonder I was alive at all. It took me over a day to become fully sober, and the first thing I remember when I was sober enough to be coherent, pumped full of chemicals that sober you up but make your mind feel like it's being scraped across asphalt, was Aed sitting down right across from me, looking me straight in the eyes, and saying with a dead serious voice, 'Nathella, I love you, and because I love you, I am not getting up from this chair until you admit you have a problem with alcohol.'

"I was trapped and pressured, and that was the most loving thing Aed ever did to me. Not marrying me; that was a close second, and that's the second best thing that's ever happened to me. No, third; coming to know God was a slow thing, not all at once, and it is the best thing I've ever known. But Aed staring at me as I made jokes, tried to cajole him, threatened to break up with him, and tried every other way I could think of to evade and deny him was the best thing that ever happened to me. He did apologize for his treatment of me the day before, by the way; he felt terrible about it, and has never behaved like that again. After five hours, he was hungry, thirsty, weary, and immovable as a rock, and I said the most painful thing I've ever said. I said, 'I'm an alcoholic.'

"Taberah, being an alcoholic is Hell on earth; I believed it when another alcoholic said that in Heaven, you can have as much wine as you want, and in Hell, you can have as much wine as you want. The first steps of recovery are even worse than being an alcoholic; it's like you had a festering wound, and now there's a surgeon going in with a knife to get the bullet out and stitch things up. It hurts, and it has to be done, and there's no anaesthesia. But it heals. Aed and I both needed support; when you're wounded like I was, you wound those close to you, and he's been healed too, even though he never drank more than four drinks in a day, usually not four drinks in a week. I've been dry for -- how long has it been? Over twenty years, and I am healed -- really and truly healed. I sometimes long for home, and I sometimes long for drink -- believe me, there are some days when I ask Fiona to sit me down and distract me and make sure I don't go to a liquor store. But I am now free of that chain -- and happier than I ever believed alcohol would make me.

"My faith... My faith is strong like I wouldn't have imagined. There's not much of me on the surface; most people don't pay me much mind. But underneath, God has given me a strength I would have never dreamed of. Childlike faith meets trial and testing that it may become childlike faith. Some people who hear my story ask me how I can have faith after experiences like that. I ask them, how can I *not* have faith after experiences like that? Even when I was dead drunk -- especially when I was dead drunk; even when I admitted I was an alcoholic -- especially when I admitted I was an alcoholic -- God was *with* me. He has never abandoned me. Never."

Taberah sat in silence for a moment, and said, "I'm sorry I asked you for wine."

Nathella smiled and said, "Taberah, there's nothing to apologize about. You didn't know I was an alcoholic, and asking for wine is a perfectly reasonable thing. Why don't you go out and have a drink with Aed tonight? I can't drink, but I know God blesses other people through the fruit of the vine... Taberah, I know what you're thinking. I see it in your eyes, and I've seen it in other people. I'd like to tell you another story, this one a story that didn't happen to me.

"My best friend in college, Naomi, was the daughter of a competent insurance salesman. Her father was friends with the vice-president of sales, whom he invited over one day for burgers and beer.

"After they arrived from the office, Naomi's father realized that he had beer but not burgers, and drove to the store to buy some food, and the vice president raped her. It was the worst day of her life, and the days after were made worse by the fact that nobody believed her. They merely told her that that was serious business, and she was too old to be telling stories anyway.

"She noticed something peculiar when she began seeing a counselor and sharing this with other people. Many men were afraid to touch her. They knew she had pain, and mistakenly believed that another man touching her body would automatically bring back traumatic memories -- at least that's how they thought about it; the way she usually put it was 'They won't even give me a hug!' It's a shame, too; Naomi was one of the touchiest people I've known, not as in easily angered, but as in liked to touch and be touched -- she always gave me a kiss when she saw me, and she very much enjoyed a man's touch -- rowdy as well as soft -- be it in an arm over her shoulder, a crushing bear hug, or in horseplay.

"Some people who've been abused need not to be touched, and it's good to ask what's OK and what's not OK when you find out someone has wounds. But apart from that, people who are hurting need hugs most of all, and not touching a woman because she's been hurt -- it's meant well, but sometimes it's just the wrong thing to do. Naomi learned to be very careful, as an adult, who she told about her experience -- most people believed her, but some men in particular, with the best of intentions, never treated her the same way again.

"When there's a person in a wheelchair, by nature people will see the wheelchair but not the person. There's nothing to feel guilty about in having to counteract that tendency, but it needs to be counteracted. The standard advice used to be, 'See the person first and the condition second.' Now that has been refined a little bit to 'See an organic whole in which the condition is part of a person.' Naomi sometimes needed to be treated differently because of her trauma; there were days when she just needed to be left alone -- and days when she just needed more hugs and more listening. It would never have helped her for me to forget she was human and treat her as something whose nature was 'wounded'. Pierce us; do we not bleed? Poke us; do we not squeak? Taberah, I am a woman -- human -- with the full range of human emotions, laughter and silliness and joy as well as pain and worry and trouble. Don't let knowing I'm an alcoholic obscure your knowing that I am a woman. I would much rather you occasionally forget and ask me to buy you a bottle of wine, than think of me as a pit of pain with whom you must always be serious, always careful not to bump me lest I shatter. I'm human, OK?"

Taberah thought for a second and said, "Ok. If you won't buy me a bottle of wine, will you buy me a keg of beer?"

Nathella laughed and tousled Taberah's hair. He had somehow managed to keep a deadpan straight face. "Honey, next time I'm out shopping, I'll buy some root beer, which doesn't have alcohol, and we can each sit down and sip a root beer. Actually, you want to go shopping now? You seemed to enjoy going out for clothing, and maybe you'll see something at the store that you'll like. No, wait; the packaging food comes in is probably not whatever you are used to. Want to come along anyways?"

Which Classes?

Nathella said, "Aed told me that you want to take some classes."

"Yes, Nathella."

"You seem to find things to do easily; I suggest that you take two classes, three at most; other students take more, but you need a lot of sleep. Come on over to the computer with me; we can look at the catalogue with me.

"Let's see... Here's 'Mathematics as a Humanity', team taught by a mathematician and an artist. When I took it, it was team taught by a mathematician and a philosopher. It was the hardest class I took -- and the best.

"In this culture, most people are taught something horrid as lower math, and they avoid it as much as they can. They don't guess what mathematicians really do -- an art form guided by intuition. Most people think a mathematician must do more of whatever they suffered through in the math classes they couldn't avoid -- more statistics and meaningless formulae. It's really sad; higher math is easier than lower math, and that course did not make me a mathematician, but it helped me appreciate what they do.

"'Modern Mythology: An Exploration of Storytelling in Postmodern Society.' This would also be a good course for you to take; it will help you see some of the good points of our culture -- and some of the bad points. I think last year they did an in-depth treatment of a classic interactive -- the title escapes me (I'm never in tune with that -- I was 20 before I saw *Star Wars*), but -- ooh! it was called *net*, and *net* was hard science fiction that somehow managed to be very popular. This class didn't look at technology much, just the timeless elements of the story -- and it is timeless. I don't know what they're doing this semester, although I can find out.

"'Philosophy of Technology'. This is a good class; it's team taught by a humanities Luddite and a technology-worshipping engineer. Aed likes to occasionally go in and sit and watch the sparks fly.

"'Psychology 212: Gift Giving. This class explores how to take basic psychological insights and use them to find a gift that will be meaningful to a friend and loved one.' I wish that one had been available to me when I was in school. Classes have been shifting towards a more practical bent. There's also 'Psychology 312: Synergy. This class explores positive interactions between people, and how to create the circumstances that give it rise.' There are a lot of good classes -- hmm.

"'Semiotics 101: A Critical Look at Contemporary Society' -- this would be an extremely valuable class to you, but not for the reasons that most people take it. It would show you how people are inculturated into contemporary liberalism, and see things into the plurality that was once a holy trinity of race, class, and gender. Taking a critical look at a course like this would help you understand contemporary academia, and perhaps a little bit of contemporary society as well.

"I know you have an artistic bent; I've seen you carving. This might interest you: 'Fine Arts 212: The Art of Tektrix'. It's a class on how to build with robotic blocks, studied as an art form.

"Here's a fun one: 'Gender Studies 315: The Wisdom of Cats. A humorous look at how our lives can be made better by living out the wisdom that cats embody naturally, and a careful study of why cats are better than dogs.' Department notwithstanding, that looks -- oh, wait. You're a dog lover. Never mind."

Taberah did not see why loving dogs would disqualify anyone from taking a course on cats, but he was too busy assimilating information too quickly to ask a question. Nathella continued, "'Communication 275: Are Sacred Cows Edible? An interpretive look at the popular comic strip and exploration of its meaning in society.' *That* looks interesting. I'm not going to try to explain it now, but you should take it. Let's see, what else?

"There's a dance art -- kind of like a martial art, but taking dance rather than combat as its basic medium. In combat between two good martial artists, there is a harmony that arises, a kind of synchronization and attunement between opponents. Neither party walks in knowing what is going to happen -- but a masterpiece emerges. A dance art does this with dance -- there are differences; in both, you learn to read your partner, but in a dance art, you also want to be readable, instead of hard to predict -- and dance art strikes Aed as very interesting. He tried one for a bit, but then left because he wasn't able to handle the structured, monotonous repetitions that low-level training took from martial arts. Maybe that's its weakness, and come to think of it, you probably shouldn't do that either, even though I have a feeling you can dance very well.

"Here we go! 'History 339: Medieval Culture.' I think this would be valuable to you as well; you would learn something about our culture in learning how it portrays your culture. Maybe that wouldn't be such a good idea; the catalogue refers to your culture as belonging to 'the misogynist tradition', and -- come to think of it, I know who's teaching that course, and she'd fail you. That professor can tolerate almost anybody whom liberalism now sees as oppressed, but someone who is from medieval society and believes we have something to learn from it -- you'd have a hostile learning environment. Let's see: what else?

"'Integrated Science 152: Heavy Boots.' I think this course would be a good one for you to learn from; it is probably the best to teach the culture of science and scientism -- as good for its purpose as the semiotics class would have been for understanding the culture of the humanities as we now have it. Another one that you might like is 'Engineering 297: Cross-Disciplinary Commonalities of Repair and Debugging. This course covers the fundamentals of how to think about technology that does not behave as intended, with application to repair of mechanical and electrical devices, and debugging of software.' What do you think, honey? Does that interest you?"

"They all interest me, Nathella. I don't know which ones to choose."

"Then we can wind to a close -- ooh! You *have* to take this one, Taberah. At least if you can get in. The professor is a cantankerous, eccentric genius. This course has been taught under a dozen department names, and now the university's simply stopped assigning it a department. You'll like it."

At dinner, Nathella said, "Have you given further thought to what courses you want to take?"

Taberah said, "Yes. I want to take the last class we talked about, the class you recommended, and -- oh, yes! Heavy Boots!"

Christmas

It seemed not very long at all before Taberah found the ground an unsteady traitor beneath his feet, and more often than not beneath his backside; he could keep perfect balance on a ship, but ice was tricky. The wind seemed to blow bitter cold through him as much as around him, and Taberah sometimes shivered even when he was inside and wearing a sweater. Taberah would have much rather been wearing heavy armor and sparring on a blistering hot day than experience *this*!

Even the cold could not damp his spirits as Christmas approached, though. He had thought about gifts for each of his adoptive family and friends for each day, starting with the first. He gave the madonna to Nathella, a riflery simulator to Clancy, pressed flowers to Fiona, and an abstract pattern to Aed. Each phoenix was given an electronic image of a stained glass window from home.

Aed received gifts in turn; he most prized the Pendragon Cycle which Nathella gave him; he would be fascinated by the historically-oriented retelling of the Arthurian legends. He knew those legends well, as well as he knew the legends of Roland and the twelve paladins, and he would be intrigued by the retelling. Seeing an American portrayal of his home gave him a unique insight into the time and place he was living with, and their conception of what is important about a place -- it did not seem as strange to him as it might have appeared earlier. The theme of Ynes Avallach, the isle of the Fisher King, struck a chord with Taberah, and he felt that here, now, he was on that isle.

The days were merry days, with much revelry and joking, and there was a relaxed energy about the house. Aed began to wonder why the custom of twelve days of Christmas was not celebrated more; it was a good custom.

Twelve days seemed perfect to grasp the meaning of the Christ child; the Kinsellas had always understood Christmas gifts to be symbolic of God giving mankind his greatest gift ages ago, but celebrating with Taberah gave a new depth of understanding to the symbol. An hour does not merely allow one to communicate twelve things, each of which can be said in five minutes; it allows communication of things that cannot be said in any number of five minute bursts. The twelve days of Christmas were not twelve consecutive Christmas days; they were part of a whole celebration that embraced gift giving but went much farther, a time of worship and enjoyment of God. Clancy wondered at the beginning how one could possibly spend twelve days celebrating Christmas; come the end, he wondered how one could possibly stop after celebrating one day of Christmas. While they were out caroling, Taberah tasted real wassail, and during the celebration Aed took Taberah to a wine bar and introduced him to champagne.

On the eleventh day of Christmas, Taberah asked Nathella, "Can you smell the incense?"

Nathella was confused. "There is no incense in this house. The only smell of incense has been on our clothing, when we came back from the Christ mass. Are you talking about that?"

Taberah said, "Not that, Nathella! The *real* incense! Can you smell that?"

"I don't understand, honey. Why would you be smelling incense?"

"Nathella, what is incense for?"

"It ascends in the presence of God, and some of it is around us at the holiest times we worship. Catholics only use it on special days; the Orthodox use incense at every worship, and believe in bringing Heaven down to earth -- ooh. Now I understand. Yes, honey, I do smell the incense."

First Day of Classes

The first day of classes was delayed by a heavy snowstorm; it was such as only occurs once every ten years, and people were in mixed moods when they finally came inside a warm classroom. The freshmen and sophomores tended to have a spirit of adventure, while the juniors and seniors more tended towards irritation.

Taberah walked into a large lecture hall, crowded with students. A professor cleared his throat and said, "Good morning. My name is Professor Pontiff, and you are in Communication 275: Are Sacred Cows Edible? In this course, we will be studying the strip of that name. If you'll excuse me for one moment..." He fumbled with an overhead projector and turned it on. A comic strip appeared overhead. It had a young man and a young woman in conversation:

> Young man: It's a shame when a comic strip becomes the medium for public discourse.
>
> Young woman: You don't like it when conversation is to the point and funny?
>
> Young man: Not that. I don't like that it has to be funny, and that you get ignored if you have a point that you can't cram into five seconds. Most theories that can be put in a nutshell belong there.
>
> Young woman: What if there was a comic strip that made its point but was not particularly funny?

After giving the class a minute to digest the strip, then said, "The term 'sacred cow' is now a bit dated, but it was popular around the turn of the century. The Hindu religion treats cows as sacred animals, and there are cows in India that people will not kill -- they would rather starve than kill a sacred cow. In a typically anti-foreign fashion, people who did not understand or respect this religious tradition took the term 'sacred cow' and made it a metaphor for an absurd belief that benighted people defend and are afraid to abandon, and which one is considered enlightened and courageous to attack.

"Or at least, that's what people who used the term 'sacred cow' understood it to mean. It worked out in practice that 'sacred cow' meant in particular the sacred cows of conservatives, but not the sacred cows of liberals. Even liberals have now come to acknowledge that liberals have just as many sacred cows as conservatives, and even that there are good if inarticulate reasons behind at least some of the norms that are branded as sacred cows. 'Sacred cow' was an anti-conservative weapon, one that could do damage without needing any argument, and it was used in sayings such as 'Sacred cows make the best hamburgers.' It was somewhat of a sacred cow itself.

"There were a number of people who began to question this, but one of the more influential ones was Anonymous. Anonymous preferred not to be known by his name, and kept his anonymity even when running for office as an independent. But that's another story I will not go into here. Anonymous was about equally likely to vote Republican or Democrat, by the way. He was influential because he chose a medium in which one person can reach a number of his people: the comic strip. The very title of the comic strip, 'Are Sacred Cows Edible?' is part of a challenge to what the term 'sacred cow' had been used for.

"On the projector is his first strip. The characters are not named; they are subservient to the idea. Even his basic idea is trying to break out of the frame of the comic strip; it shows no direct humor, but perhaps (if you look higher) some meta-level humor. And, at any rate, it bites the hand that feeds it. Anonymous was very good at that. The question, "What if there was a comic strip that made its point but was not particularly funny?" is in a sense a very pointed joke. Or is it?

"Regular attendance is expected; the class's format will have a strip a day, followed by lecture and discussion. The only textbook is the one comic book you have; I'm sure this didn't influence any of your decisions to join this class. By now, I'm sure that there are a few people in this class so industrious that they've already read the text, or a good chunk of it; I feel safe in asking an opening question that draws on some knowledge of the text: 'How does the comic strip fit among other media? How does this particular comic strip fit among other media? Are the two related or unrelated?'"

Taberah rejoiced in the discussion that followed; it reminded him of medieval reading, an activity so involved that some doctors viewed it as a form of exercise. He himself did not say anything, but paid attention both to what was familiar and what was unfamiliar: the text was viewed in a different manner, he could tell, and not as something authoritative. More of a starting point for tangents. Taberah wished to sit still and watch, come to understand what this culture meant by "having a discussion" -- and did so, until the instructor pointed to him and said, "You. What are you thinking about? You're thinking loudly."

Taberah hesitated, and said, "I was just thinking about how this discussion seems to be 'What can we jump off of from the strip?' instead of 'What does the text mean?'"

"You think we can have a discussion about the content of one strip? It's a ten-second strip."

"Maybe. I've known some good, long discussions about a single sentence. One thing which people might say is, 'How do we deal with content that does not fit within a medium's limitations?' How, for instance, do you think about something you can't say in words?"

"If you can't say it in words, you can't think it. The limitations of language are the limitations of thought, right?"

"I think things that I can't express in words. Or, at least, I think things that I can't express, and I've been told I use words well. Saying that the limitations of language are the limitations of thought is like saying that the limitations of painting are the limitations of imagination -- that, just because we can't paint something moving or three dimensional, we can't imagine it. It may well be a limit on what we can communicate, but not on what we can think. We can be tempted to this error by the power of painting -- color, shading, and perspective. We can make paintings so lifelike that we are capable of thinking they represent anything we can imagine -- but we can still imagine things that just can't be painted. My deepest thoughts almost never come in words, and it takes effort and insight to capture some of them in words."

The teacher was impressed. He said, "If you want, come in during my office hours, and maybe we will talk about how we can have a class period discussion in your style. What do the rest of you have to say?"

Taberah sat back in his chair and continued to think. He was going to like being a student.

The TA stepped forward and said, "Heavy Boots has traditionally been a student-to-student class, taught by people who have freshly learned the material, and this will be the most important class of your discipline. It tells you how to think logically, how to think about science.

"The anecdote from which this class takes its name concerns when a couple of engineering students were in a philosophy class, and the philosophy TA gave as an 'example' the 'fact' that there is no gravity on the moon: if you held a pen out at arm's length and let go, it would just float there. 'No,' one engineer protested. 'It would fall, only more slowly.' The TA calmly explained that it would not fall because there was no gravity. After a couple of things failed, inspiration struck. The engineer said, 'You've seen movies of astronauts walking on the moon, and you saw them fall down. Why is that?' The TA, who had had plenty of courses in logic, said, 'That's because they were wearing heavy boots.'"

A chuckle moved throughout the class. The TA continued, "At this point the other engineer, who was calmer, dragged our friend, who was foaming at the mouth, out of the room. They decided that night to do a telephone survey. They asked people if there was gravity on the moon. Sixty percent said, 'No.' Those sixty percent were asked the follow-up question about astronauts.

Of the people who had said there was no gravity on the moon, twenty percent went back and changed their answers, but over sixty percent said that the people on the moon stayed there because they were wearing heavy boots."

There was more laughter, and the TA said, "Science tells us how the world is, and it can be known through experiment. This class will help you learn not to have heavy boots. Are there any questions?"

A young woman raised her hand. "Do you believe in Darwinism?"

The TA said, "Darwinism is bad, but not nearly as bad as creationism, or the masks it wears -- intelligent design. It is true that Darwinism cannot explain the question of origins, but that isn't science's job. It's not subject to debate. However the world came to be, it is here, and that is what we study. As to intelligent design -- I have another story. There was an engineering professor who came in to find his class talking about heavy boots. He gave a very involved explanation of, among other things, that gravity works on the moon despite the fact that the moon has no air, explaining the whole scientific method, the idea of trying to be skeptical and open-minded at the same time, and at the end, he asked, 'Any questions?' One young girl raised her hand, and said, 'You seem to be getting very worked up about this. Are you a Scorpio?'"

Another chuckle went through the masses. "There are any number of other stories. Did you hear about the English professor who noticed that his computer was warm, and poured water in it to cool it down? Or the farmer who complained that there were holes in his computer after he played duck hunt? Are there any other questions?"

Taberah thought. Nathella was right; this course *was* going to teach Taberah a lot about the culture of science. He raised his hand and said, "Yes. Why do you regard non-scientists as having intelligence one step above that of a rock?"

The ensuing discussion was both vigorous and heated. Taberah had already begun to piece together that something besides scientific thinking that was being taught -- he could not tell exactly what, but by the end of class a good many people came to see that a disrespect for non-scientists was being taught, and some of them even questioned the equation of science with rationality. Taberah was silent for much of the discussion; he was trying to figure out what besides the obvious was being taught in that class.

A professor stepped up to the podium and said, "Good afternoon. Do we have any computer science grad students in class? Good. Any doctoral students? Wonderful. What did the B.S. in software engineering say to the Ph.D. in computer science?

"'I'll have the veggie burger and fries, please.'

"Or do we have anybody from the practical disciplines? A university without colleges of business, engineering, and applied life studies is like a slice of chocolate cake without ketchup, mustard, and tartar sauce.

"Anybody here from the English department? The English department is a special place. If you want to find a Marxist, don't go to the political science department. Nary a Marxist will you find there. Go to the English department. If you want to find a Freudian, don't go to the psychology department. Nary a Freudian will you find there. Go to the English department. If you want to find a Darwinist, don't go to the biology department. Nary a Darwinist will you find there. Go to the English department. The English department is a living graveyard of all the dead and discredited ideologies that have been cast off by other departments.

"Anyways, I'm Dr. Autre, and I would like to welcome you to the first day of class. You'll be able to remember which room we're meeting in; just remember room 20, same number as your percentage grade. This class will have no discussions, although there will be question and answer. As to discussions -- you don't really have to pay anything to hear what your friends think about a matter, but given that you're paying good money to be here -- or some of you are; the rest are sponging off your parents -- I think you are entitled to hear what a professor thinks. Someone said that diplomacy is the art of letting other people have it your way; I was never good at diplomacy. Too honest for it. Maybe some of you will do a better job at it, when you have a Ph.D. behind your name and the academic world says, 'Aah, here's a Ph.D. Here's someone we can take seriously!'

"Some of you have questions about the syllabus. The answer to those questions is very simple. There is none. I don't mean that I don't have planned material I can fall back on if I need to; I mean that the important stuff in this course is the stuff I can't foresee. The main reason I plan out course material ahead of time is that it provides me with a point of departure from which to do something interesting. As such, I do not wish to confuse you by giving you distracting information."

A young man raised his hand. "But if you have the information on hand, what harm is there in sharing it? Certainly it helps you."

The teacher said, "There was once a professor who thought his class was writing down too much of what he was saying, and thinking about it too little. At one point, he interrupted his lecture to say, 'Stop. I want you to put down your pens and pencils and listen to me. You don't have to write down every word I say. You are here to think, not to produce copies of my lecture notes. You don't have to write down what I say verbatim. Any questions?'

"One young woman frantically said, 'Yes. How do you spell *verbatim*?'

"I'm not going to spell out an answer to your question beyond that, but I am going to say that I won't always say my full meaning outright. I will leave it implied, for you to wrestle out. That requires the same involvement as discussion, but it leaves you free to hear a professor. You are encouraged to talk with your colleagues after the classroom for as much discussion as you want. Class time is for what you can only get in class time -- a professor's lecture.

"I've used a different text each time, and the registrar usually won't print how to get a text in my class. This year, I want you to get a sticky-hand, walk into Sphttp://www.powells.com/partner/24934/biblio/0684863170 Physical -- it's a mile down the street from the college, close your eyes, turn around, and toss the sticky-hand past your back. The book that the hand lands on is yours. Buy it, and study it; see how it relates to our classroom lectures, and tie it in to your discussions. I guarantee you that, after the first month, you will have learned something that I couldn't have possibly coordinated by picking the text myself. I don't just mean learning to read a text at an angle, although that is tremendously important; I mean that you will have learned something directly from the text that I couldn't have picked out. Tonight's reading assignment is pages three through ten, and the first page of the index, if your book has an index. Any questions?"

Taberah leaned back. This class was going to be a lot of fun.

Baptists

Taberah walked in after the first day of classes, excited, alert. He said to Nathella, "What does the word 'Baptist' mean? I heard someone use it between classes, and I couldn't figure it out from context."

Nathella said, "Um, that's not a five-minute question. First, do you know what 'Protestant' means?"

Taberah said, "No."

"There have been any number of reform movements in the history of the Catholic Church, and there will be any number of such movements in the future. With one of them, a monk named Martin Luther nailed ninety-five theses for reform on the door of a cathedral. The authorities questioned him, and finally asked him, 'Do you believe that the Church has actually been *wrong* in these things for all these years?'

"Luther asked for a couple of days to think about it; that was granted, and at the end of the time the question was put to him again. He said, 'Here I stand. I can do no other.'

"Then all Hell broke loose. Luther was excommunicated, and tried to set up a parallel, reformed church. The church called

'Catholic' was the one that initiated the schism, but they were not the only schismatics. Luther's church splintered and splintered and splintered. There was all manner of invective between the two sides, and they were excluded from each other's communions. It was worse than the split between Latin and Greek -- far worse.

"Over time, people began to realize that the schisms were not a good thing. There were some who said, 'The solution to the problem is simple. Everyone come over to my side, and there won't be any division.' There was the problem of communion: especially on the Catholic side, there was an understanding of communion as implying full membership in the community, which was in turn understood to mean that members not part of a particular schism could not legitimately take part in it -- this interpretation was deemed to be more important than the words, 'Take this, *all of you*, and drink from it.' that instituted a feast given to all of Christ's disciples. That's still where things are now; Rome has now interpreted Vatican II to mean that Catholics and Protestants whose consciences command full participation in their brothers' and sisters' worship may be -- what's the word, *tolerated*, in taking communion across the schism. It's a step homewards, I suppose, but we are very far off from organizational unity that once was.

"Baptists are, or rather were, one of the Protestant sects, and they added something to American culture. As to what happened --

"In the fifties, the question of abortion, the question of whether a woman has a right to kill the child growing inside her, came up with the Supreme Court. The court protected the child's life. In the seventies, it came up again, and this time the court legalized abortion, and the movement declared the controversy settled. But it wasn't.

"By the nineties... there were laws in place that offered stiff penalties for abortion protests, and RICO, a law meant to deal with organized crime, was used to inflict massive penalties on abortion protesters. There was one minister who led a protest while cautiously distancing any church involvement or statement on the protest. The courts RICOed the congregation, making a multimillion dollar settlement. Also going on were 'physical compliance holds' -- meaning pain holds used on demonstrators. Nonviolent protests of abortion received draconian punishment compared to the penalties deemed appropriate for violent protest by environmental or animal rights activists.

"When a pregnant woman walks into an abortion clinic, unsure what to do with an unexpected pregnancy, by the letter of the law she is supposed to receive non-directive counseling to help her decide how to handle the situation. What actually happens is very different. Abortion is big business; insurance companies will readily pay thousands of dollars for an abortion rather than deal with all of the expenses of childbirth and a new life out in the world. Even when there is no insurance, a couple hundred dollars is still lucrative for a ten minute procedure. Never mind that the people who perform abortions have the highest suicide rate in the medical profession; it's money, money, money. What actually happens when a girl walks in is that she receives a five-minute sales pitch that slants abortion as the only live option. Most of the abortions that have happened in this country were abortions that the girl was pressured into, that she never was allowed to say 'no' to -- same thing as date rape.

"So there was this big push to have real non-directive counseling at abortion clinics, along with a surgeon general's warning about the emotional scars that abortion can cause -- post abortion stress syndrome and all. It wasn't just Christians behind it; some feminists, especially those who had spent some time working at abortion clinics or talking with women who had gone through that trauma, had begun to suspect that they and their movement were being manipulated as pawns by forces less innocent than -- anyways, the law was passed September 1, 2012, and struck down October 1.

"The Baptists were the fastest to spearhead an initiative to get every church member into a protest -- which they didn't do; it was closer to fifty percent, but there was a massive, peaceful protest, and the police came out -- pepper spray, tear gas, pain holds, the works. The jails were filled up overnight, and it was ugly. The ugliest thing about it was that it wasn't two parties fighting each other -- it was one party attacking satyagrahi who didn't resist. The courts thought this would be a good time for an unambiguous message, and commanded a settlement of over 1.6 trillion dollars. The church could not begin to pay something like that.

"The courts lost something that day. The president of American Baptists called a press conference and said from his jail cell, 'You can force our bodies and our checkbooks, but you can never break our spirits. The denomination of Baptists in America is hereby declared to be bankrupt and disbanded. Baptists, melt into other bodies of believers. You are the heart of our ministry, not a formal structure that can be sued. Courts, you have won this battle. But *what is it that you have won?*'

"Most other Protestant denominations that participated in the protest did not do much better; Catholics were protected only by the masterful diplomacy of the Papacy. The Pope tried to be an advocate for the Protestants, too, but saving the financial viability of Catholics was making the best of a bad scenario. There were believers who left the Catholic Church -- not out of any rejection of Rome, but as a matter of solidarity, saying, 'We would rather be ill-treated alongside these righteous Protestants than be spared because our denomination happens to be powerful.'

"That single court decision galvanized the body of believers as a thousand sermons could never have done. Before then, there had been talk of an emerging post-denominational Christianity; now, people finally realized that they had bigger things to worry about than labels. It was as if two estranged brother generals forgot their dispute in the face of a battle. The Church was driven mostly underground, yes -- it had been underground at its beginning, and it will be underground again, no doubt. And people are tortured when they protest abortion, infanticide, or euthanasia -- the Constitution prohibits cruel and unusual punishment, but the courts have ruled that 'nondestructive incentives to reform' are not punishment. It is still virtually illegal to witness about your faith -- the argument classes it as harassment, and a freedom of religion defense brings a dilemma with it. If you invoke your religion as a defense, the question is which religion, and if you specify whichever area of Christianity you are from, you are slapped with massive penalties for participation in a corporate entity which falls under RICO. All of this is true and more, and the church is healthier than ever before.

"Taberah, in martial arts, I remember hearing something about you and joint locks, but I don't remember what. A joint lock is when someone twists one of your joints so that you will be pain unless you move in a certain way. This enables a martial artist to take your wrist and bring you down to the ground. What the Supreme Court learned in the ensuing years was that joint locks would no longer work against Christians. You could still figuratively twist a Christian's wrist -- break it if you pressed hard enough -- but she wouldn't go down to the ground unless you did so much damage to her that she was incapable of standing. And it is bad publicity if nothing else to do that much damage to unresisting people again and again -- so things have evolved to an unofficial 'Don't ask, don't tell.'

"Abortion is still of course legal, but now there are a lot of Christian women who can pick up on when another woman is pregnant, sometimes even before she knows it -- and tell her, 'You don't have to have an abortion,' and then talk about alternatives. The abortion industry thinks we're worse than termites -- individually not a problem, collectively a major problem, and too many to go hunting for -- and there's not that much they can do. Yes, they have advertising; yes, they control the literature that goes with pregnancy tests; yes, they do a number of abortions -- but we're able to make a sizeable dent. And the legality of killing is something that's hurting the court politically.

"There's a saying, 'Satan meant it for evil, but God turned it to good,' and the final break in dark power is that we are not angry at the court. We pray for them every night, submit to them in what we can, and go about our lives -- for God, not against the court. The court, with the worst of intentions, has created the conditions in America for Christians to deal effectively with problems that we would never have begun to treat.

"Have I answered your question, Taberah?"

Taberah thought, and said, "You have answered it and more. I would like to talk with you more some time, to better understand your form of government. You miss the Baptists, don't you?"

Deep Waters

Taberah closed his eyes for a while and said, "Nathella, you said there was a story behind your Dad wanting to make a pond. What was the story?"

Nathella said, "When I was little, I had a fantasy, an image -- of being surrounded by a gathering of many warm people, of a place where I belonged. One of my brothers, when he was little, imagined exploring a mansion, and had a very vivid image of a doorway opening, light spilling out from behind. My father had a dream like this, too. He envisioned a deep pool of water, a pool he could swim in and dive deep and meet mermaids. He liked to reminisce, and he talked about that dream from time to time. He had a better memory than most.

"One of the things that happens when you get older is that you get practical, and one of the things I accepted after a blunt remark from a young man is that 'practical' is not about getting things done; it's about letting dreams die. It means settling for less -- being happy, to be sure, but... I have come to accept my age, but I know I lost something when I gave up the bright energy of being young.

"One of my father's friends asked him, 'Why not make your dream a reality? You may be too old to swim into a pool and meet mermaids, but there are children around town who are not. They don't have a place to swim. To be sure, you'd have to put a fence around it and require parents to be around, buy one of those floating rings, but why not? Why not make a place where children can dive and meet mermaids?' He told me that a spark lit in my father's eyes -- my father said, 'I've got some stumps to blast, and I've got a field I don't use any more. I can make a pond as well.'

That friend felt very guilty when he found out what happened, but when I look back -- I think my father died well. It left on me an impression, and I've managed to keep a little more of my young openness to dreams than I might have otherwise.

"And I'm glad to have met you. You help me dream, as well. You're Heavenly minded enough to be of earthly good -- you've already changed my life for the better."

Taberah said nothing. He felt at the same time honored and slightly uncomfortable -- why was she putting him on a pedestal? Taberah now dreamed mostly of Heaven, and he was sure he would receive it. Why -- Taberah thought, and he could not think of any appropriate questions to ask. He let the matter rest.

TMC Metagame Competition

Taberah went down to the computer room, looking for something to do. He found a cool portal, and spent half the day fascinated by looking at different layerings of the human body. He particularly liked looking at a forearm end-on, with only the skeletal and nervous systems visible. It was fun, but something in his mind was still itching.

Then he heard a herald announce:

> TMC. TMC is short for TMC Metagame Competition. The objective of this game is to devise the best new computer game; players' work will be judged according to their popularity in testing votes. Points are awarded for originality, quality of game concept, quality of artwork, and another category specified by game designer. Past winners may be seen at...

This had Taberah's undivided attention. He went, sat down, and spent three hours' total playing different winners, and then, after going through the next day's classes (now less interesting to him, although he tried to concentrate), began to think in the morning.

They want something original. This culture values novelty over repetition; what can I give that is truly original?

Taberah remembered his time as a court jester, in which his role was to stand on his head, both literally and figuratively -- exalt the abased or pull down the exalted. Pleasure filled his mind, as if he were meeting an old friend. *All games that I am aware of are competitive; one wins by defeating others or possibly by gaining a high score in surmounting an obstacle. What of a game in which there is no defeating others and in which the player is not constrained by any predefined goal?*

Taberah left the computer room and began pacing in the forest. He could say those words, but what did they mean? Trying to describe a game without a conflict seemed like trying to describe a statue without a shape.

There are a great many ideas that might as well be original because of how hard people have worked to forget them. What is the one idea that is now escaping my attention, the one thing that was the air I breathed in the Middle Ages but which people do not understand now? I can't think of it -- what is the one symbol of -- symbol! -- *these people live in a world of symbols, but not as I do. It is a world of meager, half-dead symbols that do not have the courage to be. For them nature, the world is stripped of symbolic lore. A lion is not a reminder of courage -- or maybe it is the one surviving exception. They see just a yellow mass, a predator -- it is like seeing shape without color.*

How can I make symbolic meanings visible to them? How can I make a text speak to people who are illiterate? What if they could look at the green in a pane of a stained glass window and -- they can. I can make an annotated virtual world -- a cathedral and forest, full of plants and animals -- in which, when the objects are touched, a voice tells what they mean.

Aed has shown me enough that I can begin working on this now.

Results

The days passed quickly; Taberah spent every spare

moment working on his creation. He enjoyed the classes, but he rushed out quickly to be back in the joy of creation. It had been so long before he created something.

He finished just before deadline, and met with mixed results. His creation fascinated any number of people, was very popular -- and was disqualified as not meeting the criteria as a game. The metagame judges wanted something original, but interpreted in such a way as to mean something original in the creation of what you have to defeat. Taberah cried; he was hurt by the judgment, and he felt depressed not to have anything else to be working on. Yes, there were classes, and he particularly enjoyed the cartoon that said, "Tolerate this!" and showed a picture of a cross. The teacher went on to explain that liberality and tolerance did not just mean liberality and tolerance of liberal minorities, but tolerance of Christianity. This produced a heated discussion, and Taberah loved it.

The end of semester rolled around. Taberah had passed the cartoon course, aced the other humanities course, and failed the science course. He was not nearly as saddened by that grade as by the leaving of most of the students, particularly the Phoenix Society. The Kinsella's home was desolately quiet -- or at least, it was desolately quiet until Taberah received a call telling him that he was the first person to receive two Turing Awards.

Then the household was busy with preparation.

Gadfly

Taberah walked up slowly, hesitantly, to the microphone. He looked unsure of himself, but there was still a deep confidence in his walk.

He looked at the microphone for a second, and then out at members of the audience, one at a time. It was a minute of silence, and in his eyes a penetrating gaze grew.

"It was a year ago this day," he said, "that I accepted this award, and I accepted it only because it was politic. I did not and do not think that what I did then merited an award of this magnitude. All I did was look at the problem a bit differently, think a little, and see a way to cheat on the Turing test. This is not a very big deal; it was just an accident. Yes, I know that most scientific discoveries are made by accident, but this does not make an accident a scientific discovery. But this time is different. This time, I am happy to accept the Turing Award.

"This time is different. Earlier, I had merely managed to capture the accidental features of intelligence. Now, God has given me the grace to capture some of its substance, and I stand in awe. It is as if, before, I had received an award for making a statue that looked like something alive, and now, I have succeeded in making something that is vaguely alive. The difference is fundamental, and I wish to ask what lessons we have learned in the discovery.

"The first lesson I can see is that abstract thought is easier than concrete thought. Or, to put things differently, that our minds are so wonderfully made that many of us can handle concrete thought even more easily than abstract thought. (Maybe the first lesson should be that we are fearfully and wonderfully made.)" A chuckle moved through the audience. "There is much more to thought, and rationality, than is easily captured, and I've only scratched the surface of it. It took me a long time to understand that computers are logical and can do math as no human ever will -- excuse me, do arithmetic as no human ever will -- and yet that they could not think. Notwithstanding Dijkstra's dictum that the question of whether computers can think is like the question of whether submarines can swim, computers could not think. If I have managed to make a computer think, I have managed only the barest prototype of what could be done -- like those cave paintings that we can barely recognize as art, I have just stumbled on how the basic principle works.

"Or, at least, part of the basic principle. All I've discovered how to program is how to think abstractly; I still have no idea of how to tell a computer how to deal with sense input. Nobody knows how to make an artificial dog; making the robotics for a body would be easy, and making an internal chemical laboratory capable of taking in food and water and producing slobber, sweat, and the like is arguably possible, but we have no idea of how to do the intelligence. All of the abstraction in the world can't tell our robot dog how to run through a field of children without getting clobbered. We have captured one of the features of human intelligence; there are a number of features of even animal intelligence that we lack. There are other features of unintelligent life that we have yet to touch, as well. Nobody knows how to make machines that heal after they sustain damage."

"The last lesson I wish to mention concerns accident and substance, and..." Taberah closed his eyes, and said, "Mr. Chairman, I stayed up all night thinking of what to say, and manners in the country I come from are a bit less polished. I really can't think of a polite way to say it, but I really think the discipline of artificial intelligence has been running with an albatross around its neck, and my success is in large part because I somehow got on the racetrack without getting an albatross. Do I have your permission to make some polemic remarks that may sting?"

Dr. Bode said, "Mr. Kinsella, you have our full consent to say whatever you think is best suited to the occasion."

Taberah said, "I know, but I am not much older than a child, and one of the things I've learned the hard way is that people sometimes say that when they don't really mean it. Is it really OK?"

The chairman's face held trepidation for a moment; he paused, and then said, "It's OK."

Taberah said, "Thank you. And I do really mean it.

"I will not begin to attempt a full philosophical analysis of accident and substance, any more than I would attempt a full mathematical analysis of logic within this speech, were I able, but I will say this. Accident is the outer appearance of an object, what the senses can receive. Substance is what it really is, its essence, if you will. Our discipline, in this area, is the self-made victim of an incredible legacy of bad philosophy, and has many fruitless endeavors which make as much sense to a philosopher as trying to bring a statue to life by painting it and making its features ever more lifelike. We have asked the question of, 'How can we create artificial intelligence?', but misinterpreted it to mean, 'How can we imitate the features of artificial intelligence that are most computer-like?' With all due respect to the brilliant man for which this award was named, I was shocked when I read Turing's explanation of what he thinks thought is. His interpretation of human thought is like interpreting a game of chess as moving little pieces around on a board. Some of what I have seen in this community reminds me of trying to kink a cable to stop the flow of data on a network, and then switching to fiber optic to make your thinking work. But what has happened is not that you make your thinking work; you only make it stop working. The main thing I would attribute this success to is that I came from another culture and missed this bad philosophy, and I believe that the artificial intelligence community will really begin to mine out my insight when they can really escape from this bad philosophy."

Taberah closed his eyes a moment, and said, "Mr. Chairman, may I take thirty seconds for a personal announcement, as well?"

The chairman sat for a moment and said, "What you have said is a difficult thing to hear, but others have said it before, or things similar. Perhaps we just haven't taken them seriously enough. Yes, you are welcome to say whatever else you want."

Taberah looked, gazed out at over a thousand heads in the audience. All eyes were on him. Slowly, distinctly, loudly, he said, "In this whole room, I doubt if there are more than two or three of you who can hear what else I have to say, but it is something significant. I would like if those two or three would come to my hotel room after the night's festivities so we can talk about it. Thank you, and have a good evening." He closed his eyes and walked hurriedly, almost as if embarrassed, back to his seat.

There was a hushed silence, with murmuring. When he got back to his table, after waiting a minute, one of the people from an adjacent table scooted over to him, and said, "May I join you tonight?" Then another, then another. People began to walk over to him. In minutes, Taberah was at the center of a noisy swarm of people.

Taberah turned to the woman nearest him, looked into her eyes, and asked, "Would you get the chairman for me?"

In a few more minutes, the chairman was next to him.

Taberah hesitated, and then said, "Dr. Bode, there seem to be more people interested in what I have to say than there is space in my room. Would you be so kind as to provide me with a room to speak in, where these people can comfortably be seated?"

The chairman gently laughed, and said, "Mr. Kinsella, why don't you speak here? The whole room is interested in what you have to say."

Taberah picked up his glass, took a long gulp, and said, "Let me take a restroom break first. And would you announce to people that anyone not interested in my tangent shouldn't feel obligated to stay. It'll be a tad long."

When Taberah returned, not a single soul had left. The room was dead silent.

"The discipline of artificial intelligence is about how to impart rationality to computers. This is a question about computers, but it is at least as much a question about rationality. In our endeavor to make computers rational, we have paid scant attention on how to be rational ourselves. I am not saying that we should be Spocks, embodying logic without emotion. A prejudice against emotion, and a belief that rationality and emotion are antithetical, is (thank God) crumbling, but old fallacies die hard. I embrace emotion as much as I embrace being physical and enjoying music and good wine, but I do not wish to deal further with emotion now. What do I wish to deal with?

"Dick Feynman, in his memoirs *You Must Be Joking, Mr. Feynman*, included a classic speech on cargo cult science. He spoke of aboriginal people who, in World War II, had Allied food and other supplies accidentally airdropped to them, and produce a mockup of an airstrip, designed more and more to look like a real airstrip -- but, however much they worked, planes never landed. Never mind that this is very crude anthropology; there is a fundamental insight there about something that looks very much like an airstrip but just doesn't work. And it provides a key to explain something very disagreeable.

"When I came here, I was shocked at what I saw in intellectual life. It is like the shock that might come to a scientist the first time he goes to a creation science institute and discovers exactly what 'science' means in that context. Pseudo-science can incorporate a lot of material from science, and still not be science. What shocked me when I came here was that I looked for reason and found pseudo-reason."

Taberah said, "A full brain dump of what I have seen would take far too long to deliver in a speech, but I wish to give a sampling in three areas: an instance of bad reasoning I see, an instance of a bad way of thinking I see, and an instance of a possible partial remedy.

"The example of bad reasoning I see is in the area of overpopulation. The general, un-questioned belief is that our world's population is growing exponentially, much faster in the poorer areas of the world, and doomsday will come if we don't curb this population explosion. Speaking as a philosopher, I ask, 'Why?'

"The answer that is given is that people in the third world have large families to support themselves. And that's enough of an explanation to be accepted by someone gullible, but it does not stand up to examination.

"If the world's population is growing exponentially, then it has either always been growing exponentially, or it started growing exponentially at some point. If it has always been growing exponentially, then, as certainly as the future holds doomsday population levels, the past holds dwindling population figures. As surely as the future explodes, the past implodes. This would mean that prior to, say, 1700, all non-European continents would be virtually uninhabited. If the third world population is doubling every, say, ten years, then the population of the third world in the year 1700 would be less than ten. This is ridiculous. All accounts I know say that the poorer areas of the world have been inhabited with at least moderate density for quite some time

-- thousands of years easily. This leaves us with the other option, namely that the population of the third world has been basically stable and has recently begun exponential growth. To this possibility I ask the question: why on earth? The cultures of these people haven't changed at any rapid pace (and if they did, I would still be puzzled as to why *all* of them changed, instead of a handful -- a rapid change of unrelated cultures is about as unusual as the formation of a herd of cats); it is true that most of them cherish children and value big families, but that's been a part of most cultures since long before whenever this population explosion was supposed to have begun. The introduction of new technology to lengthen life and childbearing years? That would certainly account for a population explosion in the *wealthy* nations, but the average African tribesman has never heard of a Western doctor, let alone received enough medical care to possibly increase the number of children he leaves behind.

"Literature describing a population explosion if the third world birth rate is not curbed has been around for several decades; it used to specify a date for when, for instance, people would all be standing because there would not be enough room for anyone to sit down; those dates are long gone, had passed well before the turn of the millennium, and now there are no more predictions for when doomsday will be -- merely that it is always 'soon'. There are pieces of evidence garnered to support this -- for example, the great poverty by our standards of third world nations; never mind that this is how all nations lived before one civilization happened to stumble on Midas's secret -- but it doesn't stand up to rational examination. And there are many claims like this that free thinkers never question, because to question them is to question rationality or to question reality.

"That is one example among many of non-think; I do not presently wish to give others, nor even to ask who or why would perpetuate such a massive and propagandistic illusion. I am trying to keep this talk short. So I would like to move on to my next example, of an instance not simply of an irrational belief, but of a macroscopic way of thinking that is bad. In this area also, I have a number of choices; I choose to elaborate on the discipline of economics."

Several faces in the crowd could be seen to wince.

"The discipline of economics has had tremendous success at providing the right answer to the wrong question. The question which it answers is, 'How can a culture be manipulated to maximize the economic wealth that it produces?' The question which it ought to answer is, 'How can an economy be guided so as to best support the life of a culture?'

"I spoke with an economist about this; he said several things. The first thing he said is that economics takes people's wants to be constant, i.e. that it doesn't try to reshape people's economic desires. But this is nonsense; the whole enterprise of advertising and marketing is designed to manipulate people into buying and spending far more than even natural greed would have them do. People work overtime and go into debt to have things they don't need and wouldn't want enough to buy if there weren't ads pressuring them into it. As to the others -- there is a naive assumption that the starting point is a consumer who is both selfish and rational. Both have an element of truth, but even the vilest of men is not completely selfish. There is a motivation to do something beyond meeting animal needs that is not gone even in Hitler. Hitler went to incredible lengths to exterminate Jews; such dedication would be called heroic if it were engaged in a noble cause. It was perverse beyond measure, but it was not selfish. Not by a long shot. And as to rational -- anyone who looks at a marketing text, or for that matter pays attention to a few ads -- will see that the means of increasing market share has nothing to do with rational appeal. The real questions that economics could address -- the meaning of wealth, the right amount of wealth (not the greatest) for people to live with -- are brushed aside in the relentless pursuit of more, more, more, more.

"On points like this I could go on -- the death of philosophy, the curse of Babel upon academic disciplines so that, for instance, the work of any one mathematician is incomprehensible to the vast majority of his colleagues -- but I do not wish to do so here.

Instead I wish to turn, on a positive note, to how you can think in a better way.

"Larry Wall's classic *Programming Perl* described the three programmer's virtues: hubris, laziness, and impatience. His points with all three are in one sense tongue in cheek, but in another sense much deeper. The virtue he calls 'laziness' is another facet of the intellectual rigor that takes the one stitch that will in time save nine. It is called 'laziness' because applying that rigor will have the effect of taking less work overall; indeed it is a principle of software engineering that doing something well is easier than doing it sloppily. I wish to focus on that intellectual rigor.

"When you are thinking -- be it listening to this speech, or trying to get technology to work, or figuring out why someone is mad at you -- *don't slouch*. When you feel a faint intuition in the back of your mind that something is wrong, don't ignore it. Pay attention to it. Try to understand it. Analyze it. Analysis is one tool among a thousand, and you need to be able to let go of it before you can come to the insight Zen offers -- that much is clear to me from reading about it, even though I haven't the foggiest idea whether a Zen master would consider me enlightened or not. You need to also be able to relax, to be able to slide into things, to groove (if I may use an archaic term) -- but different things at different times. And a certain kind of intellectual rigor applies across disciplines, in sciences, in humanities, in humanities that think they're sciences. It applies outside of academia to life.

"I have thought a lot about the three areas these insights are taken from, and written them down in a sort of book. It will be available on my home room at midnight; those parties who are interested and not offended, whom I guess are few, are welcome to read it there. Beyond that, I thank you all for coming, and if my speech has succeeded, you all need time to think as much as I need time to sleep. Thank you, and have a good night."

Taberah slipped out the back door, scurried off to the hotel room, locked the door, and used both noise cancelling ear phones and ear plugs (noise rating 35); Aed had to get the hotel to open the room to pick up a cellular computer he'd left in there, and bring along security guards to see that he was the only person to go in. The traffic on Taberah's book was enough to take down a zuni server, but the Kinsellas' ISP had mirrors up in an hour. The next day, as the Kinsellas stepped into the plane to fly back, Aed said, "Taberah, I hope you're ready to be a celebrity. I've spoken with the chairman of the Turing society, and he says he can ensure us a week of peace and quiet with his clout. Beyond that, be ready for a lot of visitors."

Taberah smiled and said, "I'm not worried about it."

Sojourn

Ding-dong!

Aed came to the door, and stifled a wince. This wasn't a week's peace! He saw a short teen-ager in an outlandish role-playing costume: a long, loose, dark robe fell about him, hooded shadows covering his face, and fractal-decorated gloves covered the skin on his arms. "Mister, may I use your bathroom?" he said, his voice cracking, and then shrunk back.

Aed breathed a sigh of relief, and said, "Sure. Come this way." He led him to the bathroom, surprised at a smell of -- what? something chemical; he couldn't decide. As the door shut, Aed decided to stay; the kid might get lost, and perhaps something else in his house might get lost. It was a few minutes, and then, coming out, the kid reached around the side of his head and pulled off his hood to reveal a shaven head that looked older than he had seemed at first glance. "So," the teenager? said, his voice again cracking, "d'ja recognize me?"

Aed blinked, and did a double take. It was Taberah. No beard, no hair on his head, not even eyebrows. He looked unfamiliar, just a very short teenager whose eyes twinkled.

"I've decided to do some travelling incognito. Listen, I'm really sorry about all the publicity you'll deal with; I hadn't known how your culture works. No, that's not right; I'd guessed about publicity, but I hadn't cared. Anyways, I have learned a lot about travel and adapting back in the middle ages, and disguise came quickly -- I learned a lot at Halloween time. Um..." his voice trailed off, and then added, "You'll eventually have less attention if I disappear."

"Don't feel guilty about the journalists," Aed said. "Their presence is a side effect of making certain kinds of achievements. But Taberah, you will always be welcome here. You don't have to go."

"I know, but I need to go -- for me as well as for you. It's been great here, and I hope to come back -- but who knows what tomorrow will bring? I am a wayfarer, and I am not ready to settle down in one place for good."

"You're sure? You're taking an awful big step -- can I at least provide you with resources? I've got a fair amount invested, and it's an awfully big world out there."

"No. I can't describe it, it's just -- I have a feeling I'll be back, but I need to travel. To think. To work."

"What do you call your creation of artificial intelligence?"

"Aed, do we have to argue?" Aed noticed that there were tears forming in the child's eyes.

"You're making it hard enough for him as it is, honey. Let him go," came Nathella's voice.

Nathella walked over to Taberah, held him in her arms, and kissed him on the lips. "I'll miss you -- Taberah, what does your name mean?"

"Burning."

"Similar to my husband's name. I'll miss you, flame. I'll pray for you every day." Then she continued to hold him in silence.

"Where will you be?" Aed said. He walked over and picked Taberah up, holding him. Taberah kissed him, too, on the lips. "I think it would better as regards the media for you not to know," Taberah said. He lingered for a moment, and then disappeared out the side door.

A Mugging

Taberah walked out. It was good to be under the sky again, with a bent arm for a pillow. It felt honest. Or did it? In the year's time, Taberah realized he had grown more accustomed to luxury than he thought. There was something nagging at the back of his mind -- what? This culture was lacking in rationality, but he had to have more than rationality to give. Academic silliness was a symptom, not the problem. But what was it? He went into a store and purchased a pen and notepad; he needed time to write. He wandered about aimlessly, walking the city streets.

Taberah was snapped out of his thoughts at a sudden, jerky motion. A young man had drawn a knife; he said, "Give me your money. Now. And no quick motions -- you draw something, you're dead."

Taberah slowly reached into his pockets. "I don't have much money; only fifty bucks, plus a few coins. I know what I can give you. I have a nice, thick Swiss Army knife that my mentor gave me. It's quite useful. Would you like that?" He had fished out a fifty dollar bill, plus four quarters, one dime, and a nickel.

"Drop it on the ground," the robber said.

"Certainly. Why are you afraid?" Taberah asked, dropping his pocketknife on the ground.

"I'm not afraid," the robber said, and saw that his lie would not be believed. It could not. Taberah was relaxed; he carried a peace about him, and there was something about him over which the knife held no power.

"Why are you afraid?" Taberah repeated. "I'm not going to hurt you."

"Why aren't you afraid?" the robber said. "I could kill you right where you stand."

"That is the worst you could do. Then I would be with my friends in Heaven. And there are some saints whom I'd be really happy to see."

"You wouldn't even try to defend yourself?" the robber said, puzzled.

"I love to spar. I --"

"Then defend yourself against this!" The robber swung his knife to slash Taberah across the face. Taberah seemed suddenly distant; the knife flew through the air, and then the robber felt a fist between his eyes -- he would be reeling. Then he felt a sledgehammer blow to his stomach, far more powerful than he would have imagined such a scrawny body capable of delivering struggled to regain his balance

fell

realized he was in a full Nelson

felt himself retching

felt himself pulled back, so that the vomit didn't touch him.

Taberah released his arms, and then pulled back, crouched. "I'm sorry. I shouldn't have done that. I have learned that violence does not accomplish much, but my hands are not in on the knowing. I should not have pretended that I was sparring with my weapons master. I should--"

The robber cussed him out, and said, "Who are you, and where are you from?"

Taberah was very still for a moment, and said, "My name is Taberah. It means 'burning' in Hebrew."

"Are you a Jew?"

"I am a Catholic. That comes from Judaism."

"So where are you from?"

Taberah paused, and then, against his better judgment, said, "I can give you a short answer that won't tell you anything, or I can give you the real answer, which I won't blame you if you find impossible to believe."

"Give me the real answer."

"I'm from the Middle Ages, Provençe in Southern France. I've traveled a bit. An angel took me to this place. I --"

The robber said, "Ok; you don't have to tell me if you don't want to." Taberah did not argue; instead, he asked, "What is your name?"

The robber shook, and then began to cry, trying to conceal it. "You really care about me, don't you?"

Taberah said, "Look at me."

The man brushed his arm across his face and looked at him, startled. Taberah's eyes were glistening, too. He said, "It looks as if you've never had anyone who cared about you. I care about you."

The man wiped his mouth, spat, and then sat up, uncertain whether to glare or to quiver. Finally, he said, "My name is Elika. Don't know what it means. Don't have nobody to care about me. Don't understand you."

Taberah said, "Do you want to understand me?"

Elika said, "Maybe. No. Yes. Why? Are you going to talk about Middle Ages stuff?"

Taberah said, "I don't want to talk about the Middle Ages now. Maybe later, if you're interested. Are you confused about why I care about you? Would you like me to explain that?"

Elika said, "How did you know that?"

Taberah did not answer the question. He said, "Let me ask you another question. What do you think religion is about?"

Elika said, "Religion? That's not for me. It's about rules and feeling guilty and memorizing the Bible. It's impossible; it doesn't work for someone like me who has a tough life."

Taberah said, "Would you like to know what religion is for me?"

"Something you're good at?"

"Um, I don't know if I'm good at it, but it's something important to me, and something very different than what you have said. It's not about rules, or feeling guilty, or memorizing the Bible."

"Then what is it about?"

"One thing: love. God loves you. He loves me. We should love God and other people. Everything else is just details. It's about love; that's why I care about you."

"Look, I don't know why you are telling this to me; maybe it's something you can do, but I can't. Here's your money and your knife; I need to go."

Taberah said, "I gave you the money and the knife; they aren't mine any more. They're yours. But if you want to give me something -- $50 is enough to buy some bread, some meat, and a bottle of cider. I'm hungry, and you just threw up. Maybe we could meet and talk -- or not. You are free to leave, but I'd like to get to know you better."

This time, Elika made no attempt to conceal his tears, and Taberah softly asked, "May I give you a hug?" It had been ages since anybody had touched Elika, and he listened with interest as Taberah shared what was on his heart. "Why do you dare to keep company with me?" Elika asked. "My Master," Taberah answered, "kept company with all kinds of people, from the most respected to the least. His heart has room for me, for you. I want you to share in his joy."

They ate in a park, and talked long into the night.

Kindred

Night had slowly fallen; Taberah and Elika walked past a dark valley, from which a voice said, "I see your dress. Are you one of us? Are you one of the Kindred?"

Taberah gazed, letting his eyes grow accustomed to the darkness. "Who are you? Who are the Kindred?"

The voice answered back, "You already know that. Where were you born? And when?"

"I was born in Provençe, in the Middle Ages."

"Welcome, Ancient One. Step closer."

Taberah had an intuition that he couldn't place. In his mind, he raised his guard, but this was too interesting to pass by. "Come with us."

Elika said, "Don't worry; they're just role playing."

The voice said, "One is never 'just' role playing. Role play is never 'just.'"

The intuition in Taberah's mind clarified, solidifying. He was beginning to see that role play meant something different than it had with Fiona and Clancy.

They melted into the shadows, and emerged in a candlelit room. In the center lie a pile of wooden swords, staves, daggers, shields. The voice again said, "It is our custom that Kindred brought into our Clan must fight until all the other members have defeated them. Only then can you Enter. Choose your weapon carefully."

Taberah looked at the pile, picked up a halberd, hefted it. "And if I am not defeated? What happens then?"

"Then you are the new head of the Clan."

Taberah looked, and words began to flow through him, coming partly of his own volition, partly of something else. His senses were more acute; the world seemed to slow down. He said, "Darkness is powerful. Light is more powerful. As a sign to you, I choose to fight you armed only with this."

Taberah stood back, drew himself to a majestic height, and made on his heart the sign of the cross.

There was stunned disbelief in the atmosphere. One of the Kindred slowly stepped forward, hefted a quarterstaff, and swung at Taberah.

Taberah dodged; he swung again, and this time Taberah caught the staff and twisted it so that the Kinsman fell on his back.

Taberah used the staff to create around him an area of space; another person raised a two-handed sword, bringing it down. It broke the staff in two -- as had been the Kinsman's intent -- and Taberah's.

Taberah was now holding twin longswords.

From the outside, it looked as if a thousand things were going on; from the inside, Taberah was only aware of one thing. He kept dancing until he had struck all but one of the Kindred -- all but one. They were locked in a dance, the Kinsman skillful and masterful, possessing far greater power than he appeared to have, Taberah moving in a way that was cunning, alien, brilliant. Elika looked on intently; this was the most magnificent fight he had seen.

Suddenly, unexpectedly, the Kinsman threw down his sword, and opened his arms. Taberah followed suit, and the Kinsman reached out to grab Taberah's testicles.

Taberah, with equal swiftness, struck him on the side of the neck, knocking him out.

Taberah turned around slowly, looking, and once again made the sign of the cross.

One of the Kindred looked at him, and said, "Who are you?"

Taberah said, "I am your new leader, and I have many things to tell you. I wish to tell you about a kind of role play beyond your wildest imaginings, a role play that will give you what you search for in vain in calling yourselves the Kindred. Kindred we will be, bound much more tightly than ever a game designer imagined."

"And what is that, that will bind us?"

"It is a dirty word among your circles. Love."

There was murmuring, and a voice said, "Love is very nice for some people, but we need something more real. Something that knows pain. Something that knows angst."

"The love that I know was tortured to death."

"What is this love of which you speak?"

Taberah thought of a short answer, and then said, "That is not a little question, and it deserves more than a little answer. We are tired and bruised; let us, each of us, get a good night's sleep, and then I will give you an answer."

Discovered

The following night, Taberah spoke long, telling a tale that stretched from Eden to the New Jerusalem. The Kindred were spellbound; none of them could begin to imagine that anything so exciting and dynamic could be the ill-spoken Christian faith. He wrapped up by saying, "It means being loved by God, and loving God by four pillars: loving God with all of your heart, and all of your soul, and all of your mind, and all of your might." None of them were, as yet, convinced, but Taberah had their attention.

Taberah stood, teaching in the parks, day and night, and gradually some of the role players came to believe in what he said, and that he had a message worth spreading. Sometimes more than role players stopped by. One of the Kindred raised his hand and said, "Taberah, why don't we make a medieval role play circus to draw people in?"

Taberah thought, and scratched his head, and thought some

more. He said, "I would like to draw a distinction between 'medieval from the neck up' and 'medieval from the neck down'. 'Medieval from the neck down' is everything a circus can provide: costumes and castles, swordplay and feasting. Role play notwithstanding, that is gone, and it is not the treasure I wish to restore. I wish to restore what is 'medieval from the neck up' -- faith, hope, and love. Maybe there are some people who could be drawn into what is 'medieval from the neck up' after first contacting what is 'medieval from the neck down', but I do not wish to present a false lure."

"You lured us in from role play."

"You're right, except that then I was trying to follow God where I was. I don't feel the same rightness about putting on a show."

The discussion continued until Taberah noticed that a young woman was staring at him; her jaw had dropped. He looked at her and said, "What is it, sister?"

"I know you. I recognized you by the sound of your voice. You're the man who won two Turing Awards."

Adjustments

Taberah's Corner 9/1/2035:
Turning Back the Clock

Upon advocating that we reclaim certain things from the Middle Ages, I am invariably met with the question, "Do you think you can turn back the clock?", and it is a question I should like to address now."

There is a belief behind that question; that belief runs roughly as follows: time runs on an irreversible slope, and with that irreversible slope comes a necessary progression of ages that march forward. This belief appears to be only its obvious first part, that time is irreversible, but it is understood to mean the second part: an equally irreversible march of ages. These are almost so equated that asking, "Can we be medieval now?" is equivalent to asking, "Can we set back the physical clock to 1300?" -- but the two are not at all the same.

There is a distinction I have made between being medieval above the neck, and medieval below the neck. Medieval below the neck is all of those popular images that are conjured by the term 'medieval' -- knights in shining armor, castles, and the like. Medieval above the neck is not concerned with technology; it is concerned with thinking and living in light of the insights of the Middle Ages. Re-enactors spend short time living lives that are at least medieval below the neck, but I don't think that is a particularly important goal. What I do think is important is what I hinted at with my Turing award speech; it concerns rationality, for one thing. I know I'm fighting an uphill battle against stereotypes here; there has been a massive smear campaign, so that 'medieval' connotes obscurantist silliness and 'postmodern' connotes reasonability, but it isn't so. Medieval above the neck has never been obsolete, and never will be -- because it can't be obsolete, any more than good food can become obsolete.

As to what exactly this will mean -- I will write about different things at different times. I have some things to say about judging by appearances versus judging rightly -- but that will come in its due time.

Thank you for reading thus far; I hope you will continue reading.

The young woman's recognition of Taberah brought with it powerful changes; Taberah was for the first time of his life busy, and for the first time of his life had to escape from other people for the restoration of his soul. When he appeared, people asked autographs, and he soon learned to enter and leave restaurants through the kitchen. He had a voice to be heard, but he missed being able to walk through the streets and in the woods with Lydia. There were so many things about Taberah that people couldn't understand -- such as why he would sometimes rather sleep in a gutter than in a waterbed. Perhaps he could learn to use cosmetics to alter his appearance -- but when would he learn how to do that? He saw his fame as a responsibility, but it was more of a burden than a privilege.

He wrote and communicated all of the things that he had discussed with his friends -- and re-iterated that he did not want a circus to be put up. He had influence, but it was an impersonal influence with people he mostly didn't know. And so Taberah prayed earnestly that the burden would be lifted.

Reckoning

Taberah's Corner 10/1/2035:
Reckoning

There is a Bible story where God calls Samuel and tells him to find the future king among some brothers. Each time one comes out, Samuel is impressed and says, "Surely this is the one who is to be king!" God tells him, in essence, "I do not judge as you do. I do not judge by outer appearances." It is the last brother who is picked to be king.

I entertain doubts about holding a column at all; I suspect that most readers are reading this column because I have won two Turing Awards. If you are, I would ask you to stop; the Turing Awards merely indicate that I had some success with computers, and do not make me particularly qualified to advise society. If you are reading this column because you think I have good things to say, then go on reading it; if you are only reading it because of the weight of my awards, I would rather you were reading something else, something else that you chose because it is worth reading.

You people are greatly concerned about success. There was someone who said, "I had climbed to the top of the corporate ladder, only to find that the ladder was leaning against the wrong building." I would like to suggest that your understanding of success is like your judgment by appearances. There is something good about being famous as having won two Turing Awards; that something good is that you learn that, whatever success is, that isn't it. Success is being drawn into the heart of God, and it comes more easily when you are about to be deported by the Bureau of Immigration and Naturalization Services than when everybody and his brother wants you to be his honored guest. Success might come in many ways. It might be service of children -- and how few adults are willing to play with children? It might be keeping house. It might be running a volunteer shelter. It might be being a judge who has the guts to defend Christianity when it is attacked or challenge Islam when it is hurting our society. It might be any number of things. Perhaps it might even include being a celebrity and using your favor to share truth with others who might not have heard it -- but it is not defined by having an award attached to your name.

How can you be successful -- not at some date in the future, but right now?

On October 2 2035, 3:05 PM, God heard Taberah's prayer. A Muslim assassin, armed with a high-powered hunting rifle, shot at Taberah and hit him twice -- once in the right shoulder, and once in the abdomen. Taberah was in surgery for sixteen hours, and spent the next week drugged out. The doctor gave very firm orders that only close friends approved by both her and Aed were to see Taberah -- even then, Taberah always had a visitor when he wanted one.

In Taberah's medically enforced absence, the movement he started became independent of him. They were no longer intellectually dependent on him: Taberah was no longer a head, merely the first person to have known something. There were medieval fairs, showing people what was medieval above and below the neck. When, three months later, Taberah left the hospital, he was simply a member.

On March 6, 2036, Taberah was lying in bed, when the Angel of the Lord came to him in a vision, and said, "You have done well, Taberah; you have done what you were sent for. Which would you like: to return to medieval Provençe, or to spend the rest of your life here?"

Taberah cried, and said, "I have waited, and waited, and waited, and waited. Can't I go *home*? To my *real* home?"

His funeral was filled with mirth.

Epilogue

Yes, Eleta, I think you're right, and I think the manuscript will have to stand as it is, but I am still not happy with it. Perhaps no author is ever satisfied with his work, but I am not happy with it. You understand why I presented the events as fiction -- the idea is not without merits. Still, a critic could poke any number of holes in it. Someone who regarded it as fiction would no doubt note that good storytelling and good plot are rarely found together, that forty percent of the plot is glossed over in two short chapters, et cetera. I'm not sure that Taberah would share in all those criticisms -- he regarded those long days of conversation with the Kinsellas as the best time of his life, and his influential and turbulent time in the limelight as almost an afterthought in which he repeated impersonally what he had shared personally. At any rate, he would have found his message more important than telling a good story -- and he took storytelling seriously. Someone who knew this was not fiction and knew the parties involved would have much more serious criticisms to level. I have captured almost nothing of Taberah's sense of humor -- cunning, bawdy, subtle, clever, exquisite, and absurd. After hearing about some of the practical jokes he pulled -- from now on, Monty Python will taste like flat beer. It pales in comparison. I also did badly in failing to more seriously address the place of Islam. The influence of Islam in shaping the culture, and why it is by nature coercive is something I just barely nicked -- probably just enough to make the reader think I suffer from vulgar intolerance. You know better than that, of course; you know that I enjoyed living in a Muslim country, and that I greatly respect their emphasis on honor, friendship, and hospitality. And that it is my considered judgment -- as surely as that Christianity is invariably corrupted when it wields direct political power -- that Islam in power is inherently coercive. The role of Islam was one among *many* important elements of the surrounding culture that I failed to capture. And medieval culture, for that matter. And Taberah's "200 ways to use a magnetic paper clip" -- I just don't know what to say. It's both silly and serious, and it was one of the things to motivate me to wonder, "What kind of a mind would think of that?" And I have intentionally left out most of the miracles that occurred -- not that there were many, but I didn't want to present unnecessary strain on the reader's willing suspension of disbelief. There was plenty of necessary strain already.

The willing suspension of disbelief accompanying fiction is the real reason I chose to write it as fiction. It's not just that saying I know events three decades in the future would label me as a kook -- that's understandable enough, and the real explanation was difficult for *me* to believe, even having experienced it. The real reason I recorded this story as fiction is that our time has this terrible stereotype of medievals as backwards, and conception of the past as inferior -- and a science fiction/fantasy story is almost the only place where something labelled 'medieval' could be respected. What if I told you that an anti-Semitic campaign had taken the name of Einstein, and smeared Jewry by making his name a symbol of idiocy? The truth is that something equally anti-medieval has taken the name of John Duns Scotus, the medieval genius whom Catholics call the Subtle Doctor, and turned it into the term 'dunce'. That stereotype, and the preconception that we have nothing to learn from the medievals, is a force to be reckoned with, and I don't know how this manuscript will fare in its face.

Once one of Karl Barth's students asked him, "Do you believe there was a serpent in the Garden of Eden?" Barth replied, "The important thing is not 'Was there a serpent?' but 'What did the serpent say?'" In a similar insight, I have presented Taberah's story as fiction and tried to draw attention away from the question of "Was Taberah real?" and instead draw attention to the more fundamental question of "What did Taberah say?" -- on which account he has much to tell us. After coming into contact with him, I have come to believe that we can be medievals, too.

What do you think?

C.J.S.

www.ingramcontent.com/pod-product-compliance
Lightning Source LLC
Chambersburg PA
CBHW030820310726
48980CB00006B/559/J

* 9 7 8 0 6 1 5 2 0 2 1 6 7 *